P9-DNZ-456

JUDE DEVERAUX

A Justified Murder

mira

mira™

Recycling programs
for this product may
not exist in your area.

ISBN-13: 978-0-7783-6097-1

A Justified Murder

Copyright © 2019 by Deveraux Inc.

This edition published by arrangement with Harlequin Books S.A.

For questions and comments about the quality of this book, please contact us
at CustomerService@Harlequin.com.

Mira
22 Adelaide St. West, 40th Floor
Toronto, Ontario M5H 4E3, Canada
www.Harlequin.com

Printed in U.S.A.

Also by Jude Deveraux and MIRA

Medlar Mysteries

A WILLING MURDER

Novels

MET HER MATCH
AS YOU WISH

For additional books by
New York Times bestselling author Jude Deveraux,
visit her website, www.jude-deveraux.com.

Look for Jude Deveraux's next novel,
A FORGOTTEN MURDER,
available soon from MIRA.

A Justified Murder

ONE

Dora found the body—and all she felt was annoyance. Now she'd have to find someone else to clean for to fill out the week. Mrs. Beeson—as she insisted on being called even though there was no evidence that she'd ever had a husband—had been a good employer. She always left a hundred-dollar bill, always said thanks. At Christmas, she left an envelope containing three crisp, new one hundreds and a card that wished her a merry holiday.

Now here she was, slumped forward in the chair, face on her knees. There was a hole in the back of her head. Blood and...*stuff* was on the wall behind her. Dora didn't see a gun but she guessed it was squashed between her belly and thighs.

Dora knew she ought to call the sheriff. But if she hadn't cleaned the house yet, would she have a right to take the envelope on the desk that had her name on it?

She could almost hear her late husband, Herbert,

chiding her. "Shouldn't you feel sorry for her?" he'd say. "Poor thing was so sad that she took her own life. Didn't she have friends who could help her?"

"Not that I know of," Dora said aloud, then caught herself. She tried to keep Herbert's voice to herself and not let anyone know how often she heard it.

She went around the body, picked up the envelope, and put it in her pocket. For a moment, she looked out the window at the palm trees and thought of what her beloved Herbert would advise. She knew she needed to work up some sympathy, maybe even some tears, for Mrs. Beeson. It wouldn't do to call Sheriff Flynn sounding like she couldn't care less that her employer had just offed herself. With her shoulders braced, Dora made the call.

Deputy Beatrice answered.

"Oh, Bea." Dora was nearly choking on the memory of Herbert's funeral. "The most awful thing has happened."

"Take a breath," Bea said, "and tell me what it is."

"Janet Beeson killed herself."

Bea didn't hesitate. "We'll be right there and don't touch anything. Absolutely *nothing*."

"I won't." Dora clicked off the phone, and her tears dried immediately. "Damn!" she muttered and put her pay envelope back on the desk. With a resentful glare at Mrs. Beeson's body, she sat down in the living room to wait for whoever was going to show up.

Sheriff Daryl Flynn was the first to arrive on the scene. After Bea told him what happened, he hadn't gone tearing away, sirens blaring. It wasn't a criminal act, but the suicide of a sad old woman. He knew that Janet Beeson lived alone. He didn't think she'd even had any pets. Maybe the Lachlan website should include that article he'd read about how pets are good for old people and prisoners.

As he drove, taking his time, he realized he hadn't been this far out on San Remo Avenue in a while and he saw that the local super-Realtor, Tayla Kirkwood, had been at work here. The houses looked as manicured as the ones inside those fancy gated communities down in Plantation. For himself, sometimes he missed the days when Lachlan front yards had old cars on concrete blocks. Pretty as the place was, it lacked a sense of personality. It was as though everyone was just alike.

Janet Beeson's house was at the edge of the town limits. To his left, down Kirkwood Lane, was Tayla's ridiculously big, gaudy house.

On the right were lush palm trees. When he neared the address, there was a tall, solid steel fence that seemed to go on and on. *When did that go up?* he wondered. A wide metal gate was standing open, but he saw the lockbox nearby. The place looked like the home of some California movie star, not suited for sleepy little Lachlan. Why had no one told him about this?

He pulled into the drive that was shaded by overhanging trees, with flowering shrubs along the sides. He knew professional landscaping when he saw it. All this had taken time and a whole bunch of money.

He parked his Broward County Sheriff's car to the side, got out, and looked around the place. The house was long and low, with a red tile roof, blue-and-white Spanish tiles under the portal, expensive outdoor furniture, and a quietly splashing fountain with iron birds on it. He thought: *wealthy widow*. South Florida was full of the dears. Work-exhausted Yankee husbands died and left it all to their widows. The women moved south to Florida's divine climate and tarted up some house, then…

Then lived in isolation, Sheriff Flynn thought. Sad, unhappy, lonely women.

Dora met him at the front door. She'd lived in Lachlan all her life and he'd gone to school with her. She was a little out of it since her husband died and tended to still talk to him, but she was a good person.

"What was it?" he asked. "Pills?"

Dora didn't say anything, just turned and led the way to the back of the house.

As he followed, he saw lots of marble—cool in Florida's warm climate—and things that glittered. Tables with gold-colored legs, shiny wood, heavy curtains that shimmered. His wife made fun of the style. "Might as well put up wallpaper that says 'I am rich,'" she said.

When the sheriff entered the last room, he was almost smiling. But one look at Janet Beeson's body and he halted. Holy crap! The woman had blown the back of her head out. On the wall was…

He turned away, not wanting to see what was there. For this, he was going to need backup. He took out his cell to put in a call to the main office, but then the body started to slip to one side.

Without thinking that he was changing the scene, he made a leap forward and caught poor Janet before she hit the floor. When the body fell back against the chair, what he saw so stunned him that he dropped his phone.

"Oh. My. God," Dora said.

They both stood there, paralyzed.

Janet Beeson had a gunshot in her head and a large knife sticking out of her chest. Green vomit was on her chin and down the front of her shirt. Poison, maybe?

Sheriff Flynn recovered first. "Somebody really, really wanted her dead," he managed to say. It took a while to find his phone, but he hesitated in calling the main office. What would it matter if he took a few minutes to collect himself?

He couldn't take his eyes off the body. Janet Beeson, of all people! He couldn't remember anything significant about her. If her name was ever mentioned, it was always in good terms.

As his senses came back to him, it was as though he could see the future. He was just the local sheriff, so the big shots at Broward would take over this case. The fact that he'd lived in Lachlan all his life would mean nothing to them. They'd push him out completely. That he'd been instrumental in helping solve the last murder would mean nothing to them. He doubted if they'd even let him have a set of the photos they'd take. How could he investigate—on his own—if he couldn't study the crime scene? He needed those photos!

Before he could think about what he was doing, he called Sara Medlar's private number. She answered on the first ring. "I need you to take pictures of a dead body. Now. 2012 San Remo. It's—" Sara had already hung up.

Sheriff Flynn smiled. It was lunchtime so Jack might be home. He'd want to get here fast, so Sara just might arrive with young Jack on his dad's big Harley. About six minutes later, he heard the roar of the bike and his smile widened. At least he'd get photos! And if he manipulated the Medlar trio right, he might get more.

Yes, it would be better to call the downtown office *after* Sara had done her job. He went outside to meet them.

TWO

Kate Medlar was showing a cute three-bedroom house that had just come on the market.

"I really hate the furniture," the man said.

"So do I," his wife said. "We're more modern than this."

"I think my grandmother has a cabinet just like that." His tone held a sneer of derision.

Kate didn't grit her teeth. "Everything will be moved out as soon as the house sells." She tried to sound as though she'd never before heard what they were saying. "Let me show you the rest of the home."

She listened as they complained about every feature in the kitchen. They liked dark cabinets, not white. Hated the fridge and the stove. He despised…

Kate stepped away to let them enjoy their belief in their superior taste. She looked forward to telling them that the kitchen cabinets were Swedish and had cost about fifty grand. What she really wanted to say was that the cabinet in the living room was genuine Hepplewhite. If his grandmother owned one, it should be heavily insured.

But selling required endless patience—and keeping your mouth shut.

Kate looked outside. It was autumn and on their last call, her mother had asked if she missed the color change of the leaves in the Chicago suburb where she'd grown up. Kate had said she did, but that wasn't completely true. A couple of friends she kept in touch with had smirkingly asked how she bore the heat of a South Florida summer. She'd been more honest with them. "In a bikini in my aunt's private swimming pool." That had shut them up so well that their emails had become less frequent.

Just six months ago, Kate had arrived in Lachlan, one of many little towns attached to enormous Fort Lauderdale. Stores, restaurants, services, gyms, and entertainment were all there and easy to reach via wide, clean streets. A very enjoyable place to live.

She hadn't arrived feeling that way. She'd been scared half to death at the newness of what she was undertaking. She was going to be staying with her late father's older sister, a woman she knew nothing about. Sara Medlar was a famous writer, now retired—sort of. She still spent whole days with pen and paper writing no one knew what.

Jack said that a writer retiring was like a rehabbed drug addict taking a job in a cocaine factory. The goings-on in the world offered too much temptation to be able to resist recording them.

Jack was Aunt Sara's friend. Or as she put it, "the

grandson I should have had." At the first of the year he'd been in a car crash that had killed his younger half brother. When Kate met him, Jack was grieving and angry, and his leg was in a cumbersome cast.

Aunt Sara said that Kate's refusal to feel sorry for Jack had brought him out of his depression. Whatever it was, the three of them had found that living together in Aunt Sara's big, beautiful house suited them. Sara had a bedroom suite on one side, Kate had a suite of rooms on the other side, and Jack was in the middle. He had a spacious bedroom with a sitting area by the garage so he could come and go whenever he wanted without anyone knowing.

They shared cooking, straightening the house, and errands. What they didn't share was the remote control to the big TV in the family room. Any show too "girly" as Jack called it was to be viewed in private. Sara and Kate made a point of never obeying his rule.

Back in the spring, they'd been thrown into solving an old mystery that had nearly killed them. But they'd done it together and it had bonded them. The Lachlan sheriff referred to them as though they were just one person. *The Three*, he called them. Aunt Sara had written *Together* in calligraphy, framed it, and hung it over the TV. If she'd meant to make Jack remember that they were a team and therefore willingly share the remote, she had failed.

After the mystery was solved, Sara and Jack went back to their normal lives and Kate began a new one. Jack bought run-down houses in Lachlan and, with his crew, remodeled them. Kate worked for Kirkwood Realty as an agent. She'd already sold two houses this year and had three strong possibilities lined up. Sara filled her days with… Well, no one was sure what she did, but she was always busy. She loved photography and often showed them staggeringly beautiful pictures she'd taken that day.

The prospective buyers were still complaining about the house when Kate's phone buzzed. It was a rare thing indeed: a text from Jack.

Come now. 2012 San Remo. Near Tayla. Jack wasn't one to waste words. If he said *now* that's what he meant. Kate felt a sense of panic. Was something wrong with Aunt Sara?

It was bad for business, but Kate pretty much shoved the two lookie-loos out the front door and locked it. She ran to her car, which was parked on the street. When she drove clients around, she used her sedate, boring sedan. But on days like this, when she met them somewhere, she drove Aunt Sara's fast yellow MINI Cooper. When she floored the accelerator, the little car leaped forward.

Since Tayla was her boss, Kate had been to her house several times and knew the address. Jack was standing by the gate. All six foot two of him, sweaty T-shirt plastered to his muscular chest, was frowning.

He motioned for her to park on the far side of the road, and as soon as she was out of the car, she said in fear, "Aunt Sara?"

"She's fine. What the hell took you so long?" Turning, he headed toward the house, Kate close behind him.

She was unperturbed by the legendary Wyatt temper. "Stopped for a couple of beers. This better be good. You made me lose two clients."

"Ha! I met them, remember? They aren't buying anything."

"They— Ow!" She'd stepped on a rock.

"Where are your shoes?"

"They were heels. Threw them in the back."

Jack turned, picked her up, and carried her the four steps to the porch, then set her down.

Kate had always been clear that she looked at Jack as the brother she'd never had. But he had very different ideas about the two of them, and often found ways to demonstrate that. "If you think that's going to impress me, you—" She didn't finish her thought, because she saw the sheriff's car peeping out from under the trees, and she heard the low rumble of his voice inside. Her eyes widened.

"There's a body inside, but if you faint again I'll—"

Kate was already running, barefoot, to the back of the house. The first thing she saw was Aunt Sara, her face pressed to her beloved Fujifilm camera, shooting away. That she had it on silent—or "sneak mode" as Sara called it—made Kate look at the sheriff. He was blocking her full view of a woman sitting in a chair.

"I don't think Kate needs to see this," the sheriff said, but Sara put her camera down long enough to give him a look that meant he was to step aside.

Kate didn't faint as she'd done the last time she'd seen a dead body, but she did sway on her feet. Considering what she was looking at, it was a wonder she didn't hit the floor. There was a bullet hole in the woman's head, a huge knife in her chest close to her heart, and… Was that at the side of her mouth *green*?

Behind Kate, Jack put his hands on her shoulders to steady her.

In the distance they could hear what sounded like the sirens of an army of squad cars coming toward them.

"Get out!" Sheriff Flynn said. "No, Dora, not you. They'll want to ask you questions. *They* have to go."

Kate was still staring at the body, not sure she was even blinking.

Jack was trying to look as though he was unaffected by this, but his face had drained of color.

She took a step closer to him in case either of them went down.

"Did you get it all?" Sheriff Flynn's voice was gruff as he spoke to Sara, who'd never stopped snapping away.

She nodded. Her face was even more bloodless than Jack's.

Suddenly, a siren seemed to be just outside the house. Sheriff Flynn opened a back door. "Go!"

Jack, Sara and Kate scurried out, then went around the side of the house. They were hiding in the shrubs when four Broward County squad cars pulled into the drive. As soon as it was clear, they hurried through the gate. Jack's Harley was under some flowering shrubs and Sara's MINI was at the side of the road.

They didn't have to say anything to know what to do. Kate and Sara got into the car and Jack drove the bike across Longshore Drive to Sara's house.

Inside, they went down the hall past Jack's room,

through the dining room and the kitchen, to the family room. They flopped down on the big sofa, Sara in the middle, and stared into space.

It was a while before anyone spoke.

"Do you think Sheriff Flynn just wanted some private photos?" Sara asked.

"I'm sure that's it. He knows you're the best photographer in town," Jack said.

"Maybe he plans to share them with the Broward County Sheriff's Department," Kate said.

They looked at one another, knowing that was an absurd idea.

Sara sighed. "Maybe he knows they won't share with him, so he asked me to take pictures for him. And that's *all* he wants from us. I hope they come out well. In the kitchen I had to cut the exposure down a couple of notches."

"You took photos of the whole house?" Kate asked.

Jack leaned across Sara. "We had at least an hour before you arrived."

"I was there ten minutes after you sent your Neanderthal text. I thought maybe Aunt Sara'd had a heart attack."

"I would have explained but you—"

Sara was quite used to the verbal tug-of-war between the two of them. She stood up. "I'll put the photos on a flash drive, then I'll go to the sheriff's office and give them to him."

Kate stood up beside her. "Good idea. You can drop me off at my office and Tayla can give me a ride home."

Jack looked up at them. "We're not getting involved in this, right?"

"Absolutely *not*!" Sara said. "I took pictures and that's all."

They were silent for a moment.

"Janet helped us when we were investigating the murder of the Morrises." There were tears in Kate's eyes. "She found names for us."

"And she made that chocolate cake," Jack said. "Best I ever ate."

"She helped us so much." Kate looked at Jack. "Your mother got her for us."

Jack got up, pulled tissues from the box on the side table, and handed them to the women. Color was coming back into his face—and the color was the red of anger. "There was no respect in what was done to her."

Kate blew her nose. "I can kind of, sort of, understand killing someone but...but that was too horrible to imagine. One way would have done it. Why *three*?"

They looked at Sara. "Who hated her *that* much?"

"Obviously, a crazy person," Kate said.

"Or three," Jack added.

"You think more than one person was there?" Kate asked.

Jack shrugged. "It's a thought."

Sara sat back down on the couch. "I wonder how they'll investigate."

Kate sat down beside her. "They'll try to find out who hated her."

As Jack sat down on the other side of Sara, he gave a snort. "If haters are suspects, then everyone in this town is going to say they loved her."

"I agree," Kate said. "There'll be two thousand BFFs

of Janet Beeson. Bet there'll be a lot of tears at her funeral. They all loved her so very, very much."

Sara spoke up. "When we were planning the memorial for the Morrises, did either of you see or hear anything bad about her? Or even odd?"

"My mind was focused on what we were doing," Kate said. The women looked at Jack.

"All I remember about that day is the itching inside my cast."

They stared ahead at the dark TV, silent as they went over every minute of that day. But Janet Beeson wasn't a person you could remember very well. She was short, dumpy, gray-haired, with unplucked eyebrows, no makeup, and a quiet voice that didn't carry well. An unassuming woman, someone who faded into the background. The day she was at Sara's house, she'd silently taken a seat, opened her laptop, and started searching for whatever someone told her to look for.

The truth was that she was such an unremarkable person that it was embarrassing. They couldn't recall a thing she'd said. She didn't make jokes or complain or even ask questions. When everyone was driving Kate crazy about what food was to be served at the memorial for the Morrises, Janet had made no comment. She'd just stayed in the background, always helping, never asking anything of anyone.

"This really and truly makes no sense," Sara said. "Why would anyone want to kill her? I know at least five people in this town who deserve worse than what was done to her."

"Leave my relatives out of this," Jack said.

His semijoke brought them out of their stupor and they again stood up.

Sara looked at Jack. "Your mother seemed to know Janet well. She might have some idea about why Janet was targeted."

"You said you photographed the whole house?" Kate asked Sara.

"She even videoed it," Jack added in wonder. Sara liked still photos, not pictures that moved.

They looked at each other. They were standing in a circle, as though they meant to close out the rest of the world.

After a moment, Kate took a few steps back. "I'm not going to get involved, but I *am* going to talk to Heather. Maybe she remembers something from that day."

"I think I'd be better at talking to my own mother."

Kate grimaced. "You can't go. Heather will cook some childhood thing for you, then your sister will arrive, and you'll forget all about poor Janet Beeson."

Sara nodded in agreement. "I need to go buy some flash drives to put the photos on."

Jack frowned. "I hope you don't mean to let people see pictures of that body. My mother and sister aren't to see it. They—"

"Give me a break." Sara headed toward her bedroom, then stopped. She was looking at Kate and there was fear in her eyes. "I'm serious when I say that we shouldn't get involved in this. I don't want us to deal with the police, the sheriff's department, any of it. Are we agreed?" She didn't have to say that she was thinking about what had nearly happened to Kate when they'd investigated another murder.

"Yes." Kate's smile showed her relief.

"I agree," Jack said.

Smiling, Sara nodded. "Okay, Kate, go talk to Heather. When you get back, tell me what you learned, I'll write it up, and we'll give a report to Sheriff Flynn. Then we're done with all of this. Does that sound good?"

"Excellent," Kate said.

"Yes," Jack added. "Whoever did that to Mrs. Beeson is dangerous. And insane."

"Or driven to insanity by something that we obviously don't know about," Sara said. "We'll meet back here by six. Jack, get a couple of pounds of prawns."

"It's not my turn for the grocery. I'd have to make a second trip."

Kate knew what he wanted. "Okay! You can go with me to your mom's."

"Good idea. Maybe while you two are talking, Mom might cook something. Don't look at me like that. I missed lunch."

"Whatever," Kate said, then turned to hide her smile. She didn't relish the idea of talking about death—especially a brutal one—to anyone.

Heather's pretty kitchen was designed by her daughter and built by her son. She was at the stove finishing a pot of minestrone while Jack and Kate sat at the counter. There was a platter of snacks before them: raw veg for her, cheese and crackers for him.

"We heard about the suicide," Heather said.

Her back was to them so she didn't see Kate start to speak, then Jack shaking his head no.

"You heard through Wilson's police radio?" he asked.

"Yes." Heather was stirring the big pot. "I hate to say it, but I do understand why she did it. That poor woman."

"You know why she committed suicide?" Kate asked.

"Yes." Heather tasted the soup, then added more oregano.

"We'd appreciate *anything* you can tell us about Janet Beeson," Kate said.

Instantly, Heather looked at Kate in alarm. What had happened before when they'd involved themselves in a death had been harrowing. She'd lost her beloved stepson and had almost lost her son.

"It's for Sheriff Flynn's report," Jack said loudly. "Sara is going to write it. She's good at it and Flynn isn't so…" He trailed off.

"And you know Aunt Sara. Anything for a story." Kate gave what she hoped was a convincing smile, a *truthful* smile.

Heather took a moment to relax the tension in her body. "Good. That makes sense." She paused as she collected her thoughts. "What I remember most about Janet is that two years ago her best friend, Sylvia Alden, also killed herself."

Kate gasped.

"Alden?" Jack asked. "Was she married to Tom Alden?"

"You remember him for his boat, don't you?" Heather smiled fondly at her son. There wasn't much resemblance between them. Jack took after his father and grandfather. The woman he looked the most like was his Brazilian great-grandmother. Her dark hair and eyes had passed straight down the line to him.

"Yeah, I remember his boat. When he put it up for sale, I wanted it so bad I couldn't sleep."

"You were too young."

"I could have handled it. If Dad—"

Kate interrupted, "What do you know about Mrs. Beeson?"

"Not much. I know she showed up at our church six years ago." She looked at Kate. "I remember everything of that year. Jack had just bought three rotten old houses and I thought he was going to go bankrupt. It was a stressful time." Again, she smiled adoringly at her son. "Janet was so quiet and unassuming that at first no one paid any attention to her. But she volunteered for one thing after another in town and at church. By the next year, we were all depending on her. We were unanimous in voting for her to be the church secretary."

"What about Mrs. Alden?" Jack asked. "I don't remember her at all, but Tom was a great guy."

"They retired to Lachlan years ago. Mrs. Alden—Sylvia—stayed to herself. She attended church sometimes but not often. Her husband was a picture of health, but one day he pulled his car off the road and he was found there hours later. Massive heart attack. His funeral wasn't here. People came from the East and took his body away, and Sylvia was gone for months. But she returned to Lachlan and became even more of a recluse. We should have…"

Heather sighed. "Anyway, not long after Mr. Alden

passed, Janet Beeson came to town. I don't know how she and Sylvia met, but soon you didn't see one without the other." She smiled. "Janet was short and round and Sylvia was tall and thin. Sylvia was older, but still… You know…"

"What?" Kate asked.

"It's awful of me to repeat gossip, but when they were together, people said it was like seeing a lady and her maid. Sylvia was so very elegant. She was one of those women who could put on jeans and a sweatshirt and look couture. Of course she'd also have on a pearl necklace and tasteful little earrings."

"What about Janet?" Kate asked. "How did she dress?"

Heather hesitated.

"Janet could put on couture and still look like the dustman's daughter?" Kate asked.

"Sad to say so, but yes," Heather said. "But however they looked, they were as tight as teenage girls. Went everywhere together. I remember someone from church asking if they went to the bathroom together. Then someone else said they were probably lovers and—" She waved her hand. "Just gossip."

"But it didn't end well?" Kate encouraged.

"No. Several people noticed that Sylvia began to look bad. Circles under her eyes, that sort of thing. People asked if she was all right, but she was a very private person and told nothing."

"Did she tell her problems to Janet?" Kate asked.

"I think so. I remember seeing them in a restaurant over on University. I started to say hello but then I realized that Sylvia was crying. Janet was reaching across the table and holding her hands. I thought, *Maybe they are lovers*. I left the restaurant. Not long after that..."

"Sylvia killed herself," Jack said. "I don't remember that happening."

"I think you were in New York with Sara then. And it was over and done with so quickly we hardly knew what was going on. It was exactly like her husband. Someone came and got her. The funeral wasn't here, and later the house was emptied, then quietly sold. What I really remember was that Janet looked miserable after that. Her eyes were sunken and red from crying."

Heather took a breath. "We didn't say much about it because we were ashamed of ourselves. Right here in our midst was a woman so unhappy that she took her own life, and none of us had noticed or tried to do something. I kept thinking about how I'd walked out of that restaurant. I should have *helped*." Heather was leaning on the counter, her hands clenched firmly.

Kate reached out to put her hand over Heather's just as Jack did. For a moment they stayed that way, three pairs of hands together.

Heather went back to the stove. "I can't imagine how lonely Janet must have been after Sylvia died. It was as though two women had left the earth."

"Is that one of the reasons you asked her to help us when we were trying to find out about the Morrises?" Kate asked.

"Oh yes! Janet is—was—so efficient, so good at everything she did. Even cooking. I asked her for that chocolate cake recipe and she gave it to me. I tried it, but mine didn't come out nearly as good. In fact, I tossed it."

"What do you know about Janet's background?" Jack asked.

"Nothing. Ever since I heard, I've tried to remember but I can't think of anything."

"She had some money," Kate said. "In my estimate, her house is worth a million and a quarter."

"Is it?" Heather turned to look at them. "Why are you asking me all these questions? This goes past some report for the sheriff. And for that matter, why were you guys there? I assume Sara was with you."

"Sure, she was," Jack said. "Flynn wanted her to take pictures of…of the body."

Both Kate and Jack were looking down.

Heather put her hand under her son's chin and lifted his head to look into his eyes. "Your father could lie so well that no one guessed what he was up to. But you, Jackson, my darling son, aren't nearly as good. What's up?"

"We, uh… She…"

"Mrs. Beeson was murdered," Kate said.

Immediately, Heather's face drained of color. Jack leaped up, grabbed his mother, and led her to a stool. He got her a glass of water.

"Murder?" Heather managed to whisper. "And you two and Sara are going to…to…?"

"No, we're not." Kate's voice was firm. "We've decided that one murder investigation was enough for us. And after last time…" She looked at Jack to help her out.

He had his arm protectively around his mother. "The cleaning woman found her. She—"

"Daffy Dora?" Heather was looking at Kate.

"Yes. Dora found the body, then called the sheriff. He asked Aunt Sara to take pictures. Jack was home, so he sent me a text to meet him there. We saw her, then when the county guys arrived, we sneaked out."

Heather looked from one to the other, then back. "If Sara was here, you'd be those three monkeys of see, hear and speak no evil. What aren't you telling me?"

Neither Jack nor Kate spoke.

"Okay. It'll soon be all over town so I'll find out." Heather took a deep breath. "I have no idea who'd want to murder Janet Beeson. She was such a quiet little woman that I can't imagine anyone noticing her, much less killing her. All I know for sure is that for years she was best friends with an elegant woman named Sylvia Alden, who committed suicide. Since then, as far as I know, Janet has been alone. I don't think I ever saw her with anyone else. She was so alone that suicide was easy to believe—but not murder. How did—?" She raised her hand. "No, I don't want to hear that."

Heather looked at them. "You said she was rich. Could it have been a robbery? Maybe Janet heard someone breaking in, then they hit her over the head with something? An accidental murder?"

"No," Kate said.

"It was *not* an accident," Jack said.

Heather stood up. "I definitely don't want to know any more details about this."

"No, you don't," Jack said.

She went back to the stove, filled two bowls with

her homemade minestrone, and set them on the counter. "How about if we have something to eat, then this afternoon I pay some visits and get people to talk about dear Janet? I'll ask what they remember about her."

"That would be great," Kate said.

Heather set her bowl down across from them. "Actually, I have some photos of Janet and Sylvia together. Would they help?"

"If they were taken with a cell phone, Aunt Sara might not let them in the house," Kate said.

When Jack laughed, Heather joined him. After all that had happened to him in the past year, her son's laughter was a joy to hear—but there was still fear in her eyes. She turned to him. "I'll help with this only if you promise not to get involved."

"We do," Kate said. The sight of Janet Beeson's mutilated body was strong in her mind. "We're going to leave this to the professionals."

"Good. While you two eat, I'll look for the photos. You'll turn them over to the sheriff?" She was waiting for their reassurance.

"And the FBI and the CIA and—"

"The Secret Service," Kate added to Jack's list.

Heather stood there for a moment, looking as though she was trying to figure out if they were telling the truth about staying out of the murder. When she seemed to be satisfied, she left the room.

Kate let out her breath. "Was she like that when you were growing up?"

"Worse. She was always terrified that I was going to become like my dad."

"Was she disappointed when you turned out exactly like him?"

"I did *not*," Jack said. "Roy Wyatt was a lying, thieving—" He broke off at Kate's smile. "Very funny. Hope somebody laughs. Let's go to the grocery, then home. I have to go back to work."

"Me too. I have a showing at three."

"Serious buyers or time wasters?"

"They want a house that—" Her eyes widened.

"What?"

Kate put her hand to her face. "I have clients who want a house exactly like Mrs. Beeson's."

He groaned. "You never stop working, do you?"

"Look who's talking. You—" She broke off when Heather came back holding some photos.

"I can make some better prints but these are okay for now." She spread them on the countertop.

Kate picked up one picture. It was a group photo of half a dozen women standing in front of a pretty porch. To the right was the edge of a fountain with birds on it. "Where was this taken?"

Heather picked it up. "At Sylvia's place."

Kate and Jack looked at each other. "This is Janet's house."

"Oh!" Heather said. "That's right. I forgot about that! I was away then, but someone at church said Janet had bought the Alden house. That poor, poor woman. How lonely she must have been to buy her friend's house. Are you *sure* it wasn't suicide?"

"Absolutely." Jack stood up. "No doubt whatever." He stacked the photos. "If you have the originals online, send copies to me. Sara can include them in the report she gives to the sheriff."

"And that's it?" Heather asked. "No more investigating?"

Jack hugged his mother. "The first time was a one-off. My leg was in a cast so I couldn't work, Kate had just arrived in town, and Sara was, well, you know… being Sara, so it worked."

Heather held on to her son tightly. "And you knew the victims."

"Yeah." Jack's voice was hoarse. "I knew them." He held his mother at arm's length. "So stop worrying."

"But do ask questions," Kate said.

They both looked at her.

She shrugged. "It could only help. Just write down what you hear and email it to us."

Jack kissed his mother's cheek, picked up another piece of buttered garlic bread, and followed Kate to the front door.

Outside, they got into his truck. "Were we telling the truth?" she asked.

"Yes," Jack said firmly. "I'm sure I lost ten years of my life the last time we got involved with a murder. I am *not* going to do that again."

"So which grocery do you want to go to?"

"How about Trader Joe's?"

"Good idea." As he headed toward University Drive, they were silent, haunted by what they'd seen in Mrs. Beeson's house.

THREE

Trader Joe's was new, small, and set in a plaza with a wonderful selection of stores. It was just down the road from the big Whole Foods and the gym they often went to.

Kate was thinking that when her mother heard about the murder, she would call in fear. Her husband died when Kate was just four, so mother and daughter had been alone. Now that Kate was living in another state, her mother had a hard time coping.

The other time they'd found bodies, Ava Medlar had dismissed it as meaning nothing. But after Kate had nearly been killed... Well, it had taken a lot of talking to keep her mother from lapsing into one of her debilitating bouts of depression and demanding that Kate return home to Chicago to take care of her. Kate would never be able to talk her way out of a second episode.

"Thinking about your mom?" Jack asked as he pulled into a parking space.

"Yeah." She was getting used to the way he and Aunt Sara seemed to read her mind. "I need to promise her that I won't get involved." She got out of the truck. The sun was dazzlingly bright and she opened her bag, a Bottega Veneta that she'd borrowed from Aunt Sara, to look for her sunglasses. But Kate couldn't find the glasses. All she seemed able to see was poor Janet Beeson and what had been done to her.

Jack took the bag from her, removed the glasses, and slipped them onto her face. "Can't get what we saw out of your mind?"

"No, I can't. Who would do such a thing to a little old woman?"

Jack put his arm around her shoulders in a brotherly way and they stood still until she stopped shaking. "I like you in those heels. Really sexy. They make your legs look even longer."

Kate pushed away from him, gave him a look to cut it out, and they walked to the store. But she was grateful for his smart-aleck remark. It had brought her back to the present.

"My guess," Jack said as he got a cart, "is money. Somebody needs to look at Mrs. Beeson's will and see who stands to inherit."

Kate began tossing in bags of salad greens. "Are you saying her heirs got together and killed her? Just so they'd get an early inheritance?"

"Maybe." He was filling a bag with oranges.

"But isn't the heir being the killer too obvious?" Kate got brussels sprouts.

"You mean that killing for money has been done before, so this time there has to be a different reason?"

"I just like to think there are other possibilities. I'd really like to know why someone did that." Her head came up. "Maybe we should get Aunt Sara to tell Sheriff Flynn that if he doesn't keep us informed of what they find out, she won't give him the photos."

"That's called extortion. Or blackmail. And/or hindering a case by withholding evidence. Whatever it is, I don't think it's going to work." He tossed in a carton of guacamole. "Besides, do you think the Broward cops will tell *him* what they're doing?"

"Probably not. If he thought they would, he wouldn't have had Aunt Sara take photos in secret. What kind of grapes do you want?"

"Tart. Like my women." He grinned at her rolled eyes. "I can't imagine that they'll investigate this in the right way."

She looked at him in question.

"It'll be scientific. Lots of forensics and lab work. They'll try to find out who was where and when. And they'll look for other murders done in the same horrible way. But this is a crime of motive. Of anger. Or greed on a big scale."

"It's pure hatred, that's for sure," Kate said. "This is going to take some digging to figure out who and why."

For a moment, they paused, looking at each other in silence, not moving until a woman wanted to get to the yellow onions.

"So tell me about your clients," Jack said. One thing they shared was a love of real estate.

Kate was glad for the change of subject and they talked about work as they picked up the other items they needed and checked out.

When they were in the truck, Kate brought up the subject still strongly in their minds. "If we put our theories about Mrs. Beeson in Aunt Sara's report, do you think the higher-ups will pay any attention to it?"

"Of course not." He backed out of the parking space. "If they even find out we were there, we'll be in trouble. At the least, they'll say we contaminated the crime scene."

"If we really are staying out of this, maybe your mom should report directly to the sheriff."

"That would mean skipping Sara and I don't think she'd like that."

"Actually, neither would I." His look of warning made Kate defensive. "Okay, I'm curious. You caught me. Can't help it. Could you drop me off on Lime Key? I'm meeting clients there."

"The ones who want to buy Mrs. Beeson's house?"

"No. Those people live in Miami and believe that they're falling down on the social ladder by moving to the rural backwater that is Fort Lauderdale."

Jack laughed. "You haven't lived here long enough to have an attitude like that."

"Being a Realtor gives me a double dose of home snobbery. One woman said it was appalling that there aren't any gated communities in Lachlan."

"What did you say?"

"That the individual estates in Lachlan have private security systems."

Jack gave a snort of laughter. "Private estates! I take it you didn't show her the Medlar-Wyatt side of town."

"I did manage to avoid that area. Anyway, she wasn't buying."

"Certainly not now." He stopped the truck at the house she was showing. "Are you planning to ask Tayla if she sold the house to Mrs. Beeson?"

"No. Let the detectives do that. Someone is a lover of violence. Shooting, stabbing…"

"And poison. Wonder what deadly drug they used?"

"Your mom seemed to think this has something to do with Sylvia Alden's death."

"Her suicide. I wonder…"

"What?" Kate looked at the house. Her clients were late.

"What if Mrs. Alden didn't commit suicide? What if *she* was murdered?"

"And Mrs. Beeson found out about it? Your mom said people took away the bodies of Sylvia and her husband. That sounds like mega money to me. Maybe Mrs. Alden's heirs killed her for the money, Janet found out about it, and—"

"They killed her before she told. Wonder who 'they' are? Where did the Aldens live before here? But maybe Sylvia's death has nothing to do with this. For all we know, Janet Beeson was fabulously wealthy and had millions in jewels somewhere and…" He looked to Kate to finish it.

"And three kids from Miami broke in and stole the jewels from a secret safe. But Janet interrupted them and they…you know. Took turns."

"Not a gang rape but a gang murder. Although, the poison must have been difficult to get down her."

"Was there an empty teacup nearby? I didn't notice."

"Ah, come on. Give ol' Janet a break," Jack said. "At least put the poison in a shot glass of tequila."

"No. I'm sure Mrs. Beeson was a tea drinker. I wish I could hypnotize myself and remember her every moment at the memorial."

"Do you think it's significant that she was so very unmemorable? Don't spies work at not being noticed?"

"What's she going to spy on in Lachlan?" Kate asked. "How much money the church took in? She was the secretary so she knew that. Is there something going on in this town that I don't know about?"

"Based on what we saw this morning, there is something really evil going on that neither of us knows about. Your clients are here. They're not going to buy this place. The house is too small."

Kate saw the young couple. He was pushing a dual stroller of toddler twins and she was pregnant. "Sometimes bank accounts and square footage aren't equal."

"After they see this place, send them over to me. If they're willing to wait, I might be able to squeeze a few more feet out of one of my houses."

She smiled at him. "Thanks." She got out but held the door open. "Can you get my car to me here?"

"Sure. And what else do you want, Princess Kate?"

"Put the groceries in the fridge. Oh no! We forgot the prawns for Aunt Sara. I'll pick it up on the way home." She shut the truck door. "See you tonight."

With a nod, Jack drove away.

Kate turned to the clients and introduced herself.

As they walked to the house, the woman said, "Your husband is gorgeous."

"He's not my husband. He—" Kate cut herself off. House sales were about the client, not her.

The woman put her hand on her belly. "Be careful. You see where love for a beautiful man leads."

Kate couldn't help laughing as she unlocked the door. "I think this might not be the right house for you, but I do have something that I think will fit. It's in the Morris community. It's new and upcoming. There's going to be a clubhouse with a pool."

"And I wouldn't have to take care of it," the husband—a very good-looking man—said.

"That's all being arranged by Wyatt Construction."

"Kate's boyfriend," the woman said. "The name's painted on the side of his truck."

"He's not my boyfriend either. Just a friend." Kate was glad when the twins let out a howl that they wanted out of confinement. She didn't want to go into an explanation of her personal life.

Jack's men dropped off Kate's car and she drove home after showing the couple one of the houses in Jack's new development. With Sara as his silent partner, Jack had purchased several houses in the area of Lachlan that was the least developed. Rotting foundations, crumbling sidewalks, weeds that hid critters unique to Florida—and Australia thought it got the prize for weird and dangerous. Ha!

During the summer, Kate had worked with Jack and his sister, Ivy, an interior designer, on planning the remodel of the houses. Creating open floor plans was at the top of the list. Mom and Dad could cook as they watched the kids.

Someone had suggested that they make the house that had belonged to the Morrises—mother and daughter—into a sort of clubhouse, and they'd liked the idea. In the backyard that had once held derelict farm machinery and an old poinciana tree, they were putting in a swimming pool. The house had been enlarged and divided into two parts. One side was an apartment for a retired couple who would look after the place. The woman had been a state swimming champ so she was the lifeguard. Her husband was the handyman for the whole development that Jack had planned.

"I want to buy *all* of the horrible old houses," Jack had said.

Sara agreed. She'd grown up there, as had Jack's grandfather. And Jack had spent the first years of his life there. He and Sara had a life goal of reconstructing the whole place. "Change ugly into beauty," she said.

Kate's young couple had liked what they saw in the house and they were willing to wait for it to be completed. Jack wanted the deal done with a handshake, but she presented papers to be signed and arranged for money to be exchanged.

While they were viewing the partially completed house, the woman had asked why she wasn't putting her hooks into Jack. "If you don't watch out, some other woman is going to lay claim to him."

"Jack's for fun, not for keeps," Kate replied.

The woman had laughed in understanding. "When it comes to men, pretty packaging isn't a guarantee of the best content."

After the showing, Kate was smiling. It was all working out well. She stopped at a Publix and bought prawns, picked up Jack's favorite hot sauce, and pickles for Aunt Sara. At home, she put the seafood away, then called out, "Where is everyone?"

"Out here," Sara answered.

She and Jack were sitting in the shady part of the patio, looking out at Sara's beautiful tropical garden. "Did Jack tell you he sold another of the Morris houses?" she asked as she sat down, and Sara nodded, pleased.

There was a pitcher of lemonade for her and Jack, and some sort of electrolyte-filled drink for Sara. There was also a platter of crackers, cheeses, and vegetables.

Kate kicked off her shoes and put her feet up. "Anything happening?"

"Not even one new murder," Jack said. "Makes for a change."

Kate gave him a sharp look. She could tell that something was bothering him. This summer they'd spent a lot of time together. After Jack had his cast removed, he'd had to learn to reuse his leg. Kate swam laps with him at home, and she and Sara went to the gym with him. Planning the remodeled houses, working out together, and doing all the things that were necessary to keep a home running, had kept them busy. "You okay?"

He cut off a chunk of Vermont Shepherd cheese. "Today everyone was asking me questions about the murder. They wanted to know the details of Janet Beeson's death. *How* did she die?"

"You didn't tell them, did you?" Sara asked.

"Knife, gun, poison?" he said. "No, I left that part out. Did you get the pictures ready? I could drop them off at the sheriff's office in the morning."

Sara shook her head. "Daryl called me. Said I was to wait on turning them over to him."

"Why?" Kate asked.

"I don't know but I think something's up. He was talking so low I could hardly hear him."

"What's your gut say?" Jack asked Sara, then turned to Kate. "And speaking of that, did you get the prawns?"

"Pounds of them," Kate said. "I'll make a salad."

After months together, they were used to coordinating meal preparation, so they went into the house. When Jack saw the jar of hot sauce, he grinned. "Thanks, Red."

"I like Princess Kate better." As she got greens out of the fridge, she asked Sara to tell exactly what Sheriff Daryl Flynn had said.

"It wasn't so much what as how. I got the impression that they have a suspect."

"Who?!" Jack and Kate said in unison.

"No idea, but it was making Daryl sad."

"That means it's somebody he knows," Jack said.

"And cares about," Kate added.

"Just what I thought," Sara said.

"When will the arrest be made?" Jack asked.

"No idea," Sara said. "It was all in his tone. Whatever they've found out, he didn't like it. Remember Detective Cotilla?"

Kate and Jack nodded. The detective had headed the investigation on the Morris case. The fact that he'd figured out nothing and they had done it all, didn't keep him from accepting a commendation and endless praise.

"Since he's *so good* at murder investigations and since he knows *so very much* about Lachlan, he's been put in charge of this case. Seems the Broward people are beginning to make jokes about us. 'Bloody Lachlan' is now our nickname. One of their sayings is 'If you value your life, don't go to Lachlan.'"

"That's awful," Kate said. "Lachlan is beautiful—or parts of it are. What about all Tayla has done to bring this derelict town back to life?"

Jack, a platter of raw shrimp in hand, was behind Sara and he gave Kate a glare for mentioning that name. Sara and Tayla were *not* friends. Enemies since high school.

Sara, jaw clenched, looked down. "I forgot to point that out."

Kate refused to be part of a forty-year-old feud. She glared back at Jack. "Well, you should have! And you should have reminded him of all Jack has done to help this town. And—"

Sara looked up and smiled. "He knows all that. Anyway, I think Daryl's under scrutiny because he said we were to stay away from his office."

"For now or always?" Kate asked.

"He didn't say. He sounded bad. Whatever we don't like about him, that man loves this town. And feels responsible for it."

They picked up bowls of food and headed outside. The big stainless steel grill was Jack's department. He put the shrimp and sliced vegetables on. "So that's it, I guess. We are officially out of this case."

Turning, he looked at them and they each had a smile of relief. The other murder they'd worked on had drained them. Emotionally and physically, it was more than they could handle.

"I nearly forgot," Sara said. "The funeral is scheduled for Saturday."

"Are you kidding?" Kate said. "On TV, the autopsy always takes a long time. And don't they need the body to…to do whatever they do?"

Jack turned the shrimp. "It's probably a fake funeral."

"A—?" Sara began then smiled at Jack in adoration at how clever he was. "Of course. Used to gather suspects. Or at least find people who knew her."

"Funeral or memorial service, all of Lachlan will turn out," Kate said. "Whoever hated her isn't going to stay home while the rest of the town attends."

"Daryl said there was no need for me to take my camera to the service. I took that to mean that there would be videos made of the audience."

"Which *we* will never see." Kate sounded annoyed. When there was no reply, she looked up at Jack and Sara staring at her. "Which is a good thing since we are never, ever going to get involved. Right?"

"Absolutely right," Sara said.

Jack was looking at the shrimp. "You think your clients really are going to buy my house?"

At the change of subject, Kate let out her breath. She didn't want to do what they'd done last time, but she *was* curious.

They were quiet for a moment, then Jack started talking about adding to the house, and should it have hardwood floors or carpet? And what about the ceilings?

After dinner they watched TV but Kate's mind was

so preoccupied that she didn't notice when no one put it on mute for the ads. *Who? Why?* kept running through her mind. She guessed that maybe the same thing was occupying Jack and her aunt Sara.

They would just have to wait. Wait until the sheriff's department with all its glorious equipment found out why an unmemorable little old woman had been killed in such a vicious way. But Kate thought that if she heard the words *serial killer* she might become violent. After having seen the body, her instinct told her that this was a crime of hate. She just didn't know if the hate was directed at Janet or if the woman had been collateral damage.

It wasn't very late when they said good-night to each other and went to bed. It had been a long, tiring day.

Just after midnight Kate was awakened by the doorbell ringing. And ringing. The consistency was as bad as when a smoke detector battery gave out.

She practically fell out of bed and stumbled around trying to pull on a pair of leggings. Of course her toes jammed into a leg and she couldn't get untangled.

By the time she got to the door, Jack was already waiting. Aunt Sara was just leaving her bedroom, a white robe over her T-shirt and gym pants.

The doorbell kept going.

Kate glared at Jack. "So help me, if it's your stepmother again, I won't buy you any more bananas."

"She's in Colorado and she says she's going to stay there forever."

"Ha! That place is as cold as Chicago. She'll return

as soon as she realizes that you don't have to shovel sunshine."

With a grin, Jack looked out. "It's Megan Nesbitt."

"What in the world does she want?" Sara flung open the door. It was a good thing she was strong or else Megan's forward leap into her arms would have knocked her down. The young woman clung to the shorter, smaller, older Sara as though she were a life preserver.

Megan was crying so hard into Sara's shoulder that they couldn't make out what she was saying. "Kyle… witch…prison…he'll die…the boys…"

Kate took one arm and Jack the other as they pulled her off Sara, led her into the family room, and sat her down on the big couch. Sara handed her a wad of tissues.

"Tea or booze?" Kate asked.

Megan had her face buried in the pillow of tissues.

"Both," Sara said.

Kate went to the kitchen; Jack went to the wet bar.

Minutes later, the coffee table was covered with hot and cold drinks, and Megan's tears had calmed enough that she might be able to talk. She downed half of Jack's rum and Coke in a single gulp, then looked at them. They were patiently waiting for her to explain.

"My brother, Kyle, is going to be arrested for Janet Beeson's murder."

Kate didn't take her eyes from Megan's. If she looked at Jack and Sara, *I told you so* might appear on her face.

But Megan guessed. "You know, don't you?" The tears started again.

Sara, sitting beside her, put her arm around Megan,

and drew her head down to her shoulder. "We heard that someone was going to be charged, but not who. Why would it be Kyle?"

"Because everyone in town knows that Kyle was the reason Mrs. Beeson put up that giant fence. They all *saw* what had been done to her."

Jack looked as though he was running out of patience. "I've lived here all my life but I have no idea what you're talking about."

Megan sat up and blew her nose. "Oh, Jack, you live here, but you don't. You're always running off to New York, and besides, you have such major father issues that you don't see anything else."

Jack's eyes widened at that and Kate had to suppress a laugh.

Sara said, "I haven't lived here in years so why don't you tell me the whole story?"

It took Megan a while to get her breath. She finished the rum drink and hastily drank a cup of tea. "My brother, Kyle, and his wife, Carolyn, used to live next door to Janet Beeson."

"In that three and a half bath with the beveled glass door?" Kate asked. "Or the other side, the four bedroom with the Moorish facade?"

Both Sara and Jack gave her looks to stop it.

"Sorry," Kate mumbled. "Job hazard."

"Glass door. They loved their house. Kyle did a lot of work on it. He added—" Megan waved her hand, then took a breath. "My brother is a wonderful guy but he does have a bit of a problem with…uh, jealousy."

"Raving lunatic or a snide sulker?" Sara asked. "Spies on her? Suspicious of her every move?"

Megan nodded. "Yes. All of it. But it's understandable. You see, our mother—" She broke off. "I guess it doesn't matter *why*, just what *is*."

"Tell us what happened with Janet Beeson," Sara prompted gently.

"Kyle and Carolyn had been fighting for weeks. He thought she was having an affair."

"Was she?" Kate poured another cup of tea.

"I don't know. She says she wasn't, but… Anyway, Kyle wasn't in the best of moods. One night he was reading their two sons a bedtime story and it had a witch in it."

"Ah," Jack said and they looked at him. "You mentioned witches. Go on."

"Brandon, the oldest and a very serious boy even at eight, asked my brother about witches. Were they always women? What did they look like? That sort of thing."

Megan took a drink of her tea. "Kyle told me that he didn't mean to, but what he said was a bit harsh. He… well, he described their next-door neighbor, Mrs. Beeson, as what a witch looked like. But then, just that day, she had again returned a soccer ball the boys kicked over the little fence. It had landed in her flower beds. Mrs. Beeson said that her garden was a memorial to her friend and it was important that she keep it the way it always had been. Kyle said she was nice about it all but with his bad mood…" Megan looked at them, waiting for their nod of understanding.

"So he equated Mrs. Beeson with a witch?" Sara encouraged.

"Yes. And that caused my nephews to…to…"

"What did the kids do?" Jack asked.

Megan took a gulp of her rum drink but there was only melted ice in the glass. "The next day the boys—" she swallowed "—got a spray can of red paint and wrote *witch* in three-foot-high letters on Mrs. Beeson's garage door."

For a moment they were silent, then Kate spoke. "What did your brother do about it?"

"The good thing was that the incident snapped him out of his jealousy streak. He and Carolyn were mortified. They apologized profusely, then made the boys scrub at the paint."

"Fat lot of good that would do," Jack said. "Soap doesn't erase paint."

"But I bet it taught them a lesson," Sara said. "Including your brother."

"It did! The boys thought the world was ending. And Kyle felt really bad about it all. I felt soooo sorry for them."

"What about Mrs. Beeson?" Jack asked.

"She was nice and understanding. Kyle paid someone to remove all the paint from her garage door then repaint it."

Sara was leaning back against the couch and frowning in concentration. "And that was the incident that made Janet put up the steel wall around her house?"

"Yes," Megan said. "The paint wasn't dry on the garage door before the men came in with their machines. Kyle and Carolyn hated that she'd felt she had to imprison herself against them."

"When did this happen?" Jack asked.

"About a year ago." Megan put her face in her hands and began softly crying.

"You think *this* is why Kyle is going to be charged with murder?" Jack asked.

"Yes. Janet Beeson was the nicest person in the world. She helped everybody. Wasn't she a big part of working with you on the Morris case?"

"Yes she was, but…" There was caution in Sara's voice.

"So now you can find out who really killed her and clear my brother's name." Megan exhaled in relief and looked like she was about to leave.

"Wait a minute!" Jack said. "We are *not* some sort of local detectives. We don't go around solving murders."

"Besides," Kate said, "some graffiti from a year ago isn't enough to charge someone with *murder*! I mean, really. Kids doing rotten things is normal. Am I right?"

Jack nodded, but Sara looked at Megan. "What's the *real* reason you think your brother will be charged?"

Megan swallowed. "Kyle said Mrs. Beeson never forgave him."

"I wouldn't either," Sara said. "That must have hurt her deeply. Today, living alone is considered to be an almost criminal act. We're all supposed to be club members and partygoers and filled with love at the very thought of a huge Thanksgiving. And don't even get me started on Christmas! Poor Janet must have been traumatized by being called a witch by people who frequently desecrated her garden. She…"

At the looks they were giving her, Sara trailed off. "Sorry, but I'm on Janet's side. Older women living

alone are the target of too many jokes and snide remarks for me to sympathize with other people."

"I know," Megan said softly. "I think everyone will
feel that way. And since absolutely no one else in this
town has done anything bad to her and since everyone
saw *witch* painted on her door, they'll go after Kyle."

"I think the sheriff will probably talk to him," Kate
said. "But I imagine he'll talk to a lot of people."

"Like who?" Megan snapped. "Janet Beeson was a
gentle, kind woman whose best friend killed herself. I
remember how she looked after Mrs. Alden died. Sylvia was Kyle and Carolyn's next-door neighbor and
they adored her. She used to bake brownies and she
made Halloween costumes for the boys. We were all
devastated by her death. The boys felt like they'd lost
a grandmother."

Megan's tears began again. "Then Mrs. Beeson
bought the house and I guess we expected her to be
like Sylvia."

"But she wasn't?" Sara asked.

"Mrs. Beeson was quieter, but then she was grieving
over the loss of her friend. When she wasn't helping
around town, she stayed inside her house, not bothering anyone. She gave but didn't receive."

Megan again buried her face in her hands. "My
brother is the *only* person in town who has *ever* been
nasty to Janet Beeson."

Jack stood up. "Megan," he said firmly, "I think you
should go to Sheriff Flynn in the morning and tell him
everything. Personally, I think he's going to tell you to
go home and quit worrying. No one's going to think
your brother murdered a woman because she never

forgave him for something his kids did. Your brother made amends as best he could."

"Will you tell Sheriff Flynn for me?"

"No!" Jack said. "That's your job, not ours." He held out his hand to help her up. "I want you to go home and get some sleep. You've worked yourself into a frenzy for no reason."

She looked up at Jack and batted her tear-dampened lashes. "You think so?"

"Yes, I do." His voice was firm, allowing no disagreement. With his hand on her lower back, he ushered her to the front door.

"I always liked you, Jack," Megan said. "Remember that date we went on when you were a senior and I was just a junior? You were such a gentleman. I've always wondered why you didn't ask me out on a second date."

"Your brother…uh, asked me not to."

"He did?"

Jack opened the door and half shoved her out. "Go home and sleep and tomorrow go talk to the sheriff. Got it?"

She smiled. "I will."

He shut the door, leaned on it, and looked at Sara and Kate.

"So why didn't you ask her out again?" Kate asked.

"She was a fluffy-brained giggler. And besides, her brother said he'd take a sledgehammer to my truck if I so much as touched her."

"With a temper like that," Kate said, "maybe he did do something to Janet Beeson."

Sara gave a snort. "Ha! If I had a younger sister and

an eighteen-year-old Jack got near her, I'd have pulled out a shotgun."

"I can understand that," Kate said. "So what's changed about him now?"

Jack groaned. "I'm going back to bed. Alone. In spite of my undeserved reputation." He rubbed his eyes. "Little kids painting *witch* on a door as a cause for murder," he mumbled. "Ridiculous."

"If Janet had murdered him, I'd understand," Sara said. "But not the other way around."

Kate looked thoughtful. "Maybe Janet and Carolyn were having the affair and Kyle—"

"I'm the writer," Sara said, "so don't steal my job. But that isn't a bad idea for a story. If—"

"Bed!" Jack said and headed down the hall.

Smiling, Sara and Kate separated and went to their own rooms.

FOUR

At 2:00 a.m. the doorbell started again. This time it was accompanied by sharp rapping on glass.

Again, Kate struggled out of bed and again her foot got caught in her pants leg. "Why should I bother?" she mumbled. "Why don't I just go to the door in my T-shirt and undies? Better yet, I'll stay in bed and let Jack and Aunt Sara handle it."

The doorbell kept going in spurts, like a siren warning of an approaching tornado. She grabbed a pair of sweatpants off a hook and pulled them on.

As before, Jack was by the front door. In spite of the noise, he was leaning against the jamb, his eyes closed, half-asleep. Sara was sluggishly walking toward them. She'd put on a silky blue pajama set that looked like it was from a 1930s Carole Lombard movie.

"Who is it?" Kate asked.

"Three girls," Jack said. "I know their parents but not them. But I've heard enough to know that they travel in a Mean Girl pack. Nastiest of the nasties. You know, it would help if girls didn't become pretty until they reached twenty-one."

"Ugliness would have stopped *you* in high school?" Kate asked, yawning.

Jack didn't reply, but placed himself in front of the door, then opened it. He wasn't going to let this batch run into Sara.

Sure enough, three very pretty teenage girls ran in and slammed into him. For all that it was the wee hours of the morning, the girls were beautifully groomed: shiny, styled hair, so much makeup a circus performer would be envious, and clothes that could grace the cover of a fashion magazine.

"Oh, Jack," the middle one said. "You have to help us."

"Yes, Jack," the blonde one said. "We don't want to go to jail."

The last girl was looking at Kate. "Is this your girlfriend everyone talks about? I didn't know you liked red hair." She stroked her own dark locks. "I could dye mine if you—"

Sara spoke up. "Is this about Janet Beeson?"

"Yes," the first girl said. She was the tallest and seemed to be the leader. "Sheriff Flynn told my father he wanted to talk to us at eight a.m. We don't know what to say."

Jack was standing by the door. "How about the truth? Now that that's settled, you can go home."

The girls didn't move. The taller one started to cry in a way that didn't mess up her makeup. The others followed her lead.

Jack looked like he wanted to join them. "We have nothing to do with this case so there's no reason for you to tell us anything, and certainly no reason for you to be here at two in the morning. Save your story for the sheriff."

"But everyone in Lachlan knows *you* solved the last case," the tall one said.

"Yes." The blonde wiped her eyes—and didn't so much as smear her three shades of eyeshadow. "You were brilliant."

They were nearly afloat in self-pity.

"Come on," Sara said tiredly as she led the way to the living room. "Tell us why Sheriff Flynn wants to talk to you."

The girls sat down on the couch, the tall one in the middle. "I'm Madison and this is Ashley and Britney." She didn't tell which was which.

The blonde spoke up. "We weren't very nice to Mrs. Beeson."

Jack was still standing. "Did you kill her?"

The girls' eyes widened in horror. "No," Madison whispered.

"Then there is no problem. Just tell the sheriff that you were rotten little snakes to a lovely old woman, then go home and start being nice to people. Everyone in town will appreciate that." He half turned, his arm held out toward the door.

The girls didn't move. They just sat there looking at Kate and Sara with pleading eyes.

"Jack," Sara said, "could you get them something to—?"

"No." He sat down. "I don't want this town to hear

that we entertain guests all night long." He looked in warning at the girls. "Do your parents know where you are?"

They shook their heads.

"Tomorrow I'm going to talk to them about putting iron bars on your bedroom windows."

"Fire marshal won't allow it," Madison said. "My dad already asked."

Sara gave Jack a look to shut up, then back at the girls. "Tell us what happened."

"It all started because Mrs. Beeson was…" Madison looked at the other girls.

"Fat and boring." The dark-haired girl couldn't take her eyes off Jack.

"And she was always watching us," the blonde said. "It was creepy."

"From what I've seen of you three, you *need* watching," Jack said.

"Whatever." Madison waved her hand in dismissal. "We didn't mean for her to hear us."

"Or see us when we, uh…you know, acted like her," the blonde added.

Kate had been listening without speaking, but she was the youngest, so she had a better idea of what the girls had done. "So which one of you is the best at mimicking?"

The one who was fascinated by Jack lifted her hand.

"And you are?"

"Britney," she whispered. Everyone was quiet as they waited for her to speak. "I just pretended I was her, that's all. She walked funny and she never said much and she…" Britney looked at her hands.

"And poor Janet heard you making fun of her." Sara didn't conceal her disgust.

Madison sat up straighter. "We told them all that we were sorry."

"And we paid for it," Ashley said. "My dad grounded me for two whole weeks."

"Are you saying you did this in *public*?" Jack was aghast.

"What media did you use?" Kate asked.

Madison gave her a haughty look. "We aren't stupid. We know that using the internet means it goes out to the world. We thought we were alone. Private."

"So where were you?" Sara asked.

"We were on the stage at school, behind the curtain," Madison said. "We'd told our parents to pick us up thirty minutes after the show ended so we'd have time to hang out. We've been best friends since kindergarten."

"We didn't know our parents were there waiting for us," Ashley said.

"And why didn't they turn off the video camera after the play ended?" Madison sounded as though everything was someone else's fault.

The adults were looking at them in openmouthed astonishment. Without a word, Jack got up and poured three gin and tonics. A G&T was the only drink Sara would take. He handed them to Sara and Kate, then sat down with his.

"Could we please have—" Madison began.

"No," Jack said.

Sara cleared her throat. "So. You made fun of Mrs.

Beeson in a hateful way in front of the school's video system. Is that right?"

The girls nodded.

Kate leaned forward. "Did it play live on the big screens in the auditorium?"

They nodded.

"How many people saw it?" Jack asked.

"About twenty. Or so."

"And Janet was one of them," Sara said.

They nodded.

"And all your parents did was ground you for a couple of weeks?" Jack's tone told what he thought of that.

"With today's parents," Sara said, "be glad they weren't rewarded for being creative."

Britney's eyes lit up. "My dad said I was smack on in my impersonation. He wants me to take acting classes. And my mother said—" She broke off at the scowls from the adults.

Jack drained his glass and stood up. "Okay, you've told us, but there's still nothing we can do. So go home."

"You haven't heard it all." Madison was looking at her hands.

"I've heard about all I can stand," Jack said. "If we did have something to do with finding a murderer, I might put the lot of you at the head of my list."

The girls hung their heads and said nothing.

With a sigh, Jack sat back down. "Out with it."

"The next day," Britney said, "the texts about me started."

"I thought you were grounded," Jack said.

"We still had our phones." Madison was looking at Jack as though he were daft.

"What did the texts say?" Sara asked.

"That I was fat and ugly and—"

"We didn't send them!" Ashley's teeth were clenched. "We've told you that a thousand times!"

"But they came from your phones." Britney sounded exasperated.

"But we didn't—"

"Okay," Sara said loudly. "What you believe can be as important as the truth. What happened then?"

The two girls looked at Britney, then they held hands.

"I took some of my mother's pills. Too many of them." Tears glistened in her eyes. "I just wanted my friends back." She wiped away the tears. "Mrs. Beeson found me and called an ambulance. She saved my life."

"How did she know what you were doing?" Sara asked.

The girls looked down at their hands and didn't speak.

"Facebook?" Kate asked.

Britney nodded but didn't look up.

Sara's eyes widened. "You took pills in front of a camera? I've heard of that, but—" She took a deep breath and her voice lowered. "You didn't want a life without friends—and neither did Mrs. Beeson."

Britney's head was down and big tears were dropping onto her hands.

Again, Jack stood up, but this time he wasn't angry. "Come on, I'm going to drive all of you home."

The girls looked up in alarm.

"And yes, I'm going to wake up your parents to be

sure they know you sneaked out. Tomorrow they're going to go with you to answer the sheriff's questions."

When they didn't move, he said loudly, "Up. *Now!*"

The girls obeyed.

Kate went after him. "I'll go with you."

"No," Jack said. "Get some sleep." His face softened. "But thanks for the offer."

When Kate awoke again, it was nearly 9:00 a.m. and the house was blessedly quiet. She sent a text to her boss, Tayla, saying she'd be late, then took her time showering and dressing. She felt groggy and her mind was full of what she'd heard last night.

The smell of bacon cooking drew her into the kitchen.

Jack was sitting at the counter, his laptop open; Aunt Sara was at the big induction range.

"You okay?" He didn't look up.

"Fine," Kate said. "There weren't any more visitors last night, were there? I could have slept through a riot."

"Just two," Jack said.

"Did I really sleep through them?"

Sara put bacon on a platter. "Jack called that security firm we used last time and they came right away. They sent away the other people who felt they needed to confess."

"The guards told them to write their stories and email them to me." He turned his laptop to face her. "Like to read them?"

"No." She took the stool beside him. "Was there a motive for murder in any of them?"

"For Janet to eliminate some people, yes," Sara said.

"After all I've heard, I don't understand why she stayed in Lachlan."

Kate made herself a bowl of cereal. "So tell me what the people said."

Jack turned his computer back around. "Valerie Johnson showed up at six a.m. She felt she had to tell us that she wasn't very nice after she won a crochet contest and Janet came in second. I think Miss Val gloated about her win."

Kate yawned. "So Janet murdered her, right?"

"My thoughts, exactly." Sara put a platter of deviled eggs before them.

Jack continued. "About a year ago, Lyn Kelson, hairdresser, had a very bad day and accidentally dyed Janet's hair a greenish gray."

Kate tried to suppress a laugh but was only half-successful. "She changed it back, right?"

"Yes, but they had to wait forty-eight hours. Poor Janet had to wear a scarf over her hair for the whole weekend."

"Let me guess," Sara said. "Janet was very nice about it all."

"She was. She shamed them by being—and I quote—'absolutely lovely about everything.' She even bought a scarf that coordinated with the green of her hair."

Kate ate her high-fiber cereal and a couple of deviled eggs. "No doubt the Nesbitt boys saw her hair and that influenced their idea of her being a witch. Is it just me who thinks all this is ridiculous? Why would anyone consider themselves to be a murder suspect over such tiny things? We all gloat when we win. One time a hairdresser dyed my mother's hair a shade of apricot. I thought it was very pretty. Why do these people think they'll be suspected of *murder*?"

Jack and Kate looked at Sara.

"Why are you two staring at me?"

"Because you're the writer," Jack said. "You wrote seventy-some books so you should be able to come up with an idea of who, what, and why."

"Seventy books?" Kate said. "I had no idea it was that many."

"In the romance world, I'm a wimp. A slug. A lazy writer. Some of them write a book a month."

"We just need one more," Jack said. "What's your instinct about this?"

"My first thought is guilt. I think these people did or said more than they're telling. Valerie said she 'gloated' over her win. What exactly does that mean? Sent Janet black roses and a nasty note? Lyn said she'd had a 'bad day.' Maybe she did something else to Janet besides color. I think there's more to these stories."

"But how could they think that any of these petty arguments could cause them to be accused of murder?" Kate asked. "It makes no sense."

"No, it doesn't," Sara said.

"What's your second thought?" Jack asked.

"That this has something to do with Sylvia Alden. I can't get her out of my mind. I get the impression of mega money with her. And Janet bought her house. There's too much coincidence there." She thought for a moment. "And there are conflicting stories. Heather said Sylvia was a recluse who rarely left the house. That conjures a vision of a fearful woman peeping through the curtains. At best she comes across as shy and awkward. But from what Megan Nesbitt said, that description is far from what Sylvia Alden actually was."

"She made costumes for the boys and they all loved her," Kate said.

Jack nodded. "She wasn't agoraphobic. She did go places."

"Right," Sara said. "I can't quite put a character to her. Something doesn't add up. And why did Janet buy Sylvia's house?"

"Sentiment?" Kate finished her cereal. "Janet told the Nesbitt family that she'd even kept the gardens the same as a memorial to her friend. But what if there was something more?"

"I remember a story where the heroine's house was used to store drugs," Sara said. "She ended up being mixed up with some drug lord."

"Did she marry him?" Kate asked as she reached for Jack's computer.

Sara laughed. "*Amazing Grace*. You like that movie too?"

"*Love* it!"

"I have it on DVD. Maybe tonight we can watch it."

"Could you two come back to the present?" Jack said.

"You mean to trying to figure out a murder case we've said we want no part of? *That* present?"

Jack wasn't bothered by Kate's sarcasm. "We need to make people understand that we aren't involved."

"And that we need sleep," Sara said.

They turned to Kate, but she was looking at the past

real estate contracts she'd brought up online. "Tayla was the broker on the house sale to Janet Beeson."

At the mention of the name, Sara went back to the stove.

Jack gave a look at Kate to say, *Now you've done it.* She had mentioned Tayla. The forbidden name.

Kate was unperturbed. "I'll get the facts on this, and we'll add it to the report to Sheriff Flynn. Any word on when he wants the photos?"

"None." Sara looked up. "Wonder if anyone went to *him* last night."

"I doubt it," Jack said. "They just want to tell *us* their guilty secrets so *we* can tell them to go home and feel better."

Kate picked up her buzzing phone. "As I said, none of this makes sense. I just got a text from Tayla. She's overwhelmed with potential buyers. It looks like the news has made people realize that our town exists. I need to go." She kissed Aunt Sara, said goodbye to Jack, grabbed her bag, and left the house.

That evening, Kate got home just after five. She slammed the door behind her.

Jack was sitting directly ahead in the living room, laptop open. "Bad day?"

She sat down on the sofa across from him. "Only if you consider three reporters pretending to be clients maddening. I should've known people wouldn't be rushing to move to a town with a fresh, unsolved murder. Then there was my boss. Tayla was so nervous today that when someone dropped a box of paper clips on the carpet, she let out a little scream. Where's Aunt Sara?"

"Writing her anger away. She received a hundred and eight emails today."

"Yeow. That may be a record. Was it more people confessing they did something rotten to Janet Beeson?"

"It was mostly friends teasing that she was living a TV series about finding another murder in Lachlan. Her agent said three publishing houses were offering her new contracts if she'd tell all." He looked up at her. "No one knows for sure that we saw the body, but everyone assumes we did because of what happened last time."

Kate leaned back against the couch. "Why are you home so early?"

"Let's see. Two people came by the job site to ask if the Morris house was haunted. Four people arrived with cameras to ask me what Mrs. Beeson's body looked like. That girl Britney showed up and tried to put her hand inside my shirt. And, oh yeah, Gil shot himself in the foot with a nail gun. I had to rush him to the hospital. And before you ask, he's fine. His ego is more hurt than his foot."

Kate gave him a look of sympathy. "Anyone at the hospital ask you questions?"

"No. They just took turns telling me what a wonderful person Mrs. Beeson was. She sorted out one doctor's entire accounting system—for free. He sent her five pots of white orchids in thanks."

"I guess we can cross him off the suspect list as having done something awful to her. How many people are still a possibility?"

"None," Sara said. She'd left her writing room and sat down by her niece. "I talked to Heather. She spent the day doing deep research. She had her hair done at Best Day, looked at a Tiffany lamp at Out of the Attic, had tea at Mitfords, and… Ivy is going to kill her for this, but your mother spent an hour browsing at Caroleena's Bridal Salon. And somewhere in there, Heather had a cozy, chatty lunch with the owner of Kendal Place Inn."

Jack gave a low whistle. "Those are the gossip centers of this town. I owe her an oil change."

"I sent your mom flowers as thanks and in sympathy."

"Did anyone have anything bad to say about Janet?" Kate asked.

"Not a word. Just the opposite. She seems to have helped a lot of people. She was even nice to Eric Yates."

Jack groaned.

"Tell me all," Kate said.

"He's the local Lothario," Sara said. "Late sixties but thinks he's twenty. Flirts with all the females who come into his drugstore. He told Heather he felt bad because when Janet first came to town, she thought he was serious when he suggested they go out together. She showed up on a Saturday night at seven, dressed up in a red suit and high heels."

"Poor thing," Kate said.

"Jerk!" Sara muttered. "He did that to me when I got back, only I was repulsed. You should see him! Cigarette-stained teeth, cheap toupee, a little belly that curves down like a sack of flour resting on his belt."

Kate smiled. "That's a vivid image. I hope Janet got angry and told him off."

"Nope. Heather called a woman Eric said had been a witness. She said that when Janet found out his invitation was a joke, she was gracious. But Eric did say that Janet never returned to his store."

"I don't blame her." Kate slipped off her shoes and put her bare feet on the coffee table. "What do you think Sheriff Flynn is doing now?"

"Talking on the phone," Jack said.

"And you know this how?" Sara asked.

"One of the nurses at the hospital is a friend of Bea's."

"Who is Daryl's right-hand man," Sara told Kate.

"She runs the office," Jack said. "She said Flynn is at his desk, no visitors, but he's on the phone a lot. Not doing much of anything."

"Which is probably why everyone is coming to *us*!" Kate said.

"Seems so," Sara said. "How do we stop it?"

Jack looked across at the two women sitting side by side. "You mean other than by solving the crime? I don't know and I don't want to attempt it."

They looked at Sara.

"I agree. It's just that…"

"What?"

"I'm beginning to identify with Janet Beeson. Older people are *all* assumed to be senile and—gag me with a spoon—*cute*. I *hate* cute! Last week I called to make an appointment and the girl asked for my birth date. When I told her, she gasped. Then she started talking to me in slow baby talk because I'm—you know—on the verge of dementia. And someone my age has never used a computer. Certainly can't work a cell phone. I wanted to—" Sara took a breath. "I just feel sorry for Janet, that's all. No one seems to have seen her as a person, just an old woman—which of course means she was *sweet*."

Jack stood up and held out his hand to Sara. "Come on and let's have dinner. I vote that we send all that we have to ol' Flynn and never think about any of this ever again."

"Sounds good to me." Kate looked at her aunt. "Where did you get those blue pajamas?"

"A company called PJ Harlow. I have a pair that I haven't shortened the legs on. Want them?"

"Ooooh yes," Kate said as they walked to the kitchen.

Behind them, Jack was smiling in fondness.

FIVE

The doorbell began ringing at ten minutes after 1:00 a.m. Kate woke, pulled the cover over her head, and tried to block out the sound. *Jack will deal with it*, she thought. And why hadn't the security men stopped whoever it was?

Last night they'd taken big platters of food out to the guards. At the far end of the property was a shed that Jack had remodeled into a little guesthouse. It had a living room/kitchen, bedroom/bath so the men could use that while they watched over the place.

The doorbell didn't stop. It wasn't frantic or hysterical, but slow and steady. *Beeep, beeep*, then pause and repeat.

Kate threw the covers off. "Please stop," she whispered, then cursed Jack for having the house wired so the bell could be heard everywhere. "Why aren't they getting that?"

The answer came to her immediately. "Because

they're waiting for me," she muttered as she got out of bed. "One for all, all for one. No matter what time it is."

She snatched up a robe Aunt Sara had bought in China and lent her—dark blue with pale blue peonies—slipped it over the slinky pajamas, and left her suite. Sure enough, Aunt Sara and Jack were standing in front of the closed door, just waiting.

"It's the sheriff," Sara said. "Thought you'd want to hear what he has to say."

The doorbell was still going off as Jack looked the women in their silky jammies up and down. "Sure you two are well dressed enough to receive guests? I could wait while you do your hair. Or maybe your nails?"

"I could use some new polish," Kate said.

Smiling, Sara nodded at Jack and he opened the door. Sheriff Flynn stood there in jeans and a blue cotton shirt. There were dark circles under his eyes and the lines radiating out the side of his face were deeper.

Jack stepped back and made an exaggerated gesture of entrance.

"Sorry for the late hour," the sheriff said, "but I'm being watched closely. Not officially, but still… I sneaked out a second-story window to get here." He held out his left hand, which was covered in blood.

Sara took over. She led him into the kitchen and held his hand under a stream of cold water. "Bandages are in the—"

"I know," Jack said as he motioned for Kate to follow him. They went across the foyer to Sara's bathroom. "What took you so long to get to the door?"

"The desire for sleep. And I thought you two could handle whatever it was."

Sara's bathroom was octagon shaped, holding two sink counters with lots of drawers beneath. A large glass-walled shower was at the end. To the left, a toilet and bidet were in their own room. On the right was a tub that had windows to a private garden.

Jack went to the drawer that held first aid supplies.

"What do you think he wants?" she asked.

"To tell us he loves us and misses us. The same as the others wanted us to know."

She just looked at him, waiting for him to answer her question.

Jack handed her tape and gauze. "Flynn is going to do a sob story to try to get you and Sara on his side. He'll do his best to drag us into this, but I don't want us to have anything to do with it."

"But he…" Kate began then stopped. "Aren't we already involved? Can *you* get the sight of that body out of your mind? A knife *and* a gun, *and*—"

"I know!" Jack said. "That's the point. Whoever did this is ruthless. And now he or she—"

"It's a he. It has to be a man. It takes strength to—"

"Have you looked at those women at the gym? They have arms that make most men's look flabby. They could easily use a knife and a—"

"I get it. You don't need to be graphic." She held up the tape. "We have to take this in there. Poor Sheriff Flynn looked like he was about to bleed to death."

"And we wouldn't want blood on your pajamas, would we?"

"You could give jealousy lessons to Kyle Nesbitt." Kate left the bathroom, Jack close behind her.

"I bet his wife didn't entertain visitors wearing her nightclothes."

Kate clenched her teeth, then stopped and smiled. "I have on absolutely nothing under this. Just my skin." Still smiling, she went to the kitchen.

Sara and Sheriff Flynn were in the family room sitting on the big sofa, sipping drinks and laughing. He had a couple of cartoon bandages on his hand.

"And Cal!" Sheriff Flynn was saying. "I thought he was going to kill Roy and Randal—and me—when they wrecked that old Jeep."

"Ah," Sara said, "the back seat of that Jeep! I lost it there. Lord only knows what Randal and Roy used it for. And you."

"I'd have to forfeit my badge if I told the truth about those two, but Evie and I spent most of our senior year on those old springs. She said I gave her all my energy because she made straight A's while I nearly failed everything. Old man Lakely was—"

"He wasn't still there, was he? He was old in my day."

"Still there, still telling us he was going to give a sex education class. But he didn't know enough about the subject to tell us anything."

"Cal's Jeep should have been the guest lecturer," Sara said and the two of them dissolved into laughter.

Jack had been waiting for them to finish their stories, but when he cleared his throat, they kept laughing.

Kate stood on tiptoe to whisper to Jack, "They're talking about my father and yours."

"The saint and the devil," Jack said, then stepped

forward. "Excuse me but some of us need to get some sleep. We have work in the morning."

"Lot like his dad, isn't he?" Sheriff Flynn said to Sara.

She laughed. "More so than he thinks he is."

The two older people worked to get themselves under control while Jack and Kate—their faces disapproving—took the chairs across from them. Kate loudly dumped the medical supplies on the coffee table. "I guess you didn't need these after all."

Jack had no humor in his eyes. "You want to tell us what's so important that you had to come here at this hour?"

Daryl rubbed his hand. "The cut wasn't as bad as it looked. I always do bleed a lot. Anyway, I just wanted to know what you lot had found out."

Jack stood up. "We'll send you a report." He was waiting for the sheriff to leave, but the man didn't move.

Kate thought she and Jack must look like the parents while Sara and the sheriff were the naughty teenagers. Jack was still standing, and Kate looked around him. "You knew my father well?"

"As well as anyone could know someone like Randal Medlar. He was a difficult— Oof!"

Sara had elbowed him in the ribs.

"Randal wasn't someone who confided in people," the sheriff said. "Tended to keep his business to himself." Daryl seemed to be uncomfortable with that line of questioning and looked up at Jack. "You planning to stand up through this whole thing?"

With his jaw clenched, Jack sat back down.

Sara, who had minutes before seemed like besties with the sheriff, turned cold eyes to him. "Tell us what you know."

Daryl hesitated, as though he might refuse, but then he looked at their faces and took a deep drink of his iced tea. "No one in town really knew Janet Beeson. A lot of people could identify her, tell a story or two about a nice thing she did, but that's about all. So far, no one has been able to find out where she came from or who the Mr. to her Mrs. is—or was."

Kate looked at Jack and Sara. She wanted to say that they hadn't realized they didn't know those things. But she just nodded.

"It's being treated as a possible serial killing," Daryl said.

Involuntarily, Kate drew in her breath.

When everyone looked at her, she mumbled. "Sorry. Go on."

"We don't want the details to become public knowledge. People might get so scared that they close their houses with hurricane shutters," the sheriff said. "We don't want a panic."

"Especially since the idea of a serial killer is absurd," Jack said.

The sheriff leaned back against the pillows and smiled. "That's just what I said, but no one listened to me. They've found a couple of murders in California that sort of fit what was done to Janet and they're checking into them."

They just looked at him.

"No comments?" he asked.

"How do you reply to absolute stupidity?" Jack asked.

Sheriff Flynn squinted at Jack. "How about coming up with some evidence that shows they're wrong? What do you have?"

Kate looked at Jack and Sara and saw that they weren't going to speak. "We've heard the same as you. Mrs. Beeson was a very nice woman who helped a lot of people. No one has a bad word to say about her. She even saved a girl's life."

"Britney Mason." The sheriff was nodding. "Her parents were really grateful to Janet. They sent her lots of flowers as thanks."

"And what else?" Sara asked.

The sheriff looked confused. "What else should they have done?"

"I don't know," Sara said. "A parade. Pay off her mortgage. If she'd saved my child…" She didn't finish.

"I never thought of that," the sheriff said.

"As usual, no one seems to have thought of actually repaying Mrs. Beeson," Sara said. "She came in second in a contest and the winner gloated. Janet gave kindness in return. Her hair was dyed green and Janet was nice about it. She cleared up a doctor's billing and he sent a potted plant. And Eric—" She closed her mouth.

"And those girls were monsters to her, but she saved a life," Kate said.

"From what we've seen," Sara said, "Janet had reason to hold grudges against several people, but not the other way around. And we've heard *no* motives strong enough for murder."

"Who is it that you're planning to arrest?" Jack shot out.

There was a quick look of surprise on the sheriff's face, then he went back to showing nothing. "They found something but I don't think it means anything."

When he said nothing more, Sara said, "What was found?"

"I can't tell you. I want to, but I can't risk—" He stopped talking.

"Her connection to Sylvia Alden?" Sara asked.

The sheriff's eyes lit up. "Exactly! In the last twenty-four hours I've heard her name a thousand times. I think she has something to do with this, but no one will listen to me. How do you think they're connected?"

"That's a question we should ask you," Jack said.

"I got so sick of hearing her name that I called Sylvia's family." He reached into his shirt pocket, pulled out a piece of paper, and put it on the coffee table. "I knew her. She was a lovely woman, so tall and slim and gracious to everyone. She and Tom used to put on the best parties. The food... I always ate far too much." For a moment he stared into the distance in memory. "Then Tom died and Sylvia withdrew into herself."

Sheriff Flynn shrugged. "When Janet came to town, they started hanging out together, and that was the end of all Sylvia's outside social life."

"You think they were lovers?" Kate asked.

The sheriff gave a snort. "You young kids. It's never friendship—it's always sex. No, I don't think they were." He paused. "Evie said—" He looked at Kate. "She's my wife. High school sweethearts."

"With a penchant for the back seat of an old Jeep," Kate said.

He looked at Sara. "She's Randal's daughter, all right. Doesn't miss a thing. Anyway, years ago, Evie said that there was something unusual between those two. I asked if she meant a friendship bond. Evie said that whatever it was, it was very, very strong."

"Have you recently asked her what she meant?" Sara asked.

"I did. She said it just seemed like Sylvia and Janet *had* to be together. Couldn't bear to be parted."

"What happened when you called Sylvia's family?" Sara asked.

"It took a while to get to a person who knew her. I had to go through three household staff, all the way up to the butler. Who has a butler nowadays?"

No one answered him.

"So finally, I got Sylvia's older brother on the phone. He was a real bastard. Very cold. Said that his sister had turned her back on her family when she married. And the way she'd passed was an embarrassment to them. He was going to hang up on me, but I asked if he could give me the name and number of Tom's family. He said that they knew nothing about *that man.* Then he hung up." Sheriff Flynn looked at them in silence.

Kate spoke up. "In essence, Mrs. Alden had no real family except her husband, and after he died, she had no one. Mrs. Beeson must have been a godsend to her."

"Any children?" Sara asked.

"A daughter, Lisa. Married a lawyer named Wellman. They live in Boston, no kids. I didn't contact her, but the fact that no one in Lachlan seems to have ever met the daughter says a lot."

"I'm beginning to see why Sylvia killed herself," Kate said. "She must have been miserable. Do you know if she was ill?"

"Her doctor said no."

"How does all this connect to Janet Beeson's murder?" Jack asked.

"No idea," Sheriff Flynn said. "But we hit a dead end with Janet. No passport. As far as we can tell, she gave a false birth certificate to get a Florida driver's license."

"She was hiding," Kate said.

"Sounds like they both were," Sara said. "Sylvia ran off with Tom—*that man* as her family called him—and Janet was hiding from…" She looked up.

"From someone who finally caught up with her," Jack said.

"Is it possible that the same person who killed Janet also killed Sylvia?" Sara asked.

"Very possible," Daryl said. "The autopsy showed that Sylvia died of oleander poison. It was ground up and put over a plate of spicy food."

"But there was no investigation?" Jack asked.

"She left a signed suicide note and we all thought…" Sheriff Flynn gave a sidelong look at Sara.

"You don't have to say it," Sara said. "Older woman living alone. Widowed. Of course she did herself in. She didn't have a man so why bother to breathe? That's what people think. Read a cruise guide. Their one page on women cruising alone is all about how she can get a man. They think a woman is too afraid to walk into dinner unless a man is holding on to her arm."

Sheriff Flynn looked at Jack and Kate. "How long's she been like this?"

"Since seeing Mrs. Beeson's body," Kate said. "But she does have a point. Two older women, best friends, both reclusive, died in unusual ways. The first death was passed over for investigation and the second one is being blamed on somebody in California."

"Or maybe not." Jack looked at the sheriff, but he wouldn't meet his eyes. "What is it that you want from us?"

"Nothing," Sheriff Flynn said quickly. "I've been told that no civilians are to stick their noses into this and risk getting themselves killed."

"Like last time," Kate said. "By the way, is anyone admitting that *we* found out the truth about the Morris murders?"

"Nope. No one says that." Sheriff Flynn seemed to be waiting for something.

"What now?" Sara asked. "We jump up and down, clap our hands, and tell you how we are dying to help find a vicious murderer? And 'dying' is the key word here."

The sheriff stood up. "I better get home. Evie said she'd let the dogs out and cause chaos so I could sneak in the side door. This has been a nice visit. Sorry nobody knows anything." He looked at Jack. "You planning to sing at Janet's memorial service?"

"No." Jack stood up.

Daryl looked at Kate. "The house has been searched and they found nothing that gave any hint to Janet's origins. She was an extraordinarily clean and tidy person. Not so much as a grocery receipt could be found. We didn't find a personal computer although she used one at church."

"But she was on Facebook and saw Britney taking pills," Sara said.

Sheriff Flynn thought about that, then turned to Kate. "I persuaded Cotilla to let you have the house listing of Janet's house so you could sell it and get the commission. That okay with you?"

"Sure," Kate said.

"What about her will?" Jack asked.

"Didn't find one. Bea called several lawyers in the vicinity but they'd never heard of Janet Beeson. Did I mention that she paid for that house in cash? Almost a million. But her bank account had just four hundred and thirty-two dollars in it. Kind of odd, isn't it? Wonder where her money came from? Mr. Beeson? Or whatever his name is."

"No, you didn't mention any of that," Sara said.

"*Almost* a million?" Kate said. "But that house sold for one and a quarter mil. I saw the records."

Sheriff Flynn was blinking at her. "Eight ninety-nine went through Janet's bank account. We don't know where the money came from, but that exact amount was deposited, then a check went out to the title company."

"What about all the extras?" Kate asked. "Insurance and closing fees. Who paid the balance of what the house sold for?" She trailed off as everyone was looking at her. "I probably have the number wrong. Maybe it was less. If that's all she paid, she got a real bargain."

Sara turned to the sheriff. "Anything else?"

"Not that I can think of."

"Except what you can't tell us," Jack said.

The sheriff winced as though that thought hurt. "I'm afraid you'll hear about it all soon enough. I hope you attend the memorial service."

"Wouldn't miss it." Sara was standing close to Kate.

Jack walked Daryl to the front door and locked it behind him.

"You think—" Jack began when he got back to the women.

"I don't want to think," Sara said. "I want to go to bed and sleep."

"I agree," Kate said. "What about you?"

Jack put his hands in his pockets. "Maybe." He picked up a piece of paper off the coffee table and looked at it.

"Let me guess," Sara said. "Daryl accidentally left the name and number of Sylvia Alden's cold, snooty brother."

"He did."

"And you might do a bit of an internet search," Sara said.

"Maybe." Jack kissed her forehead and watched her walk away. He turned to Kate. "You leaving too?"

"Yes." The door to her apartment was off the family room. She turned back. "What did Sheriff Flynn mean when he said that my father was 'difficult'?"

"It was difficult to make him do what my father wanted him to do. Steal things, threaten people, get drunk, and start fights. Go to bed. Get some sleep."

Kate yawned. "I will. Good night."

Jack was looking at his computer screen as he mumbled good-night.

SIX

"Walking on eggshells." If the term hadn't already been coined, Kate would have made it up. For the last two days, everyone in their office had been tiptoeing around their boss, Tayla.

Kirkwood Realty was in a pretty house just off the Great Blue Circle, an area where cheaply built offices and ugly apartment buildings used to stand. But nineteen years ago, a widowed Tayla Kirkwood had returned to her deteriorating hometown and set about restoring it.

In the months Kate had been working there, she'd had lunches and after-work drinks with her boss. She'd enjoyed hearing Tayla tell about all she'd done to get the backing she'd needed to make the little town beautiful again. "I did everything and anything I had to, to get the money I needed. Except sex. Not that I was asked, but I would have said no. I think."

Working for and with Tayla had been a joy. She was

open to ideas and enthusiastic about whatever Kate thought of doing. Summer wasn't the good tourist season in Florida, so Kate had come up with ideas for the locals. She'd been behind two block parties and a toddlers' parade. The parade had drawn people from miles away and on that day, sales in the local stores went up 83 percent.

For Kate, the big reward had been that now when she walked down the streets, people said hello to her. Whether it was for what she'd done for Lachlan or because she'd helped solve a multiple murder was something she didn't want to think about.

Whatever the reason, Kate loved her life now so much that she sometimes got chills. Of course, there was still the problem of her widowed mother, Ava. She was living outside Chicago and without her daughter there, she was spending more time with her three older brothers and their families. In ordinary circumstances, that would have been good, but they were religious fanatics, always preaching doom and misery—and they wanted Kate and her mother to move in with them. And of course, they were expected to turn over their income to them. The uncles were very angry that Kate had escaped them, and lately Ava was starting to ask when Kate was coming "home."

Every time, she had to work not to say, "I *am* home." Instead, she said, "My job keeps me very busy, but I'll come for a *visit* soon."

As much as Kate loved her mother, she was glad there was animosity between her and Aunt Sara. It kept Ava far away. Kate thought that if she had to go back to dealing with her mother's depressions, she just might jump out a window.

But today at work, she was beginning to think about getting in her car and driving to… Oregon? Was that far enough away? Her boss's nervousness was putting everyone on edge.

Usually, Tayla was unshakable. She was tall and slim, with gray hair that swung elegantly about her face. She seemed like she would have been calm during the sinking of the *Titanic*, and she'd been the best boss a person could ask for.

But now, Tayla was jumping at the slightest sound. She constantly asked her employees if they'd done what they'd already told her they had. Maybe her anxiety was from all the gossip in town about a deranged killer being on the loose.

Today, when Kate escaped long enough to grab a sandwich, she saw Tayla in the parking lot talking with a man. He was so deeply hidden in the shade that Kate couldn't see his face, and Tayla seemed quite agitated.

Part of her wanted to run to them and ask what was going on, but the larger part wanted nothing to do with whatever the problem was. She and Jack and Aunt Sara were standing by their decision to stay out of it. DGI— *Don't Get Involved* was becoming their motto.

This morning, Jack said he was going back to work. Sara said she was going to spend the day compiling everything they'd heard or seen about Janet Beeson into one document. And she was going to add an outline of what they thought the sheriff's department should do to further investigate the crime.

"I'm sure that will go over well," Jack said.

"They'll probably send you a thank-you card," Kate said.

"And flowers," Jack added.

"Exactly." Sara was smiling.

"I get it," Jack said. "They'll be so PO'd at you for telling them how to do their job that they'll be sure to keep us out of everything."

"Clever boy." Sara kissed his forehead. "Nothing like a meddling old woman to stir up a bunch of men wearing guns. The Wild West is alive and well in Lachlan, Florida." Laughing, she left them alone in the kitchen.

"Could I talk to you for a moment?"

Kate turned at Jack's serious tone.

"I have something to celebrate today and Sara wants nothing to do with it. Would you join me?"

She squinted her eyes. "Does this involve shots of tequila with giggling girls in tiny tank tops?"

Jack laughed. "I save those times just for me. Taking you along would be like showing up with the schoolmarm."

"Thank you. That's a nice compliment."

He grinned harder and shook his head. "No, Miss Kate, it would be just you and me. I want to show you something. No tequila, but is champagne okay?"

She looked past his laughter and into his eyes. Whatever it was, it was special to him. "I'd love to."

"Great. I'll meet you at your office at six."

And that's where she was now. She looked at her watch, then at the clock. It was almost six. *Please*, she thought, *let Tayla go home early*. She needed some papers that were on her boss's desk, but she didn't want to have to go in there to get them. She didn't want to deal with Tayla asking if Kate had shown any properties, if she'd talked to the last clients about something she did two days ago.

When Tayla stood up and began shoving file folders into her big bag, Kate let out a sigh of relief. In a cowardly move, she ran to the restroom. Jack would be there in minutes so she needed to freshen her makeup—at least that's what she told herself. But really, Jack was the last person she had to dress up for. He saw her on weekends with no makeup. When she'd had a bad cold, he'd kept her supplied with tissues. You couldn't be glamorous to a guy you lived with.

She stayed in the restroom longer than necessary, and when she came out, Jack was leaning on the counter talking to fellow Realtor Melissa. She had a crush on him—as did lots of females in town—and she was looking at him with starry eyes.

"There you are, Red," he said. "You look like you're going on a date."

"No, just out with my foster brother."

With lots of drama, Jack mimed being stabbed in the heart, pulling the knife out, then staggering backward into the clutches of death.

Kate tried not to laugh, but she had to turn away to hide it. She looked at the adoring Melissa. "Is she gone?"

"Who? Oh. Tayla. Yes, she left five minutes ago and everyone ran out behind her." She looked at Jack with fluttering eyelashes. "You and I are alone in the office."

"Except for me," Kate said, but Melissa ignored her.

"I have to get some papers." She went down the hall to her boss's office. The folder wasn't on top of the desk so she looked under the papers.

"Can't find it?" Jack was standing just inside the closed door.

"How'd you escape your fan?"

"I said I might be at the Brigade later and maybe I'd see her there. I think she went home to wash her hair."

"And to put on clothes just a tiny bit bigger than a bikini." Kate opened a drawer.

"My favorite garment. They had some nice ones in the window of Moonflower. I could imagine you in the blue one. It—"

She looked up to tell him to stop, then her eyes widened as she looked through the glass down the hall. "Tayla is coming."

Instantly, Jack grabbed Kate's wrist and pulled her into the powder room. She tried to close the door but a file box was in the way. The door stayed open a few inches.

Jack pulled Kate into his arms, her back to his front, then nuzzled her neck.

She elbowed his ribs sharply.

He groaned in pain. "I think I need to go to the hospital."

When she lifted her arm as though to hit him again, he laughed against her hair.

They heard the swoosh of the door, then Tayla entered the office. They could just see her through the open space. She started frantically opening drawers in her desk, but when she didn't find what she wanted, she went to the tall filing cabinet in the corner.

When her cell rang, she put it on speaker and set it on the corner of the cabinet as she kept searching through the files.

"Carl told me to call you," a male voice said. "Where are you?"

When Kate let out an involuntary gasp, Jack glared at her to be quiet. The caller was Gil Underhill, Jack's best friend, the foreman of all his jobs. The guy who had shot himself in the foot with a nail gun.

"I'm at the office. Alone." Tayla slammed a drawer shut. "I am looking for the copies of the emails, but they aren't here. People use my office. I'm afraid Kate will see them. I don't need Sara Medlar snooping into all this."

"You gave them to me and I destroyed them, remember?"

"Right. Sorry." Tayla closed the bottom drawer of the cabinet and leaned on it. "I'm on edge."

"We all are. We just need to find Sylvia's book so we can clear her name. It has to be in that house! Are you sure she didn't tell everything in one of her other novels?"

"How would I know? I never read any of them."

Gil paused. "How's Charlene holding up?"

"She doesn't know anything has happened and I want it to stay that way."

"You can't keep her in the dark for long. This town is already on fire with gossip."

Tayla turned toward the window. "That's a perfect word choice. Fire. And witches and suicides and…and white lilies." Her voice broke.

"It's going to be all right," Gil said softly. "Carl will take care of it all."

She took a deep breath. "Have you said anything to Jack?"

"And get his temper involved? No thanks! When I was at the hospital he——"

"Hospital?" She picked up the phone off the cabinet. "What happened? Was it Carl?"

"No. Just me being stupid. But all the attention was on Jack and whether he was going to work on the murder. He says they won't and I pray that he keeps his word." Gil took a breath. "I have to pick up Quinn now. I can't risk him being alone for even minutes. I want you to calm down and keep quiet about everything."

"I'm hiding it all well. No one would guess that my life is falling apart. If I see you, don't even wave. It's better that we pretend we don't know each other."

"I agree. Go home and read one of Sylvia's books."

Tayla gave a bit of a laugh. "Not a bad idea. Her book, a tub of hot water, a bottle of gin, twenty-five or so pills, and——"

"Stop it!"

"Okay. Gil, thank you."

"Save your sympathy for Charlene."

Tayla grimaced. "When I think of that poor, poor baby… Sorry again. I hope we both have an uneventful night." Tayla clicked off the phone, dropped it into her bag, and quickly left the office.

For a moment, Jack and Kate stood together, unmoving, then he dropped his arms. When Kate looked at him, his face was a stone mask. Unreadable. But he didn't fool her. What he'd just heard had deeply upset him.

"Maybe we shouldn't go…" He didn't finish.

As for Kate, she didn't know who all the people Tayla had mentioned were. Quinn was Gil's son. But Charlene? Carl?

She knew Jack meant that maybe they should call off the celebration. And then what? He would go to Gil and demand to be told what was going on? If Gil refused, would the infamous Wyatt temper come out? It's what Gil dreaded. She filled in a word for him. "We shouldn't go separately?" She made herself sound cheerful. "Good idea. I'll ride with you."

Jack took a moment as he seemed to be deciding what to do.

"Is the champagne cold?" she encouraged.

His eyes let her know that he was aware of what she was doing. "Yeah. It is. Come on, let's go."

They didn't speak as they walked to his truck and got in. As he drove, she could see a muscle working in his jaw. When he went down Heron Lane, she drew in her breath. Suddenly, she realized what he'd finally accomplished. He'd managed to buy either the house his grandfather had grown up in or Sara's old house. For years, it had been a dream of Jack's to buy them, but the owner had refused to sell. "You didn't!"

For the first time since hearing Tayla's phone conversation, his eyes lit up and he nodded.

"Which one?"

"Both."

Kate laughed in delight. "And who handled the deal?

Did—?" She cut herself off. She wasn't going to ruin this with talk of money.

"The owner has a cousin who's a Realtor. Sorry." He pulled the truck into the weed-infested driveway of a little house that looked as though it might collapse at any moment. Sagging roof, rotting porch posts, broken windows. But she knew that to Jack it was a trophy of triumph. The house had belonged to his grandfather Cal, and through the rampant Florida growth she could see a bit of the house next door. It had once belonged to Sara's family.

She got out of the truck. The place was going to take a massive amount of work. So much so that it would be easier to bulldoze the two houses and build from scratch, but she knew Jack would never do that. He'd worked for over a year to get the current owner to sell to him. When Jack came to stand beside her, she said, "Well? Are you going to show me or not?"

"It's bad inside. I don't think—"

"Oh come on. Couldn't be worse than parts of Chicago."

He gave her a look of challenge, as though to say this was, then shoved on the front door to open it. It wasn't locked.

Inside, they heard the scurry of tiny feet as creatures ran to hide. Jack flipped a switch and a floor lamp in the corner came on. "Wiring isn't to code. It'll have to be redone."

"And the plumbing, and the roof, and the…" She waved her hand. "All of it. Put in new windows and the light in here would be good."

She could see energy beginning to return to him

as he took her on a tour of the decaying house. There was a living room that opened into a dining room. Behind it was a compact kitchen, a little breakfast room, and a screened-in porch. There were two bedrooms that shared the one bathroom. The house was outdated enough to be used as a display in a museum. *What the boys from WWII came home to.*

"What do you think?" he asked when they got back to the front room.

"Tear out the wall between the kitchen and the breakfast room, make the porch into a full bath, and I can sell it." She saw him hesitate. "Or not. Thinking of keeping it?"

"Maybe. I haven't decided."

"Is the floor plan for Sara's old house like this one?"

"Identical. There were four of them in a row."

"And she never wants to see hers again?"

"Right," Jack said. "Are you hungry? I brought food."

Whether it was from hearing Tayla or the somberness of the old house, Jack wasn't his usual teasing, laughing self. "Starved," she said. "You have anything good?"

"How about a Cuban feast? I brought a cooler and some drinks and…" He shrugged.

"How bad is Aunt Sara's house?"

For the first time, he gave a real smile. "I thought you might want to go over there, so this afternoon I did a little cleaning."

"Made it into a palace, did you?"

"I wish. Help me get the stuff out of the truck and we'll eat over there." He looked at her high-heel-clad feet. "I tossed in a pair of your sandals. Thought you might need them."

Smiling, she followed him outside. He seemed to be recovering from his shock. When she saw that he'd brought her dressy gold sandals, the ones coated in rhinestones, she didn't comment.

He carried the metal cooler while she got a blanket.

"We'll go across the path Sara and Granddad used. It's still worn down after all these years."

In the months that she'd been there, Kate had been able to piece together some of the story of her aunt and Jack's grandfather. Born the same year, lived next door to each other, best friends from birth, then lovers in high school. But at graduation, there was a breakup. Whatever happened, Sara had left Lachlan to go to college, while Cal stayed behind to run his father's auto shop. He soon married a local girl and they had a son, Jack's father.

They made their way across an old path that could hardly be seen for the encroaching plants. Palm trees and spiky palmettos, with lizards darting everywhere. A tropical jungle.

Under their feet was a serpentine walkway made of rocks, broken pieces of granite, and— "Are those flattened hubcaps?"

"Yup. One of Granddad's first construction projects."

"Made so he could get to Aunt Sara."

"So they could get to each other. There's an old concrete slab through the trees. Maybe it used to have a roof and they met there, in the middle. They needed to get away from his father and her mother."

"My grandmother," Kate whispered.

The Medlar house was in as bad a shape as the Wyatts'. But the rooms had been swept, the cobwebs brushed away. Next to the living room, which had a fireplace, was a dining room with big windows flanking French doors. The doors with their broken glass had been boarded up, but through the windows she could see the rotting framework of a pergola. Rampant growth hid the land. Inside, along the back wall was a table made from a quarter sheet of plywood set on concrete blocks. Big plastic bags were in the corner, pillow edges sticking out.

"For our dining." He was looking at Kate for approval.

"You've done a beautiful job. Thank you for inviting me." She could see that her praise pleased him.

"Go on, nose around while I set up."

When it came to houses, her curiosity was insatiable. As she walked through, she realized that both houses had a forlorn air to them. It was as though she could feel the unhappiness that had been inside them. The two young people had clung to each other in an attempt to escape their lives at home. Aunt Sara had made only a few remarks about her mother. "She couldn't stand me" had been one of them.

As for Cal, he believed there was a demon in the Wyatt blood that came out every other generation. Cal's father had been a raging tyrant who drank too much. The family hex had skipped Cal and gone to his son— Jack's nasty-tempered, drunken father. Sara once said that Jack believed in "the curse" so much that he was afraid to have kids.

When Kate got back to the living room, Jack had set it up. A pretty cloth covered the plywood and a long throw rug was on the floor between the wall and the table. Sara's good china and silver, with lit candles, were on top. Big pillows provided seats. He had done some serious planning for this evening and she smiled at him. "It's lovely. Really. It's beautiful."

Smiling, Jack opened the champagne and filled their flutes.

She raised her glass toward him. "Congratulations. I know it was a long, hard struggle to get the owner to sell and I'm glad you did it."

"Me too," he said and they drank.

For the next hour, they gave themselves over to the feast he'd prepared—with help from his mother.

There was *ropa vieja*, beef with olives and capers, and rice made with toasted cumin. Everything was delicious and Jack kept filling Kate's plate until she ate too much. When he pulled two pretty little molded pumpkin flans out of the cooler, she groaned. But she ate every bite of it.

By the time they'd finished, it was dark outside, but the candles made the room glow. Jack handed her an icy pineapple mojito made with coconut rum, a sprig of mint at the rim.

In any other circumstance she would have complained that he was trying to get her drunk. But after what she'd seen and heard in the last few days, she needed something to relax her.

Kate was sitting on a pillow, leaning back against the wall, drink in hand. Straight ahead was the big window. It was dark out, not even a flicker of light. It was time to start talking. "Who is Charlene?"

"Tayla's niece. Her sister Diane's daughter." He glanced at Kate and saw that she was waiting for him to continue. "Charlene is mid to late thirties, married, has two little boys. Smart kids. Husband is a lawyer at a firm in Plantation."

"Do you know her well?"

"Yes and no. She's very pretty and I had a crush on her when I was a kid. She moved away for a few years, but came back, met her ugly husband, and that was it."

"Ugly, huh?"

He grinned. "I think so. One of those blond guys."

Kate laughed. Blond would be a stark contrast to the darkness of Jack. "What does Charlene do?"

"She builds birdhouses."

"What?"

"Really. We toss any building scraps she can use into a big box wherever we're working. Charlene and her boys come by on Saturdays and clean it out. During the week, while her family's at school and work, she makes really nice birdhouses, then ships them all over the US. She does copies of people's houses. National Register homeowners love her work."

"How interesting," Kate said. "I'd like to see them."

"We can visit her if you want."

The way he said it made her look at him sharply. "You want to find out why Tayla referred to her as 'a poor baby,' don't you?"

"Yes."

When he didn't say any more, Kate felt herself getting angry. "Jackson Wyatt! Don't you dare clam up on me. I don't want any of your prehistoric ideas of 'protecting' me. I want to know everything you do about what Tayla said."

Jack was unperturbed at her anger. "I think you do know all that I do. I had no idea Gil and Tayla knew each other. As for Charlene, she's a sweet, funny woman who adores her family and old houses. You two would probably like each other. As for the other things, we know about the witches and the attempted suicide. I have no idea what fire she was talking about. And I don't know anyone named Carl. I can't imagine how all this is connected to Janet Beeson's murder."

"Did you know that Sylvia Alden wrote books?"

"Had no idea. But if anyone knows, it'll be Sara."

"She would have told us."

"Maybe," Jack said. "But she doesn't want us to get involved."

Suddenly, Kate froze in place. In spite of two mojitos, she felt fear run through her. Her voice lowered. "There's someone outside. I saw the light from a cell phone."

The only indication Jack gave that he'd heard was a slight widening of his eyes, then he leaned back and started laughing. "That's funny," he said loudly. "Now, if you'll excuse me, I need to make a pit stop. Stay here and have another drink. I'll be right back, baby."

As though they were lovers, Jack kissed Kate's cheek. "Don't move," he whispered, then got up and stretched a bit. He didn't seem to be in a hurry.

Kate sipped her drink and forced herself not to glance at the big, dark windows. When she'd first seen them, they were beacons of light. Now they seemed like bottomless wells of darkness.

When Jack disappeared into the house, her heart began pounding, her hands shaking. She was listening with all her might but there was no sound from him. No creaking floorboards. No opening and closing door. There were some sounds from outside, but they were just Florida noises, nothing unusual.

As the minutes went by, she thought she was going to have to move. What if Jack was hurt? There was a monster on the loose. A killer who used any kind of weapon he could find. Or maybe there were three killers. Maybe they were all outside and waiting. Maybe—

She heard a thud, like something—a body?—hitting the ground. She turned to the window just in time to see a tiny flash of light. Most of it was hidden behind the jungle that surrounded the old house.

Kate sprang up so fast she upset the plywood table-top and the bowl of rice hit the floor. She ran through the kitchen and out the back. The door had been closed and—damnation—locked. Looked like Jack wasn't going to let whoever was outside get in.

But rotten houses were no match for Kate's fear. Months of workouts under Jack's tutelage had given her new strength. She lifted her knee to her chest and slammed her foot into the old door so hard that it came off one hinge. As Kate climbed over the sagging door, the second hinge gave way under her weight. She went down with the door.

But that didn't stop her forward motion. She was running by the time she and the door hit the ground.

The house was long and narrow and surrounded by

years of undergrowth. She had to fight her way around the corner to where she'd seen the light.

When she reached the edge of what was left of the old pergola, she stopped and listened. Silence. Even the birds had stopped their chatter.

"I'm here."

It was Jack's voice and he sounded disgusted. As she tore her way through the plants, Jack turned his cell phone flashlight toward her. "Just stay there, I'll come to you."

She ignored him and kept pushing her way through.

Jack was sitting on a stump, blood running down the side of his head. "I lost him. Tripped over an old wheelbarrow. I think it was put in my way. I feel like a fool." He let out a sigh of exasperation. "Come on, let's go home."

When Kate turned, her foot caught on a tree root and Jack reached out for her. He slipped his arm around her shoulders. "You're shaking!"

"No, I'm not."

Jack pulled back to look at her, his hands on her shoulders. It was quite dark but they were in front of the dining room windows and some candlelight came through. "Everything is fine. I just ran into something with my head. No damage done."

Kate nodded but said nothing.

"On second thought, I think I'm seriously injured. How about if you take your shirt off and wrap it around my head?"

His joke snapped her back to reality and she pushed his hands away. "Who was it?"

"I've never seen him before. Skinny little guy. Older.

Look." Jack held up his cell, touched the screen, and up came a photo of the top half of a man. He was thin to the point of emaciation, but his eyes were glittering in merriment, as though he'd just pulled off some great joke. Since the photo was taken from below, Jack must have been on the ground when he shot it.

"Smart-aleck bastard," he said.

"I know him. I showed him a house today. He—"

"No! Don't tell me. Let's go home and tell Sara."

In spite of the fact that Jack's head was still bleeding, they only stayed long enough to put out the candles, then hurried to get out of there.

On the quick trip home, Kate texted Sara to meet them in the living room. "In case she went to bed early," she told Jack. "I told her to get the bandages out so she'll be wide-awake."

She was right. Sara met them at the door. On the dining table were enough first aid supplies to perform surgery. She had Jack sit down while she and Kate filled a glass bowl full of hot water and began to clean the cut on his head. It wasn't bad.

He smiled at them as they hovered and fussed over him. "I like this. Can we do this every night?"

The women didn't speak until they'd finished.

Sara stepped back. "I want to hear every word of what happened."

Kate motioned for Jack to tell the story. They moved to the couches as he started by telling about the romantic dinner he'd created.

"Your mother is a good cook." Kate wasn't going to comment on the romantic feel of the evening. "Get to the man."

"What man?" Sara asked.

Jack and Kate talked over each other as they told what had happened. Kate saw the man; Jack chased him. "When I fell, Kate knocked down a door to get to me." His voice held pride.

"It was rotting on its hinges. I barely touched it."

"Ha! I heard you, and I saw the door. That was one powerful kick. You must have been terrified that I'd been hurt." He was smiling in a smirking sort of way.

"The man!" Sara said. "Who was spying on you?"

"Him." Jack held up his phone to the photo. "Ever see him before?"

"No."

"Our Kate knows all about him." They looked at her.

"This afternoon about two, I showed a house over on Kingfish to a couple, but they weren't interested. After they left, I went back to lock the door and the man stepped out from behind a tall pine shrub. He startled me and he apologized. He said he hadn't been hiding but was picking up cigarette butts. He had a handful of them."

"Weird," Sara said as she transferred the photo to the big TV so they could look at it.

"Considering tonight, I think he *was* hiding," Jack said.

"I thought so too but he said he'd seen the house online and liked it and that he just happened to arrive when I was leaving. He said he'd really like to see the inside."

"So you went inside a vacant house with a complete stranger?" Jack's temper was rising.

"It's her job," Sara snapped. "What happened?"

"He didn't really look at the house. He mostly told me about Sedona, Arizona, and how utterly beautiful it is and how he'd lived there for years and how the climate is so different from Florida's."

"What was his name?" Sara asked.

"He said it was Grant."

"First or last name?"

"No idea. The whole thing took just minutes. We only made it to the kitchen, then he said he had to go. I wouldn't have remembered any of it except for that." She pointed at the TV. "He's very thin, isn't he?"

"Very. What else?" Sara asked.

"That's all of it," Jack said. "I think you should include the spy in your report to Flynn. I have a feeling that he's connected to the murder."

Kate looked at her aunt. "There was one other itty bitty thing. We overheard Tayla on the phone with Gil."

Sara grimaced. "That couldn't have been much. Maybe she wants to add on to that giant house of hers."

"People in glass houses..." Jack mumbled, but stopped at Kate's look.

"Did you know that Sylvia Alden wrote novels?"

Sara's eyes widened, then her face lit up. "That's it! She wasn't a recluse. She's far from being agoraphobic. There's nothing wrong with her but that she's a *writer*. Her head is full of stories." Sara stood up and looked down at the two of them. "This explains so much. She didn't go to church with her husband because she wanted the peace of a quiet house so she could write. She stayed home because she was working. Her friends were the neighbors because they were there. She sewed costumes for the kids because a sewing machine is good for giving you time to think." She picked up her cell phone and tapped in Sylvia's name, then read. "There's nothing in here about her books. She must have a pen name."

"I wonder if Sheriff Flynn knows she was a writer?" Kate asked. "I haven't heard it mentioned by anyone."

Jack, who had known Sara far longer than Kate had, said, "She may not have wanted people to know she wrote."

"Not tell people you're a *writer*?" Kate said in disbelief. "I'd think she'd shout it from the rooftops. Do you know how many people try to get published but never do?"

Sara didn't seem to want to answer that question. Instead, she said she'd use her contacts to find out who published Sylvia and under what name. "If it's out there, I'll find her."

Sara wanted to hear everything again to make sure they hadn't left anything out.

When she began to yawn, she told them good-night and went to her bedroom.

Kate also said good-night and went to her suite, closing the door behind her. The rooms had become a sanctuary for her. At one end was a living room with a big bowed window. A hallway went past two walk-in closets, a beautiful bath, then into the bedroom. Double doors led out to a pretty courtyard with a fountain of a girl dancing in the rain. Jack's bedroom was at that end of the house and he was often in the courtyard.

As she dressed for bed, Kate thought of all that was going on. Yes, tonight had been scary. Some man spying on them, Jack falling and hitting his head had been bad. But the truth was that every day she became happier with her life. Gradually, she was coming to see how *lacking* her childhood had been.

When Kate was only four years old, her mother had been widowed. She'd had to support herself and her young daughter on an insurance policy that made them have to skimp for all of Kate's life. Whenever her mother got a job, her debilitating depression made her lose it.

And then there were her three uncles, older than her mother, living with their families on twenty acres of land. They constantly made decrees of how everyone in the world should dress, behave and think. They expected Kate and her mother to faithfully obey their made-up rules.

Kate had managed to stay away from them—most of the time anyway. But they still had an effect on her and her mother.

How different her life now was! Aunt Sara and Jack were so easy to live with and they accepted Kate the way she was.

She had just found these lovely people and she couldn't bear the thought of changing it in any way. Jack's being hurt tonight had scared her deeply.

When she climbed into her bed with its cool, crisp sheets, she thought how good it was to feel that she belonged, that she was part of something.

SEVEN

Kate was showing a house to a couple whose only concern was whether or not their antique dining table would fit.

"It belonged to my grandmother," the husband explained.

She said she knew the perfect house for them and could show it to them that afternoon. They were delighted.

This morning she and Jack and Sara had been quiet. They were all thinking about what had happened since Janet Beeson had been murdered. While Kate and Jack went to work, Sara was to finish writing the report. They were going to meet for lunch, read what Sara had written, then she would email it to Sheriff Flynn.

And that would be the end of it. They strongly agreed on that.

When Kate left the house she'd been showing, Jack was leaning against her car. He opened the door for her to get in the passenger seat and she did. "Please tell me nothing bad has happened."

"Everybody is safe and alive." He pulled into the street. "We're still meeting Sara for lunch but I thought that first we could run this through a wash."

Jack took care of all vehicles, from the lawn mower to the two cars to his truck.

"So what is it you want to talk to me about?"

Jack gave a half smile. "You're beginning to know me too well."

He went to a car wash on Sunrise, drove onto the ramps, then turned to her. The loudly gushing water made the inside of the car seem very private.

"This morning I wouldn't let Gil near a saw or a nail gun. If you plugged it in, I kept him away from it. Even so, he fell down four rungs of a ladder."

"Is he okay?"

"Bloody shins but he'll live."

She could tell that he had something serious to say so she waited in silence.

"On the phone, Gil told Tayla that he had to watch Quinn every minute. I thought it was because he was a kid. But today when I asked him how his son was, I saw fear in Gil's eyes. Deep, gut-level *fear.*"

Kate felt her heart do a leap. This summer Gil had often brought his son over to play in the pool. The nine-year-old boy was smart, funny, and happy. And he adored his big bear of a father. Kate had helped Quinn put on a surprise birthday party for Gil at Sara's house. They'd bought a cake at the local bakery, and Jack had helped the child order a new hand plane from a specialty store in Vermont. At the party, it had been heartwarming to see the way Gil and his son hugged. It was as though their strength came from each other.

One time, Kate asked about Quinn's mother, but Jack just said, "She's out of the picture," then walked away.

"Quinn is Gil's life," she said softly.

Jack was looking at the big yellow brushes going around the car. "Ten years ago, Gil went on vacation to California and he met her in a bar." He didn't bother to explain that he was talking about Quinn's mother. "It was a one-nighter, but he did give her his email address. He didn't hear from her until Quinn was three months old. Gil flew back, ready to move to California and help raise his son."

Jack hesitated. "But the woman was using. Gil had a DNA test done and it was positive, so he knew Quinn was his. He gave her every dollar he'd saved over the years and he brought the baby home. He's not seen or heard from her since. If Gil is this afraid, then it's my guess that she's reentered the picture."

He paused a moment and Kate waited. "Last night I was thinking about Janet Beeson. She seemed to want to help everyone. What if Quinn's mother showed up here with a sob story? Women tend to believe whoever cries."

When Kate made no reply, Jack said, "No argument on that sexist statement?"

"Tears are usually a sign of pain. We notice, we care. Have you ever seen the woman?"

"Never. And no photos."

Kate put her head back against the seat. "Was there any paperwork between her and Gil?"

"None, and she *is* his biological mother. That carries a lot of weight."

"All this is speculation," Kate said. "We don't know that any of this is true, and we certainly have no way to connect Quinn's mother to Janet Beeson."

"Right. But we do know that Tayla and Gil are connected in some way."

"And Charlene. I want to meet her."

Jack gave her a sharp look. "We're staying out of this, remember?"

"You mean you want Sara and me to stay out of it. But if this does have something to do with Gil and his son, I'm sure you'll be there with your flaming sword out." She caught her breath. "If Janet *was* being a misguided do-gooder, you don't think Gil… I mean, he didn't… He couldn't have…"

"Murdered her?" Jack was looking straight out the windshield at the water coming down for the rinse. "If Quinn was threatened, yeah, I imagine Gil would do anything to protect his son. Even kill. But poison, knife *and* a bullet? No. That's too violent, even for an angry father."

Kate nodded in agreement. "Tayla called in sick this morning and we were all relieved. When she said 'that house' I assumed she meant the one Sylvia used to own." Suddenly, Kate's eyes widened.

"What?"

"Sheriff Flynn said that the listing for Janet's house would be given to *me*. Not to Tayla, but to *me*. Maybe that was significant. Maybe I'm supposed to do something with that house."

Blowers were drying the car.

"You think he was giving us a hint?" Jack sounded skeptical.

"Maybe. But why? I'm sure the house has been searched thoroughly."

"And yet they didn't find a California serial killer." He looked at the dashboard clock. "We need to go meet Sara. Hungry?"

"Starving. Think they have any seafood?"

"It's Florida. They can get fish from their backyard."

Smiling, Kate looked at the scenery as they made their way to the restaurant.

"It's good," Kate said as she handed the pages of the police report back to Sara. They were sitting at their favorite outdoor café, close to what passed for the downtown of Lachlan.

Jack finished the last page and gave his copy to her. "Concise, not too windy. What about the photos?"

"Flynn hasn't asked for them yet. I found this." She pulled an 8x10 printout from a leather portfolio. It was a picture of a bookcase in Janet Beeson's house. The second shelf had a row of bright, shiny novels with the name Amanda Martin on the spine.

"Let me guess," Jack said, "that's Sylvia Alden's pen name."

"It is." Sara was smiling in triumph as she put the typed pages back into her case. "It took work to find her. I called editors at four publishing houses and two agents before I found someone who knew who she was. They're romantic mysteries. The books still have respectable sales and they've developed a bit of a cult following. Rabid fans, that sort of thing. One agent said he'd really like to represent her estate."

"Have you ordered them yet?" Jack asked.

"Didn't have time, but I'll get them this afternoon." When she said this, Sara didn't meet his eyes.

Kate was looking serious. "Maybe Sylvia left the royalties to Janet and someone killed her for them."

"Sylvia had a daughter," Sara reminded her.

"Interesting that we haven't seen this daughter," Jack said. "Her mother's best friend murdered? You'd think she'd show up here."

"And who would tell us if she did?" Kate asked. "Detective Cotilla? Or maybe the governor would call Aunt Sara."

"I did autograph some books for his wife," Sara said.

"Oooooh," Kate said. "Is he as cute in real life as he is on TV?"

"Better. He—"

Jack spoke up. "Hate to interrupt you two, but have either of you seen the spy?" He glanced around at the other tables as though to see who was there.

Sara shook her head no. "That man's face is ingrained in my mind so strongly that I seem to see him everywhere, but no, I haven't."

"The Arizona man," Kate said. Sara had called him that in her report to the sheriff.

Sara held up the photo of Janet's bookcase. "I'm including your stories about the man, but not his photo or any others. Why are you two looking so guilty?"

Kate glanced at Jack.

"Your report for the sheriff is finished?" he asked. "You aren't going to add anything to it?"

Sara gave him a small smile. "Are you asking if I'm going to say that Gil might be a murder suspect?"

Kate gasped, but Jack gave a laugh. "Figured that out, did you?" He sounded proud.

"Not until I wrote everything out. I hope you two noticed that I left out the conversation you overheard in the report. There was too much bad in that and taken out of context, it could be interpreted as *very* bad. But it wasn't difficult to figure out that the only reason Gil would be involved in something secret is for his son. I fully believe that Gil would kill anyone who tried to take Quinn away from him."

"Janet Beeson," Kate said. "The town do-gooder. Saving lives, helping people."

"Quinn's mother might have stopped at the church to get information and met Janet there." Sara looked at her hands for a moment. "Are you *sure* that call you overheard was about Janet?"

Kate looked at Jack. "Now that you mention it, I don't know if Janet was mentioned. We're just so focused on this, it seems everything is connected. Maybe Tayla and Gil's problems aren't related to the murder."

Jack was looking down at his plate of fried shrimp. "Or maybe Gil and Tayla are doing *Strangers on a Train*. You take my guy out, I'll take yours." When the women were silent, he looked up. "It was just a thought."

"Not a good one," Sara said, and Kate nodded in agreement.

Jack leaned back in his chair. "We all agree that our part in this is over? Done with? No more working on the murder?"

"The end." Sara looked down at her pecan-crusted trout.

For several minutes, they ate in silence, then Kate spoke. "I have a house to show at two. What are you guys up to?"

"Putting on a roof," Jack said.

"I thought I'd wander around town and take some photos. Just street scenes. Or maybe macros of flowers and bugs."

The rest of the meal was eaten with chitchat as they avoided talking of the murder.

Kate's clients canceled the 2:00 p.m. appointment and she saw an office memo saying that a deputy had picked up a lockbox for the Beeson house. When Tayla called to say she wouldn't be there that afternoon, all the things together seemed to be a sign. It was like the cosmos was telling her what she needed to do.

In the call she and Jack had overheard, Tayla said that Sylvia had a book that could clear her name and it had to be in "that house." Kate had no idea why Sylvia's name needed to be cleared—except maybe to show her snobby brother that she hadn't committed suicide. But that might hint at murder, so which was worse? Anyway, Kate was assuming her boss was referring to the house Sylvia used to live in.

Whatever was meant, Kate knew that she needed to get inside the house and see what she could find.

With Tayla out, the office was quiet. Nosy Melissa was showing houses in Pembroke Pines so she wouldn't be back for a while. The two men were in the coffee room snickering over a date one of them had. She grabbed a canvas bag, Kirkwood Realty printed on the side, and dropped her big notebook inside.

It was easy to walk out the front door and get to her car unseen. She kept glancing at the big tree at the corner of the parking lot. That's where she'd seen Tayla arguing with a man. Was he the Carl she'd mentioned on the phone? Was Carl the skinny man who'd spied on her and Jack? Yet he'd practically posed for a photo. If he wanted them to see him, why didn't he show himself? Why hide?

She drove past Janet Beeson's house and was pleasantly surprised to see that the big steel gates were standing open. She parked about four houses away, changed into the sneakers she kept in the car, and walked back to the house. She tried to appear casual but she kept glancing about to see if anyone was watching.

She halted at the gate and peered through the shrubs to see if any cars were there. It would be better if she weren't seen. She especially didn't want to be seen by Jack or Aunt Sara since she'd agreed to stop investigating. It wasn't as though she was doing anything bad… Well, maybe it was illegal to trespass at a crime scene, but…

She didn't want to think too hard about what she was doing.

As she stepped onto the little front porch, she looked to her left at the beautifully landscaped garden. Last time she'd been here, Sheriff Flynn's car was hiding in the bushes.

The Realtor lockbox was on the door and she tapped in the code numbers Tayla had set up. It was a date and everyone in the office speculated what the numbers meant to their boss but no one had the nerve to ask her.

It worked. She quietly opened the door and—

"Guess we can go in now" came Jack's deep rumble from behind her.

Kate was so startled that her heart leaped and she put her hand to her throat. "What are you doing here?"

Aunt Sara stepped from behind him and smiled at her pretty niece. "Waiting for you to come with the code. Jack said he could get a window open and he'd push me through, but I said we'd wait for you. Who do you think left the gate open for us?"

"Flynn." Jack was making a joke. "He probably read your report, saw your picture of the books, and knew we'd want to get them."

"You could have ordered them off Amazon," Kate said.

"Or you could Kindle them."

"Ha!" Sara said. "I like those machines as much as I do cell phone cameras." Around her neck was what she called her baby camera, the Fujifilm X100F. It looked like something from the 1950s.

Kate was still standing by the open door wearing a look of disgust. It was deeply annoying that they'd *known* she was going to go to the house. Especially since she hadn't decided until the last minute.

Jack and Sara were standing there grinning at her.

"We get the books, then we're done, right?" Kate said.

"Of course." Sara filled Kate's big bag with all the Amanda Martin books, then began taking photos. This time she opened closets and cabinet doors and even drawers.

When they finished, they went outside and Sara took pictures of Sylvia and Janet's garden. Jack held back shrubs as Sara photographed the area around the tall fence.

"I bet this is where the kids' soccer balls came through," Sara said. There was a four-foot-deep planting of perennial flowers against the wall-high fence. A ball hitting them would destroy the delicate stems.

Kate was looking around the beautiful garden and at the lovely house. "I don't get it. Sylvia had all this and a successful career and people who loved her. Why did she kill herself?"

"Writers have a lot going on in their minds," Sara said. "It makes us ecstatic and miserable at the same time. We crave the ordinary but we also hate it. I'm afraid that I can understand suicide very well."

Jack and Kate had no reply to that. She looked at her watch. "I think we should go. That gate was opened for a reason and I don't think it was for us. I wouldn't want to be caught here. Do you think they'll notice that the books are missing?"

"Only if their records say that the California serial killer stole paperback novels after he did his business." As Jack looked at the house, his anger began to rise. "Suicide, murder. I don't think we've accomplished anything so far. But I'm sure Flynn and his entourage are going to arrest someone soon. I need to go back to work. If Gil comes back today, somebody has to be there to protect him."

"You're sure he hasn't said anything to you about why he's so upset?" Kate asked.

"Are you asking if Gil told me that his son's mother is threatening him? Or that he needs a half mil or so to pay her off? Or that he killed Janet Beeson in a really nasty way so no one would suspect him?"

Kate ignored his sarcasm and glared at him.

"No. Nothing. Not a word. Today when Gil picked up a Skilsaw I took it from him and he got angry. Yelled at me. Gil never yells at anybody. I put on my best caring look and asked him to tell me what was wrong. He said…" Jack looked at the women. "And I quote, he told me that I wasn't his, uh, f-ing therapist and I could mind my own f-ing business. Then he got in his truck and spun out so fast two of my men got hit with gravel. So no. Gil told me nothing."

Jack stalked ahead of them as he went to the gate, Sara and Kate behind him.

"Boxing, right?" Kate said.

"Oh yeah."

When they got home, it wasn't easy, but they got Jack to stay there and take his anger out on a boxing bag. That his friend Gil wasn't there to hold the hand pads made his anger worse.

Kate went to the kitchen to make a pot of chili— with no beans for her aunt's keto diet—while Sara snuggled down and began to read the Amanda Martin books.

"They're all brand new, unopened," Sara said. "It looks like Janet was a real fan. She probably had a set for reading over and over, and a display set just for show."

"Wonder where the old ones are?" Kate was chopping onions.

"Good question," Sara said but she didn't have an answer.

It was while the chili was simmering, Jack was pounding, and Sara reading, that Kate called her mother. The call upset her, but she didn't tell them about it.

After dinner, they went to the big couch in the living room and watched TV—their mutual form of relaxation.

Jack sat in the middle, remote in front of him, and the women took the ends. Sara was sitting sideways, reading glasses on, and deeply absorbed in the first Amanda Martin book. Jack knew her feet were always cold so he put a pillow on his lap and her bare feet on it. There was a lap robe on the back of the couch and he covered her feet.

Kate was so absorbed in her thoughts that she said nothing when Jack changed the channel to a football game. He pulled her feet onto his lap too.

"These books are her autobiography," Sara said.

Jack wasn't really watching the game. He put it on mute. "How so?"

"They seem to cover Sylvia's life. I can see why she didn't want anyone to know she was the author. The first one is about a woman in her midthirties—old to be a romance heroine—who is trapped by her older brother and her father. She makes their lives so comfortable that they won't let her marry. They scare off any man who gets near her."

"An historical, right?" Kate said.

"No. Contemporary. Finally, the heroine runs off with a handsome young plumber. He's content with his job but the heroine is ambitious and they end up opening a store that sells high-end bathroom fixtures."

"Plumbing?" Kate said. "Not exactly romantic."

"Pays the bills and then some," Jack said. "Sounds very romantic to me."

Sara pulled the novels out of the bag, arranged them in order, and began reading the back blurbs. "All the books are about this one couple and what happens in their lives. In this one, they have a daughter and struggle with the shop." She paused to read. "This is interesting. When the heroine's father dies, her older brother cuts her out of inheriting. When she protests, her brother slaps her with a lawsuit. Next book, they have money problems because the brother's suit has cleaned them out."

She read some more. "The daughter goes to college—no Ivy League as they couldn't afford that—and the heroine and her husband move to Florida to escape the brother. Uh-oh. The daughter is in trouble at school. Drugs." Sara sighed. "And in this one the heroine's husband dies and she's left alone." Sara was silent.

"What happened after that?" Kate asked.

Sara smiled. "Ah, the most glorious question a writer can hear. *What happened next?* That was the last book. By the way, the stories are all told in first person. It's all seen through the heroine's eyes."

"Is this ordinary that novels are about a writer's life?" Kate asked.

Sara started to answer, but Jack spoke up. "I'll take this one. Every word our dear Sara has ever written is autobiographical. That one about the woman finding the guy she loved in high school? He was a widower and the heroine took over his life and his son. Remember that?"

"I see," Kate said. "That was Sara and your grandfather. Oh! And the story about the young man who was always brooding about his rotten father. That was you."

"I don't 'brood' as you call it."

Kate and Sara laughed. "Heathcliff could take lessons from you. Every time you see Sheriff Flynn, your eyebrows draw together." Kate demonstrated.

Jack rolled his eyes.

Kate looked back at her aunt. "I think you should read the last book next. Maybe Janet is in it. And maybe it tells why Sylvia wanted to end her life. But then, a greedy brother, a daughter on drugs. It seems like her whole life was one tragedy after another. The only friend she had was her husband and when he died…" Kate sighed. "I'm beginning to understand her suicide."

"Well, I'm not!" Sara sounded angry. "I'm seeing that Sylvia Alden was a fighter. In every circumstance, she fought back. Her brother and father tried to keep her at home. But she eloped with a gorgeous young plumber. But all he did was repair toilets. So Sylvia opened a store that sold products that rich people would buy and she made a fortune. When her father died and her brother took everything, Sylvia left the state and got away from the bastard. It was an Up Yours gesture."

Kate was looking at her aunt in admiration. "I didn't see it that way."

"When someone hits you, you either get up or you stay down. Nothing in between. Sylvia *leaped* up."

"And the daughter?" Jack asked. "What about her?"

"I don't know yet. I need to read all the books—in order. I want to know more about this woman. I like her." Sara dumped the books back into the bag, said good-night, then went into her bedroom and closed the door behind her.

As soon as she was gone, Kate started to remove her feet from Jack's lap, but he held on to them. She really didn't want to move and she relaxed.

"Something's bothering you," he said.

"Besides murder?"

"Yeah, besides that. I saw you on the phone and you weren't happy."

"I don't see how you saw anything since you were beating on that bag so hard. Do you really think Gil had something to do with Mrs. Beeson's murder? You think he's the person Sheriff Flynn is about to arrest?"

"I don't know and don't change the subject. You were on the phone for at least thirty minutes. What's the problem?"

When Kate didn't answer right away, he tossed the lap robe back and began to massage her bare feet.

Kate closed her eyes. "I may turn into a bowl of warm Jell-O." When she looked at him, he was smiling in a way that was an invitation to a lot more than a foot rub. She pulled her feet out of his lap and sat up.

"Who were you talking to on the phone?"

"My lover."

He gave a snort.

"Okay," she said. "My mother."

"Was she in one of her depression bouts?"

Kate drew her legs to her chest and put her arms

around them. "No. She was happier than I've ever heard her." She looked at Jack. "Remember I told you that she used to fly to New York to buy fabric to make clothes for me?"

"Yes."

"Every time she returned, she'd have a serious attack. I'd come home from school and she'd be curled up on the floor. It was really hard to coax her into bed or even into the bathroom."

"You did this when you were in elementary school?" He sounded shocked.

Kate nodded. "And high school and when I came home on weekends from college. I thought her trips were the cause. I thought..."

"What?"

"That being away from me was the cause of her misery. I thought she missed me so much that..." Tears were coming.

Jack reached out his arm to put around her and drew her head to his shoulder. "What happened today?"

"She's in New York and she's been there for a week and she's happy."

"Isn't that good?"

She pushed away from him. "Don't you see? Maybe all her depression bouts were because she had to come back to me. Maybe I was the cause of them. Now that she's free, she's happy." She put her hands over her face, fighting back tears.

Jack pulled her hands away and made her look at him. "You are not the cause of your mother's depression. You didn't make it happen and you aren't taking it away. None of this is about *you*."

Kate sniffed. "But it was just us. One of us had to—"

"Really?" Jack's voice was firm. "You're saying that you are responsible for every feeling she has? Pretty powerful, aren't you?"

"I'm not. I just…" She sniffed again. "Maybe I'm hurt because she's so happy without me."

"And how are you doing without her? Living in misery?"

"I'm the happiest I've ever been in my life," she said softly.

"What was that?"

Kate stood up. "You heard me. I'm going to bed. Tomorrow I want to sell at least three houses and I don't want to think about Sylvia or Tayla or Janet or Gil."

"Or about your mother. Hey! You ever think she might have a boyfriend? If she's happy in New York, maybe it's some Wall Street guy in a three-piece suit. Or do they all wear suspenders now?"

Kate gave a bit of a smile. "Thanks," she said, then disappeared into her rooms. He really had made her feel better.

EIGHT

Kate slept late the next morning, awoke smiling, and hummed while she dressed. It was going to be a good day. No murder would fill her mind, and thanks to Jack, she felt less worried about her mother. He was probably right. Maybe something had happened that had nothing to do with her. Maybe—

She had her hand on the door into the house when she heard her aunt say, "Absolutely not. I refuse."

Jack said, "You owe the man so you *are* going."

Kate stepped into the room. Jack and Sara were glaring at each other across the kitchen counter. "Should I get the boxing gloves?"

Sara, her mouth in a grimace of anger, said, "Tell her what you want me to do."

He turned to Kate. "Arthur Niederman has invited all of us to tea at his house at four today. I think we should go, but Medlar here says no."

Kate went to the kitchen and got a cereal bowl out

of a cabinet. "I take it this has to do with the book Arthur wants you to read."

"Go on," Jack said to Sara. "Tell her the rest of it."

"The book is awful."

"And you don't want to tell him that," Kate said. "I understand."

"It's more than that," Sara said. "I've read dozens of unpublished novels and I've always been truthful about them. But without exception, the writers hate me. Not dislike, *hate*. That's because they all expect me to tell them their book is so fabulous that I turned it over to my agent and he got them a ten-million-dollar movie deal."

Kate gave a little laugh but Jack and Sara were looking at her seriously. "You're joking, right?"

"Not at all," Jack said. "Two years ago my mother conned Sara into reading the manuscript of a friend. Sara nicely told her the book needed work, and even told her how to change it. The woman got so angry I had to protect our Sara from the, uh, less than friendly language."

"How bad is the Niederman book?" Kate asked.

"He's not a bad writer, but the plot is like every other detective novel. You can get away with bad writing, but you *must* have a good plot. I can't imagine that anyone will publish it as it is."

Kate considered that for a moment as Sara and Jack stared at her. "Jack's right. We owe Arthur so we have to go today. And you have to tell him the truth about his book. He helped us so much with the Morris case and critiquing his novel was the price."

"I know," Sara said, "but I bloody well don't want to do it."

Jack put his arm around her small shoulders. He was over a foot taller than she. "We'll be right there with you. I have to go to work now so I can protect Gil from himself, but I'll be back before it's time to leave." He kissed the top of her head.

"Hope you have a good day," Kate said.

Jack turned his face to the side and tapped his cheek, meaning for her to kiss him goodbye.

Kate hesitated.

"How's your mom?" he asked. He was reminding her that he'd helped her last night.

She kissed his cheek.

"Ah, at last. I think I'll shellac over that spot so it never goes away."

Smiling, Kate shook her head. "I'll meet you back here no later than 3:45 and we'll go to tea."

"Think I should wear my pinafore?"

"Yes. The pink dotted swiss. Or maybe the lilac chiffon. Or the yellow—"

Laughing, Jack went out the back way to the garage.

As soon as they were alone, Sara said, "What's up with your mother? Throwing a fit for you to return to her?"

"Actually, it's the opposite." As Kate ate her cereal, she told her aunt the story, including what Jack said.

Kate knew her mother and her aunt didn't like each other, so she expected Aunt Sara to say something sarcastic. But she didn't. In fact, she didn't even mention the mystery of why Ava Medlar was so happy in New

York. Instead, she talked about what a wise and caring person Jack was.

Maybe Jack wasn't her biological grandchild, but Sara treated him as though he was. Loved him like he was.

Minutes later, Kate left for work. When she was told that Tayla was taking the day off, she breathed in relief. She wouldn't have to deal with her boss's histrionics. She had a young couple who wanted to move to Lachlan so she was to show them eight houses, and take them to lunch. She hoped she'd get done by three thirty.

She got home at three forty and Sara and Jack were waiting for her. It was already decided that they'd go in Jack's truck and he would drive.

Aunt Sara looked so glum that Kate wanted to say she didn't have to go. In the truck, they were a silent trio.

Arthur Niederman was just a few years younger than Sara and they had gone to the same high school. He liked to tell how Sara had never so much as looked at him. Her eyes were only on Callum Wyatt, Jack's grandfather. Arthur said Sara was always hurrying home after school because she had to "take care of" her younger brother, Randal, Kate's father. Kate had asked Aunt Sara what that meant. His mother didn't have an outside job, so why was Sara required to look after him?

When her aunt quickly changed the subject, Kate was reminded of how extraordinarily good Aunt Sara was at avoiding questions about her younger brother.

"You brought his manuscript?" Jack looked across Kate sitting in the middle.

Sara nodded, but said nothing.

Kate squeezed her forearm in reassurance. When Arthur Niederman was a young man he'd fallen off the roof of a warehouse owned by some big company. He never walked again. Since the accident was the company's fault, a lawyer showed up the day after Arthur fell and offered his services to sue. Arthur easily won and was awarded millions. He was in a wheelchair, but he lived comfortably in his lovely house with his books and his garden.

During the summer, Kate had stopped by several times to visit him. He was an excellent observer of people and she loved to hear about what he'd seen and heard.

"When you're in a wheelchair," he'd said, "it's as though people think you've lost all your senses, including your hearing. Couples have arguments while standing right next to me. If a walking person goes by, they shut up. I seem to be invisible."

Kate had grown quite fond of the man.

By the time they reached his house, Sara looked like she was on her way to a guillotine.

Arthur didn't wait for them to knock, but was sitting by the open door. He was a tall man and kept the upper half of his body in good shape. He had strong arms from pushing the big wheels on his chair. Kate knew that a nurse came twice a week to give him massages and work his legs. For his household needs, he used delivery services.

She kissed both his cheeks. "How are you? How are the Vandas you ordered?" Arthur had a screened porch full of orchids.

"Happy and blooming." He led them to the dining room where a long table was covered with plates of food.

As Kate looked at the table, she laughed. "You lovely scoundrel. Look what you did."

The food was divided into three sections and labeled. One was low calorie for Kate. Little round slivers of bread piled high with slices of cucumber, chocolate muffins hardly bigger than her thumb, a bowl of tiny wild strawberries. For Jack there were thick beef and pastrami sandwiches and cold beer. At the end was for Sara. Her keto diet's no-sugar and no-carbs rules had been obeyed. Bacon wrapped around asparagus, almond flour scones with whipping cream, salmon with sour cream and sprigs of dill.

Kate looked at her aunt and saw her expression soften. Arthur had made a lot of effort to welcome them. They took their places at the table. Jack and Sara were at the ends, Kate and Arthur across from each other. His plate of food came from each of the three sections.

They were just tucking into the feast when Arthur looked at Sara. "Well?"

They all knew what he meant. His book.

Sara had already eaten the asparagus and was on her second cup of tea—the Assam she loved—and she was happier. "It's very well written. You have a knack for good sentence structure. Never once did you begin three sentences in a row with 'he' or 'she.'" She filled her mouth with food.

Kate looked at her aunt. Was that all she was going

to say? She glanced at Jack. He had his head down, eating. He was staying out of what was going on.

"That sounds good." Arthur ate in silence for a moment. "I've always been curious about something. When an author such as yourself who has had umpteen books make the *New York Times* Best Seller List and has… What is it? Sixty million in print?" He waved his hand. "Anyway, when *you* turn in a book, how much praise does your publishing house give you?"

Sara nearly choked on her derisive laugh. "None whatever. You pour your heart out in a novel, send it in, and no one reads it for months. When they do, the best you can hope for is 'It's fine.' After that, you get masses of people telling you what's *wrong* with it. They—" She broke off as she looked at Arthur's pleased expression. She stuffed an almond flour scone into her mouth.

"That's what I've heard from other people. So now you want to tell me the *truth* about my book?"

Sara hesitated a few seconds, wiped her hands, and said, "Okay, you asked for it. Your book is one big cliché. Your FBI hero is the same as in everyone else's book. He has PTSD so he goes crazy and kills the bad guys? Then all his boss does is bawl him out, but lets him go free? Really? I've read that a thousand times. A flawed hero is all the rage right now. But I'm telling you that if you want people to read your book, you have to do something *different*."

She looked him up and down. "Maybe your hero is a retired cop who's in a wheelchair. He can't use his legs but he can use his brains. He's rich so he hires the gardener's gorgeous son to do the legwork, but the kid always gets in trouble with women. Every book needs sex in it. If you write about something that has meaning to *you*, your readers will feel it."

Kate's eyes were wide. There'd been a lot of passion in her aunt's diatribe and she didn't know how Arthur was going to take it.

He blinked for a moment, then said, "Can I include a smart-mouthed, retired romance writer who he's had a crush on since he was a kid?"

"Only if she still looks good in a bikini," Sara shot back.

As they all laughed, Jack winked at Kate, his way of telling her that he knew Sara could handle her own argument.

"I vote for a pretty young woman who has inherited her father's lawn maintenance business," Kate said. "The retired detective does a makeover on her. From L.L. Bean boots to Prada heels."

"I do love Pygmalion stories," Sara said.

Jack said, "How about if the cop also has a very handsome nephew and he works *with* the gardener girl, and how high are the heels?"

Arthur said, "I like it! The nephew is a doctor—or maybe a lawyer—and the very brainy uncle put the kid through school so he owes him."

Jack smiled. "And the girl takes one look at the nephew and falls in love with him. On day one they jump into bed together. Then they—"

"Booooo," Sara and Kate said and Arthur joined them.

"He can get any woman but her," Kate said.

"It's all perfect," Arthur said. "But I just don't

know where I'm going to get ideas for such a plot. *Why* wouldn't every woman fall for a tall, dark, and handsome hero?"

They were looking at Jack as though he had an answer to the question.

He lifted his hands in surrender. "That's what I ask myself every day. Every hour. Why? Why? Why?"

They turned to Kate.

"A girl wants more than dessert."

The others groaned, but Kate was unperturbed. "Arthur, you have to figure that out. It's *your* book."

"But it seems to be *your* life," he shot back.

Their explosion of laughter was a great relief after the misery of the last few days.

Sara started to say something, but the doorbell rang. Only it didn't ring once. Someone was pushing it in short, angry blasts. Frowning, Arthur rolled away from the table to go answer it.

"Déjà vu," Kate said. The bell was like what had happened to them just days before.

"Not the same as ours," Jack muttered. "This one is in daylight."

They heard the front door open then slam shut.

"Niederman!" bellowed a male voice. "Where the hell is she? You said you'd get her here, so where is she? I don't know why you think a—" his voice was a sneer "—a *romance writer* could help me. I was willing to try, but—"

"Shut up!" Arthur yelled.

Jack and Kate looked at Sara in alarm, but she just shrugged. She'd heard this all her long career.

"What?" the stranger's voice said. "It's not like you ever have a houseful of company. You didn't—?"

Arthur must have done something because the voice abruptly halted and they heard whispering. The only clear thing they heard was the man say, "I am dead."

Jack looked at the women. Whoever the visitor was, they wanted nothing to do with him. He stood up and looked toward the back door.

The women silently agreed. Leave before whoever it was entered the room.

They moved quickly and were at the back door when the man rushed into the dining room. He was round and pink-faced, his skin so pale and soft he looked like a reincarnated mole. Had he *ever* been outside in the sunshine?

"Please don't leave." His eyes were begging. "I'm really, really sorry. My life is falling apart and I can't think correctly."

"Get in line." Jack was referring to Tayla having said the same words.

"He's a writer." Sara's tone was the same a person would use to say someone had a highly contagious, deadly disease.

"An investigative journalist," he corrected. His tone said he was above a romance writer. He was carrying a thick envelope, which he tossed onto the dining table, then plopped down in the chair where Jack had been sitting. "I have been afflicted with a need to *know* all my life. I ask, I find out, I write it down. I can't stop." He had tears rolling down his cheeks while he began eating the food that was left on the serving platters.

Arthur was behind him, his wheeled chair half in,

half out of the room. It was as though he hadn't yet decided whether to flee or take part.

"I really am sorry," the man said, his mouth full. He was devouring everything, cleaning plates with the gusto of a cartoon character. "I'm usually a very nice person but the internet has ruined my life." He looked at Sara, his eyes asking her to understand.

She was by the door, flanked by Kate and Jack as though they were her bodyguards.

"You can relate to that, can't you? Remember those divine women with their grocery carts? They'd throw books and magazines in with the chips and the chops. Bestsellers were created over bags of pork rinds. Oh! It was a glorious time. But now what? Somebody shoots people and within hours everything is on the internet. For free. By the time a real writer gets an in-depth story out there it's old news. Who wants to read about it?"

"Retire." There was no sympathy in Sara's voice as she put her hand on the doorknob.

The man acted like he hadn't heard her. "I had an idea to dredge up some old cases and solve them, then maybe someone would listen to me. I got some good publicity but it was all on tiny local shows. GMA is too busy touting the latest shoe sales to talk to writers." He was eating so much so fast that it was falling down his chin.

Sara gave Kate and Jack a look of *I've had enough* and turned the knob.

"If Janet Beeson hadn't given me hope, I would have taken that job my ex-father-in-law offered me. Writing sales catalogs for his three furniture stores.

Just because I know *it's* from *its* doesn't mean I—"
He stopped at the looks on their faces.

Jack, Sara and Kate had frozen in place, their eyes
wide.

"Oh, I see. You didn't know that I knew about her,
did you?" He pushed the last empty plate away. "I think
I better go to Sheriff Flynn and tell him what I know.
I'm sure the authorities will be able to handle it." The
man got up and turned toward the front door.

The three were blinking at him, unable to move.

Arthur deftly wheeled his chair so the doorway
was blocked. "Cut out the dramatics or I'll call Soggy
Drawers Flynn and tell him you know all about the
murder of Janet Beeson. Wanna pay a lawyer to defend
you? Three hundred bucks an hour?"

"Murder?" he whispered and the pink color drained
from his face. He turned to the trio by the back door. "I
apologize deeply for the crack I made about romance
writers. But my future success rested on Janet Beeson
and when…when I heard that she'd killed herself, I lost
it. And now *murder*?" He looked at Arthur. "Do you
have any water? Everything is sticking in my throat."

"Throat of a pelican," Arthur muttered as he went
to the kitchen. "Eats everything. Hope my plates are
intact."

The four of them were staring at one another. To the
left was Arthur's living room, the furniture set wide
apart to make room for his chair. No one wanted to
make the first move.

Arthur came back, shoved a glass of water at the
man, then went into the living room. He positioned his

chair into a place made for it, across from a couch, a big chair to his side.

Everyone seemed to know where to sit. The three were close together on the sofa, the man alone in the chair. "I'm Everett Gage," he said with pride, then waited for some recognition, but they didn't react. "I wrote about D.B. Cooper and the Unabomber."

"So did everyone else." Sara's look was not friendly. "Even some romance writers."

"I deserved that," Everett said. "Okay, so I didn't do anything unique or even different, but back then…" He looked sad.

Sara relented. "I know. They bought whatever you wrote. Oh, those beautiful women spending hours in one of the many bookstores."

"And the airports! They used to read on the flights. Now even the cheap seats show movies."

Sara smiled in nostalgia. "And the publishing houses begged to send you on tour. And the parties! I miss those. People from *PW* used to attend."

"Publishers Weekly." Everett's voice sounded faraway, as though speaking of nirvana.

Jack cleared his throat. "You said something about Janet Beeson?"

Everett looked like he was going to start crying again. "I heard gossip about her death. Everything from suicide by gunshot to murder by an axe, but we weren't sure what happened." He waited for them to reply but they were so stoic they didn't even blink. He looked at Arthur. "I knew they wouldn't let me in on anything."

Arthur glared at him. "Why don't you stop feeling

sorry for yourself and tell them about you and Mrs. Beeson?"

As with all professional storytellers, there was nothing Everett liked better than an audience's rapt attention. He took his time as he got up, retrieved the envelope off the table, and sat down by the four of them. He tossed the envelope onto the coffee table. On the cover was taped a picture of some little white flowers and what looked to be a newspaper headline. "Not Found Yet," it read. "Janet knew who did it. She had the solution to a case that held the attention of the country for days. She knew…"

When no one said anything, he settled back in the chair. "July 1994? Atlanta, Georgia? The news was full of it." He looked at the three on the couch. "Surely you remember the White Lily Kidnapping."

He didn't see the almost imperceptible nudge Jack, Kate and Sara gave one another. "White lilies" is what Tayla had mentioned on her call with Gil. They didn't want that to be known so their expressions didn't change.

Their lack of reaction obviously disappointed Everett.

"Sorry," Kate said, "I hadn't been born then. But Jack was in his twenties so he probably remembers."

"I was eight," he said with disgust.

Everyone turned to Sara. "I was writing twelve hours a day. I didn't notice what year it was, much less what was going on in the world."

"Then I'll start at the beginning." He didn't seem upset at having to do so. "In June 1994, Mrs. Anna Crawford gave birth to her second daughter, a pretty baby she named Jeanne after her mother. Mrs. Crawford also had a three-year-old daughter who she named Della after her mother-in-law."

"Diplomatic of her," Kate said.

"And guarantees free babysitting," Sara added.

Everett gave a little smile. "Exactly. And that babysitting was the cause of everything. On Friday, the eighth of July, there was a department store in downtown Atlanta that was having a going-out-of-business sale. They were opening their doors at seven a.m. and everything in the store was seventy to eighty percent off."

He paused to let this sink in. "Mrs. Crawford was worried that her three-year-old was feeling left out because of the attention the new baby was getting. She wanted to buy little Della something special to show her that she was still loved, but with the new baby…"

"She was broke," Sara said.

"A tight budget. The problem came when both mothers-in-law were ill. Some of the reports said they had hangovers from a party the night before, as the two women were friends of long standing." He waved his hand. "Whatever the reason, Mrs. Crawford was faced with the dilemma of not going to the sale or taking her month-old baby with her."

"So she went." Arthur sounded as though he wanted him to get on with the story.

Everett ignored his tone. "Mrs. Crawford dressed the baby carefully for her debut into the world. She put on the white cotton dress that had been made by her mother. On the front she had embroidered in pale colors of green and cream a sprig of lily of the valley. It was summer but Mrs. Crawford knew the store would be air-conditioned so she put little Jeanne in the sweater set her mother-in-law had bought on a trip to Italy. It was fine gauge pink cotton with matching booties tied with a pink silk ribbon."

He opened the envelope and pulled out a photo. "Mrs. Crawford thought her daughter looked so good that she took a photo of her. Mind you, this was before cell phones when everything is photographed. She used a real camera."

"Nikon? Minolta?" Sara asked.

They all turned to look at her.

"Sorry. Just curious."

Everett handed Kate the photo and the three of them looked at it. It was faded color, slightly blurry, but still clear. A very cute baby with wispy bits of blond hair was sitting in a blue stroller. She had on a delicate white dress, pink cardigan, and little booties.

"Tell me she wasn't…" Kate began. "I mean, kidnappings often don't end well."

Everett gave a smug smile. He wasn't going to ruin his story by prematurely telling the ending.

Arthur put the photo on the coffee table and they waited for Everett to go on.

"Mrs. Crawford went to the sale, baby Jeanne in tow, and took her straight to the shoe department. Her daughter Della had recently announced that she wanted to be a ballerina so her mother was determined to get her ballet slippers. Tables were piled high with boxes and Mrs. Crawford soon found the toddler area. She positioned her foot against a wheel of baby Jeanne's stroller and started looking for the correct size. Unfortunately, lots of other women were also frantically searching through the boxes."

Everett paused for effect. "The tower of shoes collapsed. Some people said a woman tripped and fell and that's what caused them to fall. Others blamed the stock boy. He'd stacked them too high. Whatever the reason, about a hundred boxes of shoes went crashing. Lids flew off, shoes were launched, and tissue paper seemed to attach itself to hair and clothes. For minutes, they were blinded."

Everett gave a shrug. "No one knows what happened but when everyone righted themselves, the stroller was about six people away from Mrs. Crawford and it was empty. Baby Jeanne was gone." He leaned forward. "In the seat was a handful of lily of the valley sprigs. They weren't something from a florist but looked like they'd been pulled from a flowerpot. There were roots with dirt on them."

Everett settled back into his chair and smiled, but said nothing.

"Get on with it!" Arthur ordered.

Everett took his time. "When Mrs. Crawford saw that her baby had been taken, she let out a scream that made people's hair stand on end. As it happened, the jewelry department was close by and they had a panic button. A fast-thinking young clerk pushed it and instantly, every door in the building was locked. The button also alerted the police and they showed up six minutes later."

He looked at his audience. "The baby wasn't found. They searched every inch of the store, interviewed every customer and employee. No one had seen anything. The baby had just plain vanished."

"I'm not sure I want to hear any more of this," Kate said.

Everett continued anyway. "The story caught the imagination of the American people. For four days a manhunt ensued. The photo of baby Jeanne in her stroller was flashed on every channel. There was a lot of information turned in, but it led nowhere."

He took a breath. "On the fourth day, the baby, clean and healthy, wearing the white dress and the pink cardigan, showed up in a cardboard box at a fire station. Only the booties were missing."

Everett emptied his envelope and handed out photos and newspaper clippings encased in clear plastic. They passed them around.

"And no one ever found out who did it?" Kate asked.

"No. There were no fingerprints, nothing. There were no surveillance cameras then and no one saw anything."

Sara looked up from the photo of the baby in the cardboard box. "But you think Janet Beeson knew who did it?"

"Yes," Everett said. "She…" He took a breath. "She showed me a pink bootie."

"Could have been anyone's," Arthur said. "Maybe you fell for a con."

"No. You see, there was something never released to the public. This past spring I spent a month in Atlanta and I did my best to interview anyone who had been there that day. I talked to the store manager and three of the clerks. They knew nothing that hadn't been in the papers. But the police…"

He looked at his hands. "I was sworn to secrecy on this, but—" He looked hard at Sara.

"We won't tell," she said.

Her words seemed to reassure him. "One of the policemen who was there that day—he's now retired—told me Mrs. Crawford's mother-in-law was a staunch Catholic. Inside each of the booties she'd sewn a tiny cross way up under the toes where you couldn't see it. When Janet handed me that single baby slipper—she made me wear gloves—I turned it inside out. There it was, sewn tightly inside. Even Janet didn't know it was there. That slipper *did* come from baby Jeanne."

"And you think Janet Beeson knew who had done it?" Sara asked.

Everett leaned forward. "If Mrs. Beeson was murdered, maybe it was by the kidnapper."

Sara frowned. "But that was over twenty years ago. Why now?"

"Janet told me that the evidence has been hidden all these years."

"Hidden by her?" Jack asked.

"Either her or the kidnapper," Everett answered. "We didn't have enough time together for her to tell me." He looked like he was going to start crying again.

"You said 'exposed to the public,'" Jack said. "Who else did she show it to?"

"I don't know!" Everett almost shouted. "She was a very secretive woman."

"Did she say where she got the baby shoe?" Kate asked. "Maybe she found it in a secondhand store. You knew about the cross so maybe other people did. Janet was very good at research."

Everett sniffed. "She certainly knew who owned it because she said she wasn't sure she should tell me. If she did, it would ruin that person's reputation forever."

"Come on," Sara said. "She must have given you some clues. Some hints."

Everett was silent.

Arthur spoke up. "If you don't tell everything you know, no one will help you find out the truth, and you'll never get your story published."

Everett didn't hesitate. "Did Janet have a best friend?"

The trio's gasp was audible.

"She did," Sara said, but didn't explain.

"I'm not sure, but I think maybe that friend was the kidnapper."

NINE

They were silent as Jack drove them home. Kate knew they were thinking what she was: How could Sylvia, who had been described as elegant and kind, steal a baby?

When they got to the house—the guards were gone—Jack pulled into the garage and they went through the back hallway. He usually let the women out in front. That he didn't do so today showed how upset he was.

They began preparing dinner as mechanically as though they were robots. After all they'd had for tea, no one was very hungry. Jack put some shrimp on the outdoor gas grill while Kate and Sara cut up vegetables for a salad. The iced tea seemed to make itself.

They ate outside in Florida's soft, warm weather.

"I bet Janet knew," Kate said when they sat down. "Sylvia confided in her."

"Probably needed to relieve her conscience," Sara said.

Jack, who was good with numbers, said, "In 1994,

Sylvia was forty-seven and her daughter was eleven. Think it was a last-ditch effort to have a second child?"

"Baby lust is powerful," Sara said.

"With boxes flying and people pushing, maybe she saw an opportunity and took it."

"Okay," Jack said, "maybe she picked up the kid, but how did she get away with it? Police were searching all over the place. Where did she hide a month-old baby? In her handbag? Those little critters are noisy."

"Maybe—" Kate began but couldn't think of anything. She and Jack looked at Sara for a writer's answer.

"They hid somewhere no one thought to look." She waved her fork about. "In real life a person can do something you don't expect but in a novel, you damned well better lead up to it. But from what we've heard of Sylvia Alden, it doesn't fit. Her daughter went to college and got involved in drugs. My guess is that the girl was probably always a handful. Sylvia had a husband she adored, a business she was running, a brother who was suing her. But she yearned for an infant to take care of? I can't see it."

"So now what?" Jack said. "We run to tell Flynn this?"

"Why?" Kate asked. "Sylvia didn't kill Janet. He's interested in that murder, not an old kidnapping."

Sara said, "Maybe the real kidnapper is…"

"Still killing?" Jack said. "Protecting his or her reputation at all costs?"

Sara pushed her plate away. "I'm going to bed and reading more of Sylvia's books. I'm about to start number three. I really don't believe she's capable of stealing a child. My impression of her is that if she saw an unguarded infant in a stroller she'd protect the baby."

"Think people's good memories of Sylvia will stop this guy Everett from writing about her?"

"No," Kate and Sara said in unison.

Sara grimaced. "It won't take long for him to hear about Janet's friendship with Sylvia. That she committed suicide will make him sure he's found the guilty one, and Sylvia Alden will be declared a kidnapper. People will say that she was right to kill herself. That story will—" She broke off, not seeming able to say more. She stood up. "Good night."

After she left, Jack and Kate cleaned up, and said little. Kate went to bed, tried to read, but couldn't. She spent a restless night and awoke the next morning feeling groggy.

When she went to the kitchen, Jack and Sara were there. He was looking over a set of blueprints. Sara's eyes were red and she looked like she hadn't slept.

Kate mumbled good morning, then sat down to her bowl of cereal.

Jack pushed his plans aside. "I have an idea. I have a couple of boxes of scraps in the shop that I've been meaning to give to Charlene, and her house needs some repairs. Why don't we meet for lunch then go visit her? And take pictures." He looked at Kate. "She has a couple of horses, a lot of chickens, and a big screen house full of lettuce. It's a nice place."

"And she makes birdhouses," Kate said, her spirits beginning to lift.

"As long as 'she' isn't there," Sara added.

Kate groaned and Jack shook his head. They knew she meant Tayla and they were giving Sara no sympathy.

"Okay, okay," Sara said. "Chickens win over enemies." She looked at Kate. "What our Silent Hero here isn't telling you is that he built—and designed—everything. Horse barn, chicken coop, Charlene's studio, and a screen house with concrete beds that can withstand a hurricane."

"Did you?" Kate asked.

Jack smiled modestly.

"All for your crush on Charlene. I want to meet her. And her ugly husband."

"Ugly?" Sara said. "You should see Leland. Suave, sophisticated, and very intelligent. I only met him once but—"

Jack cut her off. "Hate to interrupt your fan club but do you two want to go or not? Or maybe you don't want to be seen with a man who wears a tool belt and drives a truck."

"Oh, Jack." Kate was batting her lashes. "I just love your hammer. And all those nails. What woman could resist?"

Jack stood up. "Be here at noon. We'll go to the Brigade for lunch. Unless you two ladies are so dainty you have to have Los Olas." He didn't wait for an answer but went down the hall to his room.

"What's Los Olas?" Kate asked.

"Gorgeous. High-end. We'll have to do a girls' day there."

"Can't wait."

Charlene lived in tiny, rural Southwest Ranches, a place that used to be all small farms. But rich people had bought most of the land, torn down the little farm-houses, and put up mansions.

Stirling Road, which ran through the area, had a speed limit so low that runners were faster than the cars. But children on horses, sauntering tortoises, and families of ducks took precedence over motorized vehicles.

Charlene's house was set back off the road, down a quarter-mile driveway that was full of potholes. Compared to the neighbors, her house was small. Jack had remodeled and expanded the original farmhouse, and the old-world Spanish exterior was lovely. When they arrived, Charlene was inside on the phone, so Jack took them around. He tried to not let his pride show but Kate and Sara saw it.

Close to the house was an L-shaped building with a deep, shady courtyard surrounded by fruiting citrus trees in big pots. Jack said it was Charlene's studio and he'd let her show it.

The chicken coop was like a small house. It had two doors in front, each one leading into its own fenced area.

"When the grass on one side is worn down, Charlene switches to the other side," Jack said. He sounded proud.

The screen house was sixty feet long, with beds that were full of a large variety and color of salad plants. "Charlene sells to top restaurants all over the city."

He walked ahead of the women. Kate whispered, "He sure does like her, doesn't he?"

"It appears so." Sara seemed as surprised as Kate was.

There was a pond, some trees, and behind a copse

of trees was what had to be the cutest barn ever built. It was small, with a steeply pitched roof and a covered area to one side. Inside were two stalls and wide double doors that opened at both ends. A mare recognized Jack and trotted out of a shady, fenced area to snuggle her head against his shoulder. He pulled an apple from his pocket and held it out to her as he stroked her head.

Kate and Sara stood back, watching with raised eyebrows. He certainly seemed at home here!

Jack grabbed a shovel and began cleaning out a stall—something he seemed to have done before—and Sara started snapping photos.

Kate wandered outside and looked around. She was admiring the pond, looking at the fish swimming just below the surface, when she saw a woman walk from the house to the studio.

She was about Kate's height and had long dark hair pulled into a twist at the back of her neck. A little ornament in her hair caught the sunlight and glittered. She had on black linen trousers, flat sandals with tiny straps, and a green T-shirt. She was slim and lithe and moved like she'd had some dancing training.

Sometimes in life you see a person and think, *I like her.* Or him. But with men it was usually the ol' sexual attraction.

With this woman it was just a feeling of *like.*

Kate hurried around the pond and caught her before she opened the door to the studio. "Hi."

When she turned, Kate saw a pretty woman, younger than she thought she'd be. Her skin was lovely.

"I'm Kate Medlar." She held out her hand to shake.

"Charlene Adams." She shook Kate's hand warmly. "Jack never shuts up about you."

Kate was surprised at that. "I didn't know he was here that often."

"Nearly every Friday. He's in love with Belle."

"Oh?"

"Our horse." Charlene was looking at Kate in speculation.

"There's nothing between Jack and me," Kate said. "I mean—"

"I know. He told me." She opened the door to the studio. "Would you like to see where I work?"

"I would love to."

The inside of Charlene's studio was like Santa's workshop. It was a long space with a tiny powder room to the side. Huge north-facing windows had a worktable beneath.

There were miniature houses everywhere. Victorians, French chateaus, southwest adobe style, Nantucket houses with their widows' walks. Some houses were half-finished, some seeming to just need paint. All of them had holes and perches for birds to enter.

"Wow" was all Kate could think to say.

"You can see how far behind I am." Across the room was a giant bulletin board with photos and drawings attached to letters. "People write to me asking me to please make a birdhouse like their home. Those photos are ones I have to get to."

Kate looked at huge shelves divided into cubbyholes full of materials. Tools were on a pegboard. A band saw was in the middle of the room. There was a painting booth with goggles hanging at the corner. "I'd like to help."

Charlene laughed. "You have enough to do. I'm sure—" She saw that Kate was serious. "That would be nice. Tell me, is Jack cleaning out the stables?"

"Yes."

"Oh dear. He does take on responsibility. And he loves to let me know my husband doesn't know one end of a horse from another. But Aunt Tayla gave Belle to my sons and…" She shrugged. "What could I do?"

"I can tell you hate your little farm."

"Oh yes."

They laughed together.

"Would you be willing to help me make two big pitchers of lemonade? The boys will be home from school soon and Jack can drink half a gallon at one sitting so…"

Kate was realizing how familiar Jack was with this family, but he'd never mentioned them. Had he meant to keep them as his own secret? Or was it just that this was none of Kate's business? "Sure. I'd love to."

"Let's go in the house. You have to see the kitchen Jack made for me."

The inside of Charlene's house was beautiful. Artwork was everywhere. There were framed pictures of her two sons' drawings, along with photos of them, as well as weavings and pottery.

"Did you do this?" She was touching a tall weaving hanging from the ceiling to the floor. It was done in shades of red and it was extraordinarily beautiful.

"I did. Majored in art in college. I was going to set the world on fire with my fiber art. The next Lenore

Tawney." Charlene waved her hand. "Great weaver. But anyway, I met Leland and never looked back."

Kate picked up a photo of a very good-looking man, older than Charlene. He was sitting in a lawn chair, drink in hand. He seemed to be relaxing but he had on a shirt and tie. "Is this your husband?"

"Yes. He's a lawyer."

There was love and pride in her voice. Charlene pulled two cans of thawed pink lemonade out of the fridge.

The kitchen was indeed beautiful. Tall white cabinets in an L-shape, with beautiful stainless appliances, pure white countertops. But the big, stand-alone island had a breathtaking piece of granite that was reddish-orange swirled with cream. Only a true artist would have chosen it. Kate loved it! "Do you like to cook?"

"I do. I've certainly had a lot of experience at it. I used to cook for Aunt Tayla and Uncle Walter."

"Can I help?"

"Sure," Charlene said. "Sit there and talk to me. I live with two little boys and a husband who reads briefs all evening. I am starved for old-fashioned *talk*."

Kate sat down at the counter. "When did you cook for Tayla and her husband?"

"I moved in with them when I was sixteen. I think I was too much for my parents to handle. Besides, looking after me gave Tayla an excuse to stop being a slave to her domineering husband. He sure loved to give orders." Charlene poured the lemonade into two big glass pitchers.

"You two returned to Lachlan."

"Yes." Charlene smiled. "Aunt Tayla hadn't been

back here in years so she was shocked. The cute little town she remembered was gone. It was like a badly repaired war site."

"But Tayla fixed it." There was pride in Kate's voice. "It's why I came here. To work with her."

"I figured it was to meet your aunt."

"That too." Kate ran her hand along the porch of a birdhouse that was at the far end of the counter. It was a Victorian with two towers. "What I really wanted was to hear about my father. You wouldn't remember him, would you? No, of course not. You're too young."

Charlene had her back to Kate. "I guess you mean Randal."

"You *did* know him?"

When Charlene turned around, she was smiling. "He was a lovely man."

"Really? I got the idea he was a bit of a…scoundrel."

"He was. But that made him exciting. He was so good-looking…" She stirred the lemonade. "You know how some men have all the confidence in the world? They just seem to know that they're going to be wanted. Accepted."

"Not really," Kate said, "but I can imagine it."

"That's how Randal was. He believed people were going to like him so they did." She smiled in memory. "Every teenage girl in Lachlan had a crush on him."

"He wasn't in school with you, was he?" Kate wondered if Charlene was older than she looked.

"Heavens no! When I was in high school, Randal was…" She thought for a moment. "Thirty-eight, thirty-nine. Somewhere in there. But charisma doesn't age, does it?"

"Tom Selleck."

Charlene laughed. "You and me both. My husband is twelve years older than I am. I tend to like a man with some experience in the world. What about you?"

"Haven't decided yet. I do like a man who can *do* things." Charlene was opening packages of cookies and arranging them on a tray. "Can you tell me more about my father? Every time I ask Aunt Sara, she clams up. And speaking of that, do you know why our aunts hate each other?"

"I've asked about that but I got no answer." Charlene lowered her voice in secrecy. "However, I did hear Aunt Tayla in one of her many arguments with Walter. I think that back in high school he did something awful to Sara and Tayla took his side."

"What was it?"

"No idea." She sighed. "Walter was a crass and rude man. The exact opposite of Randal."

"Tell me," Kate said eagerly.

"Randal wore a tuxedo like he'd been born in it. Champagne was his favorite drink."

"But I heard that he and Jack's father were friends. Roy wasn't exactly the tux and champagne type."

"Yes and no. Jack's dad wore leather and rode a giant Harley, while Randal was invited to the poshest parties in town. They were kings in their own societies. I think they respected each other."

"I heard—" Kate started to say that Aunt Sara had hinted that he stole diamonds but she stopped. "What made them friends?"

"Well…" Charlene hesitated. "Neither of them…

uh, paid much attention to rules, and that included the law. Randal was the brains and Roy was the muscle."

Kate's eyes were wide as she listened, but then the noise of two little boys, running in after having been imprisoned in school all day, cut them off. She watched Charlene envelop them in hugs. Then they ran outside yelling, "Jack is here." Kate helped Charlene carry the lemonade and cookies outside.

She was glad she'd heard some about her father but she wanted more. And more and more.

Sara was in the little barn taking stills of the tackle. She was underexposing and opening the aperture to get as much light as possible. She bracketed to get black and white as well as soft and vivid color. When she heard a sound to her left, she swung around, never taking the camera from her eye. The wide double doors were open to bright Florida sunshine and coming in was a tall woman leading a horse. The backlighting made her a dark silhouette, more a cutout than a portrait. Perfect! Sara snapped half a dozen shots before she lowered the camera.

When she saw who it was, she turned and headed out.

"Would you stop it!" Tayla said.

Sara halted but she didn't turn around.

"It all happened so long ago. And you were right. Walter was a jerk. Sorry I didn't believe you about him at the time."

Sara turned around to face the woman she hadn't spoken to in many years. Kate had told them that lately her boss had been agitated, upset about something.

And they'd told Sara of the overheard conversation. It went through her mind that it was time to put old feuds into the past.

Tayla tied the horse to the stall. "But then, Randal was worse."

In a single second, Sara went from feeling forgiveness to rage. "My brother didn't drug high school girls. He didn't tear their clothes off. He didn't—"

"No," Tayla said calmly. "Randal was merely a seducer of fifteen-year-old girls. Namely, my niece, Charlene. You didn't know that, did you?" She pulled the saddle off the horse. "I've kept this knowledge to myself for many years but I think it's time you knew. She and your brother had an affair. It didn't last long. A week or so, but she was oh so willing for it to go on. She was heartbroken when he didn't show up at their meeting place. Torn apart. No one knew what was wrong with her because your brother was so very good at keeping secrets, wasn't he?"

Tayla dropped the saddle onto a hay bale. "But then, you're not bad at holding in secrets either, are you? What happened to your beautiful, spoiled, no-conscience little brother? He just disappeared. Vanished. No explanation was ever given."

"I don't have to listen to this." Sara turned and left the barn.

TEN

Tayla watched her former friend leave and felt bad at what she'd said, and especially at the way she'd said it. Their first meeting after all these years should have been sweet and gentle. But right now there was nothing inside Tayla but anger. No, that wasn't right. It was fear—and it was building up inside her until she was about to implode. How long was it going to take before the secret she'd been hiding for so long would come out? She'd blurted only a tiny bit of it to Sara.

There were rumors around town of a reporter who was asking everyone questions. And of course there was Sara and her little entourage of would-be detectives. They were snooping into everything. It was being said that Sheriff Flynn was helping them.

Tayla left the barn and walked toward the house. The boys were home from school and they were begging Jack to turn them upside down and toss them into the air. Nothing was too rough for them. But then, their lawyer father was more likely to read to them. Leland was older, groomed to the point of obsession, and Charlene was mad about him. To Tayla, he reminded her too much of Sara's little brother.

Sara was taking photos, and standing to the side was Kate, her auburn hair glinting in the sunlight. It was a perfect gathering of people who cared about one another. People who had a reason to laugh. *How long will it last?* Tayla thought.

She went back to the barn, picked up the brush, and started combing down the sweaty horse. Riding miles in the heat hadn't helped her mood. She could *not* take away all that Charlene had now. Whatever she had to do, she wouldn't let it end.

As she brushed, she thought back to that summer so long ago.

July 1994
Atlanta, Georgia

What's more complicated than family? Tayla thought as she pulled into the driveway of her sister Diane's mega mansion. Tayla rolled her eyes at the sight of the house. It was a fake Tudor. Next door was a reproduction French chateau. Next to it was… The whole suburb was full of huge houses that were modernized copies of some time period that had nothing to do with Atlanta.

She got out of the rental car to get her suitcase from the back.

Yet again, she wondered why she'd allowed herself to be bullied into doing this. But her mother and Diane had piled masses of guilt on her. Diane and her rich husband, Garett, *had* to go to Brussels. *Had* to attend some conference. "He's the keynote speaker," her mother had nearly shouted. "You *must* do this."

"All right," Tayla snapped back. "I'll see if I can get away."

"No," her mother said. "Not see, but *do*." She'd slammed down the phone.

Family obligations, Tayla thought in disgust.

Her mother wanted Tayla to fly to Atlanta and stay with her niece, Charlene, for the week Diane and her husband would be away.

Tayla's husband, Walter, had loudly protested. If she was gone, who was going to run his office, his house, his *life*? When he told Tayla it wasn't possible for her to go, she'd booked a plane ticket. Sometimes you had to choose your battles. She was much more afraid of her formidable mother than of Walter.

She leaned against the car and looked up at the big house. Everyone in her family was angry at her. Her mother, her sister, her husband. Her fancy brother-in-law was probably angry too but at least he hadn't yelled at her.

It was all about Charlene, her sweet, adorable, quiet, docile niece. She was what now? Fifteen? No, she'd turned sixteen. Damn! She forgot to send a gift.

Tayla knew that none of her family understood the amount of work she and Walter did. Halfway through college, when she and Walter married, his dad gave them a small strip mall outside Philadelphia. It was nearly derelict, but Walter was a salesman at heart and Tayla knew how to work. They now owned four lucrative malls. She didn't have time to pop back to Lachlan for every Thanksgiving, Christmas, or even for the birth of her sister's only child, Charlene.

But then, Tayla had had a lifetime of being compared to her younger sister. According to their parents, Diane was the epitome of the "good daughter." She'd married the son of a rich family from Fort Lauderdale. Since his job at the family's firm was there, they'd stayed in Lachlan. Perfect Diane had had a baby. That Tayla—or Walter—was infertile gained no sympathy from her parents.

When Charlene was thirteen, Diane's father-in-law wanted his son to move to Japan and start an office there. Tayla wasn't sure exactly what went on—she was too busy with work to listen to a long saga—but Charlene stayed behind in Lachlan with her grandparents. "Until she finishes high school," her mother said on the phone.

Last year, they'd changed plans again. Diane and Garett had abruptly left Japan, moved to Atlanta, and Charlene left Lachlan High School to live with them.

Tayla had a feeling that something had "happened," but no one would tell her what. Was it some scandal concerning Diane's perfect husband?

It wasn't very kind of her, but the thought made Tayla smile. Her parents weren't shy about telling Tayla that her husband was far from perfect. "He orders you around like you're his unpaid servant," her mother said. Her father was more kind. He said, "Any time you want to come home, we'll be here."

Tayla defended her husband. *Always* defended him. After all, *she* had chosen him. That damned Sara Medlar had told her not to but...

Tayla tilted her head back and looked up at the sky. It was gray and felt like it might rain. That meant she was going to be stuck inside with a sixteen-year-old. What in the world was she going to do with her? She hadn't seen her in years, so what was she like now? Tayla truly hoped the reason she'd been given this task wasn't that the kid was doing drugs. Or maybe sex was the problem. Please, she hoped she wasn't expected to tell her niece about using a condom. The old banana demo? She could hear her mother. *But you live in a city, so you know about these things.* They don't have sex in Lachlan, Florida? Ha ha.

Tayla grabbed the handle of her suitcase and rolled it up the drive. There was a shallow porch with potted plants that looked like they needed watering. Tayla was a day later than she'd been told to be here but that couldn't be helped. One of their tenants said he wasn't going to pay rent if his roof wasn't repaired. Walter told Tayla to take care of it as he had to meet with new tenants—on the golf course. So Tayla dealt with hot tar while Walter had martinis at the club.

When she was delayed, she'd called her sister's number but got only her answering machine. The same happened at her parents' house. Had her niece become such a wild child that she couldn't stay alone for twenty-four hours?

Tayla noticed that one of the potted plants had been ripped apart. It was a short plant with big leaves and tiny white flowers on a stalk. She couldn't remember the name. Oh yes. Lily of the valley. It looked like something had torn out half the plant, leaving a hole in the dirt.

She'd been told that the key was under the mat but she didn't want to barge in on her niece. After all, there was no telling what a sixteen-year-old girl was up to. Boys? Girls? When it came to that, she had no idea which way her niece swung.

She rang the doorbell, then waited. She was about to get the key when the door opened. There was Charlene, as pretty as she remembered—but at least twenty pounds overweight.

A gym! was Tayla's first thought. Long walks. Cut out the burgers. Is *this* why she'd been told to babysit? To put the girl on a diet?

They exchanged double cheek kisses.

"Come in," Charlene said. "Can I get you something to drink? Or maybe eat? I'm not a great cook but I can do pasta dishes. They fill you up."

"I would love some iced tea."

"Easy enough."

Tayla left her suitcase in the big living room. It was like something out of a magazine and she had an idea that Diane had hired someone to decorate it for her. Mushroom-colored sofas. Tasteful little tables. Colorless lamps.

"Isn't it awful?" Charlene said.

Tayla smiled. "Yes, it is."

"I much prefer the bright colors of Florida, don't you?"

"Oh yes." Tayla had forgotten how much she liked her niece. They'd always agreed on things.

They went into Diane's pristine kitchen. It was equipped to run a restaurant but Tayla had never seen her sister cook anything.

"This is Mom's joy. Beautiful, isn't it? If she knew I'd been actually *using* it, she'd be very upset. But then, I've been told to eat only salads. With no dressing."

That her sister had given that order made Tayla want to go the opposite way. "We'll have ice cream sundaes for dinner."

Charlene laughed. She was such a pretty girl with her flawless complexion and her black lashes. Her hair was pulled back in a low ponytail and she was wearing a huge cotton shirt and linen pants. *Maybe this won't be so bad*, Tayla thought. At least the girl wasn't a sulky teenager with lots of black eye makeup.

"So, tell me about Lachlan."

As Charlene made them a pitcher of iced tea, they talked.

Tayla asked about everyone she'd grown up with. So many of them had left town. It was sad to hear that Lachlan hadn't fully recovered from the damage of the last big hurricane. It was no longer the thriving town it had been, but it was good to hear about people she knew.

They spent an hour at the cozy nook off the kitchen, chatting and laughing. Tayla was still puzzled about why her mother and sister had been adamant that she stay with Charlene. They'd sounded like the child was on the verge of some catastrophe, or maybe a breakdown. But she was a lovely young lady, all smiles and good humor. Very grown up.

"More tea?" Charlene asked.

"Sure. I—" She broke off as she heard a sound. It was like a baby fussing. Not crying actually.

"Oh, she's awake." Charlene got up. "And about

time." She put her hand at the top of her breast. "Another few minutes and I'd be in pain." She hurried out of the room.

Tayla sat where she was. What was going on?

She left the kitchen but saw no one. She walked through the big house until she came to a little room in the front. There Charlene sat, her shirt open on one side as she nursed a baby that even inexperienced Tayla could see was very young.

Tayla collapsed on a little love seat and stared.

Charlene, an expression of love on her young face, looked up. "Isn't she lovely? Utterly perfect."

Tayla was in shock. Charlene was sixteen years old! And she was a mother? She started to speak, choked, cleared her throat, then tried again. "I didn't know," she managed to whisper.

"Mother didn't tell you? That was naughty of her. I told her she had to go to Brussels with Dad, that I'd be fine, but you know what a worrywart she is. She didn't want to leave me alone with a baby, but we're doing well, aren't we?" She kissed her child's forehead.

"What's the baby's name?"

"Rowena. Isn't that pretty? Makes me think of moonlight and masked men. Very romantic."

"Yes. Very. I, uh, excuse me." She practically ran from the room and grabbed a phone. First, she called her mother. No answer, just the machine. She tried not to shout but she couldn't stop herself. "She just had a baby! She is sixteen years old. You sent me here to take care of this, didn't you?" She had to click off before she started cursing.

When she called her sister, there was no answer, no

machine. Tayla hung up. She was too furious to trust herself to speak.

They had dumped this whole mess onto *her*! Did they expect *her* to sort it out? Tayla the responsible one. Tayla the workhorse of the family. Tayla had no kids of her own so why not give her this very big problem?

She wasn't sure if she wanted to scream or burst into tears. They were always nagging her that she ignored them, wasn't involved with them, so they'd lied and connived to force her into it.

They've known about this for months, she thought. Is *this* why Diane left Japan? Had Charlene lived with them for her whole pregnancy?

Tayla started to go back to the room. What was she supposed to *do*?

For a moment she closed her eyes, hands into fists at her sides. She'd always been good at organization. Start at the bottom and work up. The baby was first. Get little Rowena sorted.

Next came Charlene. Where was she going to live? She hadn't finished high school. She needed to go to college, needed to be able to support herself. She needed—

Tayla gritted her teeth. She should sue the living hell out of the male who was responsible for this.

With her shoulders back, a smile plastered on her face, Tayla went back to Charlene and the baby. She'd finished nursing and was burping her daughter. "Where's the nursery?"

Charlene kissed her baby. "I guess this is it."

Tayla hadn't looked about the room. There was an open packet of diapers on the floor. In the corner was a sort of bed made out of blankets and throw pillows. "Your parents made no preparations for the baby?"

Charlene gave an I'm-sorry look. "It's not their fault. I changed my mind about the adoption."

"Ahhh." Tayla had to work to control the anger that raged through her.

Just as her mother and sister had bullied her, they'd done it to this sweet girl. She'd had sex in high school. Heaven knows Tayla and Walter had done it often then. And Sara and Cal. And everyone.

But Charlene had been caught. Got pregnant. It was Tayla's guess that Charlene waited to tell of her condition until there couldn't be a termination. Diane and their mother had handled it by declaring that Charlene would, of course, put the child up for adoption.

Charlene had destroyed their plans by refusing to give her child up. From the way she was holding her baby, it was Tayla's guess that she took one look at her infant and refused to part with her. Love in its finest moment.

So what had Diane and their mother done about this? Dumped it all onto Tayla. "Tayla will fix it. Tayla will know what to do." She'd heard it all her life.

Well, she *did* know what to do. "Charlene, honey, tell me where I can buy a car seat. When I get back with it, you and I and Rowena are going shopping. We're going to set up a beautiful nursery. While I'm gone, you can pick out a room to use in this monster-sized house."

There were tears in Charlene's eyes as she looked up at her tall aunt. She was too overcome with emotion to speak, but she managed to form "thank you."

"My pleasure," Tayla said, and she meant it.

Surprisingly, shopping with her niece for all the baby things, including furniture, was a joy. Charlene's happiness about her baby was infectious. Setting up the nursery gave Tayla a feeling that she'd never had before. It was almost like little Rowena was the grandchild she was never going to have.

For two days, she and Charlene lived in a world of soft blankets, warm baths, and waking at all hours. Taking care of the baby ruled them. Every minute was controlled by the infant's soft, sweet needs.

Tayla was shocked at how much love could develop in such a short time. Love for her niece who devoted herself to her baby and love for the helpless being who ruled their hearts.

She didn't call her mother or her sister. At first her silence was out of anger, but by the evening of the first day, she didn't care. Maybe Diane had run away from taking on the responsibility of a newborn, but Tayla loved it.

On the second day, she forced herself to talk to Charlene about what she was going to do with her life. How was she going to support herself and her child? As she spoke, she thought how she would make Diane pay. And her mother. And the baby's father. And Walter.

Charlene's reply had been a cheerful "I have no idea what I'm going to do."

Tayla opened her mouth to tell her niece that she had a baby to take care of so she needed to think about the future. But when Tayla held the baby and looked into her eyes, she began to ask herself what she was going to do with her own life.

It was so peaceful to not be around the constant chaos that surrounded Walter. He ruled everyone around him. He fired people who stood up to him. She knew that they'd have a fight about all she'd charged for the baby things and she needed to prepare herself for that. Over the years, Tayla had learned that it was easier to give in to him. She had no heart for arguments, whereas Walter thrived on them. This time, she had to stand her ground. For Charlene. For Rowena.

When she started to talk to her niece about her future and supporting herself, Tayla began to realize that, in a way, she was in the same situation. She didn't get a paycheck, didn't own stock in her own name. She had no real job title. If she made a résumé it would read *Did whatever Walter told me to do.*

She didn't know when her life had changed to that. In high school she had been... She didn't want to think back to how she'd been then. So alive and full of hope and plans. Sara Medlar had been her best friend and they had...

She made herself stop thinking of that time. They were in Diane's bland living room—lack of color seemed to imply sophistication—and she looked at Charlene, her baby at her breast. "How about if you go home with me?"

Charlene smiled. "I'd like that. I think Mother is fed up with me."

"And me. We'll be two misfits together."

"Three."

"Oh yes. Can't forget Rowena. If we make coconut shrimp for dinner, do you think she'll like the flavor?"

"I'm sure she'll love it."

It was the night of the third day that Diane called and woke Tayla.

Diane gave no greeting, just "I guess you're still mad at me."

"You played a rotten trick on me. You should have told me when Charlene was pregnant."

"I didn't know until she was six months along. Mother called me in hysterics. Garett was wonderful. He told his dad he had to go back to the US and why. My dear father-in-law set up the job in Atlanta so we could be with our daughter."

"You told your father-in-law but not me?"

Diane sighed. "Tayla, be fair. You know what you're like."

"What the hell is *that* supposed to mean?"

"You manage people like those stores your husband owns. You would have been talking lawsuits and college for Charlene. We had a scared teenager on our hands and she needed love, not lawyers."

Tayla had to swallow at that. It was too close to her first thoughts. "What about the baby?"

"Mother took care of the poor thing." Diane's voice caught. "It broke my heart seeing Charlene holding that little boy. No one knew what caused him to be stillborn."

"What?" Tayla whispered.

"I know. It's too horrible to think about. After we got home, I wanted to stay with my daughter but…" Diane's voice began to rise. "But Garett and I had been through so much with her while she was pregnant. Nights of nothing but tears. Damn Randal Medlar! And Mother said you'd be there only hours after we left and that you'd know how to take care of everything. Besides, Charlene said she needed time alone to grieve."

But I was a day late, Tayla thought. Charlene was alone for one whole day. Tayla's body was beginning to shake. "Yes. Time to grieve." Her voice was raw.

"Are you all right? You should call Mother and ask about the funeral arrangements. Maybe you can help with the headstone." There was no answer. "Tayla? Is something going on? Is Charlene okay?"

"Everything is fine. I'm going to take her home with me."

"I don't think I can allow that. I'd miss her too much. I can't —"

"Charlene needs a challenge. She needs something to occupy her mind." Tayla was squeezing her eyes shut as she said the clichés. She *had* to get her niece away from…from whatever she'd done. "And you need a rest after what you've been through in the last months."

"I could use some time to myself," Diane said. "These past months have been stressful. With Garett's job and Charlene's pregnancy, I—"

"Six months," Tayla said. "We'll try it and if she's unhappy I'll return her." She could almost hear Diane thinking.

"Walter won't like sharing you."

"Walter can go to hell. I have to go now. I have to do…uh, some things." She hung up.

She went into Charlene's room. She was asleep, snuggled in bed beside Rowena. The baby opened her eyes and looked up at Tayla. Without waking Charlene, Tayla lifted the child and held her. "Who are you?"

The baby was asleep before she got to the living

room and turned on the big TV. It hadn't been on since she'd been there. The first thing she saw on the news channel was a photo of Rowena. They were calling it the White Lily Kidnapping because a handful of lilies of the valley had been left in the stroller.

The ones from the pot outside, Tayla thought. The white dress and the little pink sweater were hanging in the closet in the nursery she and Charlene had put together. When Tayla had admired them, she'd thought how her sister had bought those expensive clothes for the baby but not a crib. But then, the baby wasn't supposed to come home with them.

The news said there was a three-state-wide manhunt for the White Lily Kidnapper. They were talking prison and…and execution. Kidnapping was punishable by death.

For the first time in years, Tayla began to pray. She needed help in trying to fix this.

ELEVEN

As Jack drove them home, he was happily listening to Kate's chatter. Knowing that he'd cheered her up, that she and Charlene could possibly become friends, was all he wanted. He thought she spent too much time with just him and Sara. They had well-established lives in and out of Lachlan, but Kate didn't. In the few months she'd been in the little town, she'd made progress in breaking away from her domineering mother but she still had far to go. Friends would help.

Kate was talking about the different styles of Charlene's birdhouses. "I've never done any kind of crafting but Charlene made me want to try. I'd start with something simple. An adobe, I guess. Lots of flat walls."

"I have tools you can use," Jack said. He glanced across her to Sara. She was looking out the side window and saying nothing.

Jack had known Sara for years. They'd been through

a lot together and he could see that right now she was upset. *Really* upset.

Tayla, he thought, then cursed under his breath. When he was in the barn, he'd wondered where Tayla's horse was, but he'd been too concerned with Kate to think about anything else. Was Tayla there? Did Sara and she meet? Have a fight?

As Jack turned onto Nob Hill Road, he regretted not asking Charlene if Tayla was going to be there.

Kate was talking about Charlene's chickens. "The boys gather the eggs every morning. Aren't they great kids? So full of life. I'd like to meet her husband, Leland. Charlene seems to be madly in love with him. Do you like him?"

Jack was so deep in thought that the silence as Kate waited for an answer went on for seconds. "Yeah, he's okay."

Kate gave a big sigh. "Okay, what's up with you two? I feel like I'm sitting between two statues."

Jack wanted to save Sara from an interrogation. "We can't get a word in around you. Leland is a good guy if you like old men. Nobody could figure out why she wanted an oldie like him. But then, when Charlene was fifteen she looked twenty-six. She—"

"Shut up." Sara's voice was soft but it was like she was shouting.

Kate turned to her, but Jack kept his eyes on the road. Now he was *sure* Sara had met with Tayla—and it had been bad.

"What's wrong?" Kate asked her aunt.

Jack spoke before Sara could. "What I said reminds her of Cheryl Morris. I shouldn't have said that Charlene looked older." He was talking faster. "Truth is that Leland is a great guy. He was married before to a woman who did nothing but spend his money. He got away from her, found Charlene, and they now have their little farm. And a family. He's a happy man. So are you and Charlene going to meet again?"

"I guess so, but we didn't make any specific plans."

"I'll give you the materials I put aside for her and you can deliver them. It'll give you a chance to meet Leland and spend time with the kids and the chickens."

Kate was staring straight ahead. "Sure," she murmured.

Jack pulled into the driveway of their house and let the women out in front, but he stayed there for a moment. He wanted to see if Kate was going to start asking Sara questions.

When the women were inside, he pulled the truck into the garage and sat there. Living with two women was heaven and hell together. The guys at work teased him about his "harem."

"You planning to add any more women?" his trim carpenter asked. "I have a sister. Divorced, two kids. You have room in that big house for them?"

The electricians were there and they laughed. One said, "I think Jack wants Kate and just her."

Jack had an urge to start the chain saw and go after them, but he just smiled. He tried to act like it didn't matter.

Was it obvious to the entire world? Did everyone see how he felt about Kate by the way he looked at her? There wasn't one thing he didn't like about her. Even the way she sometimes dismissed him as though he were an annoying mosquito buzzing around made him like her even more. Too many women…well, made themselves too available to him. Made everything too easy. But Kate…

Right now the problem wasn't Kate, it was his "other" woman, Sara. Something had deeply upset her.

Sara Medlar had come into his life at a time when he desperately needed help. Jack was eighteen years old when his beloved stepfather died, and he'd left behind a grieving widow and a young daughter. Jack saw his greedy father, Roy, circling the bereaved family like the vulture he was. Jack could see dollar signs in his eyes. No doubt he thought that if he could entice his ex-wife to remarry him, he'd get his hands on her widow's fortune. No matter how many times he was told, Roy wouldn't believe that there was no fortune.

At his stepfather's funeral, Jack had been sick with worry. His stomach was eating itself. His hands were in fists as he tried to figure out what to do. If only there was some way he could support his mother and his half sister, maybe he could keep them out of the clutches of Roy Wyatt.

Jack was standing by the coffin, feeling like he might explode, when from behind a little utility building came salvation. An older woman came into view. He knew who she was and to him she looked like an angel sent down to grant his every wish.

She was his grandfather Cal's Great Love. The one who got away. The one Cal should have been with but wasn't. The girl who left town and became a famous writer. Cal had always said, "If you need help, go to Sara Medlar. She'll give you whatever you need."

Jack hadn't really considered the words before, but on that day, he knew he had to find out if they were true.

When the others left the cemetery—Roy clinging tightly to his ex-wife—Jack stayed behind. He needed to plan what he was going to say to Sara and what he was going to ask for. He had *one* chance and he damned well better not screw it up.

She came to stand beside him. When she slipped her small hand into his, he knew that things were going to be all right.

And they were. Sara became his silent partner in a remodeling business. She kept her part secret because she wanted Jack to get all the credit. She said she didn't want people saying that of course Jack would succeed since he had a rich old woman backing him.

Jack felt guilty at not revealing her part in his business, but she was right. At eighteen his ego needed to feel that he could succeed on his own.

Sara had helped him through it all. She lived in New York and he often went to visit her. They went over business, then they played. Restaurants, Broadway shows, miles of walking through New York streets. Sara's love of photography became part of their lives. She said she had GAS—Gear Acquisition Syndrome. Trips to B&H photo store were often on their list of what to do.

Things changed when Jack had shown up with a Realtor handout from Lachlan. There were half a dozen houses for sale in Lachlan and he was trying to decide which two to buy to remodel then sell. He had casually mentioned that he'd heard that the big house called the Stewart Mansion was going to be put up for sale.

One of the things he most admired about Sara was her ability to make up her mind quickly. But on that day he saw the professional Sara, the one who negotiated multimillion-dollar contracts in just minutes.

He heard her gasp, saw her eyes widen. "What is it?" he asked.

"The Stewart house is for sale?"

"It will be. At least that's what I heard. If you ask me, it's a white elephant. It's too big and in bad shape. Hasn't been touched in years. Anyway, who wants a house like that in Lachlan? They—"

"Me," Sara said and picked up her phone. Thirty minutes later, she was wire transferring the money directly to the owner, a woman she'd gone to high school with.

After Sara bought the house, Jack and his crew, along with several subcontracting firms, repaired and remodeled the big old house.

There had never been a plan for Jack to live in it, but then there'd been the wreck, his half brother was killed, Jack broke his leg, and… It just worked out.

Then Kate arrived—and she changed everything.

Jack had never met anyone like her. At first he'd been disdainful of her—and maybe a little jealous. Over the years he'd become a bit possessive/protective of Sara. What would happen when this pampered, adored young woman came into their lives?

But Kate wasn't as he'd thought she'd be. She was far from being pampered. She'd had a rough childhood and a mother who was given to debilitating fits of depression. Since she was very young, Kate had had to take care of her mother. In a way, Ava Medlar was as bad as Jack's father had been. But unlike Jack, Kate didn't allow herself to suffer from it. Or, as she said Jack did, "brood" about it. No, Kate didn't brood about things.

She was a person who thought, *This is the way it is, so deal with it.*

And deal with it she had.

When Jack went inside the house, it was oddly quiet. No TV, no one talking. Instead, the bedroom doors of both women were closed. Jack let his breath out. Two women in bad moods. He thought of going to the Brigade and having a few drinks. Maybe pick up a nice, uncomplicated girl and have a night of uncomplicated sex. He wouldn't even ask her name.

But as he looked at the doors, he knew he had to fix whatever was wrong. Should he flip a coin to see who would be first?

Since Kate would ask about Sara he'd better find out about her first.

He gave a quick tap on Sara's bedroom door, but didn't leave enough time for her to tell him to go away. She was sitting on her bed on top of her white coverlet, arms crossed, and staring into space.

"Out with it." He lay down on his back across the end of the bed, hands behind his head. "I want every word."

"I saw Tayla."

"Figured so. Use your right cross on her?" When she didn't answer, he looked at her.

"Tayla was really nasty. Hateful. Angry."

"You two have been at it for years, so what did you expect?"

"No. *I* have been at it. She caused the problem, not me. She's usually contrite, repentant. But something has upset her so much that she's angry about everything. This murder has caused…"

When Jack saw that she was about to start crying, he moved to lean against the headboard, put his arm around her, and drew her head to his chest. "Exactly what did she say?"

Sara took time to answer. "My brother had an affair with Charlene when she was just fifteen years old. Randal was close to forty."

Jack wasn't going to show his disgust at that. "Explains why she likes Leland." He felt her stiffen. "Okay. Sorry. It's not a matter for jokes."

"You overheard Tayla's phone conversation."

"Yeah, so?"

"When the White Lily Kidnapping happened, Charlene was sixteen."

Jack drew in his breath. "Just because Tayla mentioned white lilies, you can't think she had anything to do with it?"

"I don't know what to think. Janet Beeson knew who the kidnapper was. Maybe Tayla's niece and my brother were part of that. She said Charlene was heartbroken. That can cause you to do really stupid things. I know! I ran away from your grandfather because my heart was broken. Maybe Janet found out and Tayla had to keep her quiet. Maybe she —" She cut herself off.

"You're jumping very far ahead, and you're skip-

ping a lot. Do you really think Tayla could murder another human being?"

"If someone was threatening you or Kate, I could
kill."

Jack kissed the top of her head. "Where was Randal
nine months before the kidnapping?"

"Who knows? He never told anyone what he was
doing when. He loved to sneak around. Loved to surprise people by being where they didn't expect him
to be."

"Would his wife know?"

"I thought of asking her but she'd tell Kate I was
snooping. She would—"

"I'll ask her." Jack got off the bed. "Give me her
number and I'll call now."

"That could possibly work. Maybe."

"We can try." He took the phone and went into her
big bathroom. He didn't need the distraction of Sara
staring at him with worry in her eyes.

Twenty minutes later Jack clicked off the phone and
let out a sigh of relief. He hadn't enjoyed talking to
Kate's mother. Ava seemed to think Jack was a predator
after her helpless daughter. Jack had spent most of the
time defending himself in a way he hoped soothed her.

It had taken work to get information out of her. In
July 1994, Ava Medlar had been heavily pregnant with
Kate and her beloved husband didn't leave her side for
over a year. In fact, they'd spent the summer before she
gave birth in Mexico. "I don't know what you're im-
plying but my husband was *not* in Lachlan, Florida,
that summer. In fact, there were, uh, legal complica-

tions and he… I mean, he needed to be somewhere besides the US."

With that cryptic comment, she hung up.

Jack went back into the bedroom and told all to Sara. "I guess your brother's passport could be checked, but I don't think there's a record for border crossings. Maybe Tayla is worried about something else. She also mentioned witches, and we know that wasn't about her."

"I guess so. It's just that my brother wouldn't think twice about going to bed with a teenager. Especially since she came on to him."

"Did Tayla tell you that?"

"She hinted at it."

"Anything else you didn't tell me?"

"Just that Charlene was hurt when Randal didn't show up at their meeting place."

"So," Jack said, "a beautiful young woman—who looked much older than her years, I might add—offered herself to your brother, who was at an age when he was probably worried about getting older, and he said yes. But later he had second thoughts and ended it. It seems that he went home to his wife and created Kate. Maybe we should thank Charlene."

Sara gave a half smile.

"What did Mrs. Medlar mean when she said there were 'legal complications' that kept them out of the US?"

Sara groaned. "I'm sure it was law enforcement. My brother was *always* running from the police. But then, he stole whatever wasn't bolted down. And even then he still took it. When he was a kid I had to empty his pockets, then figure out how to secretly return the items he'd stolen."

"A klepto?"

"No. Just a thief."

"What did your mother say?"

"Her son could do no wrong." She looked at Jack. "You aren't going to tell Kate any of this, are you?"

"She knows something is wrong and she's going to ask."

"It's your answer that concerns me."

Jack thought for a moment. "I'm going to tell her the truth with as little detail as possible. Are you hungry?"

"Not at all."

"Mind if I take Kate out?"

"I think that's a great idea."

Jack and Kate were in a booth in a restaurant on Broward. He waited until she was on her second glass of wine before he spoke of anything serious. "I called your mother."

Kate choked on the wine and began coughing.

Jack handed her a glass of water.

"Tell me this is one of your jokes."

"No. It isn't."

Kate checked her phone. There weren't twenty-plus calls from her mother spaced thirty seconds apart. In fact, there were *no* calls from her. She looked back at Jack. "She either liked you or she's on a plane to here."

"Should I book a hotel?"

"Not funny. Tell me every word that went on and do not give me any more to drink."

Jack took a breath. "It's this damned White Lily

Kidnapping. Sara got the idea that Tayla might have something to do with it."

"How was she involved?"

"Don't know. But she did mention it on the phone call we overheard, and today she told Sara…"

"Told her what?"

"That your father had a short-term affair with Charlene when she was in high school."

"My *father*?" She sounded incredulous. "He was a little old for her, wasn't he?"

"Yeah. Too old, too young. A perfect match."

"So what makes Aunt Sara think Tayla, my father's…*affair*, and a kidnapping are connected?"

"The dates are right," he said softly. "Tayla said Charlene was heartbroken when…uh, your father broke off with her. Maybe she…did something." In spite of what Kate had said, he refilled her wineglass. "Drink up. I'm driving." Kate just kept looking at him. Waiting. He gave in and continued the conversation. "Why would Tayla blurt out about your father *now*, after all these years, if it weren't because of the murder? It seems to have everyone on edge, ready to confess anything."

"This is all conjecture."

He saw the way her jaw was clenched and her hands were clutching her fork as though it were a weapon. It was obvious that she didn't want to consider any such possibility about her father. If he could, he'd erase the pictures he'd just planted in her mind. "How about if tomorrow after the memorial service we go visit Charlene? You can—"

"No." Kate's voice was firm. "I'm afraid of what I

might say. 'Hey, so did you sleep with my father when he had a wife with a child on the way?' Not exactly friendly girl talk."

Jack moved a bite of his steak around on his plate. "It could have been the other way around."

"Great! If she didn't instigate it, my father did. He went after a teenager while my mother was home with her endless morning sickness. You should hear her tell of what she went through to bring me into the world."

Jack was definitely wishing he'd kept his mouth shut. Should he change the subject or try to fix this? But then, he always had been a fixer. He told her what he'd asked her mother about her father's whereabouts at that time, and was glad when he saw Kate's pretty face relax somewhat. "I know your father died when you were what? Three? What do you remember about him?"

He was glad to see her give a slight smile.

"I was four and I remember whiskers and numbers." She smiled deeper. "Sometimes his face was baby soft and sometimes it had prickly whiskers. I thought it was a magic trick."

"Razors aren't magic. They're lethal."

"Which is why you so seldom use one?"

"Don't have a pretty girl watching me shave." He was referring to the one time she did watch him. "So what about you and your dad and numbers?"

"Years ago, I asked Mom about what I remembered. She said I was a precocious child and my father was teaching me arithmetic."

"I can believe you were smart enough to learn your multiplication tables at four."

"And words." She began to quote. "'Fuzzy Chain—quick to the break. Quinella wheel 5 with 1-7. $4.'" She'd started strongly but trailed off. "I haven't thought of that since I was a kid. Confusing, right? Seems like gibberish, not the preschool arithmetic Mom said it was."

Jack looked down at his plate. Unfortunately, he had inherited his mother's ability to blush deeply. Combine that with his father's darkness and he knew his face was looking like a sunburned walnut. He hoped Kate wouldn't see it.

But of course she did. "You can't hide from me. What is it that I remember?"

"It's uh… The, uh…"

She loudly put down her fork, then clasped her hands as she waited for him to complete a sentence.

"The dogs."

"Dogs?" Kate's eyes widened as she realized what he meant. "Dog racing?"

"Yes. Greyhounds." He lifted his head to look at her.

"My father used to read dog racing forms to me? And my mother lied about what they were?"

"Looks like it."

She picked up her fork and went back to her scallops. "That's a Florida sport, isn't it?"

He knew where she was going with her question. Maybe her father *did* return to Florida. Maybe he'd had an affair that lasted past what could be called "brief." Maybe—

"Your father and mine were friends. Sheriff Flynn was friends with them both. Your dad could have placed bets through them. He didn't have to be here."

When Kate's eyes cleared of some of the worry, he was pleased. All in all, he'd had enough talk of what may or may not have happened so long ago.

"What are you planning to wear to the memorial service tomorrow?" As he'd hoped, the question about fashion made her smile.

"I have a black silk blouse and a black straight skirt. But maybe all black is overdoing it. What about you? Sure you don't want to sing?"

"Very sure. How about dessert? Something with chocolate? Or they have vanilla ice cream with those tiny flecks in it."

"From a vanilla bean. I shouldn't."

"We'll order one and I'll eat most of it. Besides, to-morrow afternoon we can go to the gym. I'll work the calories off of you."

"That's not going to counterbalance—" She halted. "Oh, who cares? Yes! I'd very much like to have dessert. After what I've heard, I'd like to slide into a tub full of chocolate mousse and eat my way out of it. Maybe it would help me forget."

The image was so vivid—so luscious—that Jack almost couldn't speak. "Could I help? Please?" he whispered.

Kate laughed. "Absolutely not."

Looking like a sad clown, Jack signaled the waitress and ordered.

Just as they'd predicted, the church was packed with people for the memorial service. Every person who'd had anything to do with Janet Beeson was there to show their innocence.

"I guess we're standing," Kate said as she looked at the crowd. People were spilling out the doors.

Sara nodded toward the front. A short section of the third pew on the far right, next to a side door, had been cordoned off with yellow tape. "I think that might be for us."

"Even after we made it clear that we weren't going to be involved?" Jack said.

"No one ever accused Sheriff Flynn of being a good listener or obedient," Sara said. "Come on, follow me and I'll find out."

There were times when being small was an advantage and making her way through crowds was one of them. Sara twisted and turned, slipping through mere inches of space between people. Behind her, Kate and Jack did their best to follow.

Sure enough, Sheriff Flynn was standing by the door, waiting for them. "'Bout time you got here. I have some news." He motioned for them to sit down in the cordoned-off area.

The space was small and they were jammed together. Jack, then Kate and Sara, with Sheriff Flynn on the end. Everyone in the church seemed to be talking and the organist started playing. To hear each other, they had to lean in close, like a huddle of sports players.

Sheriff Flynn began. "First off, time of death was between seven and nine a.m. When Dora got there at one, Janet had only been dead a few hours." He paused to let this information sink in. "Yesterday a man came to me. He's the source of info to that reporter who's been hanging around town and asking millions of questions. That guy even wheeled the pastor into telling him who was going to talk today, then he went to them. I hear he's good at getting secrets out of people. I was told that he wrote their speeches for them, then rehearsed them." When they showed no surprise, the sheriff gritted his teeth. "I *knew* it! You know about him. You—"

"*Who* is the source of information?" Sara snapped.

With a glare at her, he continued. "His name is Chester Dakon, Chet for short. He's retired now but he used to be the chief of police for Atlanta. When he was young, he was one of the cops on the White Lily Kidnapping case." The sheriff grimaced. "Looks like you know about that too. That reporter talks too much! I should arrest him for having a big mouth."

Sara leaned back in her seat. She wasn't going to listen if he didn't get on with the story.

Flynn knew when he'd lost. "Anyway, Chet never forgot the case. In fact, he became so obsessed with it that it became known as Dakon's Lily. He had a special file cabinet in his office just for whatever he could find. He never came close to solving it, but then about a month ago this newspaper guy went to Dakon and said some woman in Florida knew who the White Lily Kidnapper was. That woman was Janet Beeson." Their expressions made the sheriff tighten his lips. "You know about that too!"

Kate, always the diplomat, said, "Yes, we listened to Mr. Gage. I'm sure he'd love to fill you in on all the details."

"I want you three to tell Dakon everything you know or suspect or even thought about."

Sara was aghast. "How many times do we have to

tell you that we want nothing to do with this? We were tricked into listening to Gage's story. You're the sheriff, you should talk to him and leave us alone. He can—"

Sara broke off as the side door opened and a man walked in. He was in his sixties, under six feet, and built like a bulldog: thick and muscular. He had a *very* handsome face, the kind used to sell products. It was the face of a man to be trusted.

"Is that Dakon?" Sara sounded breathless.

"Yeah, he's—" Flynn began, but Sara stood up, her eyes on the man.

He was looking about the room, his blue eyes seeming to do the proverbial "casing the joint." When he saw Sara, he halted. Not just stopped, but froze in place. His eyes seemed to shoot sparks of blue fire.

Kate nudged Jack. "What in the world is up with them?"

Jack put his lips near her ear. "I think it's called a 'sexual attraction.' A lightning bolt worth of it. Ever hear of it?"

"No. Explain it to me."

"Call your mom and ask her."

"I mention sex and she'll run here faster than a jet. But I can't see Aunt Sara and that…that man together. Not like that. I mean, they're…"

"Old?"

"I guess so, but that's not very PC of me."

Sara didn't look down at Sheriff Flynn as she told him to move.

"He can sit over there." The sheriff sounded petulant.

"Now. Go."

With an eye roll, the sheriff got up and gave his seat to Chet Dakon.

Curious, Kate leaned across her aunt to look at the man. He smiled at her but said nothing. As for Sara, she was staring straight ahead, looking at no one. "I'm Kate. This is Jack."

"So I assumed," Chet said. His voice was deep and rough.

Kate leaned back in the pew and whispered to Jack, "If Aunt Sara doesn't want him, I'll take him."

Jack's groan was covered by the pastor speaking into a microphone. While they'd been giving their attention to the sheriff and the newcomer, chairs had been set up behind the pulpit. Seven people sat there, including the four who'd gone to Sara's house after the murder.

The pastor said it was a time to remember the good of a person's life, not the bad that had ended it. He stepped aside to let Megan Nesbitt take her place by the microphone.

Megan had note cards with her and she read a highly edited story of the kindness of Janet Beeson. She left out the part where her brother had described Janet as what a witch looked like. Megan made the story of painting "Witch" on the garage sound like the innocence of children. It was just play. She ended with "But Janet forgave them."

Kate drew in her breath. That was the opposite of what Megan had told them. "Janet never forgave her brother," she whispered to Jack.

He turned to her with a frown and nodded. He also saw the change.

Next came the three teenage girls. Again, it was a different story. This time around the girls were humble, taking all the blame onto themselves. No bragging about Britney's talent at mimicry.

Britney said, "I felt so bad that I didn't want to live anymore."

The girls looked at the audience, then put their arms around each other.

"But Mrs. Beeson saved her," Ashley said. "She saved all of us."

What they said and the way they presented it was so well-spoken, so well played, that Jack and Kate turned to Sara.

"Everett Gage," Sara said in disgust.

At the same time, in the same tone, Chet Dakon also said, "Everett Gage."

In delight of their words spoken in unison, the two older people looked at each other as though they might start giggling.

Jack and Kate leaned back against the hard oak pew. "Now I wish he'd go away," Kate muttered.

"Get in line," Jack said.

The next person up was Valerie Johnson. They hadn't met her but the guards had spoken of her. She'd won the local crocheting contest. "I gloated," she said. "I had the sin of pride and I played it up to dear Janet." She looked at the audience. "Later, when my studio burned down, it was Janet who helped me. In spite of everything I did, she was a good friend to me."

It was then that the sobbing began. Loud, deep, soulful sobs. A broken heart was showing itself in tears. And it came from one person.

The four of them turned to look. Two rows behind them, Everett had his head on the back of the pew in front of him and was crying hard and loud. It was genuine misery.

"He sees his father-in-law's furniture catalog before him," Jack said.

Chet whispered something to Sara, then she whispered to Kate and Jack. "No one else is crying."

They looked around the church. There were at least two hundred people there. The walls were ringed, the pews packed. Everyone was staring and listening. But there were no tears being shed.

Chet was the first to turn back to the front. Another woman was at the podium. She told how kind Janet had been to her after an accidental bad hair dye job in her salon.

Last came the only man. "Drugstore," Kate whispered.

It was Eric Yates, the pharmacist. "I made a fool of myself but Janet forgave me" was all he said. His face was red with embarrassment.

After he sat down, two women and a man got up from the front pew and sang "Tears in Heaven."

After they finished, the pastor led the congregation in prayer. When the service was over, the people began to leave. What little they spoke was done in whispers.

Outside, all four of them went to Jack's truck and leaned against the long bed. They were watching the people file out.

"I don't know about you guys," Jack said, "but I feel like I've just come out of a two-hour therapy session."

"The question," Sara said, "is whether we were the patient or the doctor."

Chet gave a snort of laughter at that, then stepped forward and looked at them. "I don't mean to intrude, but I'd really like to talk to you three. Flynn says you know a lot about this case."

"We told him everything we know." Jack sounded hostile.

"There were a few things we left out," Sara said. "Were you the one who told Everett about the cross sewn into the baby bootie?"

"Yes." He nodded toward a big green SUV. "That's mine. I brought some boxes of info about the case with me. I thought I'd get a hotel somewhere, unload them, and you could look at what I have."

Since his eyes never left Sara's as he said this, they weren't sure if his "you" was singular or plural.

"We can put them in my dining room." Sara walked with him to his car.

"Think *we* should check into a hotel?" Jack muttered.

"I'd tell you to be nice but I feel the same way," Kate replied.

When they saw Sara get into Chet's SUV, Jack opened the driver-side door of his truck.

Kate got in and scooted across. "My suggestion is that we make a run to Chipotle and pick up a lunch for four. Otherwise, you and I will probably be relegated to being houseboys."

Jack and Kate looked at each other and smiled. It felt good to be *together* on this.

It took over an hour to go to the restaurant on University, then get back to Lachlan. As they neared the house, Jack said, "Maybe we should go see a movie. Give them time alone."

"Good idea," Kate said. "However… I am a tiny bit curious as to what files he has on the White Lily Kidnapping. Do you think Aunt Sara will tell him about hearing Tayla on the phone, then about…? You know?"

"Your father and Charlene?"

Kate nodded.

"Your dad was Sara's brother. I don't think she's going to tell his ugly secret to a stranger."

"I hope not."

"I wonder—since he's former police—if he knows anything more about Janet's personal life. Where she came from, her family, that sort of thing."

"How long ago was it that he talked to Everett?"

Jack nodded. "And what else did he tell that blabbermouth that Gage didn't tell us? He certainly sugarcoated their stories at the memorial."

"Oh yeah. When the teens told us, they were…"

"Insufferable," Jack said.

"Right, but today they had a studied remorse." She looked at him. "It was perceptive of Mr. Dakon to notice that no one was crying."

"Except Gage. But then, his life as a reporter might be over. No wonder he was bawling."

"Catalog writing! Pretty horrible fate. But if he could help break the White Lily case, it would all change."

Jack was turning into the driveway. "I wonder where Janet got that bootie?"

"And where is it now?" Kate asked.

Jack pulled into the garage and turned off the engine. Sara's MINI was in place and he'd seen that Dakon's SUV was in her favorite spot to the side of the house. "Maybe we could be of some help in figuring out the answers."

"Yeah, maybe." Kate could feel a bit of excitement running through her. "It really is a mystery of who, why, how. *Was* Janet's murder connected to an old kidnapping? What did Sylvia have to do with it?"

"If anything."

Kate looked at him. "The photo!"

Jack smiled. "Ah yes. The man who got away."

"The one who *wanted* his picture taken. Maybe Chet could find out who he is."

"So, it's gone from Mr. Dakon to Dakon and now it's Chet?"

"You should tell about Kyle's extreme jealousy since you understand it so well."

He ignored her jab. "Megan left out the jealousy part in her oh-so-clean little speech, didn't she?"

"Everyone left out all the juicy bits. In fact, no one told how truly nasty they'd been to Janet Beeson."

"But she forgave them all."

Kate opened the truck door. "I'm hungry. You hungry? Maybe Chet wants to eat. Maybe while we're being chummy over green chili, we can ask him a few questions."

"Are you saying we should suck up to this intruder who seems to be stealing our beloved Sara away from us?"

"Jack, you are reading my mind." She got out and closed the door behind her.

Smiling, he grabbed the big bag of food and followed her into the house.

Inside, it wasn't what they'd expected. Not that they'd discussed it, but Kate and Jack were surprised. The kitchen table was covered with unfurled rolls of plans of the houses Jack had remodeled.

Chet, his back to them, was bent over the plans. Sara was standing inches away from him. "Jack does a brilliant job in the design as well as the construction."

"I like this kitchen," Chet said. "I need a lot of work space as I make a mess when I cook."

"What do you like to cook?"

"Meat." Half turning, he looked her small body up and down. "I bet you're a vegan and do Pilates."

From behind them, both Jack and Kate gave snorts of laughter.

The older couple turned to look at them.

"She's a carnivore and she boxes." Jack's tone was like a put-down but it backfired.

Chet turned to Sara and looked her up and down again, only this time in a predatory way. "Yeah? Boxing?"

When Jack started to say something, Kate stepped in front of him. "You like the plans? You should see the Morris community. Jack is making it into beautiful affordable housing. They have a clubhouse and a pool."

Chet was looking at her fondly. "I saw it yesterday. Flynn drove me over there."

Jack's face had not lost its look of contempt. "Sheriff Flynn showed you *my* work? That's hard to believe."

Chet's handsome face turned serious. "He had nothing but good to say about you. He told me of your father and how you overcame everything to become a leading citizen of Lachlan."

"A…? Leading?" Jack just blinked, unable to speak.

Chet turned to Kate. "And I hear you're Kirkwood Realty's number one salesperson."

"Well…" she said modestly. "I've had help. I—"

Jack put his arm around Kate's shoulders in a possessive way. "Don't let her fool you. She eats, breathes, talks her job. A snowbird family drives through town and Kate is there telling them she can rent them an apartment cheaper than a hotel."

She slipped out of his grasp. "Not quite, but I do look for opportunities."

Sara spoke for the first time. "Is there food in that bag? Why don't we eat while we talk?"

Kate began rolling plans while Jack pulled plastic containers out of the bag. She nudged him to look at the kitchen. As though they'd known each other for years, Sara and Chet were preparing drinks. She pulled lemons from the fridge and he smashed them down over the juicer.

It didn't take long before they were seated at the round table. Outside was the pool and Sara's beautifully landscaped terrace. In other circumstances they would have eaten out there, but they all knew that there were serious things to discuss. Palm trees and warm breezes didn't lend themselves to talk of murder.

"When did—?" Chet began.

Jack cut him off. "Tell us about yourself." It was spoken like an order.

Chet's eyes sparkled as he looked at Jack in amusement. "Been a cop since I was a kid. Never known any other job. Married my high school sweetheart when we were twenty-two and—"

"Married?" Kate sounded alarmed.

Chet went on. "Not blessed with children until we were early forties. A daughter." He looked at Jack in an appraising way. "She's twenty-six now, a lawyer. Tall and blonde like her mother. I spend a lot of my life nagging her to give me grandkids."

Jack blinked a few times then looked down at his plate.

"Your wife?" Kate asked again.

Chet looked away.

Sara's voice was soft. "She died three years ago. When she was diagnosed with cancer, Chet resigned as the chief of police in Atlanta and moved to Sarasota. It's where his wife grew up."

Chet looked back at them. "Where she lived until the tenth grade anyway. Her dad's company transferred him to Atlanta. Carol Jean walked into my English class and that was it. Neither of us ever looked back."

Like now, Kate thought. *With my aunt.* She glanced at Jack and knew he had the same idea. She looked down at her plate, piled high with guacamole. *What about the romance that Sara's one true love was Jack's grandfather?* she thought. Something had separated them so they didn't spend their lives together, but Kate had been told they spent a lifetime yearning for each other. Jack had even hinted that maybe his grandfather and Sara had met at times during their lives. Maybe—

Everyone was looking at her. "Did I miss something?"

"You just looked a million miles away," Sara said.

"Chet was telling us that his daughter works in Miami and he's been thinking about moving closer to her."

"Think you can find him a house?" Jack asked.

Before Kate could speak, Chet said, "How about Janet Beeson's house? I'd like to buy it and take it apart. I'd put it under a microscope."

"Got a million and a quarter?" Kate asked.

"That's not what Beeson paid for it."

"You have done your homework," Sara said.

Jack pushed his empty plate away. "What else do you know about her?"

"She had a tough life."

"Oh?" Sara encouraged. "Let's go to the living room. Jack? Kate?"

They knew what she meant. They could clean up from lunch.

"Houseboys," Jack whispered when he and Kate were alone.

"I think he's staked you out to be his son-in-law. How tall do you think his daughter is? How blonde? Natural color or a box? And a *lawyer*. You know what they say about 25,000 lawyers at the bottom of the sea. A good start." She put the trash in the bin and firmly rolled the door shut. "Bring the pitcher." Turning, she left the room.

It took Jack a few moments to lower his eyebrows from where they'd risen up under his hair. It couldn't be possible but it almost sounded like Kate was, well… jealous.

Couldn't be, he told himself, then dumped a bag of bakery cookies onto a plate, grabbed the pitcher, and carried both into the living room. He took a seat beside Kate, facing Sara and Chet on the other sofa.

"Not much to tell," Chet said. "Janet Parker lived a very ordinary life. Only child of comfortable, not rich, parents. It was while she was at the University of Wisconsin that things changed. Her father was a mechanic and he invented something…" Chet waved his hand. "He created a gadget that made air conditioners work better. He sold the patent for millions. Mr. Parker immediately retired and he and his wife began to travel. Enjoying the good life."

Chet took a drink, picked up a cookie, took a bite, and said, "Until right after Janet graduated, that is. Her parents went skiing in Colorado and they were never seen again. Their bodies were never found."

"I guess Janet inherited everything," Sara said.

"She did. Millions. But the odd thing is that she kept on working. Nothing serious, just—"

"By serious, do you mean like being a lawyer?" Jack smiled at Chet.

"Exactly!" For a moment he looked back and forth from Kate to Jack, as though trying to analyze them. "She never stayed anywhere for long. In 2004, she married her widowed boss, Carl Olsen."

When the three listeners drew in their breaths, Chet stopped. "What bell did I just ring?"

"We've heard the name Carl recently," Jack said. "They lived in Arizona, right?"

Chet smiled. "Put that together, did you?" He sounded proud.

Sara went into the family room and returned with her big iPad, the foot-wide one, and brought up the photo Jack had taken of the man who spied on them outside the Wyatt house. "Is this her husband?"

"Could be. I'm not sure. The Carl Olsen I saw is about three hundred pounds. I'd have to run it through facial recognition software. You have other photos?"

"A few," Sara said modestly.

Chet looked at each person in speculation, then back to Sara. "I read the report you gave Flynn. Very well written. Most police reports are barely readable, but that one should be published."

"That's what Everett hopes," Sara retorted.

Her smart-aleck remark made them smile, but Chet's eyes were calculating. They were seeing the man who'd worked his way up from the bottom to the top of the police force. "Anyway, Janet left Arizona and changed her name to Beeson."

"That's why it was so hard to find out about her past," Jack said.

Chet nodded. "So what happened to make you think this man was Janet's husband?"

"Bits and pieces," Sara said.

The three of them closed their lips tightly. They weren't going to say that Tayla—one of their own— had said the name.

"All right." Chet stood up. "Maybe I could show you a *small*..." He emphasized the word. "A *small bit* of what I've found out about the White Lily Kidnapping over the years."

"Did Janet and Carl divorce?" Kate asked.

Chet gave a smile, letting her know that he had no intention of answering that question. "I'll get a box or two. Just a few of them." He quickly went out the front door, closing it behind him.

"I think we hurt his feelings," Kate said.

Sara let out a laugh. "Ha! He's playing us—and giving us time to decide what to tell."

"You sound like you know him well," Jack said.

"Kindred souls. Now! What's our vote? Tell or not tell?"

But Jack wasn't through with his bashing. "Are you sure *we* are the ones to ask? You and he seem to—"

"Tell!" Kate said loudly. "I vote we tell him everything. My hunch is that he won't go to the sheriff and blab."

"I agree," Sara said, then she and Kate looked at Jack.

Reluctantly, he nodded. "He seems to be set on show-me-yours-I'll-show-you-mine. If we want to find out anything, I think we have to tell what we know."

"I agree," Sara said. "However, he might be persuaded to show you photos of his tall blonde daughter." She went to the front door.

"What is it with you and blondes?" Kate asked as they followed. "Cheryl, then that newspaperwoman, and now the lawman's daughter."

"I've never even met her! She's probably built like him and plays rugby."

"He said she was like his wife, not him. She's probably a pro volleyball player and built."

"In that case, yeah, I'd like to meet her."

In front of them, Sara was grinning broadly.

TWELVE

Jack and Kate went outside to help bring the boxes in. When Chet lifted the back door of the van, they gasped. It was jammed with file boxes, all labeled with a date and subject matter.

It took a while to get them out, carry them inside, and pile them up in Sara's formal dining room. They filled the one wall that wasn't all glass.

Once they were in place, Chet stood there, waiting. To open or not? seemed to be his question.

"We decided to tell you everything we know," Sara said. "But you first."

He nodded, pleased that a deal had been struck.

Chet looked at Kate. "You asked about a divorce. Yes, they did. He filed, and Janet took nothing from him. Appears to have been as friendly as those things can be. But…" He paused. "After the divorce, Carl Olsen moved a lot. I had a hard time tracking him. My guess is he's a bit of a squirrely character. She did well to get away from him."

Kate nodded. It fit with everything they'd heard about Janet Beeson.

Chet pulled three boxes off the top of the stack, put them on the table, and opened them. Inside were thick file pockets, some of them tied together with string. Some were old and worn, a few were new and plastic. He was showing them twenty-plus years of collected data. The first box contained printouts of the original interviews with each of the customers and the sales staff of the store. The hundreds of pages had notes in different colors of ink.

"I use colored pens too," Sara said and she and Chet looked at each other as though they'd discovered yet another cosmic coincidence.

Jack and Kate rolled their eyes.

Chet began talking about the contents. There were many boxes of data from the first year after the case. Two boxes held ledgers with records of every call that had come in, crank and otherwise. It seemed that many people had seen Mrs. Crawford go into the store. They had noticed the pretty baby in her pink-and-white outfit.

When the alarm went off and half a dozen police cars arrived, people outside the store had stopped to see what was going on. Within minutes, there was a crowd. Many of those people had also been interviewed.

Chet picked up a handful of papers. "Everyone said the same thing. They saw the baby in the stroller go in but no one came out carrying a baby. Right after the kidnapping, the whole city seemed to shut down.

Everyone was involved. I arrested two drunks who got into a knife fight. One said the baby was dead, the other said she was alive. They were willing to kill each other over it."

"But little Jeanne was found," Kate said.

"In the fire station. I talked to the men who found her. At first I suspected one of them, but…" Chet's head came up. "I'm not proud of the way I was back then. I was obsessed. I wanted to know who had done such a heinous thing. I *needed* to know. That's why later, I put ads in the papers. I went on the radio asking people to come forward and tell what they'd seen or heard. Anything."

"You did this *after* the baby was returned?" Jack's meaning was clear: Why?

Chet glared at him. "Yeah." His belligerent tone said that he'd been asked that question before and he didn't want to hear it now.

Leaning back in his chair, Jack gave a smile. "Don't blame you a bit."

Sara explained. "We were the same when it came to finding out about the Morrises. We *had* to know." She put her hand on his wrist. "Were you given a lot of grief because you persisted?"

Chet put his hand over hers. "Endless. But the captain understood. He said there were cases in his past that he wished he'd pursued. And he was afraid it would happen again. Whoever did it, didn't get the first kid so maybe he/she would try again. We sent out alerts to hospitals to watch out. And we kept up with the questions about who and why."

He pulled out a box about four down from the top.

"We got a lot of theories. One guy said a baby adoption ring had tried to steal the child but gave up under all the publicity. Others said the baby was going to be used for child porn. One woman who used to work at the store told us that a baby could have been stuffed in a heat register and taken out later. Someone else said the sliding doors under the jewelry case could hide an infant."

"I guess you checked it all out," Sara said.

"Everything. And we were glad because we stopped some creeps who were selling babies. Found two porno sources. We got a heating company to send a man through the entire system of the store. We hoped we'd find a torn piece of clothing, or something. But there were just dead rodents, bugs, and a little bag of diamond rings that we think had been there since the 1950s. We never found out how they got there."

Chet picked up another box, set it on the table, and opened the lid. He began pulling out plastic bags. Inside were pink sweaters in various forms of decay. One had a plastic flower glued onto it. They ranged in size from something for a doll to one that would fit a two-year-old. None of them came close to the description Everett had given.

"Should you have these?" Kate asked. "Aren't they evidence?"

"The case was closed years ago. The new guy who replaced the old captain said there never really was a case. He thought maybe it was all mistaken identity. Some woman got her kid mixed up with another one and panicked when the sirens went off."

"Because women do silly things, right?" Sara said.

Chet smiled. "Exactly. He didn't last long at the job. But by that time, I'd started my own evidence file." He lifted a bag. "For about five years after the kidnapping, people turned in anything that looked like what baby Jeanne was wearing when she was taken. What we didn't tell the public was that when she was returned, she was wearing the same clothes that she'd had on when she'd been taken. Whatever they found couldn't be her clothes."

Sara nodded in agreement. "My guess is that you wanted people to doubt that it was the same baby. Keep the case going."

"Quick, aren't you?"

"She writes this kind of thing," Kate said.

"And I bet you're really good at it." His voice was so smooth, so flattering, so suggestive, that Sara smiled warmly back at him.

"Did it?" Jack asked loudly. "Is that what happened?"

Chet straightened up. "Yeah. Exactly. We got a lot of letters telling us we had the wrong baby. That the real one was… Well, fill in the blanks. Half a dozen so-called psychics called and told us we had the wrong baby. People began ratting on their neighbors. Anyone who had recently brought home a baby was under suspicion."

"It couldn't be true, could it?" Kate asked. "I mean it really was little Jeanne, wasn't it?"

"Yes. There was a birthmark and we compared footprints. It was her. But still, we followed up on every clue we were given."

"Who is the 'we'?" Jack asked. "The police force and you or just you?"

Chet's mouth quirked at the corner. "Just me. Weekends, evenings. I checked out everything. Found a couple of cases that were later prosecuted, but nothing about the Crawford baby."

Sara spoke up. "I'm curious about the cross that Everett found in the bootie. When was that made public?"

"It wasn't. Not ever. I was the only one who knew about it and the only person I told was my wife." He took a breath. "I stayed in touch with the Crawford family. She had another baby, a boy, and she told me to leave it alone, that she had her daughter back and that was all she wanted. But the grandmother who had given the sweater set agreed with me. She wanted the culprit caught. Just days before she died, she asked me to visit her and she told me about sewing a cross inside the toe of each bootie. She said she'd kept it to herself because she wanted something she could use to verify the baby's identity. 'Someone has that little slipper,' she said. 'Someone kept it. You find it and you'll find the bastard that tried to take my grandchild.' She held my hand and asked me to swear to never give up. I promised that I wouldn't."

He paused for a moment. "I kept my vow. Even though I got promotions and was made chief, I kept looking. It got to the point where no one in the office remembered the case, but that didn't stop me from searching."

Sara took a deep drink of her lemonade. "I don't know about anyone else, but I'm ready for a story. I want to know what *really* happened to make you dedicate your life to this case."

"The injustice of it. A baby stolen, the grief of the parents, the…" He trailed off because Sara obviously wasn't buying it.

"People are self-centered beings," she said. "We do things that interest us, that we have a connection to. What happened that made this case touch you? Personally *you*?"

Chet took his time in answering. He sat down on one of Sara's comfortable dining chairs, picked up a bag containing a pink cardigan, and turned it around in his hands. "Her." Chet's voice was a whisper. "I think I saw her. The woman who kidnapped the baby." He let out his breath. "Outside of my wife, you're the first people I've told that."

Sara shook her head. "How you managed to keep that secret is beyond me."

"You could identify her but you said nothing?" Jack sounded on the verge of anger.

"No," Chet said. "I couldn't identify her. Not well enough to testify in court."

"But you said—"

Sara looked at Jack. "Let's let him tell his story, shall we?" She said they should move to the more comfortable couches in the living room.

When they were settled, Chet still hesitated. But then, he was about to tell a story he'd revealed to only one person, yet it was something that had driven his life.

"I think you know the basics. It started at a frantic, going-out-of-business sale. The big store was packed with customers, almost all women, who were snatching and grabbing and… It was a state of war. In the midst of the chaos, a woman started screaming that her baby had been taken. A clerk was inches from an emergency lock-down switch. He pressed it and all the doors locked. There wasn't time for anyone to push through that crowd to get to an exit door. We got there just minutes later and began questioning everyone, but no one had seen anything. Certainly no one frantically clutching a baby."

The way he was talking sounded as though he'd said it many times before. It was a memorized speech.

Chet stopped and for a moment, he looked out the window, then turned back. "I was young, inexperienced. I'd never been on a case like that before. I was used to giving out tickets and breaking up bar fights." He let out his breath.

"I was told to check the women's lavatory. It was not something that I wanted to do, but there were no female cops so I was given the job. I can't describe my embarrassment when I saw a young woman sitting on top of the sink counter, breastfeeding her baby. I kept my eyes down."

Chet looked at them. "*Eyes down* is an important fact. Anyway, I saw that the baby was wearing denim overalls, and a blue T-shirt. It was obviously a boy and we were looking for a baby girl."

His face had a pleading look. "You have to understand that at that time my wife and I were trying to have a baby. It's what she wanted more than to live. She talked about it, dreamed of it. Babies were at the center of our lives."

For a moment, Chet closed his eyes. "I only glanced at her face, then down at the baby. I can still see it. It was a beautiful scene, like something out of a Renaissance painting. The mother and child were so perfectly content. I've never seen such a look of…fulfillment, I guess. It was as though this young woman had found her own soul. I thought, *That's how mothers should look at their babies*. I was thinking that I was seeing what having a baby meant to my wife. They were both so happy, so at peace." He stopped to calm himself.

"Finally, the woman said, 'Seen all you want to?' That brought me back to reality and I felt like a pervert."

Chet shook his head in wonder. "I left. I turned around, went out the door, and left them there. To me, it was obvious that was *her* child and he was a boy. It wasn't the baby we were looking for."

He let out a sigh. "We were on lockdown for hours and every inch of the store was searched but we didn't find the baby." Chet looked out the window, his jaw muscles working as he thought about what he'd just told.

"Did you see the woman from the restroom again?" Jack asked.

Chet turned back to them. "No. I was stuck in a room interviewing a lot of tired, angry people. One of our questions was if anyone had seen someone carrying a bunch of white lilies, but they hadn't. We described the missing baby's clothing. The truth is that I was so busy that I didn't think about the woman I'd seen. Besides, if I had, I would have assumed that someone else had interviewed her." He raised his hands in helplessness. "But then, it never entered my mind that it wasn't her own baby."

"When did you begin to think she was the kidnapper?" Sara asked.

"Not until about three days later, after I'd had some sleep. It hit me like in a fog. Gradually, I realized that I'd probably seen the kidnapper."

Sara shook her head. "If she was nursing the baby, then she must have recently given birth. And maybe she'd lost her own baby."

Chet nodded. "That was my guess. I didn't tell what I'd seen—I was too afraid of losing my job to reveal that—but I asked everyone in the squad if they'd seen her. Red hair—"

"Red?" Kate asked. "Like mine?"

"Lighter," Chet said. "You're more mahogany. She was more…"

"Strawberry blonde?" Sara asked.

"Yeah. A sort of blonde with red in it."

"What about her face?" Jack asked. "Pretty girl?"

"As I said, I just glanced at it. Very quickly. I didn't see her very well," Chet said softly.

Kate said, "If she'd just lost a baby and that had driven her to kidnapping, I'd say that at that moment she wasn't in her right mind."

Sara said, "Okay, so you realized you may have seen the kidnapper. What did you do next?"

"I got a sketch artist to draw a picture for me. I lied, said it was for another case." He got up, went into the dining room, and opened a box. When he returned, he held out a drawing. It did indeed look like a Renaissance painting. The head was too long, too perfect. No one looked like that in real life.

"It's a bit fanciful, I know, but that's how I remember her," Chet said.

"You're right." Sara was looking at the drawing. "No one looks like this. You didn't see anything identifiable?"

Chet took his time answering. "She had a heart-shaped birthmark very low on her left breast."

"You *can* identify her!" Kate said.

"So who do we arrest? Women with faces like an angel and a heart-shaped birthmark in a place that isn't exposed in public? That lineup would draw most of the squad in to look."

They took a while to imagine that. No, it wouldn't have worked.

Kate changed the subject. "Okay, so let's look at the facts. Janet Beeson had a bootie that was part of an old kidnapping."

"A very brief, long-ago kidnapping," Sara said.

"Right," Chet said. "The statutes on it ran out years ago."

"That means there's no danger to the person who did it?" Kate asked.

"Maybe not jail time but morally…" Sara said.

"Yeah," Chet said. "Morals and misery. If Gage reveals who did it, her life is over. She'd have to move to Timbuktu to keep the press off her door."

Sara smiled at Chet. "I've been there."

"Have you? I'd love to see the world. I've been to London and that's all."

"I've been—"

"Excuse me!" Jack said loudly. "We're trying to solve a murder. You two can visit the Outer Hebrides later."

"I've been there too," Sara said. "It's—" She cut off at Jack's look. "So where did someone as bland as Janet Beeson get a baby's slipper that was part of a kidnapping?" She glanced at Kate's disapproving expression. "Really! The woman was a bully's delight. Picked on by everyone. Humiliated when she was noticed, but mostly ignored."

"Poor woman," Kate said.

"She sounds like the perfect serial killer profile," Chet said.

"Only *she* was killed, not the other way around," Kate retorted.

"Darn!" Chet said. "And here I thought I'd solved the case."

Even Kate smiled at his joke.

Jack spoke up. "My guess is that she found out something she shouldn't have and stupidly opened her mouth. Probably told the people involved that they should 'do the right thing.'"

"How'd she find out what she shouldn't have?" Chet asked. "I didn't have time to do a search of her recent life. Did she have a job in Lachlan?"

"Church secretary," Sara said.

"Ah," Chet said. "That could be embezzlement, maybe with money laundering. Give it to the church, write it off your taxes, money is given back to you by someone in the church. Janet found out about it. Murdered to make her keep her mouth shut."

"She reorganized a doctor's files," Kate said.

Jack put his hand up to keep Chet from speaking.

"Someone spread an STD. Could ruin a marriage or two."

Kate said, "What if she found something hidden inside Sylvia's house? People are always leaving things behind. Top of closets, fallen behind something. In Chicago, we had a family who moved out and forgot they had an attic. It was full." She looked at Chet. "We've toyed with the idea that Sylvia didn't commit suicide but was murdered and Janet found out about it."

"Maybe Sylvia had the bootie," Sara said. "Sylvia and Janet were besties, so maybe Sylvia told her the story behind the kidnapping."

"Mom said she saw Sylvia crying," Jack said.

"I need to know more about this woman Sylvia," Chet said.

"Very elegant," Sara said. "Her husband died and someone took the body away. They—"

"He died very unexpectedly," Jack said. "I wonder if there was an autopsy? We should ask—"

"Sylvia ate oleander," Kate said. "Janet cried for a—"

"The neighbor's sons painted *Witch* on the garage door," Sara said.

"I heard that, but at the memorial, that woman, Megan, said Janet forgave them," Chet said.

"We've heard contradictions on that," Jack said. "Megan told us that Janet never forgave any of them."

Sara's voice rose. "Everett wrote what was said today. Never trust a writer! Professional liars, all. He is making it up as he goes along. He just needs a punch line."

"You mean a killer," Jack said.

"And a kidnapper," Kate said.

"They—" Sara began.

"Hey!" Chet said. "Don't mean to interrupt, but could someone tell me the story in a coherent way?"

They turned to Sara.

"Don't look at me. I tell with pen and paper. I can't even type a story. As for talking, I'm the pits."

They turned to Kate. "I sell things. People don't listen after three sentences."

They looked at Jack. "Me? Are you crazy?"

"You could sing it to us," Kate said and that made them smile.

"All right," Chet said. "I'll ask questions and you answer them. One at a time. Any paper and pen around here?"

"I think I can find something." Sara got up and went into her writing room. She returned with a black-and-red Prada bag filled with a notebook, loose paper, pens in eight colors, and a pretty lap desk of pale bamboo.

Chet gave her a look of admiration, put the board across his legs, and took out the pens and the spiral notebook. "Let's start with stats. Name, birth, where, when, who."

Sara gave Jack and Kate a look to say, *He's good, isn't he?* then they began telling everything they knew about Sylvia Alden.

They were as concise and succinct as they could be, but they had a lot of info to relay.

After going over the facts, Sara told what she'd read in Sylvia's books, how they were almost autobiographical. "She kept her pen name very secret. Obviously, there were people she didn't want to know that she was writing."

"What did she write at the time of the kidnapping?" Chet asked.

"Didn't mention it. Her heroine was busy with her child and husband."

"Have a date on that kid?"

Jack told him that Sylvia's daughter was eleven at the time of the kidnapping.

"The books stopped about the time Janet arrived in Lachlan," Sara said.

"No mention of finding a friend?"

"None," Sara said. "Sylvia was trying to adjust to widowhood and asking herself what to do with her life since she'd lost her best friend. Her agent told me that book sold the best of any of them. Not spectacular, but it did well. The reviews were excellent."

"But you said—" Kate began but stopped.

Chet turned to her. "Said what?"

Kate looked at her aunt. It was up to her to tell or not.

When Sara was silent, Jack spoke. "What no one wants to say is that someone posted bad comments on review sites. *Really* bad."

Chet looked at Sara and waited in silence.

"Yes, there were some truly hideous reviews. Meant to hurt." She said this with her jaw clenched, her hands in fists.

"I take it that you've had that done to you." When Sara nodded, Chet squeezed her hand. "I think cyberbullying should be a whole new branch of the police force."

Kate said, "As long as people support it, it will never stop."

"So who wrote these bad reviews?" Chet asked.

"Different people," Jack answered. "They really were vile. Said the author should give up writing, should never have started. They were *personal* attacks."

"Could they have come from Mrs. Alden's brother?"

"Maybe." Sara was regaining her composure. "When I read them, my heart went out to Sylvia. I wondered…" She looked at Chet.

"If they caused her suicide? It happens. I've seen too much of it. The person feels like they'll never recover. The suicide takes seconds but lasts forever." He looked at his paper. "Anything else you know about Mrs. Alden that may have made her want to end it all? She lost her husband and her career was torn apart on the internet. Maybe she—"

When his phone rang, he looked at the ID. "This is probably info." He went outside to answer the call and they watched him through the glass. From his expression, the news wasn't good.

Chet came back inside, sat down by Sara, and pulled up an email. "It's a time line." He looked at them as though he dreaded telling what he'd just heard. "Four months after Sylvia Alden died, her daughter, Lisa, went to jail for eighteen months. Seems that in college she transported drugs. A dealer ratted on her and some other college kids in exchange for a plea deal. He got six months. The kids got one to three years."

The four of them were quiet. More reasons for Sylvia to commit suicide were being found.

"That day in the restaurant, I bet she was crying over her daughter," Jack said.

"Possibly," Chet said. "Husband gone, vicious reviews of her books, daughter going to jail. It's a lot. She may have felt so helpless that she couldn't bear it, so she poisoned her own food, and got out of the whole mess."

"Loneliness combined with age..." Sara didn't finish.

Jack sighed. "Does this take us back to the beginning? No suspects, no motive?"

"I don't think we can fully eliminate Mrs. Alden," Chet said, "but it doesn't look like she had anything to do with the kidnapping. I'll do more research and try to find out where she was that day. Maybe she was there at the store and saw something. Maybe—" He broke off as he knew he was just trying to make them feel better.

"I'm not so sure about any of this," Sara said. "Kate, if you get sent to jail, I'll be waiting for you when you get out. I'm certainly not going to remove myself from life because I'm sad."

"What about me?" Jack asked.

"I'd petition for you to spend your time in solitary. Half your dad's friends were put in prison because they listened to him. Your life would be in danger."

Jack blinked a few times, then laughed. "Nice to think I'm wanted by so many."

It was getting dark outside and they'd been talking for hours.

Chet closed the notebook. "Mind if I keep this? I'd like to go over some of these facts."

"Please do," Sara said.

Chet stood up and stretched. "So where's a good motel nearby? Not too fancy but clean. And cheap."

"You can stay here," Sara said. "In Jack's room."

Jack gasped. "I don't think—"

Sara cut him off. "You'll have to bunk in with Kate. On her sofa."

Kate stood. "He cannot possibly stay with me!"

As though Kate hadn't spoken, Sara stuck her arm inside Chet's. "Let's go get your bags." They went out the front door together.

Jack turned to Kate, grinning, then frowned when he saw that she was truly upset. "I promise I'll behave. I won't sneak into your bedroom, if that's what you're worried about. I'll—"

She waved her hand. "Do stop fantasizing. I'm not in the least worried about you. Aunt Sara likes him. Really, really *likes* him."

"In the least?" Jack quoted. "You're not worried—?" When Kate walked down the hall to his bedroom, he followed her.

"Get your shaving things and I'll get your clothes." She opened his closet door and stepped inside. "Why don't you ever wear this shirt?"

"It's pink. Ivy bought it for me."

"Your sister does have taste." She tossed it onto the bed.

Jack had grabbed some shaving gear and put it in a leather bag. When he saw Kate frantically flinging his clothes onto the bed, he tossed the case down and went to her. He took her by the shoulders, set her down in a chair, then knelt in front of her. "Tell me what's bothering you."

She took a moment before she spoke. "It just hit me that someday I may have to move into my own place. Alone."

Jack put his hand under her chin. "You won't be alone. You won't be abandoned."

"It's just that I grew up so isolated. It was just Mother and me. Then I went to college and it was great being with other people. But Mother needed me so I went back home and we were alone again. When Mom told me that I had an aunt I was jubilant. And I came here and now…"

"And now you have a family."

She looked at him. "Yes."

He took her hands in his. "You won't lose it. If I have to I'll build you an apartment building and fill it with my relatives. You haven't met half of them. You'll have so much family that you'll crave peace. You'll call me and say, 'Jackson! You better get me out of here or I'll send my mother to move in with *you*.' But by then I'll be living upstairs in the penthouse so that means your mom will be just above you. She…"

Kate was laughing. "My mother would straighten you out in two days."

"One call with her just about did it. She is a bit of a terror, isn't she? I was scared to death. Started sweating."

She put her hands on his shoulders and kissed his cheek. "Thank you."

"Anytime." Jack stood up.

They heard a door close, then laughter. Jack looked at what Kate had thrown onto the bed. "We better move these things." He picked up a white shirt. "I am *not* going to wear this."

"It's nice."

"It has *lace* on it."

"It's not lace, it's white on white embroidery. Here!" She grabbed the hanger tops and handed them to him, then picked up the shaving gear. "Let's go!" She started to go through the house, meaning that they'd see Chet and Sara, but Jack said no.

He led her through the garage to the little courtyard at the side. The fountain of the girl dancing in the rain was encased in golden light.

They went through the door to Kate's bedroom, past her first closet, past the bath, to the second walk-in, which was empty.

"A whole closet to myself?" Jack said. "This is great!"

"It's temporary, so don't get used to it."

They hung up his clothes, put his toiletries in the bath, then looked at each other. Now what did they do?

"I don't know about you," Jack said, "but I am sick of murder and suicide and hearing that college girls get sent to prison. How about if you and I go to the Brigade and have beer and beef?"

Kate hesitated. "I…"

"They have a live band. Want to sing with me?"

She smiled but said nothing. She was still deciding.

"They have chocolate things. From the bakery."

"I'll be ready in three minutes."

Jack didn't complain when he had to wait thirty minutes for Kate to get ready. She had a closet full of clothes from the designer Elaine Cross and she had put on a dark green, fitted dress.

She was standing in front of the tall shoe rack, trying to make up her mind, when Jack stepped behind her. He reached over her head and pulled down her tallest high heels. "These."

"What is it with you and heels?"

"Give me an hour and I'll tell you. Come on or that loquacious ex-cop will be in here asking more questions."

"Loquacious, huh?"

"I've been around Sara too long. It's like living with a dictionary. Are you ready yet?"

"I just need to—" She smiled. "Yeah, I'm ready."

They went out the back to Jack's truck. "Think they'll miss us?" she asked.

"Not at all. Not one little bit."

THIRTEEN

Kate had heard of the Brigade, which was next door to the fire station, but she hadn't been to it. That was probably caused by a lifetime of her mother's three older brothers telling her that if she stepped inside a "beer joint" the floor would open up and drag her straight down into hell. She knew it was nonsense but still… one developed doubts.

Jack opened the door for her and the place made her smile. It was like looking at a fire station of about 1904. On the right was a long antique oak bar with a fireman's boot at the end. A calligraphy sign said it was for donations for domestic abuse victims.

A mirrored wall behind the bar held shelves full of sparkling clean bottles. At the end of the long room was a raised platform with musical instruments, a dance floor in front. To the left were booths and tables.

Jack bent and said in her ear, "Like it? My sister designed it." There was such pride in his voice that she smiled broadly at him. Seconds later, they were greeted with what seemed to be dozens of people calling hello to Jack.

"Where've you been? Haven't seen you for weeks." From the bartender.

"Why didn't you call me?" From a pretty blonde woman.

"Jack! When are we goin' out again?" Another pretty young woman.

"Are you planning to run a booth at the fair this year?" A fireman.

The people talked on top of each other as Jack answered and led her to the one booth that was vacant.

"Been here before?" Kate asked as she slid across the seat.

"A time or two. I—" He stopped because a tall, very good-looking, blond man was standing at the end of the table. "What do you want, Chris?" Jack's tone was telling the man to go away, but he didn't move.

Chris was looking at Kate. "I know you. Or at least I've seen you before."

"She sells real estate for Tayla. Half the town has seen her."

"No," Chris said. "It was somewhere else."

"I know," Kate said. "When I first came to Lachlan, you and another man were outside the fire station. Do you really have a dalmatian?"

"It's tradition. You mind?" He motioned to sit beside her.

"No, of course not." She moved to the side and he sat down beside her. She ignored Jack's glower.

"So you really sell real estate?"

"I do. Need something? A house? An apartment?"

"Actually, I've been thinking of getting my own place. I have two male roommates now."

"Ah." Kate realized he was telling her that he wasn't married and had no live-in girlfriend.

"Would you like to go out with—"

"No!" Jack said. "She's busy. Very, very busy. I think Bill's calling you."

Chris smiled. Nice teeth. "No, he's not." He looked back at Kate. "How about I stop by your office on Monday at ten a.m.?"

"That would be perfect. What are you looking for?"

"Small, cozy. Somewhere I can grow tomatoes."

"I know just the place."

He stood up. "I look forward to seeing you then. Jack." He left.

"Did you just make a date?" Jack sounded incredulous.

"A business appointment." She was smiling.

The waitress came and they ordered beers and nachos. "And a couple of Reubens," Jack said without consulting her, and the waitress left.

"What if I want a salad?"

"Do you?"

"Heavens no! After this week I may take up drinking whiskey."

"With random firemen?"

She gave him a look to behave himself. At the end of the room, some musicians were beginning to set up. "Do you sing with them?"

"Sometimes."

"Really?"

He laughed at the way she sounded like a preteen groupie.

When the nachos arrived, he ate a couple of the hot cheese–dipped corn crisps, and leaned forward. "How are you doing about…you know. The case."

"Which part? Murder? Suicide? Lies spoken in church?" She lowered her voice. "Or my father?"

"That last one."

"Every time his name is mentioned, I find out something new. And none of it has been *good*."

"At least people *liked* your dad." He ate a clump of chips and drank of his beer.

"I still can't see our fathers as friends. Would brains and brawn fit together? But then, that's like you and me and we get along well enough."

Jack grinned. "You think I'm brawny?"

"I think I'm the brains so you get whatever is leftover."

Jack gave a snort of laughter.

"The more I hear—all told in tiny pieces, by the way—I think our fathers may have been more alike than we think. The same but opposite."

"You mean that my father was loud so yours was…"

"Quiet. Mine escaped, but yours…"

"Got caught. Often," Jack said.

"My father was a cat burglar while yours was…"

"A six-gun outlaw."

Kate sighed. "Mine may have stolen diamonds." She looked at him to reply.

"No one knows where Dad got the money for that big Harley. It just appeared one day."

"Think our fathers rode away together on a stolen

motorcycle while clutching a bag of misappropriated jewelry?" When Jack didn't laugh as she'd expected him to, she looked at him. He wasn't smiling.

"My father had a big mouth. He loved to brag, thought it made him seem tough. But from what I hear of your father, he kept things to himself. If he did anything illegal, he did it alone and didn't tell anyone."

"You're saying that Roy was what he seemed but my father, Randal, hid inside a facade of charm."

"Pretty much."

"What you're really saying is that we don't know what happened with... I guess with anyone."

"We sure know a lot of facts, but we don't seem to have put them together at all. Sylvia, Janet."

"Tayla, Gil."

"And maybe Carl Olsen. Fat now skinny. Skulks around but no one knows why. I think—" He broke off when the band began to play. "I think we should forget it and dance." He held out his hand and she took it.

It was a slow dance and Jack pulled Kate close. He was half a foot taller than she was, but with her heels, they fit together perfectly.

"What shampoo do you use?" he whispered.

"Behave or I'll dance with Chris."

"You should know that half the women in town have dumped him."

She pulled back to look at him. "Did you know that when you lie your left eye twitches?"

"Until last year, Chris lived with his mother."

"Like you live with your honorary grandmother and me, your sort of sister?"

"You are destroying my manhood."

"I think there's enough of it that you can afford to lose a bit."

He started to speak, but laughed instead. "Is it possible that there was a compliment in that?"

"I think you should stop the loquaciousness, feed me, then dance my legs off. I *need* movement. I *need* to clear my overworked brain."

Jack twirled her out to arm's length. "Did I ever tell you that you are what I've always dreamed of in a woman?"

"But I'm not blonde."

When the music stopped, Jack was laughing.

"Hey, Jack!" the lead guitarist called. "Sing with us."

"Gotta feed my girl, then maybe."

To one side four firemen were sitting at a table. They had on tight T-shirts and jeans and they were so fit, so muscular, they looked like they were ready for their calendar photo shoot.

When Kate smiled warmly at them, they lifted their beers in salute to her. "If you want to sing, I'll be fine. Really and truly *fine*."

Jack put his hand firmly on the small of her back and half pushed her to their booth.

On their way there, they passed two old men sitting at the bar. One grabbed Jack's arm.

"She's Randal's daughter and you're Roy's son."

The second man smirked. "Lock up your women and your jewels."

Kate saw that the remarks made Jack angry. She stepped between him and the men—who looked a bit drunk. She put on the most flirtatious manner she could conjure. "Roy's son has learned to combine them both and I can assure you, gentlemen, that he never locks *me* up." She winked at them. "Not too often anyway."

"Really?" Jack asked as soon as they were back to the booth. "My reputation isn't bad enough without you adding to it?"

"From the way everyone in this place greeted you, they certainly seem to like you. Did you ever think those men were teasing you just to see the infamous Wyatt temper flare up?"

Jack opened and closed his mouth before turning red and looking down at his beer. "No, actually, I didn't."

"Well you should." The band was playing "Summer Nights" from *Grease*. "Can you sing that song?"

"Sure."

"You know all the words?"

"Are you trying to get rid of me?"

"Yes. You know that I can't stand to be around you."

Jack started to frown but then smiled. Since Kate had arrived months ago, they'd hardly been apart. "I guess you want me to show you."

"I do rather like your voice. In singing, that is."

With a chuckle, he got up, went to the band, and picked up the microphone. He came in midverse in the song and immediately, the dance floor filled. From the reactions of the patrons, Jack singing with the band was a regular occurrence—and a welcome one.

Minutes later, Chris came to the booth, held out his hand to Kate, and she took it. When she was on the dance floor with him, she saw Jack, singing away, glower. She mouthed "Wyatt" and he shook his head at her. As she started to dance, Jack put more energy into his voice, more emotion into the song. And when he started a sexy, gyrating dance, the women broke away from their partners, stopped moving, and gave their attention to Jack.

But Kate didn't want to stop dancing. Chris raised his eyebrows in question and she shook her head. She didn't want to stop. The other dancers stepped back and formed a circle around the edge of the dance floor. When all of them looked toward the table of firemen and started clapping, she knew something was up.

One of the men, about Jack's age, downed half his beer, then stood up, and did a stretch. His T-shirt strained against muscles. He had on suspenders and they looked good.

Kate had no idea what was going on, but Chris did. He let go of Kate and stepped back. It looked like he was turning her over to the other man.

"Name's Garth," the man said over the music, then took Kate in his arms.

To say that Garth was a good dancer was an understatement. Think Patrick Swayze in *Dirty Dancing*. Think Channing Tatum. Kate thought that she loved dancing so much because she'd been deprived of it when growing up. It was inconceivable that she would have been allowed to go to a high school dance. Her religious-fanatic uncles forbade it.

When she got to college, it was as though all that pent-up movement came out. Her required physical classes were all in dance. Garth, as limber as though he were made of soft plastic, brought out the best in her. Add that to Jack's singing, which grew in tempo and ferocity as it went on, and it was a three-way show. Kate and Garth on the floor, surrounded by clapping and cheering couples, Jack on the stage, his voice throaty and suggestive and powerful.

After a very long dance session, Kate was out of breath and she could practically see Garth's heart pounding through his tight shirt. Abruptly, Jack changed to a slow song, the other dancers filled the floor, and Garth pulled Kate to him. His cheek was next to hers.

"So you like Chris, do you?" Garth asked.

"Nice guy. So why's he single?"

"Same as Jack, I guess. He can't find a woman who is sweet, pretty, and mentally stable."

"Oooooh. Sounds like he's had a hard time."

"He has. Ask anybody about Bridget. He hasn't had it as bad as Gil, but—"

At the name, Kate stopped and looked at him. "Gil? What did he—?"

Their halting seemed to bother Jack as he abruptly stopped singing. One of the band members took the mic, and Jack jumped down. He pushed Garth aside and led Kate into the dance.

She had grown accustomed to his quick movements. "You interrupted at a very bad time."

"Garth is married and has a kid and a half. He—"

She moved closer to him. "Shut up and listen. He said that Chris dated Bridget who—"

"Was crazy."

Kate stepped away and glared at him.

Jack pulled her back into his arms and was silent, listening.

"Garth said Bridget wasn't as bad as Gil has it, but…"

"But what?"

"That's when you jumped off the stage and demanded my full attention."

Jack ignored that remark. "Gil is my best friend. He'd tell me if…"

"Tell you what?"

"Nothing. He hasn't told me anything. What does Garth know that I don't?"

"Maybe I would have found out if you hadn't done one of your jealous fits and—"

Jack stopped dancing, took her hand, and led her back to the table. Their sandwiches were there.

"I want you to stay here while I go talk to Garth."

"How about if *you* stay here while I go talk to *all* of them?" She picked up her drink and when the napkin stuck to the bottom, she pulled it off and dropped it on the table.

"I know those guys so I—" He broke off as he looked at the napkin.

Kate saw what he was looking at and put her drink down.

The napkin had large, black letters on it.

STOP THE COP

A second later, Jack had slid out of the booth and was looking around the room. Other than a few tourists, he knew everyone in the bar. "Stay here," he said, then hurried through the dancers to reach the back door.

Kate was a foot behind him.

"I told you—" He'd already seen the futility of trying to make Kate obey him. As they ran through the kitchen, he asked if any strangers had been there.

"Just an old guy," a cook said.

"Skinny?"

"Yeah."

Jack practically leaped to the door and flung it open. Kate caught it before it closed.

"Damned heels," she muttered. "If you hadn't made me wear them, I could —"

Outside, Jack stopped and looked around. "That's why I told you to stay inside. For your safety."

"No, you told me to stay behind because I'm a girl and therefore you think I am incapable of doing—"

He gave her a *Give me a break* look. "He's gone."

Kate pulled the napkin out of her pocket. "So now what? We go home, do show and tell, and go back to endlessly talking about murder? What happened to our vow to not get involved?"

The band started to play again. High up on the wall was a screened window and they could clearly hear the music.

Jack could see how upset she was. On impulse, he pulled her into his arms and began a slow dance with her. "You are a great dancer. Nobody can keep up with Garth, but you did."

She knew he was changing the subject and she was glad of it. "I had classes in college. I like staying agile."

"Yeah?" He pulled her closer.

"What do you think that note means? I'm guessing 'the cop' is Chet. Do you think he's getting close to the real kidnapper? Or maybe he's close to finding Janet's murderer. Maybe we should—"

Jack dropped her into a dip so low that she quit talking. "I suggest we go back in, eat our sandwiches, have a few more beers, then go home. I'll get one of the guys to drive us. Tomorrow we'll turn this over to Chet and let him figure it out. Sound like a good idea?"

"An excellent plan. When do we order the chocolate?"

"As soon as you swear to never ever again dance with Garth. My heart can't stand watching that again."

"Oh, Jack, you do say the funniest things. I'm going to dance with Garth every chance I get. What's his wife like?"

"Pregnant. Never could dance. He said it was his favorite thing about her as she would never complain that he didn't take her dancing."

She laughed. "Come on, let's go."

They went back into the bar together.

As Carl Olsen watched them from high above, he sighed in relief. His entire body hurt and it was hard for him to get down. If they'd stayed a few more minutes, he might have fallen at their feet. It had been hard to escape them. But earlier, it had been easy to disappear in the excited crowd in the bar. No one looked at a skinny old man who was hunched over and scuffling about. Those people were full of the energy of *life*, something that Carl no longer had.

As he got down, he thought how he wished with all his might that the cop would stop investigating. He wasn't worried about that reporter. That guy was so desperate that he'd make up an ending for his story, anything that would get him on talk shows. The truth meant nothing to him.

But the cop… He cared about justice, about vindicating his stupidity from the first time around. All that cop cared about was being able to say, "See, I figured it out. I wasn't a fool after all." The consequences of revealing the truth meant nothing to him.

But Carl cared very, very much about the consequences. And when it came to *true* justice, he needed it even more than the cop did. In fact, he was willing to give up his life to get it.

One of Jack's friends drove them home, and another one drove the truck. The two men left together as Kate and Jack entered the house through the garage.

"You sure do have a lot of friends," she said.

"What can I say? I'm a likable guy."

Kate smiled. But then at the moment she was feeling no pain, so everything made her happy. "I guess you're staying with me."

"Yeah." Jack seemed to be thinking of something else. "You go in and go to bed. I'm going to take this to Dakon." He held up the napkin.

"Okay, but tell me what he says." Kate walked through the courtyard to her bedroom, grabbed her nightclothes, and went to the bathroom. The dancing had made her sweaty so she got into the shower and washed her hair. It felt good to be clean, even better to have had an evening away from the image of a woman in a chair with a knife in her chest—not to mention what was on the wall behind her.

When she got out, she dried off and put on one of

her old nightgowns, the *Sister Wives* kind she'd worn while living with her mother. Uncle approved.

She thought Jack would probably be outside the door, his eyes teasing, making sexual innuendos, faking horror at her high-necked, long-sleeved gown. But he wasn't there.

She got a robe—plain and pale pink—out of her closet and went into her living room. The couch had been pulled out to make a bed and covered with white linens. No doubt done by Aunt Sara.

Jack was fully dressed and sitting on the edge of the bed, his eyes downcast.

She sat down beside him. "What's wrong?"

"Noth—"

"No! Don't patronize me. What's upset you?"

"Dakon wasn't in my room."

"Maybe he's watching TV. Did you check?"

Jack looked at her.

"Yeah, of course you did. Think he went somewhere?"

"I think he's spending the night with Sara. In her bedroom."

They looked at each other.

"How about tomorrow we give them some privacy? I have a boat," he said.

"Do you? I guess you haven't been out on it since I've been here."

"Nah. Too busy solving murders. I vote that we leave early in the morning and spend the day on the water. It would help clear our minds."

"You can tell me about that apartment building you're going to build for me and all your relatives."

"Forget the boat. Let's get married tomorrow and I'll buy us a house."

His joke made her laugh. She stood up, covered a yawn, then bent and kissed him on the forehead. "We'll do the boat. I like that."

Jack was looking at her hard. "My offer was real."

"Yes, I know it was. But just to be clear, if you repeat it tomorrow I'll jump over the side and ride an alligator to shore."

Jack gave a half smile. "Old man Dakon scores but I don't."

Kate was walking toward her bedroom. "If *he* had asked me I might have said yes." When a throw pillow hit her in the back, she laughed and kept walking.

FOURTEEN

Early the next morning, they left a note for Sara. Her bedroom door was still closed, but then neither Jack nor Kate wanted to see them just yet. They moved about Kate's rooms quietly.

"What clothes should I take?" she whispered.

"None" came his answer, making her smile. She put on her 1940s-style outfit of Bermuda shorts and a halter top. An inch of midriff showed.

Jack ran his finger along the bare skin. "Hope you have sunblock for that."

She patted her big canvas tote bag. "Three tubes. And a swimsuit, towels, a couple of books and—"

"Won't need the books." He held the door open for her and they went out the door toward the garage. Sara's MINI was there and Jack's truck.

"We should take the car. Think Dakon can handle a three-quarter-ton pickup?"

"I think he could drive a tank right over it."

Jack tossed fishing gear in the back. They had breakfast at First Watch by Sawgrass Mall, went to the nearby Fresh Market, then Jack drove them to A1A. He kept his boat docked on the ocean side of southern Florida. He told her that last night he'd called ahead so the boat would be ready: cleaned and gassed.

His boat was long and sleek, mostly white but with a dark blue stripe along the side. There was a tall mast with a navy sail wrapped around it. A raised area had stairs that led down into a cooking/sleeping cabin.

It was a beauty!

"Impressed?"

"Very," she said.

"It was my first big purchase. I wanted to prove to myself that I could own something and pay it off. I wanted to be in debt."

She smiled at him in understanding. It was her guess that after his stepfather died, buying the boat was something he needed to do all on his own.

A tall blond young man came out to greet them. "I had to call in a team this morning to clean it up," he said. "Sorry but you're going to get a big bill, but it's clean now and fueled."

Jack was frowning when the young man left.

"What's wrong?"

"I haven't been here in weeks. I think somebody else has been using my boat."

"Isn't that what security is supposed to prevent?"

"Alarms are put in houses but they still get robbed. Let me go in first."

She watched him disappear through the door into

the hold, then waited until he stepped back out and motioned for her to get onboard.

"All clear," he said, then began untying it from the dock and they pulled away into the open water.

As Jack said it would, the wind and the water cleared their minds. Death and kidnapping seemed far away.

Jack was an excellent sailor. He seemed at one with the sea.

Kate didn't put on her swimsuit. The sun was so hot she thought enough skin was exposed. She slathered on sunscreen, stretched out in the shade, and told Jack to sing for her.

"There was a woman from Nantucket," he began.

"No, no. Something nice."

He stood by the mast and began to sing an aria in Italian.

Kate didn't know much about opera, but she knew it was a love song. She closed her eyes. Between Jack's singing, the water, and the warmth of the sun, she was sure she was in heaven.

When he finished, she opened her eyes and raised her hands to applaud him, but someone else was already clapping.

Kate sat up so fast she banged her head on the side of the boat.

Jack, still by the mast, was staring in openmouthed astonishment. "Who the hell are you?"

"I'm Zelly."

Kate was rubbing her head as she looked up to see a thin, scraggly-haired blonde woman standing by the door that led down into the boat.

"Zelly?" the woman said. "Gil told you about me, right?"

They were silent.

"He should have told you. I'm *real* important in his life." She said the last almost as a threat.

Jack and Kate exchanged looks. They had an idea who she was: Quinn's mother.

"Do you have anything to drink? It was hot in that closet and besides, it's been hard living here and having to sneak out to get food. That guy that runs the place watches everything. But he's cute, isn't he?"

When no one moved, she reached for Kate's canvas tote bag.

But Jack grabbed it first. "What do you mean that you've been living here? On my boat?"

"Well, yeah, but Janet said I could."

Kate had recovered enough to get up. She opened her bag and handed the woman a bottle of water.

She drank deeply of it. "Yuck, it's warm, but I guess that's okay. So where are we going?"

"*We* aren't going anywhere," Jack said. "I want to know why you're here. And it was Janet *Beeson* who said you could stay here?"

"Yeah. You have something to eat? I like candy a lot."

"I think we should sit down." It was the first time Kate had spoken. "I'll get the food. Sorry, no candy."

"You two look like you go to a gym." She had an unnaturally thin face, as though she hadn't eaten in a long time. She had on red shorts, a blue tank top, and flip-flops that looked to be years old.

Kate got the bags of food from below and when she

came back up, Jack and the woman…was Zelly short for something?…were sitting far apart on the cushioned seat. He was staring at her as though he'd found a feral animal. Was it poisonous or not?

Kate didn't open the grocery bags but put them by the woman, then went to sit by Jack. It was clear that the two of them were on one team and she was on the other.

"Why don't you start at the beginning?" Jack said.

"Well, Janet said—"

"No. From the real beginning. With Gil."

She was picking through the bags, pulling out sandwiches and salads, cheeses and crackers, fruit. She sneered at all of it. "No hot dogs? No cheese doodles?"

No one answered.

She took out a roast beef sandwich, peeled off the plastic, then leaned back against the seat. "Okay, so I guess it started with my mom. She was sick—cancer, but not too bad—and I took care of her. She had some money so I didn't have to get a job. That suited me. It was all fine until I broke my wrist." She was chewing, her mouth full. "It hurt like hell. You have any ketchup?"

"No." Jack was glaring at her.

"So Mom shared her pain pills with me, and it felt so good to not hurt that she bought me some more pills. She got them from a guy that lived downstairs. He and I were a couple for a while but it didn't work out. He *still* wanted me to pay for the pills. Can you imagine?" She took a bite. "So one night I met Gil at a bar. You're his friend, right?"

Jack nodded, but didn't speak.

"I'd had a few drinks—they made the pain pills work better—and this big guy asked me to dance. He was just so *clean* and he smelled so good. Well, we ended up back at his motel. I guess we never would have seen each other again, but the next morning he drove me home in his truck. I picked up a bill off the seat. It was for wood for fifteen grand so I knew he was rich. I got him to give me his email address."

"It wasn't his bill." Jack's jaw was clenched shut. "It was for *my* company."

"Oh?" She looked at Kate. "You're smart to go after him. All that money!"

"I don't—" Kate decided not to put herself on the defensive. She waited for Zelly to go on.

"Six weeks later I was throwing up. I was preggers. I thought I'd go to a clinic and you know, have it out, but Mom said she really wanted a grandbaby and we could raise it together. By that time her cancer was…" She looked at Kate to supply the word.

"In remission."

"That's right. You a doctor?"

"No. What happened?"

Zelly looked annoyed. "My mom made me eat foods I don't like. She loved green. Anything green and she made me eat it. And no pills of any kind. She even flushed the Tylenol. And I'm not sure but I think maybe she was the one who called the police on the guy downstairs. He didn't come back."

"I like your mother," Kate said.

For a moment, Zelly turned away to look out at the water. "Yeah, me too," she said, then looked back at them. "I had the baby. He was…" She waved her hand.

"Needy. Every minute of every day he needed something. Then my mom got sick again and…and…"

"So you contacted Gil," Jack said.

"Mom did. She said the baby deserved better than the two of us. She asked me about the father and I told her about Gil, how clean he was and all that. Mom was afraid he was like Joe downstairs, but I told her he wasn't."

"And Gil came right away."

"Yeah, he did." Zelly shook her head in wonder. "He took one look at that baby and wouldn't put him down. Even when the kid smelled bad, he still held him."

"What about the money?" There was anger in Jack's voice.

"Well… Everything costs a lot now."

Kate spoke before Jack could. She could see his anger rising. "Gil had a DNA test done, didn't he?"

"Yeah. He and Mom did all that. They talked about money and she wouldn't let Gil take the baby with him to his motel. Gil kept saying no to the money but when the test came back and he saw that he was the father, he…" Zelly shrugged.

"Gil gave you every penny he had in his savings, sold the stocks in his retirement plan, and later put a second mortgage on his house. He sent you that money too."

Zelly was unperturbed by the anger of Jack's tone. "Gil got what he wanted so he was happy."

"Were there any papers signed? A lawyer involved?" Jack asked.

"No. Gil wanted that but my mom said it was a deal of 'honor.' And…"

"And what?" Jack asked.

"Mom said that maybe someday I'd change my mind. I told her I didn't want a kid hanging around me, but she said I might. I laughed, told her she was crazy."

There was a pause as Jack and Kate thought of the ramifications of this lack of paperwork.

"What happened after that?" Kate asked.

"Mom and I moved to a nicer place and for years everything was fine. She made me go to rehab now and then but it never worked with me. I had a few jobs but I got bored and quit. Then…" She took a breath. "A year ago in May, Mom… Mom…"

"Passed," Kate said gently.

"She didn't even tell me she was sick again! Didn't tell me the doctor said there was no hope." Her voice was rising, her eyes filling with tears.

"When did you meet Janet Beeson?" Jack's tone was gentler than it had been.

"Just a few months ago. After Mom…passed, there wasn't much money left. I needed to cheer up so I threw a few parties. Not many, but the landlord told me I had to get out. I ended up getting a job as a waitress at a Denny's and I had a one-room place that—" She took a breath. "Anyway, it was awful, but then one day I walked into the dining room and there sat my mother. Or that's what I thought. I dropped my tray and screamed. The boss yelled that I had to pay for the broken dishes, but I didn't care."

"Was it Janet?" Kate asked.

"Yes, and she looked so much like my mother that I freaked. Her hair was pulled back like Mom's and she had on a white blouse with a little blue and red scarf around her neck. I gave one like it to Mom when I was eight years old. She wore it all the time. And on the collar was a little butterfly pin like the one I gave Mom when I was eleven."

"Did you talk to her?" Kate asked.

"Oh yeah. Sure. I was about to finish my shift so we went out to lunch to a real nice place. Talk about angels looking out for you! She was there because of Gil."

"Gil knew Janet Beeson?" Kate asked. "Socially?"

"She was Sean's Sunday School teacher and he'd told her—"

"Sean? Do you mean Quinn?" Kate asked. "Gil's son?"

"I get the name mixed up, but he's my son too! That's something Janet taught me. She said a mother has rights and that children need *two* parents."

Jack and Kate looked at each other, their eyes asking *Why did Janet Beeson do that?*

It was as though Zelly understood their silent question. "The boy, Quinn, told Janet he'd been born in Asheville, North Carolina, and that his dad said it was a really pretty place. That's why Janet was there on vacation, and she was alone and I was alone, so we had a vacation together. I got fired from my job for not showing up, but I didn't mind because Janet paid for everything. She even paid my back rent. It was like being with my mom again and I told Janet everything. I said I'd been totally sober ever since Mom passed but you know what? My life didn't get any better. Rehab tells you that if you can just stay sober you'll suddenly have a wonderful life, but mine was really boring. I hated it."

They waited for her to say more but she was digging in the bags looking for food. She didn't seem to like anything she found.

"So Janet offered you a new life?" Kate asked.

"I think it was more me asking her," Zelly said. She picked up a banana, looked at it as though she'd never seen one before, then tossed it back into the bag. "Janet told me about Gil's job and showed me photos of the kid's birthday party. He's cute and he looked real happy. And I saw pictures of Gil's new house." She looked at Jack. "Did you know that he built that house himself?"

"Yes."

"So anyway, by the time Janet was ready to go back to Florida, I wanted to go with her. She said yes, but I thought…"

"Thought what?" Kate asked.

"That I was going to live with her but she said no." Zelly leaned forward. "Between you and me, I think she had some secrets she didn't want anyone to see."

"So you moved onto my boat," Jack said.

"Janet said it would be all right because you were Gil's best friend and you were so busy with your red-haired girlfriend that you never used your boat. Janet said it was sad to waste housing when I needed a place so very much."

Suddenly, her face began to turn red with anger. "Janet and I were going to work things out with Gil. We had a *plan*. I was going to move to Lachlan and live with him in his big new house. Janet said that I'd be so happy that I wouldn't miss Mom anymore. So happy that I wouldn't even want drugs. Janet said that I'd had post-something after the baby was born."

"Postpartum depression," Kate said softly.

"Yeah, that's what Janet said I had, and if Gil hadn't taken my baby away from me, I would have got over it and Mom and I would have been happy." Zelly's hands were in fists. "But then I saw a newspaper. Janet was *murdered*!" She shouted the word. "Who could do that to such a nice and kind old lady? Only my mother ever cared for me like she did. She said that Gil would love me when he got to know me, but no matter what, I'd always have her. Always have Janet. She—" Zelly put her face in her hands and began to cry.

Jack and Kate looked at each other in silent communication. This time, it was one word: *Gil.*

Did Gil kill Janet Beeson when he heard that she'd brought his son's newly sober mother to Lachlan? Or when he heard that Janet had told the woman that she was going to live with Gil in his "big, new house"? Was it an act of passion? Uncontrollable rage? Gil would have seen that there would be a bitter custody fight coming. A judge would hear that the mother had suffered from postpartum depression and decide that Gil had used that illness to steal the baby from her. No doubt a lawyer would say that her doing drugs had been caused by what Gil had done. But she was now sober and wanted her son back—at Gil's expense. At the very least, Zelly would be given joint custody—or maybe full custody since Gil would be called a thief, maybe even a kidnapper.

What would Gil do to keep his precious son out of this woman's clutches? Anything? *Everything?*

Jack turned the boat around. He didn't need to ask Kate what she wanted to do. They both wanted to go back to Lachlan and…and… *What* could they do about this? Go to Gil and ask him if he'd murdered Janet? Used poison, and a knife, then shot her?

"What's he doing?" Zelly sounded alarmed.

"We're going back to land," Kate said. "So tell me more about your plans for you and Gil and Quinn. Don't you think you'd be bored staying home all day?"

She gave a smirking smile. "I *do* have a plan, a good one. As soon as Florida legalizes marijuana, I'm going to open a shop. I know lots about grass and I could help cancer patients, and people like that choose the best brand." She leaned forward. "I know some really important dealers and I have some good contacts. A few of them are dead now but there are enough left that I could make it work."

Jack was near enough to have heard this and he was staring at her in silent horror.

Zelly looked from one to the other. "Listen, I'm sorry that I messed up your time away from that old woman you two live with. Smart of you to do that because she's so rich. But if you want to go downstairs and do it, that's fine by me. In fact, if you want me to, I'll join you." She looked at Jack. "No? Well, I just thought I'd ask. I'm pretty good with my mouth. Had a lot of practice, if you know what I mean." When Jack took a step forward, Zelly stood up and moved away from him. "Hey! I meant no offense. It was just an offer. Janet said—"

Jack's voice was calm, low. "You either sit down and shut up or I will throw you over the side. No one knows you're here so no one will miss you. Do I make myself clear?"

Zelly nodded and sat back down.

FIFTEEN

By the time they got back to land, Jack was utterly sick of the woman. She was a chatterbox, never stopping to think about what she was saying. Also, she seemed to be controlled by her mother and Janet, always quoting their opinions on everything from what she should eat to where she should live. The fact that they were both deceased didn't seem to hinder their influence on her.

She constantly disparaged Florida. "Mom said the state was full of really weird people and Janet wondered if I really and truly like palm trees. She said coconuts and foxes fall on people's heads. Sometimes, it kills them."

Jack started to correct her but Kate put her hand on his arm. She was right, his temper was about to explode.

"I think you mean foxtail palms. The fronds are indeed quite heavy."

"The what? What kind of word is that? You mean the leaves?" She started laughing in such a derogatory way that Jack had to lead Kate away before she told the woman off.

After that, they just worked to keep calm as Zelly talked and talked and talked some more.

When they finally reached land, Jack jumped onto the dock. The first thing he was going to do was go to the management company he paid to look after his boat. Kate grabbed his arm. She didn't have to say anything but he knew what she meant. Keep the Wyatt temper under control.

He did. He didn't yell, didn't curse. Instead, his tone was what he'd used when one of his men had forgotten to lock up a chain saw over the weekend. When Charlene came by to get the lumber left for her, one of her clever sons managed to start the thing. Nothing bad happened but it could have. By the time a calm, quiet-spoken Jack finished, the guy was shaking in fear. He never returned to the job.

Jack went back to the two women waiting for him and they went to the truck. Zelly tried to sit in the middle but Jack wouldn't allow it. He put her on the end, next to the door.

On the drive across Fort Lauderdale to Lachlan on the west side, Zelly kept up a chatter about her future life. Seems that Janet had rhapsodized about Asheville. "I don't know why we have to live *here*," Zelly said. "Gil could build us a house in Asheville. I have friends there. And Mom is buried there. It's my *home*."

"It's where the marijuana dealers live?" Jack asked.

Kate gave him a look to stop it but the woman didn't seem to realize that he was being sarcastic.

"Yes!" Zelly said. "They do. I could—"

Jack tuned her out. His mind was on his friend Gil. *This* is what he was facing. A lifetime with this greedy, stupid woman. If he didn't put up with her he could lose his son. No paperwork! Jack grimaced at that thought. There wasn't a shred of evidence saying Gil hadn't taken the child from a bereft mother.

Zelly had told them that Janet said she would help her in any way possible, even to paying her lawyer's fees. "She was an angel," Zelly said. "Put on this earth to help others."

"I don't think that's the way Gil sees it," Jack mumbled. With all this going on, no wonder Gil shot a nail through his foot, he thought. No wonder he'd driven away cursing.

Why didn't he tell me? Jack asked himself. Why didn't Gil come to him and tell him of the situation?

Because of what Kate called "the legendary Wyatt temper"? Or because Gil thought he could handle everything himself? How? By killing Janet Beeson? Without her backing, the idiot Zelly wouldn't be able to pay a lawyer, wouldn't have the courage to pursue a goal she only thought she wanted. He couldn't imagine her living in Gil's new house, helping Quinn with his homework, and going to church on Sundays. She wouldn't last two weeks!

When they got to the house, Jack saw that Chet's van was still under the trees. In the garage was Sara's MINI.

They went through the courtyard and into Kate's

suite. He turned to Zelly. "I want you to stay in here. Take a bath. Wash your hair. Watch TV. Whatever you do, don't leave here until Kate or I come and get you. Do you understand me?"

"Sure. You want time to tell the old lady about me. She—"

"Do not call her that." Kate's tone was of repressed anger.

Zelly looked at both of them. "Okay, I get it." She looked out at the canal with a clump of palm trees to one side. "Are there alligators in there? And what about falling coconuts?"

"Yes," Kate said. "Lots of danger out there. Stay in here."

Jack opened the door into the house and let Kate go first. He closed the door behind her.

"No jury will convict Gil," she mumbled.

"I wish that were true," he said.

They were standing by the kitchen and neither of them wanted to go any further. The original idea of the boat trip had been to get away from thoughts of the murder.

But Zelly had taken over everything. Their time together had been all about *her*.

"Ready to see our houseguest?" Jack asked softly.

"I guess so. You wouldn't start acting like a dad with a shotgun and Sara as your virginal daughter, would you?"

Jack smiled. "You should help Sara write her books. I swear that I'll behave. I'll—"

He broke off when the doorbell rang. They heard a door inside the house open and the house was filled with the sound of a man's weeping. Loud, full of agony—and they'd heard it before.

They looked at each other. *"Everett,"* they said in unison.

They hurried into the house. Sara and Chet were standing in front of the round, pudgy Everett. He had his hands over his face and tears were squeezing through his fingers.

When Chet turned, he blinked a few times in surprise when he saw Jack and Kate, but Sara didn't.

"Get him a cold drink," she said to Jack. "Cold washcloth," to Kate.

It took a while to get the weeping man to a couch in the living room. Chet sat at the end, and Sara took her place on the couch.

Everett drank deeply of the ice water Jack handed him, then rubbed his face with the cold cloth.

Jack and Kate flanked Sara on the couch.

"I did it," Everett said. "It was all my fault. I may not seem so but I'm a very religious man. I'm going to hell for this. That poor woman. All because of *me*."

Jack started to say something but Sara beat him to it. *"Who?* Tell us what happened. *Now!"*

"Tayla. She—" He sniffed.

Kate reached across the coffee table and handed him a wad of tissues.

He blew his nose loudly. "Tayla. She—"

Sara and Jack looked like they were going to strangle the man.

Kate asked, "What did Tayla do?"

"You haven't heard?" He looked at them. "I thought the sheriff would have called you."

Sara squinted her eyes at him.

"Tayla confessed to the murder of Janet Beeson."

They all gasped, even Chet.

That Everett had astonished them with a writer's beloved weapon, a story, seemed to perk Everett right up. He took his time finishing off his glass of water, then waited while Jack went to the fridge door and refilled it.

Chet spoke. "Tell us everything that happened. *Why* did she kill the woman?"

"She didn't," Sara said. "She isn't—"

The look Chet gave her made her stop talking. They were so quiet that the birds outside sounded loud.

"Well," Everett began, "as you might remember, I was a bit perturbed during dear Janet's memorial. Such a lovely lady. I miss her very much."

So many words came to Sara that she began to choke. She coughed to cover herself, but she said nothing.

"After the service, Tayla invited me to lunch at the Mandarin in Miami. She is a very interesting woman. She told me she'd read everything I'd written and thought I was an undervalued writer. She said—"

When he saw Chet's face, he stopped that line of the story. "Anyway, it was a very nice meal."

The three on the couch sat up straight. Who lived in Fort Lauderdale and took people to a meal in Miami? Tayla must have had a *very* serious purpose. And considering what she did, yes, she was more than serious.

"I, uh…" Everett looked ashamed. "I drank too much. But then Tayla ordered a fifty-five-dollar bot-

tle of wine and oh, it was delicious. Fruity, tart, and—"
He cleared his throat. "I told her everything."

"About what?" Chet asked.

"About my book. About the kidnapping."

They didn't dare look at each other for fear that
they'd give too much away.

"What *exactly* did you tell her?" Chet asked, and
they knew they were hearing the voice of a man who
had gone up through the ranks to become chief of police.

"I, uh… I, uh…" Everett took a breath, then looked
directly at Chet. "I embellished. I told Tayla that you
could identify the kidnapper."

Sara, Jack, and Kate turned to Chet. He gave a
barely perceptible shake to his head. No, he had not
told that.

"I'm sorry," Everett said. "I made it up. I—"

"Why did you do that?" Jack asked. "Now you're—"

Sara broke in. "Because that's what writers *do*. Give
us one fact and we can stretch it into a book. Go on,
tell us how you came up with that idea." She sounded
almost proud of him. Some writer's bond, maybe.

He glanced at Chet, then back at Sara. "I knew he
was hiding something. I could feel it. And there *had*
to be a reason he was so obsessed. It made sense that a
rookie cop saw something but was too dumb to report
it. Later, he realized what he'd seen and regretted it."

Only a slight widening of Chet's eyes betrayed that
Everett had guessed the truth.

"What makes you think Tayla had anything to do
with the kidnapping?" Sara asked.

"I've asked around about people."

"Right," Sara said. "Looking for stories. But what about Tayla?"

"No kids. Probably her husband's fault. He wasn't a likable man." He looked hard at Sara. "But you know that very well, don't you?"

Sara glared at him.

Everett leaned back on the couch. "Did you know that Tayla's sister lived in Atlanta at the time of the kidnapping?"

"She's Charlene's mother?" Kate asked even though she knew the answer.

"Yeah, but the kid was here in Lachlan. She lived with her grandmother while her parents lived in China."

"Japan," Sara said.

"Oh right. Japan."

Chet said, "So you think Tayla Kirkwood was the White Lily Kidnapper?"

"I think it's possible," Everett said. "Sometimes women want a baby so much that they'll do anything to get one. Maybe Tayla was there in Atlanta and saw an unguarded baby and took it."

"How did she hide from us?" Chet asked. "The police were there in minutes."

Everett was silent.

"He hasn't made that part up yet." Sara's voice held less pride than it had.

"So," Jack said, "this morning Tayla confessed to murdering Janet Beeson."

"I guess Janet found out," Everett said. "That's why she had the bootie. Maybe Tayla kept it as a souvenir and Janet found it."

"And Tayla killed Janet?" Sara said.

"Poisoned her?" Kate said.

"Stabbed her?" Jack said.

"Then shot her brains out." Chet sounded disbelieving.

"I don't know," Everett said. "The deputy called me and asked if I knew what was going on."

"The deputy called you?" Chet asked.

"Yeah. Dave. He's been a great source of—" Everett gave a cough. "I mean, yes, he called me."

"Where did Tayla turn herself in?" Chet asked.

Everett shrugged. "I guess not to Flynn."

"He wouldn't have believed that she did it," Sara said. "Tayla's not violent. She let Walter push her around before she married him. He liked her because she's a workhorse."

"And she was from the right side of town," Everett said. "Whereas you and Cal—"

Jack stood up. "Do you have anything more to tell us? Other than that you got drunk and blabbed a made-up story that caused a woman to confess to murder?"

Again Everett's eyes filled with tears. "I didn't mean to cause anyone any problems. I just wanted to bring a kidnapper to justice."

"And revitalize your career." Sara stood up by Jack. "I think you should go home. I want you to write down every word of your dinner with Tayla. Don't leave anything out. Then put it in a PDF file and send it to me. Got that?"

"Yes." Everett stood up. "I took a taxi here. I didn't trust myself to drive."

"Chet will drive you home," Sara said, then looked at him.

He nodded. He knew she wanted to be alone with Jack and Kate.

As soon as they left, Sara turned to them. "It wasn't her."

"Of course not," Kate said and they went into the kitchen to start dinner.

Sara pulled a package of chicken out of the fridge. "I've gone skinny dipping with Tayla. There is no heart-shaped birthmark anywhere on her body."

"What about Charlene?" Kate whispered as she started a salad. "Who had an affair with my father."

"Maybe Tayla confessed to protect her niece," Jack said. He was pouring hot sauce into a bowl.

"It's what I'd do," Sara said. "Tayla and I don't have much life left, but Charlene is young."

"It would destroy her marriage, her children," Kate said.

They had filled the counter with food and they looked at each other.

"What do we do?" Kate asked.

Sara tightened her lips. "We do *not* let Chet see Charlene. Just in case we're right. And maybe we're not. They all just happened to be in Atlanta at the right time and the bootie was brought here to Lachlan. I'm sure there are other explanations. But Chet is *not* to see Charlene."

They nodded in agreement.

They were on their way out to the grill when the doorbell rang.

"Probably Chet," Sara said.

"You didn't give him a key?" Jack was smirking.

"Keep on like that and you'll find yours missing."

Kate and Jack went outside while Sara went to the door.

"Keys," Jack said as he turned on the grill. "My boat was locked up. How did she get the keys?"

"Good heavens! Zelly. I forgot about her. I'd better go check on her."

"No!" Jack said. "Leave her alone. We have enough to deal with now. We can—" He broke off because Sara had opened the door. Behind her was Sheriff Flynn, and he looked like he'd aged about ten years.

Sara pointed him toward a padded chair and he flopped down in it. She went to Jack and Kate. "His wife is out of town so we're going to feed him."

They put the chicken on the grill and closed the lid. Jack got beers for everyone, then they sat at the big table across from the sheriff. He did indeed look awful. His uniform was dirty and his eyes were sunken. They didn't say a word, just waited for him to speak.

"I guess you heard."

They nodded but didn't speak.

"Tayla went over to Broward HQ and confessed to the murder."

Again, they nodded but kept silent.

"Tayla sold Janet the house, and you know how Realtors are. Until those papers are signed, they're your best friend." He looked at Kate and she shrugged in a way that said it was part of the job. "Tayla said Janet was going to ruin her reputation around Lachlan." The sheriff looked up, his eyes bleak. "She said she gave Janet tea poisoned with oleander. They sent forensics over there and sure enough, there was a metal box full of poisoned tea. Really strong stuff. It was labeled *Syl-*

via's Tea. Maybe it was in the house when Janet bought it. Maybe Sylvia used it to kill herself."

The sheriff ran his hands over his face. "Who kills someone over a lawsuit? I don't get it. Tayla could have hired a super lawyer and—"

"What?" Sara asked. "A lawsuit? What are you talking about?"

Flynn looked puzzled. "Didn't that reporter tell you? Janet Beeson was suing Tayla over the sale of the house. Janet said she paid full price but Tayla pocketed thousands and made no record of it. Janet said Tayla did that with a lot of houses. A case like that would have been in the courts for years. Even if she won, I can't imagine that Tayla would have any business left after that battle. And she'd certainly be broke."

He looked at the three of them, staring in wide-eyed shock. "So Tayla killed the woman to keep her quiet. But her conscience got the better of her and she confessed."

Sara was the first to smile, then Kate. Jack grinned wide.

"What the hell is wrong with you people?" the sheriff said. "I tell you of a murder confession and you're *happy*?"

They got up and Jack waltzed Sara around in a circle, then Kate. The big punching bag was nearby and Sara did a dozen or so punches—but not hard enough to injure her writing hand.

Sheriff Flynn was leaning back in his chair and gawking at them.

Chet came through the door. He too was smiling. "Looks like you heard." He spun Sara around.

Sheriff Flynn picked up his hat and started for the door, but Sara caught his arm and led him back to the chair. "Of course Tayla didn't kill her and the motive is ridiculous."

"Yes," Kate said. "House sales are registered."

"Just get a few witnesses and a truckload of papers and her motive is gone," Jack said.

"But..." the sheriff began.

Chet sat down across from him. "They're right except for..."

"For what?" Sara asked.

"It looks like Tayla did kill her," he said. "She knows too much about the murder scene to be innocent."

That deflated them and they sat down.

"How do you know so much?" Jack asked.

"Called someone," Chet said, but didn't explain further.

"Murdered over a lawsuit?" Sara said.

"I don't believe it," Kate said.

Chet looked at them. "What other possible motive could she have?"

Sara said, "I think you better look at the chicken."

"Are you changing the subject?" Sheriff Flynn asked. "What do you know that I don't?"

Sara had opened her mouth to give a lie when the patio door opened and in the evening light stood Zelly. She had on one of Kate's best dresses, a red sleeveless one suited for elegant dinner parties. She'd draped herself in what had to be most of Kate's jewelry. Half a dozen necklaces were piled on top of each other. Bracelets went up to both elbows. She was a garish-looking wraith.

"Are there any alligators out here?" she asked.

The sheriff didn't miss a beat. "Only Jack and he does bite."

The look of fear on her thin face seemed to hit something in them. Murder, confessions, it was all too much.

Spontaneously, they burst into laughter. It was a great relief to all of them.

Zelly seemed to be pleased that she had been the cause of the laughter and she stepped outside. Jack felt so good that he handed her a cold beer.

"If that's made with coconuts, I don't want it," she said.

Her statement made them laugh harder. Jack turned the chicken over and filled the grill with vegetables.

When the sheriff asked who Zelly was, Sara said she was the daughter of a friend and didn't elaborate.

Sixteen

As was her habit, Sara woke early the next morning. She was glad to be alone in her bed. Her one night with Chet had been wonderful, but it wasn't something she wanted forever. She'd had a lifetime of people pitying her because she was alone—meaning unmarried. But the truth was that she'd met only one man who she'd ever wanted to share closet space with: Cal Wyatt.

She was glad for her thick carpet as she went past the closed door of her study because Zelly was in there. Last night, by silent mutual agreement, they'd not talked more about the murder. They'd not mentioned Tayla at all. Zelly was a stranger and therefore not to be trusted with their secrets.

At nine, Sheriff Flynn went home looking better than when he'd arrived. Laughter had healed some of his misery.

Sara quickly dressed and put on makeup. She truly believed that the use of cosmetics was a sign of respect for other people. She was considerate of what they had to look at.

The study door was still closed when she went past it. It was dark outside and she loved the feeling of being the only person awake.

She'd been intrigued by the forensics people finding a tin marked *Sylvia's Tea*. Had it been there when they'd seen the house? Was it in one of her photos but they'd not seen it?

She put the pictures on the big TV in the family room and started going through them. There was a spice rack in the kitchen and it did have some small boxes of herbal tea. One of them was metal and it was turned so the label didn't show. No one had thought to turn it around.

She was annoyed with herself for missing something so blatant. Why hadn't her curiosity been piqued by an unlabeled tin?

She sat on the couch and watched the other photos go by. Had she missed things in them too?

When the photo Jack had taken of the man came on the screen, she paused.

"That's Lisa's friend."

Sara turned to see Zelly standing behind her. She had on the sweatsuit Kate had lent her. Zelly said that she wanted the pink negligee she'd seen in Kate's drawers, but she was told no.

"I take pictures too." Zelly sat down by Sara. "I have selfies from everywhere."

Sara had to stamp down her urge to walk away from the woman. She didn't like her and Virgos have a hard time dealing with people they can't stand. "You know him? And Sylvia's daughter, Lisa?"

"I just saw him for a minute, but Lisa is nice."

None of them had considered that this unappealing woman knew something about the case. "When did you meet her?"

"It was like this. I mean early morning. Mom said that I could live in a black room and I'd still know when it was four a.m."

"Me too," Sara said. "Interesting things happen this early."

"Yeah. One time when I was about six, I—"

"Lisa," Sara said. "I'd really love to hear about her. If it was Sylvia's daughter, that is."

"I don't know. She said her mother used to own the house."

"Yes!" Sara felt her heart speeding up. "Tell me everything. From the beginning."

"Well, it was like I told you. No wait, I told Jack. Or maybe it was Kate. Anyway, I thought I was going to *live* with Janet but she said no. But I did stay one night."

"And you woke up early?" Sara encouraged.

"Yes. I was looking out the window. My mom and I always lived in an apartment so I wasn't used to flowers. Palm trees scare me because of the coconuts. Did you know that people get killed when they fall on your head? They can—"

"You were up early," Sara said.

"Oh yeah. There's a little, uh…building in back of Janet's house and I saw someone there so I went out to say hello. That's when I met Lisa. She was looking for something. She—"

"What was she looking for?"

"Her mother's book. Well, not really a book book, but a flash drive. She said her mother *wrote* the book. Can you imagine that? I have trouble writing a text but she—"

"Did she find it?"

"No," Zelly said. "She had a metal tool with her and she was going to take up the floor but she said she'd better not. I think she was afraid she'd get in trouble."

"What kind of trouble?"

Zelly looked at Sara as though she was an idiot. "It wasn't her mother's house anymore, was it?"

Sara had to bite her tongue to not point out that Zelly had been staying on a boat that didn't belong to her. "Did she tell you about the book?"

"Oh yes. She said it was her mother's last book and it would show that what happened was just…"

"Just what?"

Zelly put her fingers on her temples. "Just-something. Ask Kate. She's good with words."

"I am too. What did the word sound like?"

"Longer."

"It was longer than 'just?' Oh. Justified?"

Zelly nodded.

Sara leaned back on the couch. "Lisa said that if she found the last book her mother had written it would show that what had happened was justified."

Zelly smiled. "That's it exactly. You're good with words too."

"Thank you." Sara looked up at the screen. "So when did you see Carl?"

"He came to the fence and told her she had to leave. I don't think he saw me. He's really skinny, isn't he?"

"He is," Sara said. "What else was said? What else did you see?"

"That's all. I don't think Lisa liked that I saw her there, and she didn't want Carl to see me."

"How do you know his name?"

"Lisa said it. She stepped in front of me then said, 'Carl, you scared me.' Then she grabbed her bag and left."

"That's everything?"

"All of it. She picked up the gun and ran out."

Sara drew in her breath. "She did what?"

"Picked up the gun. It fell out when she grabbed her bag. I know it's easier to reach a gun if your bag has an open top but it's not safe to do that. I tell my friends that all the time."

"That's, uh…good advice." Sara was blinking at her. "So, Lisa had a gun with her. A pistol?"

"Probably a .38. Looked like one. I like those. Not as much kick as a .45."

"Yes, of course. The kick."

"Hey! Do you think maybe Lisa killed Janet? If she did, that makes me really mad. I don't know what I'm gonna do now. Janet was going to pay for the lawyer I need to get to Gil. She said he ought to marry me, then I'd have a place to live forever. I left Asheville to come here *for him* so Gil owes me for that, doesn't he? He ought to pay my expenses. Janet said—"

She stopped because Sara stood up. "How about if you and I keep what you told me to ourselves?"

Zelly stuck out her lower lip. "Now you sound like Mom and Janet. They were *always* saying that to me."

"What did Janet tell you to keep secret?"

"About staying on the boat. I had to sneak in and out of it. I still don't know why I couldn't stay with her. She had room or she could have gone online to get me a motel."

Sara was standing, looking down at her. "Did you ever see Janet with a computer?"

"Yeah. All the time. She had three of them. I asked if I could use one but she said no. Right after that she said she had to go get some keys then she was going to put me on a beautiful boat. You know what? After she left I looked for a computer but couldn't find any of them. Which is strange because her place was really clean, so they should've been easy to find. If you ask me, that house of hers was too clean. It needed some pictures around the place. My mom had pictures of me everywhere."

"You want some breakfast?"

"Sure. You have any Frosted Flakes?"

"Fresh out, but I can make you an omelet."

"Eggs. Yuck. But okay. Then maybe we can go see Gil. I bet he's gonna be surprised to see me."

"Oh yeah," Sara said. "*Real* surprised."

Sara got Zelly nestled in front of the TV and put on a surfing movie about Laird Hamilton.

"He's old but he's hot," Zelly said. "Do you remember things like that?"

"I do remember last night, yes." Sara smiled at the young woman's look of confusion, then went to the kitchen to start breakfast. She mixed up a batch of carrot muffins for people who were not on the keto diet—which was everyone but her.

Kate came into the kitchen at 7:30 a.m. She nodded toward Zelly on the couch, saw that her eyes were glued to the TV with its pictures of men surfing. "What's with her?"

Sara kept her voice low. "She's a veritable fount of information. Sees and hears a lot but has no idea what it means. Where's Jack?"

"Not with me. His bed was empty."

They looked at each other, then Kate took off running. She was back in minutes. "His truck is gone and Chet has the door closed but he's talking to someone. So last night you two didn't...?"

"Spend the night together? No." Minutes later, Sara was taking the muffins out of the oven when Jack threw open the door to Kate's suite. From his look, something bad had happened. "You talked to Gil."

"Without me there?" Kate sounded hurt.

"Yes to both." He glanced at Zelly but she was absorbed in her movie. He went into the kitchen. "Gil wouldn't talk to me. Said it was none of my business. How can he say that when we've been friends since elementary school?"

Sara put her hand on Jack's chest and half pushed him onto a stool. "He's worried. He's terrified. He thinks that being quiet will save him."

"Not with *her* calling in lawyers." Jack kept his voice low. "One word about postpartum blues said with tears and a judge will—"

Kate turned on the blender to drown him out.

Sara split a muffin, buttered it, and gave it to him on a plate.

Jack took the hint and shut up.

"What do we do next?" Kate whispered as she handed Jack a smoothie of orange juice and kale. He took one sip, grimaced, and handed it back to her. She took a big drink.

Sara spoke up. "Lisa was at Janet's house looking for a flash drive copy of her mother's last book. She said it would show that what had happened was justified."

"Does that mean Sylvia's suicide or Janet's murder?" Jack asked.

"I don't know but Lisa had a gun."

Jack and Kate blinked at her.

"I think we need to go searching," Sara said. "Tear up the floorboards."

"To do that, we'd have to get permission," Kate said. "Ready to sit down with the Broward County authorities and tell all?"

"Then they arrest Lisa before we talk to her?" Jack said. "I don't think so."

"Oh yes," Sara said, "Carl came to get Lisa. It was him in the photo, the skinny man who was spying on you two. Janet's ex."

"You got all this from *her*?" Kate nodded toward Zelly curled up on the couch.

"Every word. And Janet had three computers but when she left the house Zelly couldn't find any of them."

"There's a hiding place in that house," Kate said.

"Computers and flash drives," Jack said. "I think we definitely should go have a look."

At that moment, Chet came down the hall. "Wherever you're going, it has to be postponed. We're going to visit Tayla in jail." He looked at Sara. "But not you."

"I wouldn't go anyway."

"Thought not. I had to call in some favors and show some credentials, but I got us in." He sounded excited, as though he was dying to do this.

"What are you going to ask her?" Jack was cautious.

"*Not* about the lawsuit. Certainly not if she actually did steal money."

"She didn't," Kate said and they looked at her. "She's a good person and she has her own money."

"Maybe," Chet said. "I want to know about the kidnapping. I need to shave. Be ready to go in thirty minutes." He grabbed a muffin and went back down the hall.

For a moment, Jack, Kate, and Sara were silent.

"What if—?" Kate began but stopped.

"What if Tayla is protecting someone's entire life?" Jack asked.

"A young family's life," Sara said.

Kate sat down on a stool. "How do we rescue Tayla without giving away that we suspect what may have happened years ago?"

"I have no idea," Sara said.

"If you were writing it?" Jack asked.

"My character would find Lisa and Carl and prove them guilty of the murder," Sara said. "Then Tayla would be freed and nobody would ever know anything about a long-ago kidnapping."

"And Chet?" Kate asked.

"He'd go *home*!" She said it so fiercely that Kate and Jack laughed.

"I like it," Jack said. "Let's go see Tayla and do our best to tell her we're trying to get her out."

"Without letting *him* know," Kate said.

"Agreed."

Kate was texting her office to let them know she wouldn't be there. Melissa would have to show Chris an apartment. Jack saw what she was doing and he smiled all the way down the hall.

To get to the cell where Tayla was being held, Jack, Kate, and Chet had to pass a lot of people in uniform.

"Hey Jack!" an older man said. "Good to see you again."

"Jack! We miss Roy a lot. Especially Moose. He likes to entertain us with what he'd like to, uh, say to your dad." This was followed by laughter.

"Jack, have you had any trouble with Wayne since he got out? He was pretty mad at your dad."

"Long time, no see. What'd they get you on this time?"

"I'm waiting for you to call me back, baby." This was said by a pretty blonde woman.

Through it all, Jack gave vague smiles and mumbled nonanswers. And he absolutely would *not* meet Kate's eyes.

Tayla was waiting for them in her cell. Without makeup and with eyes that said she'd given up hope, she looked her age. Her usually sleek hair hung in flat tendrils and looked rough and disheveled. Her prison uniform was too big for her and swallowed her slim figure.

A folding chair had been set in the cell. She took it and the three of them sat on the hard bed across from her.

Kate was sitting next to Chet and she could feel his heart beating rapidly. He'd been involved in the White Lily Kidnapping case for most of his life and right now he might be close to an end to it.

"We want to know the truth," Chet said. "What happened in Atlanta on—"

"How are you?" Kate asked loudly. "I brought a bag of cosmetics and moisturizer but they wouldn't let me bring it in. I'll transfer money into your account."

"Thank you," Tayla said.

"We—" Kate began.

Chet cut her off. "We don't have much time. Where did Janet Beeson get the baby bootie from the White Lily Kidnapping? Who wrote *Stop the Cop* on that napkin? Was it Janet's ex?"

Tayla looked at Kate. "You need to stay out of this. Let me deal with it. Only I can stop it."

"By taking the blame?" Jack asked.

Tayla's eyes were intense. "I did it. I killed Janet Beeson."

Kate didn't so much as blink. "Did Lisa give you the gun?"

"No! She—" Tayla took a breath. "I poisoned Janet. I swear it."

"Because of a lawsuit?" Jack's tone was of disbelief.

Chet had been impatiently waiting. "Look!" he said angrily. "We need information from you. We believe

Janet's murder has nothing to do with some lawsuit and everything to do with the kidnapping. What do you know?" He shouted the last.

Tayla didn't seem perturbed by his aggression. "You think this is one of your investigations, but you don't know anything. You think you've found out all about witches and teen girls being nasty but they mean nothing. You haven't come close to the hatred involved—or the evil that controls it."

She looked directly at Chet. "You want to find a way to forgive yourself for your stupidity when the kidnapping happened. And you think it's all right to do *anything* to achieve your goal. You believe you will be satisfied, so other people don't matter."

She stood up and looked down at them. "You have no idea of the depth of hatred that you're trying to bring into the light. It will eat up the good."

After a quick glance at Kate, she called the guard and he opened the door for them to leave. Her dismissal of them didn't make Chet soften his attack. Obsessions aren't destroyed by a few scary words. His voice was barely more than a whisper. "Just so you know, I *can* identify the kidnapper. Cross my heart." He made the gesture on his chest where he'd seen the birthmark. When Tayla's face went pale, he got up and walked out without a backward glance.

Jack paused by her. "Sara is on your side." He stepped out of the cell.

Kate kissed Tayla's cheek, but she said nothing. There wasn't anything she could say.

Tayla caught her arm. "Nobody is what they seem." She started to say more but the guard separated them.

* * *

Carl was hiding again. His weight loss was good for slipping into small spaces and his age and lack of good looks were assets. No one paid any attention to a skinny old man.

As he waited for the young woman, he thought back to when it all began.

After his dear wife died, he'd been so alone. They'd been together since they were fourteen. It had been her idea to start manufacturing ink cartridges. She said, "Someday every house in America is going to have a printer and they'll need ink." The bank thought the idea was ridiculous—you just pour the ink into the machine, right? Ink was cheap so there was no money to be made in that. Carl and his wife had borrowed and hocked things until they could start a small company. It flourished. Eventually, he bought a high-rise and rented out the floors his company didn't use.

For years, he'd been a happy man. They weren't blessed with children but they had each other.

She died when they were in their fifties. She had a headache, took a nap, and never woke up. People said he should be glad she hadn't suffered. But Carl hadn't been glad about anything.

One thing that had especially distressed him was that he was suddenly considered "a catch." He had money in the bank but he was also fat and losing his hair—but still women went after him. All of them seemed to think that he needed to have "fun." To them, that meant getting drunk and dancing all night. He just wanted to watch a movie, or sit in the shade and read a book.

Wherever he went for lunch, a restaurant or in his office, some female would "accidentally" show up there.

Out of frustration, he took his packed lunch and went into a broom closet to eat. He did this three times before he was disturbed. One day the door was opened by a woman. She was fortyish and not especially pretty, but then, neither was his late wife. He wasn't attracted to the supermodel type. She was curvy, also like his wife was. She jumped in surprise when she saw him, and he had to coax her to stay. He found out that she worked on another floor and didn't know who he was. She said she was escaping giggling girls in her office who wanted to spend lunchtime talking about men. "There's some guy on the twelfth floor who is a recent widower. All of the women brag that they're going to get him. I feel sorry for the poor man. They're clearly after his money." He didn't tell her that he was their prey.

He and Janet began to meet in the closet every day. She shared her home-cooked lunches with him. He managed to keep his identity secret from her for weeks, but when she found out, she was hurt. She suffered in such a sweet way that he felt strong and protective.

However, it didn't get serious between them until he found out that her parents had left her money. She had her own wealth, so even though she knew about his money, she didn't see him as a living bank account.

When they were married three months later, Janet had insisted on inviting every female who worked in the building Carl owned. All two hundred and seventy-one of them. At the reception, she told him that she wanted the women to see that she'd won. Carl Olsen had never seen himself as a prize to be fought for, but it certainly felt good. For the second time in his life, he had found someone who saw him as a person to be treasured. His second wedding was as happy as his first one.

That was years ago and he didn't like to think about what happened after the wedding ended. But that was the cause of what he had to do now.

He'd followed Sara Medlar to a hotel because she had Zelly in her car with her. He knew that Janet had practically adopted the young woman, but he'd also seen Zelly with Lisa. She thought Carl hadn't seen the scraggly-haired woman hiding behind her, but he had. He knew of Zelly's connection to the women but he didn't know how much she knew.

Carl waited by the pool, unnoticed, until Sara left, then he checked into the hotel. After he'd purchased swim gear and a change of clothes in the gift shop, he went out to the pool. As he'd expected, Zelly was there in a tiny bikini and flirting with the staff.

He would have liked the time to draw her in, but he couldn't afford it. He told her that he was Janet's ex and that Chet Dakon and he used to work together. Chet had asked him to look after her. "For Janet's sake."

"That's good," she said. "Those people are too dumb to know when there's trouble. I tried to tell them but they wouldn't listen."

"Yeah, that's what Chet says too. I bet you know a lot."

Zelly smiled. "More than they think I do. They talk

when I'm around 'cause they think I don't understand what's going on."

Carl laughed in a way that said the joke was on them. "I bet you saw the files." He'd seen them being unloaded.

"They tried to keep it a secret, but I think he has a picture of some kidnapper."

"Oh." Carl swallowed. "A photo?"

"Maybe. But those three—you know?"

"Jack and Sara and Kate?"

"That's them. They keep whispering that they know something they don't want him to know. I think they're hiding something really *big*. They're worried what will happen if that cop finds out what it is."

"I would imagine that you're right," Carl said. He closed his eyes behind the expensive designer sunglasses. It looked like his warning of *Stop the Cop* had had no effect.

Too bad, he thought. *Really, really too bad.*

The ride home from the jail was in silence. Kate wanted to talk to Jack, but she wouldn't say anything in front of Chet. She didn't like the way he'd acted with Tayla. What she'd said about him, that he cared only for clearing *his* name, seemed to be right on.

When they got home, they saw that Chet was furious. His face was red to his ears—and it was all rage.

"Are you going to help me find the kidnapper, or not?" he demanded.

"That's what we've been doing," Jack said.

Kate was glad to see that Jack's temper didn't match Chet's.

The older man squinted at them as though trying to read their minds. "I'm leaving for Atlanta. I need to check out some facts. I'll get my things later." Turning, he went to his van and sped out of the driveway.

Inside, Kate and Jack sat down with Sara. She told of taking Zelly to a hotel and leaving her at the pool. She'd instructed the manager about bills. There were to be *no* parties. "I'll send her back to Asheville as soon as…" She didn't finish. As soon as what? Tayla was put on trial?

Sara looked at Kate and Jack. It was their turn to speak. They went over every word that had been spoken in Tayla's jail cell. Then they told her that Chet was going away for a while. It made them breathe a sigh of relief.

"I think we should stay out of this. It's what Tayla told us to do," Kate said. "She seemed really afraid."

"And leave her to the wolves? Or worse, to the lawyers?" Jack asked.

Kate looked at him. "I thought you were planning to marry Chet's lawyer daughter."

"I am. We can have a double wedding with you and Chris."

"I'm holding out for Garth. We'll dance all night."

"Oh yeah? And who is going to sing for you?"

"Could you two please take a break?" Sara said. "The problem now is Tayla. We have to do something to help her."

The faces of Kate and Jack said they knew she'd solve the problem.

"I do know a few lawyers. One of them deals with criminals."

"Think he'll take her for a client?" Kate asked.

"He likes cases that he can't possibly win, so when he does, he's jubilant."

"I like him already," Jack said. "Maybe he can get Tayla to stop telling everyone that she's guilty."

"Did she say anything about stabbing or shooting?" Sara asked.

"Nothing," Kate said. "Tayla said she *poisoned* Janet. Swore she did it."

"Interesting," Sara said. "If I were writing this…"

"Yes?" Kate and Jack said in unison.

"I'd have an autopsy prove that the poison didn't kill the victim, so Tayla would be freed."

"So who would be punished?" Jack asked.

"I'd have to start on page one to find that out. I'd make up some really bad guys, but of course no one would know they were bad until I revealed it."

"That's what Tayla said. *Nobody is what they seem.*"

"I can believe that," Sara said. "Sweet-tempered Gil has turned into an angry bull."

"Sylvia—who everyone adored—had a daughter who packs a weapon," Kate said.

They looked at Jack. "Chet seems sane but with Tayla he was…"

"Feral," Kate supplied. "Pushy, demanding, aggressive. I wanted to hug her. Well, I wanted to hug her even without his snapping, but that doesn't matter."

Sara was thoughtful. "Who else is not what he or she seems?"

"We wouldn't know, would we?" Kate said. "Until someone lets us inside their minds, we can't know. It's like when you read that some man killed his wife and kids. You're astonished. You just didn't *see* it."

"But it was all there," Sara said. "When you know the answer, you can look back and see what the clues were. The question now is *What have we seen that we paid no attention to?*"

They had no answer for that.

"I think I'll write all this down," Sara said. "See if I can make sense of it."

"And I need to go to work," Kate said.

"Me too," Jack added.

But they didn't move. Someone they knew was in jail. She was freely admitting that she'd poisoned a woman—but they didn't believe her.

"And you have to call the lawyer," Jack said.

"Yes, of course," Sara answered.

When they separated, they were silent. The feeling of "unfinished" hung heavily over them.

Kirkwood Realty was like a funeral parlor. Worse, everyone looked at Kate with accusing eyes. But no one said anything. Even Melissa was quiet—for about an hour.

"You found out who killed those Morris women, but Tayla doesn't matter to you enough to take this case?" Her voice was pure venom. "I bet you want this place for your own. Is that what you're hoping? To make it into Medlar Realty?"

Kate saw that the others in the office agreed with Melissa. She knew she should do the "strong woman act" and stand up for herself, but instead, she grabbed her handbag and left the office. She practically ran to her car. She wasn't sure where she was going until she realized that she was about a mile from Jack's job site.

As she pulled into the drive, her phone began ringing. She picked it up just as Jack opened the door and got into the passenger seat. "Gil is about to go after me with a sledgehammer. He—"

"It's Everett." Kate put the phone on speaker and leaned toward Jack. "Hello?"

Everett talked so fast they could hardly understand him. This time, he was in hysterics. Chet had been there. It looked like he'd lied to them about going to Atlanta. But then, they hadn't exactly been honest with him either.

"It was like the Gestapo," Everett was saying. "No. The Spanish Inquisition. I expected him to send me to the rack if I didn't answer him."

"*What* was he asking you?"

"Is that Jack? Do you two spend every second together?"

"Gage!" Jack snapped.

"He wanted me to tell him all about Tayla. Where, when, what. I told him what I remember, but he still went through my notes."

"What did he find out?" Jack asked.

"Nothing that I haven't already told you guys. But I think there was something he must have found useful because he started laughing. He skidded out of here on two wheels."

Jack and Kate exchanged looks, then he took his phone out of his pocket and brought up a name. "Answer, oh please answer," he whispered.

"What's he saying?" Everett asked.

"Nothing. Gotta go." Kate clicked off her phone.

Seconds later, Charlene's stressed voice come over his phone. "Oh, Jack. Tayla is—"

"I want you to leave town now. This minute. Take nothing unless you have some cash. Don't pack. Go! I'll get the kids from school. Do you understand me?"

"Yes," she said, then shut down the phone.

For a moment Jack and Kate just sat there, looking out the car windshield. His crew was putting in new windows of the house they were remodeling. Outside the car, everything seemed normal. Inside, the air was full of…of danger.

"What do we do now?" Kate whispered.

"Pray that we were in time," Jack said.

She nodded. What if Chet got there before they did? What if he saw Charlene? He said he wouldn't recognize her face, but was that true?

He was so obsessed with the kidnapping, would he bring it into the open again? Had Tayla given up her life to protect her niece for nothing?

"Let's go home," Jack said. "Sara…" He didn't have to say more. Kate knew what he meant. He called Charlene's husband and told him he was to get the kids, but gave no explanation.

The man didn't ask any questions. "I'll take them to my parents in Fort Myers."

"Good idea." Jack hung up and looked at Kate. "I think he knows everything."

"As he should," she said.

Jack got into his truck and they went home to Sara. They took only minutes to tell her what had happened. Jack said they should ask Everett hard questions.

"No," Sara said. "He's a pest but he's smart. He may put it together. My guess is that right now he's going through his files to find out what made Chet laugh."

Each of them called Chet's number but it went to voice mail. He wasn't picking up.

"I hope Chet isn't waiting at the school," Kate said.

Sara called the principal.

"Oh no," she said. "Their father took them away over an hour ago. A death in the family. Poor dears. Maybe you could pick up their assignments and send them on."

"No," Sara said and hung up.

They settled down to watch the clock. Every sound made them jump. Only Jack was hungry and he ate a bowl of cereal.

At ten, they went to their beds. There was no talk of Jack going back to his own room, but then, Chet's things were still there. He pulled out the couch in Kate's suite, stripped down to his underwear and got into bed.

When the doorbell rang at 1:00 a.m., they were still awake.

Jack got there first then waited only seconds until Sara and Kate arrived. "It's Flynn." His voice was bleak. What news did the sheriff have that was so urgent it couldn't wait?

In silence, they opened the door and he came in. He didn't speak until he was seated on a couch, across from them. They waited until he was ready to tell them what had to be awful news.

"Don't know how to tell you this," he murmured.

Sara was in the middle and she took the hands of Jack and Kate.

"Chet Dakon was killed in a car wreck."

They stared at him, blinking.

"I almost saw it. I was on my way to see Charlene and—"

"Charlene?" Sara said.

"I thought I'd talk to her about Tayla. Not that I could say anything good but—"

"Chet?" Kate whispered. "Killed?"

"Yeah. In Pembroke Pines. Eyewitnesses said he lost control and ran into the side of a building. He was doing about seventy. If he'd swerved left he would have hit oncoming traffic, but he went right and…" The sheriff shrugged. "Poor guy. They had to cut him out of that van but it was too late."

Sara had strong hands from years of boxing and Kate thought her fingers might be breaking. She had to work to disengage her hand from her aunt's.

"It was an accident?" Jack asked.

"Why wouldn't it be?" the sheriff asked.

"I need…" Sara said. "I mean… Chet was…"

They looked at Sheriff Flynn. "Right. I know you liked him. I better go. Broward takes the murders but leaves me cleanup for this. I got hold of some people in Atlanta and they'll be here tomorrow to get the body. They're going to do a full honors burial for him." He nodded at Sara. "You might want to go."

When he saw that she was on the verge of tears, the sheriff heaved himself up off the comfortable couch and went to the front door. He paused. "Is there anything I should know about this?"

"No," Kate said. "Nothing."

"Sounds like he was going too fast," Jack said.

"What I want to know is *why* he was racing to go down south. To see someone? He was only a few miles from Charlene's house. I know you saw Tayla yesterday. Did she tell you anything?"

"Just to mind our own business," Jack said.

"Seems like she'd want your help."

"I'm getting a lawyer for Tayla," Sara said. "If you don't mind, I need some time to…"

"Yeah, sure," the sheriff said. "I need to go home and get some sleep. I'll think more about this tomorrow." He looked at Jack and Kate in a way that was almost threatening, a warning maybe.

"We'll be glad to see you." Jack opened the door and closed it behind the sheriff.

SEVENTEEN

The next day was a Tuesday, a workday, but no one spoke of leaving the house. It was over a week since they'd seen Janet's poisoned, stabbed, and shot body. Kate's boss was in jail and a man they'd befriended was now dead. The stacks of boxes of files on an old kidnapping case filled a wall in the dining room. Sara's eyes were red from a night of crying, while Jack and Kate were so down they could hardly lift their eyelids.

Kate made coffee and Sara managed to brew a pot of tea so strong you could almost stand a spoon in it.

They weren't talking. But then, there was no need to speak of what they were thinking. It was their fault that Chet had been killed. If they hadn't stuck their noses into the murder of Janet Beeson, he'd still be alive. If they hadn't encouraged Everett Gage to keep looking… If they hadn't…

"We're going to the gym," Jack said.

"No, I need to work on—" Sara began.

"You're not," Jack said. "Whatever you want to do, you can't. We're going to go to the gym and hit the bags."

Kate went to her bedroom to put on her gym clothes. She could hear Jack in the living room of her suite. When she came out, he was in his workout gear and she nodded at him. She wasn't sure she'd ever fully smile again.

"I texted Flynn and he's sending a deputy over to get Chet's personal things. We'll leave the garage door unlocked."

"What about the files?"

"It seems that no one wants them. Flynn said he was told—I quote—'that old kidnapping case was Dakon's bugaboo. It has nothing to do with the Beeson case.'"

"But—" Kate began then stopped. "Right. It's their case. Has nothing to do with us."

"Exactly," Jack said.

Sara was at the truck waiting for them. Her sixteen-ounce red boxing gloves and gel hand protectors were in a Ringside sling bag. She had on long black pants and a green T-shirt.

Jack drove to the LA Fitness on University and they went into the basketball court to box. Kate was new at the sport but she'd picked it up quickly. "It's DNA and anger," Sara had said.

"I got the DNA from you and Dad, but no anger," Kate said.

"Your mom's depression bouts didn't make you angry?" Sara asked.

"And your uncles saying your naked knees were inspiring lust in men didn't do it?" Jack asked.

"How about your isolated childhood?" Sara asked. "And—"

Kate slammed into Jack's pads so hard he had to remove them and shake his hands to relieve the pain. "Okay, so maybe I do have a teeny bit of strong feelings."

Even with past experience, Jack wasn't prepared for the strength that came from the two women. Brutally hard slams, left then right. Uppercuts so violent the pads almost hit him in the chin. He could feel the muscles in his chest crying out to stop.

But the women went on and on, taking turns in three-minute rounds of hard hitting, then switching to the bags. None of them rested.

Only Jack added kickboxing. After thirty minutes of holding the pads for the women, he tossed them down. He released some of his own anger by kicking the big hanging bag so hard it bent in the middle. When the bag touched the wall, Sara and Kate got behind it and held it with their shoulders. Jack's strong kicks pounded into their bodies.

Leather hitting leather echoed through the gym. They didn't realize it but they had an audience. Outside the glass doors were half a dozen trainers and gym rats, all watching in awe. It didn't take much to know that they were witnessing a physical manifestation of fury.

Sweat ran down the faces of the three of them, the drops so big they could be heard hitting the wooden floor. Their eyes burned from the salt, but with the big boxing gloves on they couldn't wipe it away.

When Jack's legs were screaming in pain, he put the pads back on and the women starting hitting again.

It was two hours before they stepped away. Jack tossed the pads down and the women clasped the gloves between their legs and pulled them off. They looked at one another, dripping wet and shaking with fatigue. Jack opened his long arms. They went to him, arms around his hot, sweaty torso, and began to cry. Jack's tears joined them. They were a huddled threesome of unhappy, weeping people.

Outside the door, the watchers left. What they were seeing was too intimate to behold.

It was a while before they recovered enough that they could separate. Silently, they picked up gloves and pads and put them in their gym bags.

They didn't shower there. Sometimes they went to one of the big grocery stores nearby, but not today. Today they just wanted to go home and try to get back to lives that didn't involve dealing with a murder.

Jack had parked the truck in the covered parking garage near the exit.

"That was quite a show you put on in there. It was almost like you gave a crap."

They turned to see a man, midthirties, quite handsome, but his face was distorted by a sneer. "But you gave it up, didn't you? Walked away. Did you have too many suspects to choose from?"

Jack had stepped in front of the women, using his body as a shield. He was Megan's brother, Kyle, and he looked ready for a fight. "I don't know what your problem is, but we don't want it." Jack protectively started to usher the women to the truck.

Kyle didn't move. "I'm one of the people who hated Janet Beeson."

The three of them turned to look at him.

"Nobody hated her," Sara said.

The man's handsome face looked incredulous. "Nobody…?" he whispered. "Of all the stupid—" He took a breath.

"Your sister talked to us," Kate said. "You had problems in your marriage."

"Your kids painted *WITCH* on Janet's garage door," Sara said.

Kyle was shaking his head in disbelief. "Do you really not know? Everyone said you were good at uncovering the truth, but it looks like you know *nothing*." When a car pulled into the lot, Kyle jumped out of sight, waited until the car passed, then stepped back into the light. "Did you see that?" His voice was rising. "I have to hide. I can't be seen. Do you know why?"

"No," Sara said. "We don't."

"Because my ex-wife has a restraining order against me. I can only see my sons under supervision. And this is *all* Janet Beeson's fault." He paused to look at them. "I can see that you don't believe me. No doubt you've been told that I have a temper. That I'm jealous. You think you know all about me, and that Janet Beeson was a good person. Long-suffering and caring."

Another car drove in and Kyle stepped to the side. "My wife lost her phone for a day. I found it and there were texts from a man on it. She said she didn't know him, but I thought… I went crazy. I know it was that Beeson woman! She—" His lips tightened. "I can see that you don't believe me, but there are lots more like me. Talk to those teenage girls. The snotty ones. She nearly *killed* one of them."

"Janet did?" Sara asked. "But they said she saved them."

"Girls like that think evil is posting bare-breasted photos of their ex-friends online. They haven't lived long enough to understand people like Beeson. They don't even *know* the truth. But if you're as smart as people say, you can figure it out." He was walking backward. "Or are you going to let Tayla swing for a crime she didn't commit? I should have killed the bitch myself. I'd probably have more visitation rights if I were in prison." Turning, he hurried toward the exit.

"All this because your kids painted on her garage?" Jack was derogatory, disbelieving.

Kyle didn't look back. "Yes!" He ran across the street and disappeared around a building.

It was another silent drive. They were stunned by what Kyle Nesbitt had said. His sister had given the impression that her brother was unreasonable, a person of unpredictable temper. But then, Jack had said Megan was "a fluffy-brained giggler," so perhaps her perceptions weren't correct. On the other hand, maybe Kyle was one of those people who blamed others for their misdeeds. Like alcoholics who said, "I wouldn't drink if you didn't do ____." Fill in the blank.

Or maybe Kyle was telling the truth.

At home they saw that Jack's room had been cleared of Chet's belongings. Everything from shoes to shaving gear was gone.

"You'll like having your own bed again," Kate said.

"I guess," he answered. He'd liked seeing Kate first thing every morning. Had even liked sharing a bathroom with her. All her ointments and salves smelled good.

When they were clean, they met in the kitchen. Jack grilled burgers and vegetables while Kate and Sara put together the rest of the meal. Until they sat down at the table, there was only necessary talk.

"Do we believe him?" Sara asked as she reached for the mayonnaise. Her keto diet didn't allow carb-rich buns but she needed lots of fat.

"Not much," Jack said. "He seemed crazy angry to me. His wife was probably right to leave him."

"And a judge decreed that he shouldn't be alone with his kids," Kate said.

"But then, we worry that a judge will give joint custody to dumb Zelly," Sara said. "Judges aren't infallible."

"Whatever, we can't get involved," Kate said. "Chet…"

"Right. Chet. We can't risk something like that happening again," Sara said. "I called Daryl."

"And what did our illustrious sheriff have to say?" Jack asked.

"Chet's body is being transported back to Atlanta today. It seems that for years his colleagues said that the White Lily Kidnapping case would someday kill him. Consensus is that he was driving too fast while chasing another pointless lead and lost control."

"There won't be an investigation?" Kate asked.

"No. There's no suspicion of foul play. To the authorities, Janet Beeson's murder has been solved."

"They believe Tayla poisoned, stabbed, and shot the woman because of a lawsuit?" Jack asked.

"Yes," Sara said. "That seems to be the case."

Kate leaned back in her chair. "And what do *we* think happened?"

Sara took a deep breath and let it out. "That Chet was killed because he was too close to finding out the truth."

"Which is?" Kate asked.

They looked at one another.

"I think someone wanted to protect Charlene," Jack said.

"You don't think her husband…?" Kate trailed off.

"Fixed Chet's van?" Jack asked. "No. But maybe somebody did."

They knew he was thinking of his half brother, killed less than a year ago when the brake cables in Jack's truck were cut.

"It was *us*," Sara said. "*We* did it. Our snooping cost Chet his life."

"I guess this means we're going to, as Kyle said, *Let Tayla swing.*"

"Nothing else we can do," Sara said. "The best thing—the *only* thing—we can do now is go back to our lives." She looked at Kate. "You need to go sell some houses."

"That will be fun. They think it's my fault that Tayla isn't being set free. And I'm not getting her out of jail because I want to open a Medlar Realty."

"If you do want your own business, I'll back you," Sara said, but the look Kate gave her made her mumble, "Sorry."

"So we leave it alone," Jack said. "That right?"

"Yes, exactly right," Kate and Sara agreed.

But they didn't leave the table, didn't start clearing away. No one mentioned actually going back to their jobs.

"Wonder what he meant about those girls?" Jack asked.

"He said they probably didn't even *know* the truth," Sara said.

"I am curious to know what he was talking about," Kate said. "Of course it's all ridiculous. His own sister told us Kyle was a problem."

"And everyone knows about the deep love between siblings," Sara said.

Kate pursed her lips. "Are you talking about your brother? *My* father? With Charlene? Is this all *his* fault?"

Neither Jack nor Sara replied to Kate's rising temper.

"Too bad we can't invite the girls over," Sara said. "We'd just ask them…"

"Ask them what?" Jack said. "They told us everything. Nasty, spiteful, selfish. I still feel sorry for Janet."

"Britney tried to kill herself and Janet saved her," Kate said. "Where is the bad in that?"

"It sounds to me like Kyle Nesbitt is a sore loser," Sara said. "Blames others for his problems. One time a man told me that my novels caused his divorce. I told him my books were a symptom, not the disease."

"Bet that went over well," Jack said.

"Let's just say that I got away from him very fast."

For a few moments they were quiet.

"If we had those brats come here, we'd be telling

the town that we haven't stopped working on the case," Jack said. "And we'd be telling whoever may or may not have gone after Captain Dakon that we are actively involved."

"Too bad we can't do something to make them climb out their unbarred windows," Kate said. "Not our fault that they showed up here. Ha ha."

"We could set a giant trap," Jack said.

"Bait it with the juiciest gossip they've ever heard," Sara said.

Kate looked at Jack. "We could use *you* as bait. The girls seemed to want you more than the latest Prada bag." She waited for Jack to make his usually cutting reply, but instead, his eyes widened. "What is it?"

"Bait," Jack said.

"The boys," Sara said.

"Okay, so now I'm feeling left out. What are you talking about?"

Sara stood up and began cleaning the table. "If we could meet with the girls for something far removed from a murder, maybe we wouldn't set off any alarms."

Jack began to help put things away. "We'd say the case is closed. Done. Nothing more for us to do. We'd—as they say—get on with our lives."

"But we'd talk to the girls in secret." Sara smiled at Jack. "Think we can do it? Will they come?"

"Sure. But it'll cost me."

"Give them your Harley."

"Over my dead body," Jack said.

"Who?!" Kate shouted. She was still sitting and looking up at them.

"Mike," Jack said.

"Max," Sara said.

Kate squinted her eyes at them and they sat back down.

Sara spoke first. "Jack has some sixteen-year-old cousins who—"

"I told you I have lots of relatives," he said. "Sorry, go on."

"The boys are so beautiful they make Jack look like a troll."

Kate looked at him, expecting a protest, but there was none. Instead, he nodded in agreement.

"We'll just get them to come stay with us and ask those girls to show him around," Sara said.

"And you think these kids will come?"

"We Wyatts are a mercenary lot. Offer them enough and they'll move in with us."

Jack had to pay a heavy bribe to get the boys to come to Lachlan. They knew their cousin wanted something big so they made the most of it. The negotiation went on for thirty minutes. New iPhones and iPads, of course. Max wanted to work on Jack's construction crew during the summer. Mike wanted a summer survival camp.

Jack agreed to it all. Since the boys had only their learning permits, their mom gladly volunteered to drive them down from Sarasota that night. She said she'd stay in a hotel, see a movie, eat meals in peace, go shopping, then pick them up on Thursday morning.

"That should be enough time," he said when he hung up.

"I'd say that two hours would do it," Sara said.

"They're that good?" Kate asked.

"Oh yes," Sara answered.

"Interesting," Kate said. "I can't wait to see them."

When Jack said the boys were human beings, not things to be ogled, the women laughed.

The boys arrived that night and Kate had to agree that they were beautiful. Identical twins with all the Wyatt dark good looks.

Kate had seen a video of Jack as a child and she'd said he looked like an angel. Of course she'd added, "What happened to you?"

The boys were young enough that they still had that angelic aura—and they knew it. They were courteous, helpful, smart, and all-around adorable.

"It's an act," Jack said, sounding like he was jealous of the attention the women were giving the boys.

Kate called the principal and arranged for the boys to spend the next day at the high school. The story was that their family might be moving to Lachlan and they wanted to see how the twins fit in.

"I don't know," the principal said. "This is awfully short notice."

"They play football."

"And basketball," Jack said and Kate repeated it.

"Okay," the principal said. "I'll get the coach to show them around and—"

"We know Ashley, Britney and Madison so maybe they could escort the boys."

"That's highly unusual but—"

"They also run track," Jack said into Kate's phone.

"Sure," the principal said. "Bring them at nine."

Since Jack hadn't moved out of Kate's suite, the boys stayed in his room.

The next morning, he took the twins to the high school. He walked through the halls ahead of them— and it was a Red Sea parting. The boys weren't just beautiful but were also tall and athletic. And they had the air of being descended from Olympus.

The students stopped talking and flattened themselves against their lockers, gaping in openmouthed astonishment.

As for the boys, they smiled modestly, as though they had no idea what was happening.

"Knock it off," Jack murmured.

"Jealous, old man?" Max smiled at a dumpy girl who had probably never before been noticed by a boy. He picked up the book she'd dropped and handed it to her.

Mike winked at another girl who looked like she was about to faint.

"This doesn't last long," Jack said under his breath.

"You mean that someday we'll be old and alone like you are, cousin?"

"And we won't be able to get a hottie like Kate?"

"We saw the bed in Kate's living room. So you've spent nights near her but nothing happened? Are you *that* old?"

"Would you like me to show you how old I am? A few kicks to the side of your head should do it."

"Wouldn't want you to strain yourself. At your age you might not recover," Max said.

"About Kate," Mike said, "if you can't get her, mind if I try? She's more my age than yours. She—"

Jack gave them a look of such threat that they laughed—and caused a dozen girls to give loud sighs.

"Is that them?"

Ahead of them were the three girls. The other kids were plastered against the walls, but not Ashley, Britney, and Madison. They were the Queens of Lachlan High and they knew it. Their hair was shiny, faces made up like in a magazine, and their clothes were designer. They had no idea that never again in their lives would they have the extreme, unbreakable self-confidence they did at that moment.

Even so, at the sight of Jack's young cousins, their eyes began glowing like something out of a sci-fi movie. No green screen work needed.

"Uh," Jack said, looking at them. The magnetic poles of the earth didn't have a stronger attraction than those kids did to one another. However, Britney did glance at Jack in question. She seemed to say, *Three girls and just two boys?*

Jack turned and nearly ran out of the school.

At home, the adults weren't sure the girls would show up that evening. After all, they were still grounded from the last time they'd escaped. The parents had been bawled out by Jack, the sheriff, and the fire chief.

But the boys had been so sure they'd come that they prepared for a party. Jack drove them to the grocery and loaded up on disgustingly unhealthy food and drinks. At home, the boys calmly sat down in front of the big TV to wait.

The adults talked about what they were doing.

Would the killer know? Guess? Put it all together? They had no answer.

At 5:00 p.m., the girls showed up—and behind them came most of the senior class.

"I didn't expect this," Sara said in horror.

When Jack's mother, Heather, arrived, Sara hugged her in gratitude.

"I've been through three teenagers," she said, "so I know what it's like. Go. Do whatever. I'll take care of them. Here! Yes, you, Jason Lombard. Do *not* stand on the furniture."

Sara practically ran into the sanctuary of her library. Minutes later, Jack and Kate arrived and in front of them were the three girls. Their smiles were now sulks.

"We need to—" Madison said.

Jack cut her off. "If you complain, it will take longer. But if you answer our questions quickly, then you can go. Your choice."

The girls sat down, mouths closed. Sara and Kate sat across from them.

"We want to know more about your time with Janet Beeson," Sara said.

"She found me after I took my mother's pills," Britney said. The music was so loud they could hear it through the thick walls of the house.

"Tell us more about what led up to your attempt at…?" Kate's voice was full of caring.

The girls had their heads turned toward the music. Martyrs had suffered less than them.

Jack was standing and he leaned toward them. "If you don't talk to us, I'll take you out the back way and drive you home." He narrowed his eyes. *"And you'll never see my cousins again."*

The girls snapped their heads around to face him.

"We had a fight," Madison said.

"Why? Over what?" Kate asked.

The girls tightened their lips and said nothing.

Jack got his truck keys out of his pocket.

"We vowed to never speak of it again," Ashley said.

"Break that vow. Now," Jack said.

"They texted horrible things to me." Britney's eyes filled with tears. "I told you. They said I was fat and ugly and not up to their standards and my dad is poor and my mother smokes cigarettes. They said I should end my life." She put her hands over her face.

"We did *not* do that," Ashley said. "We've told her and told her that we didn't do it, but she won't believe us."

"But it's all true. I *am* fat. My mother *does* smoke. My dad—"

"Then who sent them?" Sara asked.

Britney said, "They were from *their* phones."

Kate looked at the other girls. "Did you ever lose your phones? Even for just a day?"

The girls stared at her like she'd asked if they'd forgotten to attach their arms.

"Then who did write those texts?" Jack asked. "Who dislikes you that much?"

The girls looked at one another, then back at him. "Jessica Williams. She is our main enemy."

Jack ran his hand over his face. "As opposed to minor ones, I guess. Why did you declare her to be at the top?"

"She used to be one of us," Madison said.

"But she stole Maddy's boyfriend."

"And of course the boy had nothing to do with it," Sara said.

Their expressions showed that they didn't understand what she meant.

"How did you get back at her?" Kate asked.

The girls said nothing.

"I'm guessing you posted naked photos of her," Sara said.

"She deserved it!" Ashley said. "She—" The looks of the adults made her shut up.

"How did you know it was us?" Madison demanded.

"Somebody told us," Kate said. "Okay, so Britney, you assumed they were going to do the same thing to you."

The girl nodded.

"And you didn't want to be thrown out and ripped apart," Sara said.

"No."

"And Janet Beeson saw you on Facebook taking the pills?"

Again, Britney nodded.

"After Janet found you, what happened?" Sara asked. "How did you get back together?"

"Our parents met with us," Ashley said.

"Glad to hear that your parents are at least somewhat involved with you three," Jack said.

Ashley spoke. "My mom told us that she had three best friends in high school and they separated because of silly arguments. She said she still missed them so she wanted us to stay friends forever."

"Our moms made us swear to forget the past and move on," Madison said. "We promised to never speak of it again, even when we were alone."

Britney said, "I still don't know who else could have told me I should kill myself." She cut her eyes at the other girls.

"It was *not* me," Madison said fiercely.

"Or me," Ashley said. "I told you that—"

Britney cut her off. "I forgive you both."

"Forgive us? But we never—"

"I think it was probably a fourth party that did it," Sara said.

The girls looked confused. "There are only three of us."

"And it was *no* party!" Britney said.

Sara coughed to cover a laugh. "I think you can go back inside."

The girls stood up and started firing questions.

"Are Mike and Max really going to move to Lachlan?"

"They don't have girlfriends, do they? We asked but they wouldn't answer."

"The coach said he'd give his right—" Madison looked at Sara. "He'd really like for the boys to be on our school's football team."

"No one knows the answer to any of that," Jack said. "Go back in there and in forty-five minutes I'll drive you home. And I'm going to talk to your parents. Again."

"That isn't fair," Ashley said. "We gave you information. We helped you."

"Yeah?" Jack asked. "What exactly did you tell us that we didn't already know?"

"That…" Madison was unable to give an answer to his question.

"I think Jack is right," Britney said.

"You *always* think Jack is right," Ashley said. "Did you tell him about the brides magazines you bought?"

"And how you write *Mrs. Jackson Wyatt* everywhere?"

"And—"

"Out!" Jack shouted and the girls left the room. He firmly shut the door behind them. "I feel sick."

EIGHTEEN

Heather helped them get rid of the kids. "Did you find out what you wanted to?"

Kate said, "We have no idea what you mean. If you're referring to the Beeson murder, that case is closed."

"Yes, of course," Heather said. "If I know nothing, I can't tell anything."

"Mom!" Jack said.

"Don't worry, my dear son. I'm sure you're just helping your cousins by shelling out two months' salary. By the way, if you don't keep those boys occupied, they'll get into trouble."

"I think I can handle a couple of kids," Jack said.

"That's what everyone thought about you." Laughing, Heather left the house.

The boys had gone to Jack's room so the three were alone.

"You didn't leave your spare truck keys in your room, did you?" Sara asked.

"Locked them in Kate's jewelry drawer and I put the key back where she hid it."

"You did what?"

"How about the door into the garage?" Sara asked.

"Bolted from the outside and I put the alarm on. They open a door and we'll hear it."

Kate was still glaring at Jack. "How did you find the key to my jewelry drawer? And when did you search for it?"

"When I needed a hiding place for the truck keys." He yawned. "Anyone else ready for bed?" He smiled at Kate invitingly.

Her eyes flashed anger. "I'm staying with Max."

"Then can I have your bed?" he shot back.

"Much as I enjoy hearing the foreplay of you two," Sara said, "I'm done in. Good night." She went to her bedroom and closed the door.

For a moment Jack and Kate stared at each other. Arguing wasn't as much fun without an appreciative audience.

In just a few days they had become used to each other's routines. Twenty minutes later they were in their separate beds and asleep.

Kate was the last one to get up the next morning. She put on black trousers and a lovely Elaine Cross top, and she was careful with her makeup.

"You're going to work today?" Jack asked when he saw her.

"As long as Tayla is in jail, I don't think they want me there."

"Then why…?" Enlightenment hit him. "For the boys? You're all dressed up to impress a couple of *kids*?"

"Ah. The jealousy of Jack Wyatt. Legendary. It—"

Sara spoke up. Loudly. "Do you think Janet had anything to do with those nasty text messages sent to the girls?"

"Just to one of them, wasn't it?" Kate got out cereal and a bowl.

"Easier to hack that way," Jack mumbled. He was still looking at Kate.

She took the stool next to him. "I don't know anything about hacking but I see it done on TV. I'm sure there's a way."

"How doesn't matter." Sara put a full plate of eggs, bacon, and toast before Jack. "What's important is *if* she did it."

"I don't see it," Kate said. "That was a really, deeply nasty thing to do. To try to get someone to kill themselves? Because of a kid mimicking you?"

"Kyle said she took away his children because they painted WITCH on her garage," Jack said.

"And how could she do that?" Sara asked. "Was she there in the courtroom? Did she bribe the judge? It all seems too farfetched to be real."

"Besides," Kate said, "everyone liked her. You heard the praise about her. She had a good effect on people's lives."

"It doesn't matter," Sara said. "Good or bad means nothing."

Jack and Kate looked at her.

"We've all met rotten people. In my long life I've met—" She waved her hand. "You aren't allowed to kill them, no matter what they do to you. They can beat you, steal all you have, whatever. People can do horrible things to you but you can't kill them. You can't even get them back by doing what they did to you. If they steal from you, that doesn't give you the right to steal from them."

"So Janet had no right to…?" Kate began.

"I mean that whoever killed Janet shouldn't have done it."

"But we do need a motive," Jack said.

Sara picked up a notebook off the kitchen desk. MOTIVE, she wrote at the top. "Tayla may be protecting her niece."

"Gil didn't want Janet helping his son's mother."

They looked at Kate. "It's possible that Janet did something to the teen girls."

"And maybe to Kyle Nesbitt," Jack said.

"That's four motives for murder," Sara said. "Not sure who would have done it for the girls."

"Britney's dad," Jack said. "I would have if it was my kid."

"That would mean that her parents *knew*," Kate said.

Sara was looking at the paper. "Did just one person know—if any of this is true, that is? Or did all of them know?"

"Maybe three of them killed her," Kate whispered. "Like in *Murder on the Orient Express*."

"So Tayla is taking the blame for a *lot* of people?" Jack asked.

"I wonder…" Sara said.

"What?"

"If there are others."

"Four motives and multiple suspects aren't enough for you?" Jack asked.

"Remember the woman with the crochet story?" Sara asked. "She came after we'd called the guards. They said she was really upset and wanted to tell us how good Janet had been to her."

"At the memorial service several people sang her praises," Kate said. "Janet the good."

Jack pushed his empty plate away. "Too bad we can't talk to them and see if they would tell the real truth. If there is an alternate truth to all this, that is."

They were silent as they thought about this. If they went around town asking questions, whoever had killed Chet—and probably Janet—would know.

Sara sighed. "There was a problem with a hairdresser. Maybe Kate and I could get our hair done and ask about Janet. We'll make it sound like gossip and nothing else."

Jack snorted. "I'm sure you'll be told, 'I hated her enough to kill her. Please put me on your list of suspects.'"

"So how do we get them to tell what they know?" Sara asked.

"Numbers!" Kate said loudly. "In the sexual harassment cases, no woman wanted to stand up by herself and say, 'He did that to me.'"

"Because she wouldn't be believed," Sara said. "For all our 'enlightened' age, if a woman says a man assaulted her, people will say it was *her* fault. She wore a tank top in 1986 so of course the man went after her. *Not* his fault. Hers!"

Jack and Kate waited for her soapbox tirade to finish.

"Sorry, just my opinion. You were saying?"

Kate continued. "That there's strength in numbers. If we could get them together, and one said a bit, then another—"

"Would say more," Sara said.

"So how do you get a passel of women together without setting off alarms?" Jack asked. "Advertise a murder evening? Put on a grand ball?"

Kate gave a little smile. "If only we knew someone who had something everyone wanted."

Jack seemed to understand and they looked at Sara.

She backed away. "Oh no, you don't. There will *not* be another open house! The town has seen every inch of where I live. There are photos of my bathroom on-line. The caption says—"

Kate grabbed one of Sara's novels from the book-case and waved it around.

"Oh," Sara said. "You mean a book club, don't you? One of those things where they ask me questions. What computer do I use? I say that I write by hand. Then a woman will start telling me that I could use a computer if I'd just have confidence in myself. Then another one says she'll help me…" She looked defeated. "Couldn't I just slice open a vein and bleed a quart or two?"

"You'd be given crackers afterward and they're not keto," Jack said.

Sara sighed. "Please not a book club."

Kate's face didn't soften. "We'll have an invitation-only book club and a reading of—"

Sara gasped. "Read from my own book?! I can't—"

Frowning, Kate got louder. "We will promise whatever we have to to get them here, then we'll drill them about Janet Beeson. No reading, no questions."

Sara's face lost twenty years of accelerated age. "Yeah? We talk about murder? I don't have to read a scene I wrote thirty years ago, then explain why I wrote it, and by the way, what do I do about writer's block—which they assume I have often?"

"Nope. None of that."

Sara stood up. "I'm going to make a pitcher of strawberry iced tea. Anybody want some?"

"I'll take a beer," Jack said. "And some of the leftover junk from the kids."

"It's too early in the morning for beer," Kate said. "And besides, it's bad for the boys to see."

"You dressed up for them, but I can't—" He broke off because Sara and Kate were staring at each other. "What?"

"The boys can deliver the invitations," Kate said.

"We'll dress them up."

"Jack's clothes should fit but they may be a bit small," Kate said.

"Small?" he sputtered. "Like hell they are. *I* can deliver the damned notes. We don't need—"

"Need what?" the twins asked as they entered the kitchen. They had bed-tousled hair, no shirts on, and low-riding jeans. They looked like tall angels come to life.

Jack saw the smiles on the faces of the women and stood up. "Get dressed, you brats."

When no one moved, Jack half pushed the boys down the hall. The giggles of the women echoed behind him.

* * *

It took them less than an hour to make out invitations to a book club for that afternoon. *Tea with Sara Medlar*, it read.

"It's very short notice," Kate said, "and it's a weeknight, but I still think they'll come."

"Unless they get suspicious," Sara said.

"Or more likely that will make them come," Jack said.

Sara and Kate looked up at him. He was wearing a shirt with a collar and black dress trousers.

"Where are you going?"

"The bank." Jack's face seemed to go pink.

Kate and Sara stared at him. They didn't believe him.

Jack sighed. "Okay. No bank. I thought I'd go see Leland."

Sara turned to Kate.

"Ten minutes," she said. "Meet you at the MINI."

"I don't think—" Jack began.

Sara spoke up. "*You* are going to talk to Leland alone? You're practically in competition for his wife's favor."

"And you'll lose your temper," Kate said.

"I won't do that. I—" He gave up. "Ten minutes, then I leave without you."

"Sure you will," Kate said. "Good one."

It took thirty minutes as they had to organize the boys. They couldn't drive without an adult with them and their mother was unreachable. The hotel said she was having a deep tissue massage.

In the end, they took Kate's car. Jack and Sara were

in the front bucket seats and the boys sandwiched Kate in the back.

"Let's drive home," Max said as he smiled at Kate. "Only take a few hours."

Jack made them get out near Valerie Johnson's house. "Just give her the invitation, then leave. You have other stops to make and you can walk."

The boys winked at Kate and waved goodbye.

"Their father needs to take them down a peg," Jack muttered as he drove away. He acted like he didn't hear the smothered laughter of the two women.

By the time they got to Southwest Ranches and pulled into the long drive to Charlene's house, they weren't laughing. Their minds were back on the murder—or murders.

The gate was open and they pulled in. No one answered at the house or Charlene's studio. They walked around, but the place had a feeling of abandonment. No one was there.

They were about to leave when a sleek blue BMW pulled in. The man behind the wheel was Leland, Charlene's husband. The look on his handsome face told of his misery and worry. And his fear.

He stood beside the car for a moment as he looked at them, unsurprised to see them. With a movement of his head, he motioned for them to follow him inside.

Kate thought how her first visit there had been so happy. Charlene had been laughing and talking about how wonderful her life was.

Leland sat down heavily on the couch, while the three of them sat across from him and waited in silence.

"If you need to talk to my wife, I don't know where

she is. She doesn't have a car or credit cards or her passport. I—" He ran his hands over his face, then looked out the window for a moment. "I guess you want me to tell you what I know."

"Yes, we would," Sara said softly.

He nodded. "I just got back from seeing Tayla."

Kate drew in her breath.

"Yeah," Leland said. "Exactly. She's taking the blame. She—"

He took a moment to compose himself. "I didn't know of the bootie until Tayla told me this morning." He blinked back tears. "Where do I begin? Janet—" He swallowed at the name. "Janet Beeson babysat our boys four times. We thought she was ideal, a sweet little old woman who said she'd taken care of hundreds of children in her lifetime. She said she used to teach school." He looked at them for verification.

"Not that we've heard," Sara said.

"Our kids and the Nesbitt boys were friends."

Again, Kate gasped.

Leland shook his head. "I guess you've met Kyle. He *hated* the woman. Said she complained about everything he did. Trees, noise, deliveries. Everything displeased her."

"The boys probably heard his complaints," Sara said.

"Kyle said he figured that's part of why the kids thought she was a witch." Leland looked up, his eyes brimming in tears. "I didn't believe him. I like Kyle, but he gets angry too easily. I felt sorry for the woman. She—" He took a breath. "So we said yes when she said she'd love to babysit for us."

"Did the boys like her?" Sara asked.

"No. But we didn't believe them either. We thought the Nesbitt kids had told them what Kyle said."

"The trickle-down effect," Kate said.

"Exactly what did your boys tell you?" Jack asked.

"That Mrs. Beeson poisoned them."

Jack, Kate, and Sara were too stunned to make a reply.

"I punished them for that. No iPads for a week. And to prove my point, I asked Janet to stay with them overnight." He paused. "Today Tayla said Janet probably drugged the kids so she could search the house."

"To get rid of them so she could look for secrets," Sara said.

"Yes," Leland said. "I think so."

"And she found a big one," Jack said.

"I didn't know it—and neither did Tayla—but Charlene had an old tin box with newspaper clippings and the pair of booties in it."

"I would imagine that it was so she'd never forget how fortunate she is to have her life today," Sara said.

"*Why* was Janet so angry at Tayla?" Kate asked.

"I think it was because Tayla sold Sylvia a house."

"You mean for charging too much?" Kate asked.

"No," Leland said. "A few years ago, Janet went away for a couple of months. While she was gone, Sylvia bought a house through Tayla."

"Why would that make Janet angry?" Kate asked.

"You ask *me*? My life is coming apart and I'm supposed to know why some old woman wanted to hurt people? Why did she bring up a twenty-plus-year-old…? I can't even call it a kidnapping. Charlene was sixteen years old." He stopped and looked away.

"Would you tell us?" Sara asked softly.

"I guess you deserve that." Leland took a moment to collect himself. "Charlene shouldn't have been left alone. I guess you know that just days before her parents left the country, she'd given birth to a stillborn baby, a little boy. She was still…" He made a motion around his chest area. "You know." He looked up. "My wife is brilliant at concealing pain. She said all the things her mother and grandmother wanted to hear. She told them she was glad it was over so that now she could *get on with her life.*"

"The catch phrase that everyone thinks buries the past," Sara said.

"Yes!" Leland's hands were in fists. "Her mother shouldn't have believed her, but…" He looked up.

"Tayla was coming," Jack said.

"Yes, that was it. The problem and the solution all in one person. Tayla was supposed to arrive about two hours after the parents left." Leland grimaced. "That whole damned family *loves* to dump responsibility onto Tayla. They think she can do anything, that she can solve any problem. So they turned over a frightened, half-crazy teenager to her—but they'd kept the whole pregnancy secret from her. Tayla walked into a monumental problem knowing nothing about any of it!" He got up, went to the window, and looked out for a moment.

When he turned back, he was calmer and he sat back down. "To be fair, I think Charlene actually believed she was okay. When Tayla left a message saying she'd be a day late, Charlene decided to get out of the house. She felt so good that as she left, she pulled up a bunch of flowers from a pot by the door."

"Lilies of the valley," Kate said.

Leland nodded. "Charlene slipped them into her pocket, then caught a bus to downtown. When she saw the sale signs at the store, she went inside. But…" He looked up, his eyes bleak. "Right away, she saw the children's department. Infant wear." He paused for a moment. "I think that's when she realized what she'd lost. She was holding an outfit for a little boy, for her son, when suddenly boxes and racks collapsed."

"And there was the baby," Sara said.

"Yes," Leland said. "A baby in a stroller, crying in fear at the noise, stopped at her feet. On its dress was embroidered lilies of the valley. It seemed to be fate. She picked the child up, put the flowers in the stroller, and went into the restroom. She changed the baby into boy's clothes, then fed it, nursed it. She was a mother and that's what mothers do." Tears were rolling down Leland's cheeks. "Charlene doesn't remember hearing any sirens. It was just her and the baby."

"And that's how Chet saw her," Sara said. "As a young woman who had *found her soul*."

"That's probably a very good description. I asked but she doesn't remember seeing anyone."

"How did she get the baby out?" Sara asked.

"The child went to sleep after it had nursed. Charlene held her under her big shirt and it looked like she was pregnant. She told the young police officer at the door that she was having contractions. He got her a taxi."

"Sorry to say this," Jack said, "but if she could come up with that lie, it sounds like she was beginning to realize what she was doing."

"Yeah." Leland's eyes were downcast. "That's exactly what the lawyer in me thought."

"I don't think Chet knew about a pregnant woman leaving the store," Sara said.

"Probably another rookie afraid he'd screwed up," Jack said. "Like Chet, he was afraid to tell anyone what he'd done."

"What about Tayla?" Kate asked.

"By the time she got to Atlanta, Charlene was… was…"

"Living in a dreamworld?" Sara asked.

"That's being kind," Leland said. "She thought the baby was hers and for a while, so did Tayla. When she realized what was going on… I give it to Tayla. It was a miracle that she managed to stay calm. She left the baby at a fire station, then she took Charlene home to Philadelphia with her. They never told anyone what happened. At least not until right before we married, then Charlene told me."

"And how did you react?" Sara asked.

"Shocked but it didn't change my mind about her. Love is love."

Sara was smiling at him.

"Looks like the family was right," Kate said. "Tayla *did* fix the problem."

"Right now, it doesn't feel like it was ever fixed," Leland said. "All the secrets were hidden inside a tin box that a vicious old woman went searching for."

For a moment, they were all quiet.

Jack spoke up. "Did Sylvia remodel the house?"

"How would I know that?" Leland was puzzled by the incongruous question.

"It might explain some things," Jack said softly.

"I don't know…" Leland wiped his eyes. "No. Wait. One time Tayla made a remark about Sylvia's new kitchen. It seemed to puzzle her. She said that when Sylvia bought the house she'd liked the kitchen very much, so why did she tear it out?"

When they were silent, Kate whispered, "Was my father…?"

"Yes." Leland's eyes bored into hers. "He was the father of my wife's baby. If it makes you feel any better, it was once and he never knew about the consequences. Tayla's mother said, 'Why ruin more lives?' She meant that your parents shouldn't be told, especially since you were on the way."

Leland stood up. He seemed to have finished as much of the story as he could handle. "I need to… I don't know what has to be done. Water things. Feed animals. It's Charlene's domain. She—"

Sara stood up. "Go take a shower. It'll make you feel better. We'll feed and water everything."

Leland didn't protest but went down the hall to the bedroom.

Quietly, the three of them left the house and walked to the barn. There were two horses there. Jack directed them in the feeding and watering and they went about it in silence.

When they got to the chickens, Sara spoke. "Sylvia. It always goes back to her."

"Why would Janet be angry because Sylvia bought

a house?" Kate asked. "I assume she had one when she lived with her husband."

"Sure, but it wasn't like the one she bought," Jack said. "What I want to know is why I wasn't asked to do the kitchen. Tayla and I are friends. She would have recommended my company to Sylvia to do the work, but she didn't call me."

"Your question is why you didn't get the business?" Kate sounded almost angry.

"All I'm saying is that this is yet another odd thing."

"Sylvia's husband was a plumber. I'm sure she knew building contractors," Sara said. "A new kitchen is nothing compared to Janet drugging kids so she could search for secrets. She was angry at Tayla and got her back by trying to hurt who she loves the most: Charlene."

"That makes no sense." Jack threw out meal to the chickens. "If she was angry at Sylvia, why didn't she go after *her*?"

They looked at one another.

"Maybe she did," Sara said.

"There's more to this than just a house," Sara said. "If I were writing it I'd have the house built on top of something valuable. *Touch Not the Cat*."

They looked at her.

"It's a wonderful old novel. Valuable Roman ruins were under the house, and people wanted the place."

"Chet wanted to tear up the floorboards of the Janet-Sylvia house."

At the mention of him, they were silent for a moment.

"Where did Sylvia get the money for the house? Her books didn't make any," Kate said.

"Not with those brutal reviews that put people off." Sara sounded bitter.

"So what's so damned valuable about *that* house?" Jack asked.

Sara looked at her watch. "I'd say we should go there now, but we have the, uh, the thing. The book club."

"I think you'd rather face a firing squad," Kate said.

Sara's eyes brightened. "It would sure be quicker."

Kate rolled her eyes and Jack laughed.

They got home at 3:30 p.m. In the shade outside the front door were three coolers. The tea shop beside the bakery had delivered boxes of sandwiches and cakes.

They carried them inside to the dining room and halted. Chet's big boxes of files were still stacked against the wall.

Jack got a handcart and began wheeling the boxes down the hall to the garage.

Kate and Sara did double time as they hurried to set up the table with food and drink. Loose tea was put into the pot. It just needed water for the brewing.

At five to four, Sara said she doubted if anyone was going to show up. She sounded hopeful. At one minute to four, the doorbell rang.

Jack said, "I'm going to look for the boys." In a very cowardly way, he scurried out the back.

They had invited four women, but six of them showed up and went straight to the dining table. Behind them, his shoulders bent, his face tired and drawn, was the only man.

"Eric Yates," he said to Sara. "I think you've heard of me."

"From the memorial service, yes." She gave no other information.

He followed the others into the dining room, where Kate had started pouring cups of tea. She stepped away to stand beside her aunt Sara. "Do you think they know what this is about?"

"I do. Men don't usually invite themselves to tea parties," Sara said. "So how do you plan to start this?"

"You sit over there and begin autographing."

Sara started choking.

"Just kidding. Do whatever it was that I saw you planning, then I'll take over. Unless you want to run the show."

"No! You. Not me."

They waited until 4:30 p.m. to begin. It was a solemn group, talking in subdued voices of gardens and the problems caused by the non-native iguanas.

When they were full of tea and smoked salmon and puff pastries, Kate directed them into the living room. They filled the two couches and the chairs, then looked expectantly at Sara.

She stood at one end, a pile of 4x6 index cards in her hands. "As I think you know, we have some serious matters to discuss. Things we don't want other people to know about. At least not yet."

She looked at the cards in her hands. "If you've ever read a murder mystery you know how important alibis are, so I'm going to give you one." She handed the cards to the woman on the end for her to start passing out. "We all understand that husbands want to believe they know all, but they don't want to listen. So I'll explain writing in a few sentences. Memorize them so you can parrot them back to your hubby or whoever asks and sound as though we really did have a book club meeting."

On the card was written:

> *There are no secrets to writing. Put your butt on a chair and* do *it. One sentence at a time. And* never *say you want to BE a writer. Say that you want to write.*

She gave the women time to read the cards. "The book club portion of the evening is now completed. You know all there is to know about writing. I turn this over to Kate."

Kate didn't tiptoe around. "We want the truth about Janet Beeson." As she expected, there was no answer. "It doesn't have to be a truth that you know for sure. It could be something that you believe. Your gut instinct. A feeling."

There was still silence. Kate looked at Sara as though to say that this had been a failure. But when she turned away, Valerie Johnson stood up and moved to stand before the window.

"I think Janet Beeson burned down my studio."

She paused for a moment as she gathered the courage to tell the rest of her story. "My husband had it built for our thirty-second anniversary. It was very cute, and north facing so the sun wouldn't hurt my eyes. He put in a powder room so I wouldn't have to go into the house. It was his last gift to me and he knew it. After he passed, I nearly lived in there. It made me feel close to him. It was in there that I created a baby blanket for the grandchildren I was never going to have. It won first prize in four contests before I entered it in the Lachlan fair."

She swallowed. "On the day I entered it, Janet smiled and said it was a good effort. She was letting me know that it wouldn't win. I didn't tell her about the other contests. I just let her think that was my first. When I won, I said, 'I guess the judges chose the best one.' It was arrogant of me. I should have been more humble. She looked at me—" Valerie crossed herself. "With hatred. Pure hatred. She made the hairs on my entire body stand on end. I was *afraid*. Over a local crochet contest!"

She took a moment to breathe. "Two days later, my studio burned down. The fire chief said it was an electrical problem. To me, it was like I'd lost my husband a second time."

Valerie's face changed from sorrow to anger. "The embers hadn't stopped smoldering before Janet showed up with a huge basket of supplies. The finest yarns, silk from India, and needles from Switzerland. Those needles! I think she ordered them *before* my studio burned down. I looked at her smiling face and I knew she had done it. I just plain *knew* it."

She sat down, tears on her face. The woman next to her put her arms around her.

They were quiet for a moment, then Lyn Kelson stood up. "I know that look of hatred. It chills the soul. Janet gave it to me when I accidentally dyed her hair green. My son was in the hospital and we didn't know if he was going to live or die. My husband and I took turns going to work and being with him. I wanted to be there the whole time but I owned the salon. I ran everything and my employees needed the work."

She looked down at her hands. "I messed up. It was a mistake. I was in tears of sorrow, but I couldn't repair her hair for forty-eight hours. I was afraid it would fall out."

Lyn took a breath. "Two weeks later someone bought the old hardware store across the street from me. Within a month a new salon moved in. They had equipment I couldn't afford and I couldn't compete. Six months later I had no business. Even my regulars went to them. But then, somebody sent them seventy-percent-off coupons."

Lyn paused. "I thought it was all just something that had happened. Bad luck. But a couple of weeks after I closed down, I saw Janet. She said she sure hoped the new salon didn't dye anyone's hair green. The way she said it made me think, *She did it. She bought the building and financed the new salon.*

"My suspicion was so outrageous that I didn't even tell my husband what I thought. But I couldn't get rid of the idea. I wanted to know the truth so I went to Tayla and asked if she could find out who had bought the property. It was a week before she got back to me. I was right. Janet Beeson bought the old store and the franchise that moved into it. It did so well that a year later she sold it and doubled her money. I work for them now."

Lyn's hands were fists. "I accidentally dyed Janet Beeson's hair green and in retaliation she put me out of business. And I was so afraid of what she might do next, that I told no one. Only Tayla knew."

Sara looked at Valerie. "Have you told anyone else about your suspicions?"

"I tried to tell my sister but she said I was crazy. She said, 'Nobody would burn down a building over a crochet contest.' I didn't mention it to her again, but soon afterward, Tayla came by. She gave me the Wyatt Construction card and said that Jack would rebuild my studio and he'd give me a good price.

"I got angry because she didn't seem to understand that it wasn't just a building but my last real connection to my husband. I didn't mean to but I said, 'Besides, she'll just burn it down again.'" Valerie didn't say any more.

"So you told Tayla?" Sara asked.

"Yes. She asked me what I meant and it all came spilling out. She listened. I think Tayla believed me."

"What did she say when you finished?" Sara asked.

"To keep my mouth shut. To tell no one anything. The way she said it made me obey her. Until tonight I've done nothing but sing the praises of Janet Beeson. Even in church, I lied. I—" Valerie couldn't go on.

They took a break after Valerie's revelation. The other women and Eric had sat through it in silence. Listening but saying nothing.

They brewed more tea and the rest of the food was soon gone. The looks on the faces of the people was *Who's next?* Who would be the next to confess and therefore make themselves a murder suspect? The rumor around town was that Tayla was just one of the suspects. More were to be arrested.

When one of the women passed Kate on the way

to the bathroom, she slipped a folded piece of paper into her hand.

Kate thought, *How juvenile. Just like kindergarten.* She shoved the note into her pocket and hurried to the kitchen to help Sara. "The blonde gave me a note," she whispered to her aunt. "Didn't read it yet."

"It's probably about Jack. Is he dating anyone?" She paused, a tray in her hands.

Kate opened the note and her face paled.

I'm Sylvia's daughter. Janet Beeson killed my mother.

"Get Jack back here," Sara said.

"I'm on it." Kate sent him a text. Home. NOW.

For the next hour, Sara and Kate worked to not stare at the pretty blonde woman sitting at the end of the couch. Three more women got up to tell their stories. None of them were as drastic as the first two and they were just as circumstantial. They'd done something Janet Beeson didn't like and right after that something bad had happened to them.

"Shades of the Salem witch trials," Sara murmured. The only one with any proof was Lyn. Janet had bought an old building and financed a hair franchise. When she sold it, she made a lot of money. Any lawyer would argue that the new salon was an investment, not an act of revenge. And certainly not after Lyn had proven that Lachlan needed a competent salon.

Jack returned but he didn't join the group. He entered Kate's suite through her bedroom and made sure she saw him. She excused herself and went to him.

"What's up?" he asked.

She handed him the note.

"Lisa's here?"

"I guess so. Any suggestion of what to do? Aunt Sara and I are afraid she'll escape. We don't want to say who she is or—"

Jack had left the room.

She followed him and watched as he went to the woman.

"Lisa, how good to see you." He practically pulled her upright, kissed both her cheeks, then led her into the suite and closed the door.

Kate looked at Sara. They were dying to hear what Lisa had to say.

Eric was telling how Janet Beeson gave him brownies laced with drugs so he became addicted again. Unfortunately, there was no proof of this.

One after another, Kate's and Sara's phones rang. Jack was giving them a way out.

"Yes, I do," Sara said into her phone. Jack had hung up but that didn't matter. She looked at the people in her living room. "Okay, we have to end this. You need to keep everything said here today quiet. Don't tell anyone what you've told us. Agreed?"

"Yes," Val said. "But I want to make it clear that I didn't kill her."

"Of course you didn't," Sara said.

"Did Tayla…you know?" Lyn asked.

"I doubt it." Sara was ushering them out the door. "Thank you for coming." She closed and locked the door behind them.

In the next second she and Kate were running to her suite. Sara was older but she was small and lithe.

She got there first and flung the door open so hard it almost hit Kate in the head.

Jack and Lisa were sitting across from each other. Sara sat beside him, and Kate by Lisa.

For a moment they stared in silence at one another. Now that they knew who she was, they saw that she looked like the photos they'd seen of Sylvia Alden. Tall, slim, naturally blond hair. And she had a kind of gracefulness about her that was like what they'd heard about Sylvia. At the same time, there was a light in her eyes that said she'd fit in well with a bunch of guys at the Brigade. She was a combination of beer and champagne.

"I don't know how much Carl has told you," Lisa said.

"We haven't met him." Kate found the photo on her phone. "Is this him?"

"Yes, that's Carl. He—" She stopped herself from finishing the sentence. "My mother wrote some good books."

"I've read them," Sara said. "They're autobiographical, aren't they?"

"One hundred percent. Mother said she had no imagination at all, but she had been blessed with such a colorful life that she didn't need one. It sounds good but it caused a lot of problems."

"With her father and brother," Sara said.

"Exactly. They are…" Lisa didn't seem to know how to describe them.

"Couldn't be worse than *my* family," Kate said. "Religious zealots. Think they know everything."

"My grandfather was the same and my uncle still is.

But their religion is money. My mother's problem was that she could organize the earth. She was brilliant at it and they *needed* her."

"Like my mother needed me to manage my little brother," Sara said, then looked at Kate. "Sorry."

"I think Tayla would say that you should have worked harder."

With a snort of laughter, Sara turned back to Lisa. "Sylvia escaped them through Tom."

"Oh yes." Lisa was smiling. "My father was a very handsome man and a darling. He used to say that if he'd been left on his own he would have been cleaning sewer lines when he was sixty. But Mother swooped him up and made him into a king."

Lisa looked out the window for a moment. "They were a very happy couple. On the day they left me at college, they went out to dinner and my dad said, 'It's your turn.' He said that she'd given up her whole life to her father, her brother, her husband, and her daughter. So now it was her turn to do whatever she wanted to—and he'd follow her."

"I like him," Kate said.

"She wanted to get away from her birth family," Sara said. "I understand that."

"Mother wanted to live somewhere warm and she wanted to write about her life. In secret."

"If they saw the way she portrayed them, they might sue her," Sara said. "Her portrayals of their greed aren't flattering."

"And it was all true. I was shocked when my parents told me they were selling the business and moving to Florida. I didn't know about the books until long after they left."

"I believe that in college you had other things on your mind," Sara said.

Lisa looked at her hands. "I didn't behave well in school. I had been raised with pink cashmere and white pearls. I was fascinated by the… I guess you'd say, the dark side of life. I experimented. I…" She pursed her lips. "It was bad. *I* was bad."

She paused. "I came out of it enough that by the time Dad died, I was in a better place. I was engaged to a man my grandfather and uncle thought was perfect. I was sad about my father but…" She shrugged.

"You had a life to live," Sara said.

"I did. It wasn't until after I married that I found out what true hell was. My husband was like my uncle. I could take that but what I couldn't abide was that they wanted me to be my mother."

"A manager."

"And an organizer. They wanted me to keep track of every business deal they made, but I inherited my father's ability with numbers, which is none at all."

"Bet they told you that you were a failure." Kate's voice told of her experience in that area.

"Every minute of every day. They never let up on me. I don't know if this makes sense but I blamed my mother."

"It's hard when you're constantly compared to another human being and always found wanting." Sara didn't look at Kate, but they knew she meant how she had been compared to Kate's father.

"I'm ashamed to say that for years I had little to

do with Mother. I told myself that she'd left me, that she wanted nothing to do with me. I pictured her as a Merry Widow, with no cares in the world. Dancing all night with no thoughts of me or Dad."

"But your mother had Janet," Sara said.

"You have done your research."

"We're finding things out," Sara said.

"Tell us about her," Jack said. "About Janet."

"I don't know where to begin."

"When you met her," Sara said. "Stories must begin at the beginning."

"That would be when I realized that I needed my mother. In spite of all my nasty thoughts about her, there was no doubt in my mind that she'd take me in."

NINETEEN

When Lisa arrived at her mother's house, she was wallowing in self-pity. It was like she was in a vat of black oil that she couldn't swim out of. It was all she could do to keep her face lifted enough to breathe. But she wasn't sure she wanted to do that.

Divorce. That's what her husband wanted. He and her uncle had been together when they told her. With exaggerated patience, they'd explained that she wasn't pulling her weight with the family business—and therefore she had to go. Out of the business, out of the marriage.

She was thirty-two years old and a failure at everything she'd tried. She'd been a teenage rebel, always angry about… She wasn't sure what made her angry. She just *was*.

In college she'd sunk very low, like barely-escaping-going-to-jail low. After she'd cleaned up her act, her uncle had introduced her to a young man who swept her off her feet. Oh! But it felt good to be *wanted*.

They were married in a beautiful—but economical—ceremony and had a lovely four-day honeymoon. When they got back, her husband and uncle had turned over what seemed to be the entire management of their businesses to her. She found out that at the wedding her uncle had signed her husband on as a junior partner. To Lisa, it felt like a bride price had been paid. Or in this case, it was that a husband had been purchased for her.

They were angry when she failed at everything they gave her to do.

"I'm like my father," she told them. "My mother is the controller."

At least that's how she thought of her mother. The woman who'd abandoned her to a husband and uncle who expected her to be what she could never be.

But when she was very coolly told that there was to be a divorce—her uncle said she would be given "severance pay"—all Lisa wanted was to be with her mother.

She flew to Lachlan, Florida, and fell onto her mother. As Lisa knew she would, Sylvia took over. She coddled and cosseted and listened to her daughter. Agreed with her, sympathized, and often brought her food so Lisa didn't have to face the world—meaning outside the one room.

Lisa was there for three days before her tears began drying up. The anger that was so natural to her began to spark a bit.

She got up early and walked around her mother's new house. It was quite nice, with big windows that framed a beautiful garden. The furnishings were subdued, quiet, tasteful. They showed her mother's conservative New England background.

The kitchen was new and in it was the dumpy little woman Lisa assumed was the housekeeper. She'd seen the woman often, but had paid no attention to her.

Lisa began opening cabinet doors as she searched for the cereal her mother had bought for her.

"I threw it out."

Lisa looked at the woman. "Threw what out?"

"That cereal. It has too much sugar."

Lisa was too shocked to speak. Her family's home—where she'd lived since she graduated—had several staff members. They did what she told them to. "Where is my cereal?"

"I told you. I threw it out."

That little fire inside her sent forth a flame. "Who gave you the right to—?"

"Good morning!" Sylvia said loudly. She kissed her daughter's cheek. "I see you and Janet have met."

Lisa's eyes were hard. "She threw out my cereal."

"Did she?" Sylvia sounded vague. "I'm sure it was for a good reason."

The woman gave Lisa such a look of triumph that she wanted to smack her.

"This morning," the woman said to Sylvia, "you are to have whole wheat pancakes, but just two of them. You know how you have to watch your weight. And one third of a cup of sliced strawberries. I measured out your coffee. Only half a cup today. Mustn't get too wound up, what with all the turmoil of the last few days."

"What the hell?" Lisa muttered. "Mother! What is going on?"

"Thank you, Janet," Sylvia said. "That sounds lovely. Perhaps after breakfast I may work in my garden."

"May" as in asking permission.

"That will be all right." Janet handed Sylvia a stack of papers.

At the grimace her mother made, Lisa took the papers and read them. They were printouts of the most recent reviews of her books from over the Internet.

"Should give up writing."

"Worst book I've ever read."

"I want my money back."

Lisa dropped the papers into the trash bin.

"I'm sorry, Janet," Sylvia said and retrieved the papers. "Of course I'll read them. I know they are constructive criticism and I can learn from them."

With her back to Janet, Sylvia mouthed *Shut up* to her daughter.

After the meager breakfast, Janet told Sylvia how long she could work in the garden, and how much time she could spend writing.

It wasn't easy, but Lisa managed to stay quiet.

At 4:00 p.m., the odious little woman left the house.

"Come on," Sylvia said. "We have about an hour."

They went to Sylvia's bedroom. She stretched out on the bed, her daughter beside her, as they did when Lisa was a child. "Now tell me your latest thoughts about your divorce."

"Screw that." Yes, indeed, fire was coming back into Lisa. "Who the hell is that horrible woman?"

Sylvia seemed to wrestle with her own mind. What to tell? What not to tell? "Shall I start at the beginning?"

"Yes."

"All right, but are you grown up enough to keep secrets?"

"I believe I am."

"You know how my novels are autobiographical?"

"Yes. It was embarrassing to read about myself, though. I wish you'd lied, or at least sugarcoated it."

Sylvia kissed her daughter's forehead. "After your dad died, I ran out of the bio, the *life* part. With him gone, I no longer had a reason to be social. I just wanted to stay home with my garden, play with those adorable Nesbitt boys, and write. But *what* did I write that would be interesting to a reader? Baking brownies with the neighbor's children?"

"So what was your solution?"

"I got Janet to tell me about her life."

"She doesn't seem like someone who's very interesting."

"Oh, but she *is*. She is fascinating. She has the oddest philosophy of life. She believes that other people make her do bad things."

"Lots of people believe that."

"But not like she does. She has no internal scale."

"What does that mean?"

"If you murder someone, your punishment is worse than if you are, say, rude to a person, right? But not to Janet. A big transgression against her carries the same weight as something minor."

"Everyone is quirky."

"How do I explain this? Say you're in the grocery store and a woman hurries forward and gets in front of you. What do you do?"

"Give her a dirty look."

"But you don't slash her tires, do you?"

"Of course not."

"What about finding out who the woman is, then leaving notes in her car that are supposedly from other women to her husband? Or posting nasty comments from the husband about his boss so the boss can see them?"

"That didn't really happen, did it?"

"Yes. Janet did all those things to a woman who pushed in front of her at the grocery."

"You can't stay here with someone like that. You have to leave. Now."

"Not yet. I'm finding out too much to quit. I just have to be careful of what I ask her and how I say it. Above all, I have to be on her side and give her lots and lots of sympathy."

"Sympathy? For what?"

"Janet lives in a world where she sees others as being out to get her. They *want* to hurt her. They think about her all the time and plot to cause her downfall."

"She certainly sees herself as important, doesn't she?"

"You have no idea! Empress of the World. The Center of the Universe."

"Mother! She is a horrible person."

"She is, actually."

"But you nearly *live* with her."

"I consider it research. Like Nellie Bly."

Lisa looked blank.

"She was a nineteenth century reporter who did things like commit herself to a mental institution so she could write an exposé. I want to write a true crime novel about how an ordinary person can be the epitome of evil."

"Evil?"

"Her parents very conveniently died before they could cut her out of their will."

Lisa looked at her mother. "You think Janet *killed* them?"

"I don't want to believe that, but sometimes I think she is capable of it."

"Mother! You have to get out of here. You can go back home with me. We can—"

"No," Sylvia said softly. "I can't leave now because, well... The secret part is that Janet has a hold over me."

"You? You haven't done a bad thing in your life. You—" Lisa paled. "But *I* have. I've done..." She didn't want to say things out loud. Transporting drugs. Selling them. Back then, she did what she thought was necessary to pay for her habit. "Is Janet threatening you about me?"

Sylvia didn't directly answer her daughter's question. "Something I learned a long time ago is that things happen for a reason. I was very lonely after your father died. Then this woman showed up and introduced herself. She told me I was the author of her favorite books and she'd worked hard to find me. She seemed quite proud that she'd been able to sleuth me out. She went to a conference and asked—" Sylvia waved her hand. "How she found me doesn't matter.

Janet said she was moving to Lachlan and she and I were going to become best friends, that we were going to start doing everything together."

Lisa gave a snort. "Didn't her presumption put you off?"

"Oh yes. I was quite firm in telling her that I wasn't interested. I needed a friend but she wasn't exactly my type."

"Understatement," Lisa muttered. "Why didn't she take the hint and leave you alone?"

"But darling, empresses think they're honoring a person with their presence. Truth is that I wavered between being amused and horrified by her—but the horror won out. As kindly as I could manage, I told her no."

"Then what?"

"Janet is brilliant at finding out things about people. Like how she got past the so-called secrecy of my pen name. I don't know how, but she found me. Anyway, she went away for a month and when she returned, she had evidence about…about…"

"Me." Lisa thought about who knew of what she'd done and how to find it out. A bit of research into the records of her roommates, a talk with their angry landlord, a police record or two, and a lot could be discovered. After a serious near bust, they'd dispersed, and Lisa got clean. But she knew Phil was living in LA. He always was a snitch. Give him a hundred bucks and he'd tell all. "She threatened you with me, didn't she?"

"Yes," Sylvia said. "But it's okay. In a way, she and I are good together."

"She bosses you around, tells you what to eat, what to wear."

"I know, but in return I listen to her. She can talk for hours about the awful things that people have done to her—and how she has repaid them. I write it all down. I have nearly a book's worth now."

"What if she finds out what you're writing?"

Sylvia gave a little smile. "It's all well hidden. Not a scrap of paper or anything on a computer. Only one tiny flash drive."

"How can anything be hidden? She's everywhere."

"I did a bit of remodeling on this house and let's just say that I have a place no one will easily find."

"You can't—"

Sylvia hugged her daughter. "I'll tell you another secret, something I've been working on for a long time. As soon as your divorce is final, you and I are going to go away. Out of the country. We're going to change our names, our identities. Your father and I did well when we sold the shop and my books make some money. When my crime novel comes out, I definitely don't want to be where Janet can find us."

"But—"

"It's going to be okay. I have a friend here in Lachlan who is going to help us. She was my Realtor who sold me this house." Sylvia paused. "Janet was furious when I bought it! I did it while she was out of town. She went away to do something dreadful to her ex-husband. That poor man! She never leaves him alone. He can't escape her. That's how I know that you and I can't continue to live in this country. Especially not after the book comes out. But Tayla will help us. She's had some tough times in her life so she understands."

"I don't like this," Lisa said. "Let's leave now. Today."

"No, not yet. Your divorce has to be final. We can't have my brother's lawyers searching for us. In another few months, you and I will fly away and never return. We just need to choose a place. Italy? France? Maybe a country house in England."

"From the sound of all this maybe we should move to Afghanistan. A war zone might keep her away."

"It's going to be fine. You'll see. I've been planning this for a long time. Let's go to England and marry you off to a duke."

"I'd rather have a blacksmith. I love those arms."

Sylvia laughed. "Come on, let's go eat. I'm starving."

"How about two whole wheat pancakes and half a cup of coffee?"

Sylvia groaned. "Wherever we end up, let's stop in Paris and eat our weight in pastries."

"Agreed," Lisa said.

With arms linked, they went to the kitchen.

TWENTY

Lisa abruptly stopped her story and looked at the others. "The next day I flew home and on the next, I turned myself in to the police."

Kate gasped.

"I couldn't bear for my mother to have to endure that woman because of what I'd done. I figured I'd serve my time and when I got out, Mother and I would go away. She'd just have to wait a while before her book could come out. I thought she was right when she said it was all going to work out."

"But it didn't," Sara said.

"No." Lisa had tears in her eyes. "I never saw my mother alive again. When I was told that she'd killed herself, I started screaming that she didn't do it. But no one believed me."

"That's because they assumed that a woman without a man is a miserable being," Sara said. "Of course she'd want to end her life."

"How long was it before…?" Kate asked. "You know."

"Before I was taken into custody? Just weeks."

"And when you got out, you went looking for Janet," Jack said.

"No, I didn't. The woman terrified me. I wanted to put all the bad behind me. I got a job. I got away from my relatives." She stood up. "What happened to me doesn't matter. Besides, the rest of the story is Carl's. You should talk to him."

"We'd love to," Sara said. "How do we reach him?"

"You can't. The poor man has had years of experience in escaping Janet's wrath so he's good at hiding. He'll contact you when he wants to." She walked to the front door and the others followed her.

"There's one thing we haven't spoken of," Kate said. "Who killed Janet Beeson?"

"And Chet Dakon?" Sara added.

"Don't you think Janet orchestrated her own death? She was like an evil plant and she nurtured herself."

It was obvious Lisa wasn't going to answer their questions. She left and they locked the door behind her.

There was no need for words. They knew what they had to do next. They practically ran to Jack's truck. He tossed a couple of toolboxes in the bed, then got in, and backed out of the garage.

"Should we tell him?" Kate didn't specify who she meant, but they knew.

"Don't want to," Sara said, "but there's that damned *tampering with evidence* thing."

Kate took out her phone and sent a text to Sheriff

Flynn. We have news. On our way to Janet's house. "That should do it."

"He'll probably beat us there," Jack said.

He did. When they got there, the sheriff was standing in front of the locked gate, key in hand. "I was in the neighborhood." He nodded toward Kirkwood Avenue. Tayla's big house was down there. Had he been searching it?

They waited for him to explain but he didn't. He unlocked the gate and Jack drove through.

Jack planned to use a laser beam to measure the rooms. If he put the sizes on paper, they'd be able to find where there was concealed space. But first, he looked around with a builder's eye.

Right away, he found a wire hidden in the crown molding in the master bedroom. "I suspected this. The room was bugged." He looked at Kate and Sara. "Anything that was said in this room was heard and probably recorded."

The women looked at each other. That meant that Janet had heard everything Sylvia and Lisa said. Sylvia had said she despised Janet so much that she was writing a true crime book about her. Sylvia said Janet was evil. And Janet heard Sylvia's plan to run away, to hide from her.

Janet also heard that somewhere in the house was a secret room. But where? They continued searching.

It was Sara who figured it out. "The unread romances," she said as she stood in front of the tall bookcase. "Janet said Sylvia was her favorite writer. I wondered why the spines weren't broken from being read again and again."

Jack turned his laser on the two bedrooms that were behind the bookcase. "Clever." In the next second he was searching behind the books looking for the latch.

Sheriff Flynn turned to Kate. "What's the story that led to this?"

Jack answered. "Sylvia had some out-of-towner remodel her house so she could create a secret room. She needed to hide things from Janet."

Sheriff Flynn blinked. "That's a jump from Janet the Good, Sylvia's best friend, to hiding things from her. So maybe your book club wasn't about putting your butt on a chair after all?"

Sara smiled that he'd already heard about that. "Maybe not."

Jack stopped searching and grinned. There was a click and the bookcase swung out. He didn't so much as glance inside but turned to the sheriff.

"Don't touch anything. Not any surface. Nothing."

They nodded in understanding, then stepped inside.

Sylvia'd had a foot taken out of each bedroom and had repositioned two closets. It gave her a room of about six feet by twelve.

What was in it now had belonged to Janet. Along one wall was a long table with four big computers, each with a separate screen. A shorter table held six laptops and half a dozen iPhones. A single chair was used for all of them.

"Wow," Kate said. "She was a super techie."

"Which one was?" the sheriff asked.

"Janet," Sara said. "I bet Sylvia had a comfortable chair and a single laptop in here."

"So what's on all these?" the sheriff asked.

"I don't know for sure," Sara said, "but my guess is bad internet reviews that Janet wrote. And a way to send texts from the wrong person. Lots of messages that are lies. All sorts of things that destroy lives."

There was a curtain in the middle of the facing long wall and a button beside it. Sara put her shirttail over her finger and pushed the button. The curtain started drawing open.

"I told you not to—" the sheriff began, but cut himself off.

The four of them stood there, staring with wide eyes. The wall was a shrine to Sylvia Alden. Photos, framed and not, were hanging on the wall. Sylvia and Lisa. Sylvia and Tom. Tom holding a young Sylvia in front of a shop named Alden Classics.

In the center was a framed photo of Sylvia and Janet smiling at the camera. Short, plump Janet was leaning toward the elegant Sylvia. "A lady and her maid" was what they'd heard and it suited the picture perfectly.

"Her relatives came and got the furniture," the sheriff said.

"They probably threw these out," Sara said.

The sheriff turned full circle to look at the room. "You know, don't you, that this makes things worse? You're proving that Tayla had a lot of reasons to kill Janet Beeson. The woman would have ruined Tayla's life, as she did to others. And if Tayla knew what Janet did to other people..." He looked at them and Sara gave a curt nod. "All this makes it understandable why Tayla killed her over something as small as a lawsuit."

"We think Janet killed Sylvia," Jack said.

The sheriff shrugged. "What does it matter now?

They were friends, fell out, one poisoned the other. They're both dead so no one can be prosecuted. That reporter is the one who's going to benefit the most from all this. He'll write everything with drama and fireworks. Damn who he hurts."

Sara kept looking at the wall of photos while the others turned to the computers.

"I bet we could find out who Janet terrorized in Lachlan," Kate said. "Maybe there'll be some evidence that Kyle Nesbitt was innocent and he'll be allowed to get his family back."

"And Charlene will—" Jack stopped talking. Chet had paid the ultimate price for nosing around about the White Lily Kidnapping so there was no reason to add to it.

"What about her?" the sheriff asked.

"Nothing," Jack said. "She's upset about Tayla's confession."

"You're not good at lying." Sheriff Flynn was frowning. "You three want to tell me what you've been doing?"

Jack and Kate were silent.

"No." Sara was still staring at the photos. "There's no need to tell anything. Janet Beeson was a horrible person. She hurt a lot of people."

"Tayla still shouldn't have killed her." The sheriff's voice was sad. Tayla was his relative.

"Right." Sara put her arms up, elbows out, as though smoothing the back of her hair. When she pivoted around, an elbow hit three photos and knocked them to the floor. Sara let out a yelp of surprise.

The noise in the closed-in room was startling. In

a swift gesture, Sara used the tip of her shoe to kick something toward Jack. He put his foot over it.

"I'm so sorry," Sara said. "Should I pick them up?" She was a study in innocence.

"Leave them," the sheriff said. He was looking at them in suspicion, but could see nothing wrong. He held his arm out to the door. "I think we should leave."

"Of course," Kate said, then put her hand on the sheriff's forearm. "How are you holding up under all this? There must be a lot of pressure on you."

"Thanks for asking," he said. "I'm okay, but my wife…" He kept talking as he led them out. He didn't notice that when Jack checked his shoelace, he palmed the tiny flash drive that Sara had sent scurrying toward him.

When they were in the truck, Kate said, "Okay, what did you two do?"

"I have no idea what you mean," Jack said.

"Elbows hitting the pictures? Aunt Sara screams? Out with it!"

Smiling, Jack took the flash drive from his shirt pocket and handed it to her.

"Think it's what Lisa was looking for?" Kate turned to her aunt.

Sara shrugged. "It's in half the mysteries I've ever read. Picture frames are great hiding places, and considering Janet's vanity, what wouldn't she hurt?"

"The photo of her and Sylvia," Kate said. "She might burn Lisa's and Tom's pictures but not her own."

"Exactly what I thought," Sara said. "I kept staring at that picture with its wide wooden frame and the lower left corner seemed to be smoother than the other ones."

"Fingers touching it," Jack said.

"My thoughts exactly."

"So you sent it skidding, the flash drive fell out, and—"

"And I hid it," Jack finished.

"Now what?" Kate asked.

"Now we go home and open it and I hope we see Sylvia's book," Sara said.

"But…" Jack trailed off. He didn't need to say what he was thinking. Sylvia's account of all the horror Janet had done wasn't going to clear Tayla. As Sara had said, *You can't kill people no matter how horrible they are.*

Kate clasped the flash drive in her hand. "Maybe this will satisfy Everett enough that he'll forget about the White Lily Kidnapping."

"Ha!" Sara said. "He'll write about Janet, then about Charlene. He'll make a trilogy of it. Base a career on it. He'll—"

Kate put her head on her aunt's shoulder. "We'll do what we can."

"Yeah," Jack said. "All that we can."

When they got home, Kate and Jack sat on each side of Sara as she put the flash drive into the side slot of her computer and brought up the contents.

"A woman after my own heart," Sara said. "Sylvia used WordPerfect."

The title page read *Evil at Home*.

"Not pulling any punches, is she?" Kate said.

Sara flipped to the first page. *Janet Beeson says she wasn't born evil but I don't believe that. She left too many tears in her wake. Too many dead bodies. What else is the definition of evil?*

The three of them drew in their breaths.

Sara closed her computer lid.

"Can she do that? Use a person's real name?" Kate asked.

"No," Sara said. "Not while the person is alive. No wonder Sylvia was planning to leave the country. But then, maybe she was going to change the name in the book to something fictional."

"Do you believe she was?" Jack asked.

"No. I think Sylvia Alden had come to the point where there was only one thing in the world she cared about: her daughter. If she could get Lisa out of danger, I think Sylvia planned to expose Janet."

"To keep her from hurting others," Kate said.

"That would be my guess."

"Mind if we read more?" Jack asked.

"I think I should print out two copies," Sara said. "Jack and I get one, and Kate, you can read on the screen. We'll make notes and later…"

"We'll share our horrors?" Kate suggested.

"Exactly."

Sara ran the 321 pages off on her fast black-and-white printer, then handed Jack his copy and gave Kate the laptop.

They went to their separate bedrooms and began to read.

After two hours, Sara went to the kitchen. Kate heard and joined her. Jack came in behind them.

"Where are you?" Sara asked.

"She just killed her parents," Jack said. "Traveled

to the ski lodge under a false name, pushed them over a cliff, and watched them sink into the snow."

Sara looked at Kate. "She's planning to beat the other girls at winning Carl."

They turned to Sara. "I skipped ahead to Charlene and Gil. I think it's possible that they mur—"

"Don't say it!" Jack said. "Tayla is taking the blame. She—" He stopped. "I just need a sandwich then I'm going back to read more. Why did nobody tell anyone what this woman was doing?"

"She was threatening them where they were most vulnerable," Sara said. "If someone had done that to me about you or Kate, I'd pay and keep quiet."

"I guess," Jack said.

Sara handed him a fat BLT and a can of beer and he went down the hall to his bedroom.

Kate and Sara made salads and read while they ate.

No one turned out a light until well after midnight, which was why they were still behind closed doors at ten the next morning. Jack was just waking up; Kate was dressing; Sara was writing her thoughts about Sylvia's book. It hadn't been finished and Sara knew she was the one to do it.

The doorbell went off like an explosion, the sound filling every room in the house.

"Whatever this person has to tell, we already know it," Jack said as he hurried to the door. Sara and Kate were close behind him. "It's Flynn." He opened the door.

The sheriff didn't wait for permission to enter but plowed ahead. At ten feet in, he turned. "Tayla is to be released."

"Thank heaven," Kate said.

"Why?" Jack and Sara asked.

"Carl Olsen confessed to all of it. He poisoned, stabbed and shot his ex-wife."

"Any evidence?" Jack asked.

"He has the gun that shot her and a detailed knowledge of every minute of that morning. And he has masses of motive. He has a box full of legal papers. The poor guy was pursued by Janet all over the world. He said he couldn't take it anymore and ended it."

"So why'd he let Tayla take the blame?"

The sheriff looked at them. "He says he was waiting for something to happen before he came forward. He wouldn't say what it was, but I think he was waiting for you lot to find out the truth about his ex."

Sara led the way to the living room and sat down, Jack and Kate beside her. The sheriff took the opposite couch. "So he really has been watching us."

"Every minute of every day, as far as we can tell."

"What happens now?" Kate asked.

Sheriff Flynn looked at his hands for a moment. "Remember that Carl Olsen used to be a really big guy? He's thin now because he's dying. Cancer. The doctors can't believe he's been able to move around for the last month. Most people would be in a hospital bed with tubes in them at this point."

"Hate," Sara said. "An emotion as strong as love— you'd be surprised how either one can keep you going. Where is he now?"

Sheriff Flynn took a breath. "That's why I'm here. He's in the hospital and he's named you three as his next of kin. He'll only talk to you. He said he wants to talk to people who can *understand*."

"This is for his trial?" Kate asked.

The sheriff's look answered that. Carl wasn't going to live long enough for a trial. "My car's outside. I'll drive you there."

"But no siren," Sara said.

The sheriff didn't smile.

Sara and Jack left to get dressed, but Kate stayed. "How's Tayla?"

"Crying a lot. She held it together for a long time but when Carl confessed, she collapsed. And before you ask—because I don't know anything about it— Tayla called Charlene. She's coming home from her 'vacation.'"

The sheriff got up and for a while, he looked out the window, then back to Kate. "The big shots at the head office saw Carl's papers, and heard his confession. They think he has more motive than Tayla did with her lawsuit from Janet."

"So they don't need to know any more about what else Janet Beeson did? About what she knew of the kidnapping?"

"That's my thoughts. What about you guys?"

"I don't have to consult them to know that we agree with you on this."

"What about that reporter? Think he'll keep the details to himself?"

"Aunt Sara will take care of him. I have no idea how, but I'm sure she'll fix it. The outside world won't hear about Lachlan's secrets."

The sheriff let out a sigh that seemed to deflate him.

He seemed to blink back tears. Tayla and Charlene were related to him and he loved them.

Minutes later, Sara and Jack returned and they got into the sheriff's car and he drove them to the hospital.

TWENTY-ONE

In the big white bed, Carl looked even smaller than
he had the other times they'd seen him. His eyes were
sunken, his skin gray and thin.

Sheriff Flynn left them at the door and the three of
them took seats by Carl's bedside. There was no need
to make introductions.

"I want to tell you about her," Carl said.

"I think that after what we've been through, we deserve that," Sara said.

For a moment, Carl put his hands over his eyes.
"Where do I begin? First, you need to understand that
Janet liked to win. Winning was what ran her life. She
set a goal then worked to achieve it. She didn't care
how she won, just so she did."

"It seems that you were a trophy," Sara said. "We
found Sylvia's book."

Carl closed his eyes for a moment. "Yes, I was. Janet
worked in a small, menial job in the building I owned,

but she didn't need the money. She just liked to spy on people."

"Liked to learn their secrets," Sara said.

"One fateful day, she was in a restroom with half a dozen women. They were plotting about me. How to get me. Fat, plain-faced, boring old me."

"But you had a bank account and that's what they wanted." Sara spoke from experience.

"Yes," Carl said. "That was the *real* prize. The problem was that they ignored Janet. They didn't consider her competition. She vowed to *win* no matter what she had to do. Never mind that the prize was a human being."

"Let me guess," Kate said. "She researched you."

"Went to the town where I grew up and asked people about me. What I like, that sort of thing."

"She did that with Gil and Lisa," Jack said.

Carl smiled at him. "You three have been so clever in uncovering the truth."

"What happened after the marriage?" Sara asked.

Suddenly, there was light in Carl's eyes. They were seeing some of the hatred the man had felt for years. "To her, marriage meant that she'd won so she didn't have to make any more effort. She hated sex and affection. She didn't cook. Didn't clean. Didn't want to go anywhere. She spent a lot of time on her computer, and I had no idea what she was doing."

He paused. "It made me sad. My idea of a marriage is what I'd had with my first wife: love and affection and great heaps of delicious food. But it was okay with Janet. It wasn't bad, just sort of nothing."

He paused. "But then, a few months after the wedding, one of the women in the office, Elaine, brought me brownies. I took them home to share with my wife. I was shocked when Janet became furious. She didn't yell, just looked at me with hate in her eyes, then dropped the brownies into the garbage disposal.

"The next day Janet came to the office. She was so smiling and happy that I thought everything was fine. But two hours later, Elaine was rushed to the hospital. She had to have her stomach pumped. She nearly died.

"At the time I didn't connect it all. I never thought anyone would poison a person over some brownies." A machine he was attached to started loudly beeping and Carl took a moment to calm his breathing. Talking was depleting him.

"When did you realize the truth?" Sara asked.

"There wasn't any one moment. It was a hundred things. Objects in my house began to disappear. If it had a hint of my first wife, it would go missing. If I asked Janet about it she'd get angry—and her anger was out of proportion to what I was asking. I began to keep my mouth shut."

"You got so you did anything to avoid the rages," Sara said.

"That's exactly right. It was better to keep the calm. I'm not sure when I started being afraid of her. Maybe it was when I went to a sales conference three states away. I was at dinner with potential buyers, all men, and I looked across the room and there was Janet. She didn't wave or say a word. She was just *there*. Staring at me. It creeped me out. One of the men asked me a question and when I looked back, Janet was gone. I told myself it was probably someone who looked like her."

"Did you ask her about it?"

"Oh no," Carl said. "By then I'd learned—no! I'd been *taught* to ask no questions about her personal life." He took a breath and smiled. "But then, I fell in love."

"Elaine," Sara said.

He chuckled. "I've read some of your books. You're good at romance."

"Thank you."

"Yes, Elaine. We were very discreet, but she made me remember what I was missing. I sat down with Janet and said that our marriage wasn't making either of us happy so we should get a divorce."

"But that would make her a loser," Jack said.

"That's the way she saw it too. I denied that there was another person involved. I thought it was going to be okay, but then, bad things began happening to me. Car trouble. Credit cards canceled. Two big clients left. I slipped on marbles and broke my foot. It was something *every day*.

"I knew it was Janet, but I was determined to leave. We went to mediation, and in front of the counselor, she cried. I'd never seen her cry before. She got a lot of sympathy.

"Janet must have found out the truth because things began happening to Elaine. Someone smashed her car. Her purse was stolen. It was nothing big, just annoying. But one day her ten-year-old son didn't come home from school. Elaine panicked. By that time she knew it was Janet. She told me she loved me but her fear of Janet was stronger than her love—and she had to protect her son. She wrote Janet a formal note saying *You win. I concede.* She quit her job and left the state.

"After that, I began throwing money at Janet to make her sign the divorce papers. When I sold my company that seemed to satisfy her and she signed."

"But that wasn't the end of it, was it?" Sara asked.

"No. She found me wherever I went. If I made friends they soon looked at me with fear, so I knew Janet had found them and lied to them about me."

He paused, getting his breath. "Seven months ago, I was told that I had no more than six months to live. The doctor said that if I had anything I really wanted to do, now was the time. I had some money that I'd been able to hide from Janet and I thought about traveling. Go see the Taj."

"But you wanted something more than that," Sara said.

"Yes," Carl said. "I wanted to see Janet. I'm not sure why. Maybe I wanted to reassure myself that she had only taken her anger out on me. I knew she was living in Lachlan, Florida, so I flew here. On the first day I was sitting in an outdoor restaurant reading a local brochure and telling myself I was stupid. I should book a cruise. Then I saw Janet sitting at another table, her face hidden inside one of Sylvia's books. My hair stood on end and I expected her to plop down in front of me, but she didn't.

"It took me a while to realize that she didn't recognize me. I'd lost a lot of weight and I had a small beard."

Carl closed his eyes for a moment. "I watched Janet staring at three pretty women who were laughing. She went to them and said hello. But they didn't invite her to join them. I knew that would set her off." He shook his head. "I saw Janet drop a pill into the drink of one of the women. Ten minutes later she grabbed her stomach and ran to the restroom. It was Janet who called for an ambulance. The next day I heard what a hero she was.

"I knew then what my bucket list was. I wanted to expose her. Maybe put her in jail. I rented a house through Tayla. I hired Dora to clean my apartment. She's a great gossip. She loved Sylvia and never believed she committed suicide. I studied social media sites. It's amazing what people tell online. I saw that no one connected the bad with the good. If they did something bad to Janet, bad happened to them, then Janet showed up to be the hero. It was a pattern, but I seemed to be the only one who saw it."

He paused. "Or was I? When Dora told me that Janet and Tayla argued, I pursued that. I got Tayla to tell me about Gil and how he might lose his son."

"We met Zelly," Kate said.

"Ghastly, isn't she?"

"Yes, she is," Sara said. "And Charlene?"

"That took some time to get Tayla to tell about her. I'm sorry I didn't come forward at first but Tayla swore that you three would find out the truth. When they arrested her, I wanted it stopped, but Tayla said no. Janet *had* to be exposed, and she knew that if she was being arrested for the crime, you three wouldn't stop until you found the truth."

"But she told us to stay out of it!" Kate said. "She talked about great evil."

Carl nodded. "Tayla was willing to take the blame,

but she also wanted the truth about Janet exposed. She told you to do what was right, but she knew—prayed—that you'd keep looking. She told me that you three were the only ones who could protect Charlene and Gil."

"She trusted us that much?" Kate asked.

He looked at Sara. "She said she owes you in a very big way and that maybe this would help you forgive her."

They all looked at Sara but she made no reply.

"What about Chet?" Jack asked.

All the energy seemed to leave Carl. "I am sorry for that. Very, very sorry."

"He would have exposed Charlene," Sara said. "You killed him to stop that from happening."

"Yes." Carl was squeezing his eyes shut and there were tears coming out.

"His death was declared an accident," Jack said. "There isn't going to be an investigation."

Carl nodded but he didn't speak.

Sara stood up. "I think we better go."

Carl whispered, "I just wanted a family. My wife and I wanted children so very much. A *family*. That's all I wanted in my entire life. But I didn't get it."

There was nothing they could reply to that, so they left the hospital room without another word. Outside, Sara said, "And Chet won't see his grandchildren."

"Nothing but pain because one woman wanted to win," Kate said.

"Come on, let's go home," Jack said. "This is done."

It was a week later that Sara was in her little library, computer on her lap, and going over what she'd written for Sylvia's book.

The book stopped right after Lisa left, and it told how happy Sylvia was that the misery she'd been enduring would soon be over. When her daughter's divorce was final, they could leave. Sylvia wrote of all she'd done to prepare for their escape. She'd transferred every photo she had of her life with her husband and daughter onto a single three-terabyte hard drive. She'd secretly mailed it and several sentimental items to a friend who lived in Boston, someone Janet didn't know about. Sylvia put a couple of packed suitcases in a storage locker, along with two open-ended plane tickets to London. Her passport and five grand cash were in her bag. She would be able to walk out the door with nothing in her hand and leave the country.

What wasn't in the book was the night Janet cooked spicy enchiladas and served them to Sylvia. She ate them and drank most of a bottle of red wine. Considering what Janet usually "allowed" her, Sylvia must have thought it was a treat.

She'd had no idea that Janet overheard her plans of escape. It was difficult for Sara to make up what she needed to finish the story. It was tough putting herself into Sylvia's place and imagining what she must have felt when she realized that Janet had poisoned her. Surely, Janet told Sylvia that Lisa had turned herself in to the police. Sara wrote of Janet's delight in telling Sylvia that all she'd gone through had been for nothing.

Janet had the suicide note ready for Sylvia to sign. If she didn't sign it, Janet said she'd persecute Lisa forever. So of course Sylvia signed. She died pleading, not for herself, but for her daughter.

Sara could have ended the book there, but she

wanted to add the rest of it. The readers deserved to hear about some form of justice in the end. For that, Sara needed the details of the actual murder of Janet Beeson—and those could only come from Carl. When she went alone to visit him in the hospital, she took a notebook with her. His strength was failing rapidly but he smiled at the sight of her, and said yes, he'd be glad to tell her everything.

"But I've never been a good storyteller," he said.

"That's okay. How about if I ask you questions?" He nodded and she started. "What would you most like people to know about that day?"

"That it was an accident," Carl said.

"How could it have been an accident if you arrived with a gun?"

"I only meant to use it if I needed to defend myself. Maybe I shouldn't have been concerned about my own death, certainly not when you consider the circumstances, but…" He didn't seem to know how to finish.

"Okay, so you had a gun. Bought it? Stole it? What?"

"Bought. But not from a store. There's no documentation on the gun. You need to understand that I went there to reason with her. And I wanted to prove to myself that I could talk to her without being overwhelmed by her. Does that make sense?"

"Yes. Proving your courage, and that you've learned something. What did you talk about?"

Carl shrugged. "You know."

"Tell me."

"I wanted her to stop threatening Gil and Tayla. And I wanted to know the truth about what had happened to Sylvia."

"What was her reply?"

"Janet wouldn't answer me. She said she was going to call the sheriff. Her phone was on the dining table but I grabbed it before she did. She screamed at me."

"Did anyone hear her?"

"No," he said. "She'd run the Nesbitts off and the other neighbors were at work. She had a kettle on the stove and it went off. I decided to make her a cup of tea as a peace offering."

"Wait a minute," Sara said. "You're there with a gun and she just sat there? Why didn't she run away?"

"I was carrying a canvas bag, like the ones you take to the grocery. I had a newspaper in there and some bananas."

"And a .38."

"Yes, but she didn't know that."

"Did you leave the bag behind when you went to the kitchen?"

"It was on the end of the dining table."

"Near Janet?"

Carl paused. "Janet was never afraid of me. And the truth was that she was enjoying seeing me beg."

"So you left the gun behind and went to the kitchen to make tea. Then what?"

"I saw the canister that said *Sylvia's Tea*. I honestly thought it was a nice gesture, a calming one, to serve her the tea Sylvia used to like. I didn't know it was full of poison."

"Wasn't it kind of dumb for her to leave it there? In full sight?"

"Who was going to think that a little old woman

was a multiple murderer? Who would have kept a tin of poisonous tea on the counter at the ready?"

"I see your point. I guess she drank the tea."

"She did. Downed a whole cupful. But then she saw the canister I'd used and started shouting that I'd tried to kill her. I had no idea what she was talking about. She put her fingers down her throat and vomited into the sink. When she came up, she grabbed a knife off the rack, then threw the canister at me. That's when I realized it must contain the poison she'd used on Sylvia. I backed out of the kitchen.

"She followed me. She was raging, saying she was going to take Quinn away from Gil, going to expose Charlene. She was going to destroy everyone who'd ever done anything bad to her."

Carl stopped for a moment. "I honestly don't know what happened next. She lunged, and I swerved. I was trying to knock the knife out of her hand, but she leaped toward me. I grabbed her wrist and twisted. The knife went into her body and she fell back onto a dining chair."

Sara was listening with wide eyes. "And then?"

"It didn't kill her. She told me—ordered me—to give back her phone so she could call an ambulance. 'I'm going to make all of you sorry for this,' she said."

Carl paused. "She grabbed the canvas bag. Maybe she thought I'd put her phone in it. The gun fell out and she reached for it. I was several feet away but I got to it before she did. I was shaking all over and pointing the gun at her. I just thought of Gil and Quinn and Tayla and Charlene and all the people she was going to destroy. And the many, many others whose lives she'd destroyed."

Carl ran his hand over his face. "It was horrible! She had vomit on her face and her clothes and a big knife was sticking out of her chest. But she just sneered at me in contempt. I'd seen that look so many times before. Then she said, 'You always were a coward.'"

Carl shrugged in a gesture of helplessness. "I shot her."

He took a moment to get his breath. "I was quite calm afterward. I put the gun in the bag, then cleaned up the kitchen. Janet was always fanatical about neatness. I wiped the kettle of my prints, picked up the little canister of Sylvia's tea, wiped it and put it back into the rack. I turned its face around as I couldn't bear to see the name.

"Then I walked out. I felt bad that poor Dora would probably be the one to find her, but it couldn't be helped."

They sat in silence for a while. Sara was visualizing all that he'd told her. Carl's face was even more gray than it had been.

Sara looked at her notebook. She hadn't written a word. "I guess that's all."

"Are you *sure*? I don't want any questions to come up later. After I'm, you know, gone."

"I don't think there will be," she said softly.

"Good." Carl smiled. "The drugs they give you here are wonderful. I can almost understand addicts. Speaking of which, how is Lisa?"

"Still here in Lachlan. She's…"

"I know. Waiting for me to go. I will as soon as all

this is settled." He sat up a bit, his face alarmed. "What about that reporter? He's been a real pest."

"He's been sorted," Sara said firmly. "He's dropped the White Lily Kidnapping. I told him that Chet had planted the evidence, and that the man was kind of crazy. His imagination had blown a small case into something huge."

Carl's face seemed to age. "Did he believe that?"

"Heavens no!" Sara said. "But what he did believe is my offer to get my agent and my editor to read the fiction series that he and Arthur are going to write."

"A what?"

Sara smiled. "Arthur wants to write a murder mystery series about a man in a wheelchair and Everett is going to be a collaborator. I think they're going to move in together."

"Makes sense. Arthur is rich and alone and…"

"Everett is poor and alone. It's a perfect match."

Carl nodded, pleased. "It might work out. And Charlene?"

"She's at home. She's been talking to Jack but she hasn't told us anything we didn't already know. Tayla has put her big house on the market. She's going to give the commission to Kate."

"That's good," Carl said. "Very good. And you'll write Sylvia's book?"

"It's finished except for this last part. It will be with her name in huge letters on the cover, but mine will be small and below it."

"Because your name sells books."

"Right." Carl's eyes were drooping so Sara stood

up. "I'll see you later," she said, but thought *Maybe*. When he didn't answer, she left the room.

That had been two days ago. Carl was still alive, still hanging on to life, but not for long.

Sara closed her computer. She could hear Jack and Kate in the kitchen. They were laughing and quietly talking and Sara didn't want to interrupt them.

Her X-Pro 2 camera was nearby and she took out the SD card. It had been so long since she'd used that camera that she didn't remember what she'd last shot. She'd received a call from Sheriff Flynn and she and Jack had gone tearing out. She didn't even remember what she'd done that morning—the time when Janet was being murdered.

The photos came up. Oh yeah, she'd taken her MINI all the way over to the east side to Andrews Avenue to have it serviced. Jack said he'd do it but Sara wanted the drive. She got there at 7:30 a.m., turned her car over to the team, and started taking photos. There were men with air hoses, cars on hydraulic lifts, women dressed for work, a customer—

Sara was sure her heart skipped a beat. She enlarged the picture.

Carl was standing in the background. The camera's face recognition had caught him in crystal clarity. A quick search showed that he was in six pictures, always standing in the background and watching.

Sara brought up the info screen. The photos were taken on the day Janet Beeson was murdered. At the *time* Janet was being murdered.

Sara took her laptop into the kitchen. One look at her face and neither Jack nor Kate spoke. Sara couldn't.

She set the computer on the counter and pointed. There was Carl. She swiped through the photos. More of Carl. Sara opened the info screens. The pictures covered from 6:45 a.m. to 10:00 a.m. The MINI garage was far from Lachlan. There was no way Carl could have been there to murder Janet.

"Let's go," Jack said.

Sara wasn't sure if he meant to go to Carl at the hospital or to the sheriff—and she didn't ask.

Silently, they went to Jack's truck and got in. Kate took her aunt's hand and held it. The computer was on Sara's lap.

Sara felt that, as the oldest, she should make a decision. And of course she should be on the side of justice. Take the photos to the sheriff. Prove that Carl couldn't have killed Janet.

Then who did? *That* was what was screaming inside her mind. Maybe what Carl told her was what actually happened—but he wasn't the one who *did* it. Maybe he'd been told the details. An accidental poisoning, then an angry Janet pulled a knife. In the tussle, she was stabbed. But she wasn't dead. If she did as Carl said and threatened to ruin their lives... Lisa did have a gun hidden in her bag. Maybe she used it. But did Lisa do all of it alone? Did she make Janet a cup of tea? That sounded more like Tayla. If Janet picked up a knife, would Tayla wrestle her for it? Probably not, but Gil would.

Sara didn't want to think about what would happen if Carl's confession was proven wrong. Prison for sure. Execution? The publicity would be horrific.

But Lisa had paid for her sins. Jail time, her mother

murdered. Gil certainly didn't deserve to have his son taken from him and given to a woman like Zelly. Quinn wouldn't survive under that! And Tayla and Charlene... Their lives and those of their families would be destroyed forever.

When Jack pulled into the hospital parking lot, Sara didn't know if she was relieved or angry at herself for not protesting.

They took the elevator up, still not speaking, and went down the hall to Carl's glassed-in room. Then halted.

The room was filled with people and balloons and flowers. Happy people. Laughing. Gil and his son, Quinn, were there. Charlene and Leland were laughing with Tayla. Lisa was bending over Carl and kissing his forehead. To the side was Kyle Nesbitt. He was watching four young boys show Carl their iPads. They were Charlene's two and Kyle's sons.

On a tray was a blue-and-white cake, with one big candle. Strung across the room was a sparkly banner. *We love you Grandpa Carl* it read. It was a family. What Carl had wanted so much. What he'd given his life up to get for these few precious moments.

Sara was the first to turn away. Kate came behind her and Jack followed.

In the truck, Sara deleted the photos.

* * * * *

#1 *New York Times* bestselling romance author

JUDE DEVERAUX

continues her new series with this third Medlar Mystery novel. Old friends gather at a country estate in England to solve a twenty-five-year-old mystery. But the festive murder-mystery weekend takes a dangerous turn when the remains of someone who'd been thought to have run off with valuable jewelry are found, and the victim has clearly met with foul play.

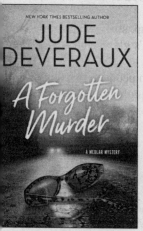

Retired romance novelist Sara Medlar is determined to get her niece, Kate, out of Lachlan, Florida, before someone from her past can cause trouble. Searching for a reasonable excuse, Sara concocts a plot the way she used to write books. She contacts an old friend in England who owes her a favor and the two agree that Sara should rush to her bedside and the friend will pretend to be dying. Sara adds to the story by suggesting they try to solve a decades-old disappearance that occured on the estate. Sara's friend eagerly agrees to invite all of the people who were there twenty-five years ago to reenact that weekend and solve the mystery. Sara also wants to encourage a romance between Kate and her friend Jack, so she insists he come along for the adventure. However, once they arrive in England, no one is who they seem to be and everyone is protecting secrets. What is meant to be a distraction becomes a real murder investigation when human remains are discovered on the property. Suddenly, Sara, Kate and Jack are trying to solve another mystery...but will it tear them all apart?

Coming soon, from MIRA books!

Be sure to connect with us at:
Harlequin.com/Newsletters
Facebook.com/HarlequinBooks
Twitter.com/HarlequinBooks

Harlequin.com

MJD989